HArVESTEr of the NOW

VOLUME TWO:

SECRETS OF
THE DARK REALM

by

Alan Smith

**Grosvenor House
Publishing Limited**

This book is published by
Grosvenor House Publishing Ltd
28-30 High Street, Guildford, Surrey, GU1 3HY.
www.grosvenorhousepublishing.co.uk

A CIP record for this book
is available from the British Library

ISBN 1-905529-90-2

For Louise Day…
The first person to ever tell me I was going to be a writer.

…and Robert Whitehouse
for laughter, silliness and eternal friendship.

HArVESTEr of the NOW:
Volume Two:
Secrets of the Dark Realm

Chapter 1: The Prophecy

Chapter 2: Patient 143

Chapter 3: The Equestrian Circle

Chapter 4: The Pig-Beast

Chapter 5: The Frozen Lake

Chapter 6: Mary Graham

Chapter 7: Secrets and Tea Cups

Chapter 8: Caged Rats

Chapter 9: The Warren

Chapter 10: Children of the Mist

Chapter 11: Shadows beneath the Dark Realm

Chapter 12: Consequences

Chapter 13: Crossing the Line

Chapter 14: The HArVESTEr

Chapter 15: The Parting

ALSO BY THE SAME AUTHOR:

HArVESTEr of the NOW: VOLUME ONE:
The Notebook Dress
(ISBN: 978-1-905529-16-2)
(Published by Grosvenor House Publishing Ltd 2006)

A SOUR PEACH
(ISBN: 1-84436-210-8)
(Published by United Press Ltd 2005)

JACK FROST'S CHRISTMAS
& OTHER PLAYGROUND POEMS
(ISBN: 1-84436-419-4)
(Published by United Press Ltd 2006)

HARVESTER OF THE NOW VOLUME TWO:

Secrets of the Dark Realm

Alan Smith is an award winning poet and author of the *Harvester of the Now* trilogy.

His writing career began in primary school when he would invent short stories to entertain his family and friends. He was encouraged by several inspirational teachers including Sheila Allan, Jackie Hampson, Helen Copper, Roshan Doug, Derek Underhill and Christine Richards and he continued to write creatively during his formative education.

At college he met Robert Whitehouse and the pair formed Rob & Al, a comedy partnership that has lasted over 13 years and spawned a wide variety of audio and visual material. They are currently finishing work on a new CD of material entitled:

Off the Cufflinks, and are in the process of completing their first play, *Hell is a Private Club*.

Alan felt he lost his creative momentum for several years as he pursued a variety of careers, until he enrolled at Worcester University in the winter of 2002. Here he began to enter his poetry into national competitions, winning a series of awards that led to his work appearing in several magazines and anthologies. He was finally commissioned to produce his first collection, *A Sour Peach*, which was published by United Press Ltd in 2005.

Shortly after enrolling at Worcester Alan began work on a novel which was to become *Harvester of the Now*. It took three and a half years to complete.

Alan is currently working on a second adult collection of poetry called Empty Voices, and a brand new novel.

His first collection of children's poetry: *Jack Frost's Christmas and Other Playground Poems* was published by United Press Ltd in October 2006. Alan writes independently for a number of magazines and performs creative writing and poetry workshops at primary schools.

He can be contacted at:
www.harvesterofthenow.com

1

The prophecy.

*B*lood splashed the stone. It dripped like a tap, though a very concise tap and echoed in the hollow black depths of the cave. Just three droplets of fresh blood were allowed to fall, and then silence followed.

In the flickering campfire light, three pairs of eyes turned to watch this strange ritual, with avid interest.

An old withered hand quickly smeared the gathering fluid across the flat stone, as though creating a macabre hand painting of a rainbow.

Into this smear, crushed splinters of maple wood were sprinkled, very slowly, as though the perpetrator were now adding seasoning to some evil looking delicacy. The wood splinters flecked out across the congealing blood, some spinning and drifting in the drying fluid.

There followed a pause.

Then finally, four misshapen stones were cast into this mess like dice. The old woman who had been preparing this strange collage let out an unexpected throat-clearing gasp.

"What is it Morquinda? What do the runes tell you?" A brittle voice broke out from the darkness, like the sudden splintering of a wind-snapped tree. From within the stillness of the cave, the sound of shuffling feet could faintly be heard, as Morquinda's three companions moved away from the warmth of their camp-fire, to see for themselves the runes' new message.

"Keep back...you will not be able to interpret them," Morquinda's high, yet strained voice ordered them. The shuffling stopped. Then a muttering began amongst the other three. Morquinda could sense immediately that she was on the brink of a mutiny. In order to quell it, she chose to speak: "The runes tell me that the Pig-Beast has killed again this night."

This time it was her companions' turn to gasp. Then immediately the chattering began again. Several questions were asked of her at once, but Morquinda chose to answer only one.

"A child...another of the Mist Children. The Pig-Beast has found their hiding place. As has our master," Morquinda coldly informed them. The muttering ceased. "He will unleash such terrible vengeance against those children, it is to be hoped that the Pig-Beast kills them all first. That fate would be the lesser of two evils."

"His Lordship fears the Beast." A defiant voice spoke out from amongst the gathered group. Morquinda turned the full malice of her bloodshot eyes on the three other old ladies, crouching in the darkness of the cave.

"He does not, Isabella. He fears only the coming of the Harvester." A shiver spread amongst the group, as though no one could quite believe what Morquinda had just said. "And well he might..." the old lady continued, "for the Harvester has come...I feel it." She broke off from her thoughts, and began swirling the runes in the puddle of blood.

"Tell us more lies from the Great Find," Isabella suddenly cried, utterly changing the sombre mood of the cave. The three old ladies took up the call, chorusing:

"Yes, you must, more Morquinda...more lies from the Great Find."

Morquinda was studying the runes with a look of anxiety on her face; she barely heard the requests of her companions. With a slight wave of her ancient hand, she lulled them all into silence.

"I will read to you more this evening…as I promised," she said, still transfixed by the runes.

"Is it not my turn to read tonight?" an elegant voice asked.

"You forget Felicia…as you always do…that you are blind." Morquinda sighed as she announced this tragic news once again.

Felicia rubbed at her sightless eyes for a second, and then softly she began to cry.

Suddenly Morquinda let out a shrill scream and swept the runes from the stone with a deft flick of her wrist. Blood splashed across the cave wall. The three old ladies who had inched their way towards her, now backed fearfully away from Morquinda. She was twirling round in a circle, the rags of her dress billowing out as she did so, one hand clasped to her throat as though she had swallowed something foul.

"What is it?" Isabella screamed out. She was shuffling madly backwards and forwards on the spot, unsure whether to assist Morquinda or not. Felicia rested a restraining hand on her shoulder.

"Elyse…you must go to your sister," Felicia ordered the other old lady, hunched by her side.

"I do not need help," Morquinda suddenly bellowed. She had stopped spinning and was now rasping harshly, trying to catch her breath. For a time she still remained bent double as though to be sick, but slowly as the feelings subsided, she stretched her bony, brittle back, and stood once again at her full height. With slow, deliberate steps she made her way along the sharp stone floor of the cave. She ignored her three companions as she passed them, and went to stand inches away from the crackling campfire.

Bathed in this hellish light Morquinda looked even more imposing to the others. Her long grey hair, although thin and wispy, jutted out at crazy angles, utterly unkempt. Her once graceful silk dress, the one she had always worn on Sundays for church, now hung from her like a funeral shroud. Torn and tattered, with several buttons missing, the dirt from the cave she now occupied had caked the material turning it from grey to black in places. She was bare foot. Her wizened feet were swollen and cold, flecked with liver spots. Her toes were curling over each other with arthritis. Each step she took caused her to wince with pain. Morquinda pulled her dress about her, enjoying the warmth the fire offered. When she finally spoke, through her broken yellowed teeth, it was to the flames, not to her companions, that she directed her words.

Jean Candicote has been lost to us," she whispered into the orange embers. "So sad she should go like that. But we did try to persuade her to stay," Morquinda justified. The three others exhaled in shock.

"How?" they asked in unison.

"The young boy…Krinn…has been most industrious it seems. She has passed into darkness. I will miss her." Morquinda hung her head.

Why? Jean Candicote was evil…she believed all the lies of the Great Find. She wanted us to go home," Elyse suddenly barked, shuffling towards her sister and wildly gesturing with her arms. "You make no sense as usual Morquinda. You are a hypocrite. Never the same story twice, that's your problem…you useless old hag." Elyse finished her rant just as she stepped out of the darkness of the cave and into the light of the fire.

The similarity between the two old ladies was immediately apparent. Morquinda had the edge with her height, but Elyse had the more striking profile. Her hooked nose drew attention towards her grey eyes that sparkled in the campfire. Her hair was thicker, and had retained hints of its original black colour. Her dress, which on closer inspection looked like an official uniform, also hung in tatters. Her posturing and incessant enunciation of her words gave her an almost bohemian air.

"It is you...my most precious sister, who is the hag. You forget more than you remember. Was it not Jean Candicote who introduced us to the Sacred Mother? Without her friendship in the beginning, Annabel would never have given us the gift and shown us the true reality. Or do you now question what is real and what is not? Do you now believe the lies of the Great Find yourself?" Morquinda demanded, spitting with rage. Isabella and Felicia cowered in her presence, but Elyse firmly stood her ground.

"You miss my point. You were amongst the first to brand her a heretic when she began to throw doubt onto our reality. Because of you the Sacred Mother told us her lies. Lies, which some of them believed, and their greed to know more led them to uncover the Great Find after the Sacred Mother left us. But it was YOU Morquinda who allowed the wild girl to read some of the writings. You, who allowed her to sew the notebook pages together and make that dress she wears so proudly..." Elyse broke off as Morquinda hissed at her, but before she could interrupt, Elyse continued her soliloquy: "Soon after, you declared the Great Find to be heresy. Claiming the books were fiction, claiming that you had stumbled upon them years before anyone else, that they were not the writings of either the boy or the girl. Your madness was contagious; it spread amongst us like disease. Soon no one knew what to believe...even now I DO NOT REMEMBER. I frighten myself into believing you...but there are so many gaps in my memory. Why do I not know the history of these lands?" Elyse screamed, wiping at tears that rolled freely down her wrinkled face. Morquinda looked on horrified by this outburst. She was fidgeting as though on the brink of another fit.

"You must stop this sister, you are scaring us all. Remember we are the Old Ones. We are as ancient as these lands, as precious as the sky. We serve only our master, the Lord of the Now. He has shown us the truth...there is no past...there is only now..." Morquinda sounded pitiful as she tried to calm the group.

"I remember the House," Isabella unexpectedly chipped in. "It had guards, corridors and hundreds of others as old as us," she continued, a vague smile creasing the side of her chapped lips. Felicia also nodded.

"There was medicine for us to take, and routines and board games..." she began.

"Listen to them Morquinda...They remember the House just as you do," Elyse argued, wiping away her tears. "The House came first...long before these lands."

"ENOUGH!" Morquinda suddenly screeched, belting Elyse across the mouth with her withered right hand. "Enough I say. You are all going mad...your diseased minds are confused, I am the only one who knows the truth...I am the only one who can read the signs, predict the future...I have the sight." Morquinda quelled them. Elyse had staggered backwards and was now dabbing at her bleeding bottom lip with the sleeve of her dress.

"You fool Morquinda...you forget that you always read tarot cards in the House...you always read tea-leaves. That is why you can interpret the runes," she vainly began.

"BE SILENT," Morquinda demanded, drawing back her hand as though to strike her sister again. Elyse fell silent, terrified by her sister's rage.

Morquinda waited a while, enjoying her small victory. Finally, when she was sure she had all their attention once more, she began to speak. "We must all calm down. We are losing track of ourselves, tripping over anagrams and puzzles that are not really there." She soothed, moving closer to the other three Old Ones. "My sister has confused her memories of a House with the story written by the boy. The story we all read. Lies...lies from the Great Find. It is a fiction, based on nothing but the avid imagination of a young boy. Like the other stories we keep here," she emphatically explained, gesturing behind her companions who all turned to stare at a large wooden trunk near the back wall of the cave.

It looked as though it had been cobbled together from broken blocks of rotten wood, and held in place by two frayed but sturdy looking black leather straps. The wooden trunk was partially obscured by branches from a weeping-willow tree, as though a vain attempt had been made to conceal it from prying eyes.

"All her lies...and those of the boy are hidden here. We have no need to look closer, my instincts...and indeed your own must tell you the writings are all lies. We came from here," Morquinda finished, gesturing all around her and bathing in the glory of her empiric victory.

"Yet...I do have memories of a past..." Isabella offered.

"False. There is no past, only now." Morquinda silenced her. "Yet it is still sad that Jean Candicote did not join us. But she has paid dearly for her hesitation. She is as evil as the girl was. Pretending to be our friend, yet refusing to accept the simple truth...there is only now," she repeated. "I mourn her passing, but I do not pity her."

For a while no one spoke. The Old Ones still stared at the trunk, not wishing to catch Morquinda's eye. Eventually Felicia spoke:

"Did the runes reveal anything else?"

"They confuse, always they speak in twisting riddles...yet some of their meanings I do understand," Morquinda confessed, slowly squatting down with her back towards the fire. The horrible sound of creaking bones accompanied this action.

"They speak of the Harvester once again. They confirm he has arrived...yet his features remain cloudy. Why has he not sought to find me?" Morquinda rhetorically asked.

"Will he be the end of us…the end of this infernal winter?" Felicia was hesitant in her questioning.

"He will bring conclusion," was all Morquinda would say.

"Then tell us Morquinda…tell us more lies from the Great Find," Isabella demanded. Immediately the mood within the cave changed, as Morquinda struggled to her feet, and shuffled towards the trunk.

The Old Ones parted to let her through and as she began to undo the straps of the trunk, a wave of excitement seemed to pass through them all. With a violent creak the lid flipped upward on its rusty hinges and several sheets of yellowed paper immediately spilled out. The Old Ones all made to reach for these, but Morquinda kept them back with a gesture.

"Only I can read them," she declared, rummaging through the top layer of papers to find what she sought.

"Be quick!" Isabella squealed with almost childlike excitement. Morquinda was methodical in her search, her movements suggesting that she did not wish to disturb the papers too much; lest they reveal something else held within the trunk. Eventually she slammed the lid shut, and retied the straps, turning back to face the others and brandishing a crumpled sheaf of papers clasped in her left hand.

"What it is? What hear? Lies must there be tonight?" Isabella was suffering catachresis in her excitement. Morquinda looked at her with disdain. She hated Isabella's inability to maintain self-control. Shuffling once again back towards the roaring fire, Morquinda gathered the Old Ones around her. They all cautiously sat down, each individually flinching with discomfort.

In the ever-flickering light Felicia and Isabella looked even more agitated. Isabella was the taller of the two, her white hair still thick but bunched neatly above her head using string. Her features appeared younger than the others. Her wrinkles were less prominent and her smile seemed almost to roll back her many years. She sat rocking backwards and forwards with excitement. She had a slight squint, as though distance proved difficult for her to judge. This caused her to habitually wipe her sleeve over her left eye as though to clean it.

Felicia sat hunched, a slight hump in her back. She was almost crippled with arthritis and could barely stretch out her arms at times. Her sightless eyes and constant fidgeting to remain comfortable had given her an unfair appearance of catatonia. Like Isabella and Elyse she wore the ragged remains of a uniform, the inscription of which remained sewn onto her torn gown: Property of Lambert House.

"It is called..." Morquinda began, ironing out the creases on the paper with the flat of her hand. "...*The history of Khynous Morf.*" The Old Ones chattered in alarm.

"Surely that *cannot* be part of the Great Find?" Elyse cried. "That is lies which have been written about our world, not the girl's." She sounded fearful, but Morquinda was grinning horribly.

"It is Annabel's handwriting," she announced, turning the paper round for all to see. Isabella and Elyse squinted to read the words, Felicia simply giggled. "I will prove to you all that anything within that chest is lies, whether written about this world or the past. I will prove just as our master has done, that there is only now." Morquinda made a sudden and violent retching sound, scrunching up the paper as her hand clenched into a fist. Her eyes seemed to bulge and strange contortions twisted her craggy face. The Old Ones watched in awe, none wishing to interrupt a ritual they had seen happen many times before.

Unaided by the runes, Morquinda was experiencing a vision.

She made almost reptilian noises, as her throat seemed to contract, forcing her breath to squeeze out of her restricted windpipe. She was pirouetting like a ballerina, though the action seemed unnatural, as if a demented puppeteer was manipulating her limbs.

Finally with a harsh rasp her vocal chords returned, and her vision cleared. She fixed the other three with a steely glare and for a second her bloodshot eyes seemed to clear. Then in a voice that sounded much younger and stronger than any she had spoken in before she cried out:

"*The white horse haunts you Peter Bettany.*"

The silence that followed this outburst was as total as it was chilling.

2

Patient 143.

To begin with it felt the way she had always hoped safety would feel. Soft and warm as though a never-ending blanket had smothered her skin.

Slowly it surrounded her, pulling, smothering and finally embalming her into the sweetest sensation imaginable.

It felt like a Mediterranean Sea washing over her skin under a clear azure sky. The waves took her under in their warm embrace, holding her till her brain had stopped panicking when she finally realised that, unbelievably, she could breathe underwater. Only then, did she dare open her eyes and see such magical landscapes.

A fortress stood on a hill, bright banners hanging down from its walls, and trumpets sounding from its battlements. And here, as she swam in the warmth of this kingdom she had found beneath the waves, she finally felt as though she had come home.

The sensation of swimming through crystal clear warm water gradually left her body, and she experienced the very real sensation of terra firma beneath her feet. Wherever she had been brought to, it felt as real as the earth. Yet something seemed very wrong.

It took her a while to realise that it was her own body that wasn't substantial. Her skin was almost translucent, and seemed to morph and shimmer in front of her eyes. Was she the dream? Or was it this place?

She realised she had begun to panic again and quickly took deep breaths to calm herself. There had to be a rational explanation for this. Her mind raced through possibilities, while her senses reeled from the experience she had just suffered. One thought shone through bright and clear.

She wasn't dreaming this.

Strangely the thought didn't scare her. If anything it acted as a comfort zone, and her palpitations seemed to ease.

The landscape remained unchanged around her, and her instincts told her to stay calm. The scenery seemed to echo these feelings. The day was bright and clear. Green healthy grass bulged between her toes, growing rampantly from the hillside. Flowers bloomed all around her, indicating that it was spring. The sky was blue, and the air smelt fresh. Even the imposing bulk of the fortress looked welcoming, despite the militaristic approach to its design.

She was being shown something.

As soon as this thought arrived in her mind, a sense of honour swept through her body. She had never believed in premonitions, or visions, and this felt too strong to be the kind a novice would experience anyway.

This was deliberate. It felt distinctly as though someone was trying to explain something to her.

Before she had chance to dwell on this, a new sensation of momentum rushed through her mind. The image became unclear; though she was aware she was running without moving her feet. Like watching a film in fast-forward she found she was travelling through the beautifully adorned corridors of the fort. Or rather, they were racing through her. Like air she filtered across the marble throne room, feeling totally at peace. The brave fighting men who feasted in the banqueting halls, bade her welcome. She sat with them while they told their story. It was a great and ancient tale, the story of Khynous Morf.

She heard how there was never, and could never be a fortress like it. Its masonry shone in the late evening sun glistening with all the colours you could ever attribute to pride. It drew to its courtyard every type of traveller. It was the place the lonely could come and never feel abandoned. It was a place of healing, where those who had survived a great terror would feel justified to come and rest.

As she flew through the tables, and hovered above the courtiers and noblemen who flocked to that great hall, she knew she was seeing a time that had long passed from these walls. A time that felt unreal.

A time that felt just like a fairy tale.

As soon as she knew this, the image vanished.

She was left alone in that mighty fort, Khynous Morf. Yet the building seemed greatly changed. Full of history, the type she had just seen; yet now, also full of great pain.

She walked despondently down the corridors, staring at the crumbling brickwork, feeling immensely saddened that all the joy had been so viciously torn from this place.

It was as though unseen hands had reached into the walls and ripped out the beating heart of Khynous Morf. It all seemed so unfair. She felt cheated at the moment of ecstasy, as though she were now being told that none of it was really how she'd interpreted it.

In her own heart she realised she had been momentarily part of a great deception. One that although clearly serving a greater purpose, was cruel in the utmost; she had been manipulated for one person's ends at the expense of everyone else.

It was a feeling that could only be compared to her earliest realisation of mortality, that moment as a child when finally it became clear that the games, the laughter, the breath of life, did not go on forever.

She had been seven years old, when her grandmother had died. It had been a day of sadness incomparable, at that time, to any other. The old lady had been lying in a hospital bed, unspeaking, just breathing for nearly nine hours. It had been hard for her, as a child, to finally arrive at the hospital, in the hope of talking to her Gran the way she had only twenty-four hours before. Gran always loved to hear how she was, what new toy she had to play with, what dreams she had to share.

She had told her Gran that she wanted to 'be a nurse when I've grown up, that way I'll be able to look after you when you stay in the hospital.' The old lady had smiled with such delight at this story, and squeezed the side of her cheek, the way she always did.

Now, twenty-four hours later, her Gran lay dying in a lonely sterile hospital room. She had been moved out of the main ward, and allowed to spend her final hours in the privacy of a small room.

How kind they were.

Because she had been at school, it was almost too late when she finally arrived at the hospital. Her Mom had met her outside the room and told her: 'Gran is very ill,' but that she had been: 'waiting for you to arrive.' None of this made sense to her at the time. Within minutes of her stepping into that quiet hospital room the old lady died.

She had barely had a chance to squeeze her hand, and say 'Hello'.

She remembered waiting for Gran to open her eyes. But she never woke up. She remembered her Dad crying, a sight she would never see again.

That was a memory that haunted her to this very day. Now as an adult she could rationalize it. Appreciate it for the impact it actually had upon her life. It taught her that no one lasts forever and that the human spirit is so strong and so precious.

Her Gran had held on for her to arrive at the hospital, held back even death so she could say goodbye.

But she could not hold it back forever.

She realised she was crying now at this memory, and tried to wipe a tear away, but her hands were liquid, they just seemed to pass through her skin. Perhaps she wasn't crying, perhaps she just felt as though she should.

In fact, was that not what this whole sensation was all about? Was it not in some way a sort of atonement or a confession?

Someone had created this fortress, Khynous Morf, from the foundations of a belief that everyone who is lost deserves to be found and deserves a chance to be safe.

The premise felt righteous enough, but the reasoning was flawed.

In order to create an ambience for the building, a history to go with the surroundings, the creator had simply made one. Khynous Morf's past was a complete fiction of soldiers, laughter and happiness all held within these empty hallways, which she now idly walked; feeling like a tourist with no guide to help her.

As quickly as this history had been created, it had been taken away.

Something fearful had happened at Khynous Morf. It could be felt within the desolation of the courtyard she now stepped into. Whoever had created this place of safety had also brought a sense of their own fear into this new world.

And that fear was now out of control.

As she stood in the empty courtyard, she began to tremble as a terrible feeling took hold of her. Her mind began to swirl and dark images filled it. She saw hundreds of ranks of soldiers all around her, marching with military precision towards their certain death.

This once proud army was being cut down by a never-ending mass of swift moving black shapes, all of them endlessly screaming, as they tore and clawed at the soldiers of Khynous Morf.

They were the stuff of nightmares, or at least one person's specific nightmare. It was a nightmare that had long been suppressed but had finally taken hold, no matter how strongly it had been kept down.

Just as suddenly the dark images ended.

Once again she was alone in the courtyard, but her terrified brain was now screaming at her with a fresh and much darker thought.

Whoever had created this world, and failed it once, would certainly try again.

~

With a scream Nurse Samantha Raynor released Patient 143's hand, and in doing so her mind, recently filled to capacity with the swirling chaos of Khynous Morf, returned to the present day with a heart-stopping thud.

It took her disorientated senses a minute to fully grasp what had just happened to her, and where she was. She was on her feet and pacing the room a second later, keen to touch solid objects with her hands so she could remind herself that everything was real, and her own skin was no longer like water.

She groaned as her mind cleared, and the pain of a migraine seemed to centre on her throbbing temples. She could vaguely remember coming down to the ward to visit 143. She knew that the coma patients had to be checked because the storm was playing havoc with the electrics. She even remembered sitting down next to 143 and taking hold of her hand.

Then the sensation of drowning had seemed to invade her mind, pulling it apart thread by thread and sucking her down into a world of which she had no concept.

Outside the window of the small hospital room, Samantha could hear the sound of wailing police sirens and thunderous rain. It seemed as though all hell had just broken loose in Great Wick Holm. She stared fearfully back at the young girl lying so peacefully on the hospital bed.

"What *have* you done?" Samantha stammered.

∽

The phone in Wick Holm police station burst enthusiastically into life for the umpteenth time that evening. No one hurried to answer it.

Cyril Bettany had barely replaced the receiver himself, when it had begun its commotion all over again. He helpfully shrugged as Police Superintendent William Toland audibly sighed and reached over his cluttered desk to answer it.

Cyril weaved his way through the growing throng of concerned locals who had all piled into the tiny police station. He waved and nodded to several he recognised, and finally found his wife, Jayne, huddled in a corner of the cramped police station.

"I've just spoken to the hospital, *everything's fine*…though no one's been admitted fitting Peter's name or description," Cyril began. The news brought Jayne very little comfort.

Above the police station the storm continued to rage, seemingly unleashing its full fury upon the little coastal village. The driving snow had now been replaced by torrential rain. The deluge was mixing with the compacted snow, and almost immediately freezing in the chilling winter winds that whipped up from Wick Holm Bay. Black ice was forming across the many twisting roads that led into the village, making driving conditions hazardous. The sky had been filled with strange and unnatural colours for almost an hour, now it had settled once again into blackness, the final rumbles of thunder had sounded very distant. Endless rain poured down on a village that had already suffered enough that night.

"Hasn't rained like this for months," one local woman moaned as she queued to speak to Superintendent Toland. Jayne overheard her comment and eyed Cyril warily. In a low voice she whispered:

"I don't think it's rained this badly since Peter's accident? Or perhaps the rain never seemed so heavy after that?" Her eyes had welled up with tears and Cyril put a comforting arm around her shoulders.

"Now, now…that young man's old enough to take care of himself. You *mustn't* worry Jayne, I'm sure he's fine. Hospital had no rec…" He was cut off by Jayne's panicked outburst:

"You *saw* the state our flat was left in Cyril…our home? Whoever did that, has probably *hurt* our son…*Or even…*" But the thought was too horrible to contemplate. She began to sob uncontrollably, and Cyril squeezed her into his protective embrace as several people in the queue began looking concernedly in their direction.

Superintendent Toland replaced the receiver of the phone, just as a member of the gathering crowd in front of his desk shouted out a fresh question. He held up his hand for silence, warily glancing back at the phone, almost daring it to ring. He stood up from his desk, bringing the full height of his six foot frame to the attention of all those gathered within his normally quiet police station. He glanced back at the phone, and with a slight hesitation, chose to take it off the hook.

He was an imposing sight, even at fifty-two. His athletic build and stature kept him respected by even the youngsters of Wick Holm. He still had a full head of grey hair, which he often had to gel, as it was very thick and troublesome to style. His face was kindly, though with a glance he could alter his expression into a perfected stare of ambivalence.

"Ladies and Gentlemen if I could just have your attention for a minute?" he requested, throwing up his hands and bringing down the slow babble of noise to a stumbling silence. "I know you're all very concerned for loved ones, and I realise you all want an explanation as to what has happened here tonight...but I'm afraid I am not going to be able to provide that answer this evening." He sighed. Predictably the murmuring restarted with gusto. Several more questions where shouted from the crowd, coupled with a few choice insults as to the way the whole affair was being handled. Toland swallowed his pride and after a few minutes of chaos he once again shouted for order. "I appreciate your concerns, really I do. But I can only repeat the facts," he insisted. "I've just been speaking with Great Wick Holm constabulary. They are sending as many officers as they can spare to us tonight. You must all appreciate that there will be a slight delay to their arrival as conditions out there..." he said, pointing at the glass front doors for emphasis, they were being pummelled with relentless battering rain, "...are treacherous. Now! I suggest that anyone who has left children or elderly relatives at home should try and make their careful way back to them, as this storm looks set in for the night," Toland pleaded. "Anyone directly awaiting news of relatives is of course very welcome to stay. Miss Bloomer and Mrs Meredith have both very kindly agreed to stay with us and make some refreshments." He gave a cursory nod towards the two elderly ladies, who were already making themselves quite comfortable in the station utility. The steady 'chinking' of teacups could faintly be heard.

Toland faced the already muttering crowd. He did feel empathy for several of the locals, who had genuine cause to be there. However, he had worked the streets of Wick Holm for long enough to appreciate that a vast percentage of the crowd were just curiosity seekers, hoping to find out what was going on so they could gossip about it.

When it became clear that Toland was not going to reveal any more about the events of the last few hours, almost half the people in the waiting room pulled on their galoshes and hoisted up their umbrellas. With a barely disguised grumble of discontent they began to file out of the police station and into the turbulent night.

Toland breathed a sigh of relief. He ran his hands quickly through his gelled grey hair, and then, eyeing Cyril and Jayne Bettany sitting on a bench in the far corner, he made his way over. "I bet both of you could do with a cup of tea?" he announced, fearing he was stating the obvious. Jayne looked away but Cyril nodded gratefully.

"I don't suppose there is any news yet Bill? Is there?" Cyril asked in a familiar tone.

"I don't know what to tell anyone if I'm honest!" Toland sighed, pulling up a chair so he could sit with them both. "It seems like our little village has gone crazy all over again. Nothing like this has happened since that Lambert House business…and that was twelve years ago!" Toland said. "Now, in one night I've got three dead bodies." He lowered his voice, casting a furtive glance over towards Louise Deane who was sitting looking very anxious near the front desk. "And at least two missing persons." His brow creased in bewilderment.

"Why only two? My son *is* missing as well." Jayne interjected, barely keeping her voice in check. Cyril squeezed her hand.

"I'm sure Bill is hoping that Peter will turn up soon… right Bill?" he hastily enunciated. Thankfully Toland took the hint.

"That's right Jayne…*I'm sorry*. I'm not classing Peter as reported missing yet. I hesitate to even put Lucy Doran in that category. I mean there's a good chance the pair of them have just eloped together?" He smiled. Cyril also managed a laugh.

"They could have picked better weather for it," he said hopefully. The sound of torrential rain drowned out the silence that followed.

"Is she okay?" Jayne finally asked, looking pointedly at Louise Deane. Toland shook his head.

"She's barely spoken since we found her at the church. Terrible business. Poor Trevor Crispin was being ambulanced out when she arrived. Whoever's done this has made a tidy mess of the church. Place looks like an *army* marched through it. Ash everywhere...but no sign of a fire." He explained. Jayne nodded.

"Our flat block was the same...and poor Jean's..." Again she began to cry. Cyril hugged her tighter, fighting back his own tears. Toland seemed unsure whether to continue, but his pause for thought had allowed Ivy Meredith to arrive with a tray of tea.

"There you go my dears!" she announced. "What a business, I'm worried sick you know?" she announced, as though no one else had yet thought about becoming even remotely concerned. "Where on earth that young girl's got to...on a night like this? I don't know? No doubt your Peter will be able to shed some light on it when he finally turns up...the pair will probably be married...about time too!" Ivy looked set to prattle on all night. Cyril hastily took a cup of tea for Jayne, and one for himself from the tray Mrs Meredith held in front of her, as though she were displaying a collection of sacred chalices. Toland rolled his eyes as Mrs Meredith continued in what she considered to be a whisper: "Won't they be surprised when they find out what they've missed? I hear some vandals destroyed the church good and proper! And poor Trevor Crispin...I know he was cantankerous but no one would have wished him any harm...except maybe Father Deane...and he is missing!" she deduced, tipping a wink towards Toland, in case he may not have foreseen this possibility. Toland dunked a biscuit in his tea and sighed. "Oh well! Can't stand chatting to you three all night," she suddenly declared. Having just spotted Miss Bloomer taking a fresh cup of tea to Louise Deane, Ivy feared she was about to miss some vital gossip. "I'll just see if Louise wants a biscuit?" she announced, depriving Toland of the packet of Digestives, just as he was reaching for his second one.

"Shame she couldn't stay," Cyril sarcastically announced.

"What is that woman like? She has no concept of what's happened here tonight at all," Toland moaned. "Three deaths… murders potentially," he continued. "I don't think we've ever had a murder in Wick Holm? That's why they've sent for the constabulary from Great Wick Holm station. They may even bring New Scotland Yard in. I'm telling you Cyril, if you could have seen what they'd done to old Arthur Green…animals." He broke off, shakily slurping his tea.

Jayne Bettany just stared out into the unsettled night. She felt ashamed that her own thoughts did not stretch to caring for all the families involved in the tragedy of this one hellish night. She knew that since Peter's accident her thoughts and concerns had become very selfish. She just wanted her only son to be safe.

3

The Equestrian Circle.

"*P*eter! *I can't breathe anymore!*" Sufi screamed at him, her face utterly contorted in pain. She was crawling on all fours across the wooden floor of her bedroom. The air was now thick with acrid smoke, and her white dress was coated in soot and dust.

Peter was still desperately searching for an escape route. He had his head out of the bedroom window, and was staring in horror at the fast spreading flames that licked at the roof.

The Still army had formed an unmoving cordon around Myfanwy. They were everywhere, bloating the landscape like spilled ink.

They were waiting for him to jump down from the burning farmhouse.

The minute he reached the ground, Peter knew he would be ripped to pieces.

"You are going to burn to death Sacred Mother."

The Lord of the Now called out to him. He was sitting astride the demonic Still-Rider watching the hellish scene play out in front of him like a conscientious objector. He had moved back behind his vast army of Still, and seemed a little uncomfortable with the rising heat from the farmhouse.

"Be certain that fire does not spread,"

he commanded Krinn, who stood a little way to his left.

Krinn was staring at the burning house, a faintly devious smile spreading across his lips.

"Frightened it will burn you...*again?*" he mocked. The Lord of the Now made to swipe Krinn, but he took a swift step backwards, and gripped the shaft of his glaive.

"You must watch that tongue of yours Krinn, or I will pull it out. You have done well tonight, though I fear for your methods sometimes."

"Everything is as it should be. The Sacred Mother is here, trapped with the Dream Blender like rats in a burning cage. I cannot help it if some other nonentities got in my way. They have been eliminated. I would have killed more of them if the void had not returned us here so swiftly," Krinn said in a tone laced with contempt.

"You are over zealous little slave...you will learn to curb your bloodlust,"

he threatened. Krinn seemed to accept this threat, and gave a slight bow of apology.

He had taken the spyglass from the folds of his cloak, and was training it on the woodlands by the river Tarn.

"What do you seek Krinn? The fire is to the west."

The Lord of the Now mocked him, but Krinn ignored the jest and continued to focus on the silent trees.

"You fear Ethanril will come here? He would be committing suicide if he chose to. Look at the army we have, nothing could escape us,"

the Lord of the Now proudly announced, spreading out his arms as though to reveal the full extent of his powers. Krinn remained unimpressed, as he took in the amassed Still with a single nonchalant glance.

"Ethanril is *already* here," he said, so casually it was almost an afterthought. The Lord of the Now stared incredulously at him.

"What?"

"He has been here all the time. Or did you not sense that yourself, my master?" Krinn was moving now, his black cloak swishing behind him like a tail as he leapt onto a tree stump, and crouched down to see directly between the farmhouse and the woodland. "The question is where he has secreted him-self...and of course the others?" Krinn seemed to hesitate in this one spot for a second, sniffing the air like an animal. Then he leapt off the stump and returned to his master. "I will take a horse and see if I can draw them out of hiding. They will not be far from here. Beware they will try to use the river Tarn to their advantage. Do not let the Still pursue them down the embank-ment, or they will lose them in the waters. They must be cut off before they reach it."

"What makes you so sure of all this?"

"The Dream Blender is Ethanril's sister, she is *trapped* in that farmhouse, and he will not let her die; even if it means *sacrificing his own life.* The Sacred Mother is their only weapon against you. I swear to you now they *will* rescue him, or *perish* in the attempt." Krinn's statement was emotionless, neither concerned nor impressed. The Lord of the Now arched his serpent-like neck downwards so his foul face was inches from Krinn's.

"If you're wrong Krinn, I will kill you. But if you're right, then you must not allow them to capture the Sacred Mother...If this Peter Bettany manages to flee the burning house, you will behead him before he escapes. Now, take the wild dogs with you, they will seek out your prey."

Krinn seemed unmoved by this rant.

"I will go alone. The dogs will *only* hinder me," he spat, and without pausing he sprinted a few feet away and jumped up into the saddle of his black horse. The great beast gave a whinny of surprise, and without glancing back, Krinn spurred it on at the gallop.

The Lord of the Now watched him go, his own feelings mixed. It was becoming clear that the powers he had bestowed upon Krinn were turning him into a highly skilled adversary. Yet he did not fear this, knowing that in a moment he could kill Krinn if it was absolutely necessary. He stared after the solitary black rider, keeping his glittering eyes on him until he disappeared into a veil of trees; finally he turned back towards the burning farmhouse, screaming out:

"Fill the air with Lepidoptera. Make the sky turn black."

Two bloated Still waddled forward to the left and right of the Still-Rider and belched forth a black cloud of newborn moths. The Lord of the Now turned his attention towards the two Still who had returned through the void carrying the unconscious bodies of Father Deane and Lucy Doran.

"Make haste back to Stilfanwyn Chasm with these two. They are not to be scarred in any way. Cage them up in the Hold and await my instructions,"

he ordered. With a short scream the Still lumbered away from him.

ॐ

"Stay as close to the floor as you can Sufi," Peter advised. He was lying next to her now, desperately trying to escape from the encroaching fumes. He wrapped his arms around the young girl and held her to him.

"I've *failed* you Peter, *I am so sorry,*" Sufi began, but Peter quickly silenced her.

"You have brought me *more excitement* in the last few days than anyone has ever managed in their life!" he said with a forced smile. He coughed heartily as they began to crawl back towards the window. Sufi pulled her hair out of her eyes and fixed Peter with a warm stare.

"I'm sorry I shouted at you *so* often Peter. *I really am*, I just *had* to try and make you see this was all real," she explained, coughing hard. Peter looked helplessly at her, realising the fumes were starting to suffocate her.

"It's real enough now!" he announced, hoisting her weakened body to her feet and dragging her towards the still open window. He held onto her hips and bent her forward so she could breathe in the early morning air. The effect seemed to work, as soon Sufi began breathing more deeply. Then she screamed.

"We're trapped here Peter," she declared, staring helplessly at the unmoving mass of Still that looked up at them from the surrounding fields.

With an unexpected roar, a blazing Still lurched upwards from its resting place just below the lip of the windowsill. Sufi nearly had her face incinerated as it tried to bite her. Peter reacted fast, pulling her back into the smoke filled room, and slamming the glass window shut against the creature's burning head. The old glass frame shattered on impact, but the blow was still strong enough to propel the creature off the window ledge and it spiralled backwards towards the snowy ground. Peter glanced furtively down and saw the Still hit the cold snow, which immediately extinguished its burning body. He looked upwards and saw even more Still moving across the blazing roof like scuttling spiders. Without the glass of the window left to protect them, the situation was looking very bleak.

Something heavy slammed against the wall.

"*Oh my Annabel!* Peter, *they're* in the house, *they're throwing themselves against the barricade!*" Sufi cried in alarm.

She was right. Already the weaker brick wall, which the Mist Children had hastily built, to cover up the doorway all those years previously, was bulging outwards from the continuous pounding. Peter cupped his hands over his mouth and nose as he stared helplessly at the ever-cracking brickwork.

"They're clever, *I'll give them that*," he shouted to Sufi. "They're hitting the bricks at their *weakest point* every time," he said, almost with admiration.

Sufi had plunged back into the haze of smoke and was trying to prise her bed away from the wall.

"Help me push this against the barricade Peter. It may hold them off for a few seconds more *while we jump*," she announced. Peter did not fully comprehend what had just been said to him, and began to move the bed with alacrity. Seconds later he looked up at her.

"*Jump?*" he said incredulously.

"*What other choice do we have?*" she screamed, pulling at the heavy bed with all her might.

At that moment, the barricade dissolved into rubble.

The noise was deafening as the final impact dislodged the supporting bricks and the whole wall caved in. There was a secondary noise, one that sounded utterly incongruous to the original rumble of masonry. It sounded like the splintering of wood and the freeing of an immense spring, just as if the workings of a large clock had suddenly exploded.

A plume of fresh brick dust ballooned into the air, mingling with the already thick smoke, which totally obscured the now exposed doorway. Peter tried desperately to block Sufi with his back so he would be the first in line for the Still, which he felt sure would any second spring through the opening into the bedroom. The sound of a man coughing harshly could be heard, and then boots scrambling over the bricks. As the dust cleared from the doorway the figure of a young man with wild long blonde hair, and wearing clothes of myriad colouring was revealed. He turned his rugged countenance towards the two huddled occupants of the room, and stepped confidently forward with his left hand clamped tightly over his mouth and nose. His right hand he offered to Peter who, utterly dumbstruck, found himself shaking it. The figure shook firmly back, smiling in a way that utterly changed the normally serious expression he wore, into an enthusiastic and amiable one.

"Peter Bettany…what an *honour* it is to finally meet you, I'm…"

"*Ethanril!*" Sufi had just poked her head out from behind Peter, who appeared utterly incapable of speech. She quickly pushed past him and hugged her brother. The brief respite of an open doorway had allowed some of the smoke to clear from the bedroom, but the air was still poisonous to the lungs. Ethanril was already on the move, upending the bed and dragging it over the rubble of bricks to wedge it into the gap of the doorway.

Outside the farmhouse, the weather had subtly altered. Snow was falling much heavier now, and a strong west wind blew across the paddock, combining to hinder the fire as it slowly spread over the roof of Myfanwy.

"I take it we're *not* leaving by the front door?" Sufi asked, placing her hands on her hips. Ethanril looked at her briefly.

"No *we're* not. The Still have utterly surrounded the farmhouse, and the fire is beginning to spread to the lower levels. I'd barely been inside Myfanwy more than a few minutes when the Still arrived here in full force. Thankfully, they *don't* know I'm in here." He had briefly turned back towards the rubble. "Shame that had to come down…still, shows how badly we built it!" he announced. "I used the grandfather clock from the hallway to break it down. If it only took *me* a few minutes, I have no idea how long the Still would have been kept out?"

"Well you designed it!" Sufi scolded with a laugh. Ethanril turned quickly towards Peter and flashed him another smile.

"I may have helped." He added quickly, "it never crossed my mind that someone might try battering it down with a Grandfather Clock!" Peter had attempted a reply but Ethanril was already moving towards the shattered window. "Not very *chatty* this new

Sacred Mother of yours!" he whispered to Sufi while hastily shaking off his wolf skin cape and throwing it over his shoulder towards Peter. "See if you can jam that under the bed, and fill that crack near the floor, it should stop any more smoke coming in…and I think there's more than enough of it in here already to keep us going!" Ethanril quipped.

The wolf skin cape practically landed over Peter as though he were a coat stand. Somehow the shock of the material falling around him, suddenly spurred him back into life. He moved quickly towards the upended bed and rolled the cape tightly underneath the headboard.

"Done," Peter said, returning to the window.

"What *happened* to you both?" Ethanril asked. He was sitting on the window ledge and leaning out backwards so he could examine the roof. "We saw the void reopen, but not here at Myfanwy. It opened near Stilfanwyn Chasm," he revealed.

"I was trapped in Peter's world for a while…" Sufi began. Ethanril had sat bolt upright at this news. "But Peter *saved me*; he found another way back to Myfanwy," Sufi said proudly. Peter wanted to shrug nonchalantly as if it was nothing, but the fumes from the bedroom just caused him to cough violently till his eyes were streaming with tears. Ethanril was smiling at him.

"We'd better get out of here," he stated. "I'm afraid the *roof's* out of the question too!" he said, beginning to lean backwards again.

At that moment a black wave of moths struck the front of the burning farmhouse. They covered Ethanril as he leaned backwards, and hundreds flew directly into the bedroom through the shattered window. They repelled Peter and Sufi, driving them further into the room. All they could do was cover their eyes as the moths attacked, and Ethanril, who was blinded by the mass of insects now crawling all over him, felt his grip loosening on his already precarious position outside the window. His back arched so he was hanging upside down vertically out of the window, flailing at the moths with both hands. He was hanging on for dear life with his legs clamping the window ledge as firmly as he could. Just as his back touched the jagged brickwork of the Farmhouse exterior he heard two violent screams. He craned his neck backwards to stare directly down at the ground, feeling the blood rush to his head. He looked on in horror as two bloated Still leapt from the snowy ground and gripped the farmhouse wall just below him. It would take them only seconds to reach him.

"*Sufi?*" Ethanril screamed out, realising he had only seconds left to live.

Inside the bedroom the moths were covering the pair like bees in a honeycomb. Peter staggered backwards, his skin alive with the insects as they swarmed all over him. He had backed against the upended bed, and stumbled over the pile of bricks that lay strewn across the floor.

Sufi raced around the bedroom, slamming herself into the walls in a frenzied attempt to crush the ash-covered moths. She saw Peter fall to the ground, and watched horror struck as his body disappeared beneath a swirling mass of insects.

Outside the window she could hear her brother screaming for help. Despite every instinct telling her to rush to Ethanril, she knew that Peter must be protected above all else. She looked down at her dress, which looked like it was moving with a life of its own as the moths spread across it. With a vicious swipe she dislodged a large percentage of them, almost winding herself in the process. Ash filled the air like dust from a freshly beaten carpet, and with a twist, she backed violently into the wall, crushing the swarming Lepidoptera that writhed up her spine. She didn't hesitate to see how much damage she had caused them. She could feel them slipping into her hair, tiny antenna probing her skin. She wanted to scratch her own flesh off to be rid of them, terror maddening her movements. She was running quickly towards the now buried

Peter. With a spring, she scrambled across the bricks and tugged the wolf-skin cape free of the doorway. Turning quickly, she spun the heavy material until it twisted like a thick coil of rope in her hand. Apologising to Peter under her breath she began to viciously beat the moths that shrouded him. They came away with each fresh strike, flying upwards and amassing across the ceiling. When Peter's body was finally revealed, Sufi billowed out the cape as though it were a bed sheet. She jumped down to where Peter lay sprawled, and covered them both with the cape.

Peter was coughing, and moaning faintly. Sufi held the cape tightly across them, feeling the material grow gradually heavier as the moths began to swarm onto it, trying to chew their way in. She silently prayed that Ethanril was safe.

The Still were screaming their hatred as they stalked towards Ethanril. They had fanned out, trapping him in a pincer movement. He looked on, held in the grip of utter revulsion as, with a horrible cracking sound, they dislocated their jaws to reveal even more rows of gleaming teeth.

Ethanril closed his eyes very slowly, focusing his breathing. He had pulled himself upward slightly, in an attempt to reach the window ledge. But as he did so, the moths that scrabbled over him, had migrated from his torso towards his legs, trying to disorientate him and cause him to lose his balance.

He exhaled slowly, and a strange sensation of calm flooded through his body:

In his mind's eye he was back in his Oak tree in Kilfanfyn Forest. Below him he could see Annabel. She was looking at him quizzically, wondering what he was about to do next...

Very slowly he relaxed, allowing his upper body to fall slowly backwards once again, bringing himself vertical against the exterior wall. His arms swung downwards towards the approaching

Still, who screamed with pleasure at the proffered feast. As his back once again brushed the wall, Ethanril felt the weight of his broadsword shift in its scabbard. With a smooth slip, it slid out of the leather holding, and arched outwards, falling fast. Ethanril's reflexes reacted like lightning, and he shot out his right hand, catching the falling sword by the hilt, just as the two Still sprang towards him with a united scream.

Ethanril cried out from the physical effort it took to twist his upper body away from the wall. Then with a precision swing, he decapitated both Still in one blow. The noise of steel slicing through the air filled his ears, and seconds later, the two headless bodies fell backwards from the wall, spiralling to the ground. Ethanril knew it would take them only seconds to recover once they hit the snow, so with a mighty lurch, he arched himself upright, and thrust his sword into the damp wood of the window ledge. It sank deeply into the rotting frame, and Ethanril pulled himself up, using the sword as a support. As soon as he was level with the window, the moths abandoned their position on his legs, and swarmed into his face, attempting to propel him backwards out of the window. Ethanril was too fast for them, he lunged into the bedroom, dropping to the floor, and scraping his hands violently over his face and scalp, dislodging the moths. As they flew upwards, he reached back and recovered his sword. He sheathed it, and spun on his heel looking for Peter and Sufi. For a second he couldn't see them, then he heard Peter's pitiful cough, drifting up from the dusty floorboards.

With a shout Sufi leapt upwards from the wolf-skin tent she had created. She brought the writhing cape up with her, revealing the spluttering form of Peter Bettany beneath. She hurled the moth-encrusted cloth behind her. It landed in a heap near the far wall, smothering and trapping a large percentage of the moths.

"They'll *soon* eat their way out," Peter spluttered as he struggled to his feet. He was spitting out ash that had accumulated on his tongue. Ethanril nodded, helping him to his feet, and noticing that already a few moths were escaping from a tiny hole in the fabric.

A vicious scream filled their ears, and the upended bed gave a sudden lurch as something in the passageway slammed against it.

"They're here!" Sufi stated, backing away from the cape, and standing next to the other two. Ethanril jumped forward and shouldered the bed, driving it back into the gap. His body took the full impact as another Still leapt against the door.

"I hate to say this…but we're going to *have* to jump," Ethanril announced.

"I *already* suggested that!" Sufi interrupted, "long before *you* got here!" She was adamant that Ethanril wasn't taking the credit for it.

"Well I think you're both *crazy!*" Peter concluded. He had rushed to the window, and was staring down once again at the grim situation outside.

The jump itself was perfectly feasible. The drop was not high enough to kill them, and if they landed in deep enough snow they would potentially escape unharmed. However, as Peter could irrefutably see, the minute they landed; the Still would swarm forward and crush them.

"It's *madness* to even consider it!' he cheerlessly continued.

The bed shuddered again, this time more violently as though a second Still had joined the assault. Ethanril cried out in pain, as once again he shouldered the charge.

"It's really simple!" he announced. "It won't take them long to realise the more Still they use the *faster* they'll break down this barricade. And then…" Ethanril began, slamming his whole weight against the bed, which forced the iron frame as deep into the surrounding brickwork as it would go, "they'll kill us," he concluded, backing away from the bed and drawing his broadsword. He spun it around with his wrist, so it wheeled in a shining arc of steel.

Sufi looked quickly towards Peter, who was staring from the doorway to the window. Neither option seemed inviting.

"O K" he said, very slowly. "*We jump.*" Ethanril stared Peter straight in the eye, his expression now one of pride.

"*Thank you* Peter," he said genuinely.

With a horrific scraping sound, the bed finally hurtled free of the doorway, driven into the room by a Still that appeared to have momentarily trapped itself within the springs of the bed. Two more cannoned into the room, uncoiling and immediately lashing out with their back claws. Sufi grabbed Peter's arm and pulled him backwards, just seconds before a claw whizzed past his face. He was staring at the vile creatures in horror, and Sufi knew she had to keep him moving or he would freeze on the spot.

Ethanril rolled forward underneath one of the leaping Still, and thrust his broadsword deep into the creature's belly. It screamed in rage as he spun round on the floor, hurling the shocked Still back out through the fresh gap in the doorway. The sound of its body crashing down the wooden stairs filled the room.

The second Still was advancing on Peter and Sufi as they backed towards the window. Sufi kept Peter behind her, watching mesmerized as the faceless beast stalked forwards, matching her step for step. Peter cried out as he felt his legs brush the window ledge. The Still tilted its head slightly to the right, and released a short harsh rasp, almost as though it were laughing.

It had them trapped.

Ethanril jumped to his feet, whirling to see the Still advancing on his sister and Peter. With a cry he lurched forward and grabbed the headrest of the gyrating bed. The Still trapped within it was desperately trying to claw its way out. Ethanril didn't hesitate; with all the strength he could muster, he toppled the full weight of the bed onto the advancing form of the second Still just as it prepared to jump at Sufi.

With a scream, the trapped Still and the iron bed crashed down on the unsuspecting creature as it began to pounce. The Still reacted too slowly to prevent the bed from crushing it against the floor. Immediately the maddened Still trapped within the springs began to attack its companion with a unmitigated fury.

Ethanril jumped over the bed, while the two Still remained distracted fighting each other. He sheathed his sword, and looked quickly out the window. His face seemed to have hardened, and he looked seriously at Peter. "We *will* die Peter…if you give up hope," he informed him. Peter was still staring at the ravaged bed, as the two Still fought on. With a roar, one ripped clean through the heavy mattress with its teeth. A plume of feathers shot into the air, as the exposed head of the Still emerged from the shredded mattress. It screamed at Peter, fully opening its jaws.

Ethanril had unsheathed his sword and decapitated the Still before Peter even had time to react. Sufi screamed, firstly in surprise, then in shocked relief.

"Let's go," she said firmly, spinning Peter round. Ethanril was already crouching on the windowpane, his sword clasped firmly in his right hand.

"You're killing yourselves. Surrender to me."

The Lord of the Now screamed at them. He was making his unhurried approach through the ranks of Still. Ethanril turned back to Sufi with a broad smile on his lips.

"Looks like there's going to be a fight!" he casually remarked, leaping out of the window. Peter gasped in surprise as he watched Ethanril's disappearing body. He was on the window ledge a second later, desperate to see him land. Ethanril hit the snow with a slight roll. He was on his feet in seconds, sword poised to repel the unmoving army of Still.

Peter squeezed Sufi's hand, enjoying one final time the feeling of warmth she generated.

"Are you ok Peter?" she asked almost comically. But Peter knew what she meant. He turned to face her.

"Yes I am." He suddenly sounded very resigned.

Behind them, the two Still practically tore the mattress in half to free themselves. The noise was as deafening as it was spine chilling. Peter didn't notice, not even the fact that the wounded Still had by now re-grown its lost head. He was holding Sufi's hand, staring into her blue eyes. It seemed only seconds since she had first come to him in Wick Holm church, and warmed his feet with her hands. So much had happened since then; so much of his life would be forever changed. Yet even in this moment, when he realised that despite it all, he was about to face the end with her, he knew he wouldn't have changed places with anyone, not for the world.

He heard the strange sound of Ethanril whistling from below them. The next second, just as the two freed Still launched at the window, Sufi and Peter jumped.

∾

Everything seemed to slip into slow motion for Pigeon. He watched dumbstruck as he saw Ethanril leap from the bedroom window of the burning farmhouse. He practically dropped the spyglass onto Fess's head in surprise.

Fess was crouched on a lower branch of the horse chestnut tree they currently occupied in the coppice near Myfanwy. Pigeon grappled with the spyglass as though it had suddenly come alive in his hands. He fumbled to keep hold of it then put it back to his disbelieving right eye.

"Ethan's just *leapt* out of the window!" Pigeon announced, utterly flabbergasted.

"*What?*" Fess shouted, as he practically fell out of the tree in surprise.

"Do you think *that* was the signal?" Pigeon asked. He was torn as to whether to look down at Fess or keep his eyes glued on the action at the farmhouse.

"He never *mentioned* anything about jumping through the window before he left us here," Fess said. He was now climbing up to join Pigeon on his branch. "I doubt he planned to do it...anyway I thought he told you quite *specifically* what the signal was going to be?" Fess accused, leaning over Pigeon's shoulder and trying to get a closer look through the spyglass. His goatee beard rubbed against Pigeon's cheek causing him to splutter in alarm.

"*Specifically...*" Pigeon enunciated, pushing Fess slightly away from him: "...is a *very* strong word!" At this Fess clouted Pigeon with the back of his hand, causing him to mess up Pigeon's spiky pink hair.

"Watch my hair!" Pigeon said, sounding more alarmed than he had been when the Still army had first swept into view an hour previously.

"Never mind *your* hair!" Fess yelled, almost drowning out the sound of harsh whistling that now whipped in on the freezing winds. "We *have* to stay alert otherwise we'll *miss* the signal...whatever it turns out to be!" Pigeon was raking his hand through his hair, desperately trying to restore some order.

Beneath the tree the four white horses stood tethered in a semi-circle. They were all bridled, their white coats glimmering in the winter sunshine. Astervarn pricked up his ears at the first sound of Ethanril's familiar whistle. He became agitated and began to pull at the leather straps that tethered his neck, keeping him close to the trunk of the tree. The other three horses also began to whinny in frustration as the persistent whistling called to them.

Fess had managed to wrestle the spyglass off Pigeon and was training it back towards Myfanwy. He felt the tree wobble slightly as the combined tugging of the four horses vibrated along the branches.

"They're going *nuts* down there!" Pigeon observed, staring through the canopy at the jostling horses. In that second the whistling stopped.

"*Thank Annabel for that!*" Fess flippantly remarked, adjusting the focus on the spyglass.

He froze.

Quickly he jiggled the spyglass and then retrained it on Myfanwy in the hope of altering the image he had just seen. As Pigeon rambled on about the distress the horses appeared to be in, Fess poked him firmly three times on the top of his shoulder, Pigeon stood up.

"*What is it?*" he hissed.

"I'm really not sure *how* to break this to you..." Fess slowly began, suddenly holding the spyglass as though it had turned into a stick of dynamite.

"If it's about my trousers..." Pigeon furiously retaliated, but Fess was staring at him, a look of shock on his face.

Again the whistling began, but this time more frantically.

"Oh blast that noise!" Pigeon said. "What's the problem?" he demanded of his suddenly frozen friend.

"Sufi..." Fess began, but upon hearing her name Pigeon immediately grabbed for the spyglass. He succeeded in retrieving it from Fess's limp grasp, but his hands were shaking so much that he fumbled it. He looked on helplessly as the spyglass fell through the branches of the tree. Pigeon audibly winced as it bounced off Lockavarn's head.

"*Sorry.*" he called down. "*Is she ok?* What was happening?" Pigeon continued to demand. He was now moving around the branch, desperately trying to get a better view.

"She just jumped out the window, holding hands with a strange man," Fess announced as though he were reading from an autocue.

"*Holding hands with a strange man?*" Pigeon cried, utterly missing the first part of the sentence and focusing solely on, in his mind, the more important issue. Fess nodded.

"Do you think *that* was the signal?" he asked. Pigeon nearly kicked him. He was about to start shouting as a way of dispersing the anger that now flooded his nervous system. However, it would have been difficult over the noise of the whistling.

"*Whoever* keeps doing that is *really* starting to…" Pigeon tailed off.

He looked at Fess.

Fess stared back at him.

A thought passed between them.

"*The signal!*" they both chorused, arriving at the same conclusion.

The two had clambered down the tree in quick leaps, and seconds later were untying the now frantic horses. They had to be careful the wild stallions didn't kick them as they fought to be free of their bonds and answer Ethanril's distress call.

∾

Ethanril, Peter and Sufi had formed a small triumvirate, commanding the west wall of Myfanwy as best they could against the horde of Still. They were overshadowed by the bulk of the ancient Oak tree, its twisted branches reaching out for them like choking arms. They bravely stood their ground as the Lord of the Now slowly rode towards them.

Ethanril's broadsword was never still in his hand, as he watched fitfully the front row of Still. All were silent, but all were watching. He knew that when they finally chose to rush forward the group would be overwhelmed, but he was determined to take down as many as he could. With a sly glance he saw that his left hand was shaking in fear, but he angled himself to hide this from the other two.

"Peter Bettany?"

the Lord of the Now demanded. The mass of Still had parted to allow him and the Still-Rider to pass through them, and arrive metres from the small group. Sufi squeezed Peter's hand as the Lord of the Now drew ever closer.

"Yes?" Peter tried to say casually, though it came out almost as a squeak. Up close now, he could see the full horrific vision that truly was the Lord of the Now. His spoiled bandages looked stretched to breaking point as they shrouded his muscular body. His mouth glittered with wet saliva and his shoulders hunched forwards causing his back to arch like a wolf's. He glared with unimaginable menace at Peter, as though his glance alone could kill him.

He looked exactly as Peter knew he would.

"We meet finally…and yet, it seems as though we have known each other forever,"

the Lord of the Now whispered almost resignedly. He dismounted, his feet crushing the snow as he landed. His whole body writhed like a King Cobra. The similarities failed to end there; his serpent like neck swung his smaller head from side to side as though he were trying to hypnotise any that looked upon him. Ethanril and Sufi inched closer together, neither meeting his gaze, but Peter stood where he was, a strange expression on his face.

"You're real?" he said with a gasp.

"Very much so…as indeed, is all this."

The Lord of the Now gestured to the surroundings. He seemed in no hurry to seize any of them, though Peter didn't doubt he could have killed them all in a second if he chose to. Behind him the Still remained immobile.

"*Its just not possible*...you burned." Peter was muttering unintelligibly. Both Ethanril and Sufi flashed him a confused look.

"*Annabel is dead,*"

the Lord of the Now announced, but before Peter could respond he had continued:

"*And now you...Peter Bettany, the second Sacred Mother, have come to meet your destiny. I have waited so very long for you.*"

The Lord of the Now took a step forward, closing the gap between them. Peter stood his ground, utterly transfixed by this nightmarish vision.

"I *always* knew you would come for me...*eventually,*" he sighed. The Lord of the Now nodded as though this was to be expected.

∽

Mundo scrabbled through the dense foliage and tried to find a more concealed vantage point. Behind him he could hear the gently babbling waters of the River Tarn. He looked up at the position of the sun. Even through the snow heavy clouds, he could see the winter sun vainly trying to penetrate the horizon.

He had expected to see the four white horses galloping past by now.

Surely Fess and Pigeon hadn't missed the signal? It had certainly been loud enough. Silently he prayed that Ethanril was safe. He thought back to their collective panic when minutes after Ethanril entered Myfanwy, the Still army had arrived. It was Mundo who had had to improvise a plan. Before leaving them to enter Myfanwy, Ethanril had said that he would signal them if he needed help. Not that he could have foreseen an army on such a grand scale cutting off all possible escape routes for him. But it did seem, with hindsight, as though Ethanril was half expecting an ambush of some kind. This thought comforted Mundo and he knew that it wouldn't take Ethanril long to work out how best to escape from the farmhouse.

"When he *is* ready to leave, we *must* send the white horses to him," Mundo had told Pigeon and Fess. "At the very least they will prove a distraction for the Still. If Ethan can just ride out on one of them he stands a fighting chance."

That had of course been before all hell had broken loose.

∽

While Mundo cut his way through the dense undergrowth of the woodland near the River Tarn, Fess and Pigeon climbed a tree to observe developments at Myfanwy. In the midst of this, chaos had torn the sky apart.

Even now Mundo had no clue as to what had actually happened. All he could swear to was the sudden change in the atmosphere as it seemed to revert back to the way it had been earlier in the evening when the void opened above Stilfanwyn Chasm. In his heart Mundo prayed that this new anomaly only heralded the return of Sufi from the Sacred Mother's world.

He was now trampling through the under-scrub. It had taken him a long time, but finally Mundo had found a suitable place to conceal himself. He cleared away the snow, pausing briefly when he heard a twig snap close by him. He stared fearfully around; unsure now whether he had actually heard wood breaking, or just the crackling of the fire that was spreading across the roof of his beloved home. As he turned slowly back towards the devastation, he heard the sound again. Only this time it was much nearer.

Mundo barely had time to roll to his left.

As he did so, the razor sharp tip of Krinn's glaive pierced the ground where only seconds previously he had been lying.

4 3

"*Wake up,*" Krinn hissed as he pulled his glaive free, spinning it in one complete circle, so that once again the skull-encrusted hilt pointed skyward. His black-clad frame gave him the look of a poised panther.

Mundo jumped to his feet and unsheathed his rapier in a second. He quickly surveyed the battlefield. The under-scrub encroached most of the area. Vicious brambles, dusted with snow penned the duellists into a small gap.

"*Krinn!* I'm ashamed I didn't hear you *slithering* towards me *you slug!*" Mundo retorted, checking the weight of the glistening blade in his hand. Krinn brushed off the insult.

"I could *already* have killed you Mundo, but it seemed such a shame to not give you at least a fighting chance," he idly remarked. Slowly he spun the glaive again.

"I should be careful Krinn…" Mundo bravely continued. "Ethanril is not far from here, and I just know he *won't* want to miss seeing you again." Krinn laughed sharply, then immediately stopped, fixing Mundo with a chilling stare.

"Your lies mask your *fears*. Ethanril is *trapped* in that burning hovel." Krinn pointed through the trees towards Myfanwy. Mundo almost lost the grip on his sword in surprise. "Surprised?" Krinn mocked. "I doubt he will escape the flames Mundo, even Ethanril is not that *lucky*. So I'm afraid there will be no audience…" Krinn's speech had slowed, as he coldly spelled out the words while preparing to strike his opponent. "…*to watch you die.*"

༺

"Bow down before me while you still have the chance. Your friends' deaths will be swift, I will promise you that. After all Peter, none of them has a future…"

The Lord of the Now was only inches away from Peter. Sufi and Ethanril stood like statues, only their eyes were moving as they glanced from the imposing bulk of their oppressor back towards his vast army of Still. Ethanril harshly whistled one final time.

"...*You waste your time Ethanril. Krinn will have found your friends and slaughtered them all by now.*"

At this revelation the whistle died in Ethanril's throat. He whirled to attack the abomination he now saw reaching out a horrifically burnt fist towards the petrified Peter.

"*Stay back boy. Your own end will come soon enough. Peter knows...*"

the Lord of the Now bellowed in triumph, fresh ash flying from his wet mouth,

"*...you have no future. You have no past. There is only...*"

But before he could finish his war cry, a low rumble shook the ground.

The small group looked at each other in surprise, even the Lord of the Now took a slight step backwards, away from Peter, as though fearing he was in some way responsible for this new tremor. His head slithered to face the direction from which the thunderous noise was erupting. Peter stared upwards, expecting to see the void split the sky apart like a cataclysm. The very foundations of Myfanwy seemed to be shaking as the heavy rumble continued. Ethanril had an expression of joy on his face as he twisted round and unexpectedly sheathed his broadsword. With two hands he took a firm hold of both Sufi and Peter, drawing them towards him.

Utterly confounded by what was happening, the Lord of the Now had stepped right back to the very front line of the Still army. He seemed momentarily unsure what course of action to take. Then suddenly he exploded with rage.

"*Tear them apart,*"

he spat with such fury at the waiting Still. With heavy steps he backed towards the waiting Still-Rider and leapt atop the foul beast.

With a united scream that shattered the remaining glass windows of Myfanwy, the vast army of Still rallied into life. Ethanril had both his arms wrapped tightly around Peter and Sufi, burying their heads in his chest so they wouldn't see the army drawing near.

He was whispering a prayer under his breath, as he stared down the advancing Still. With a final shudder of fear he too closed his eyes.

Like an unstoppable swell of white water, Lockavarn and his three brothers galloped across the snowy field of Myfanwy. The startled Still halted their advance as the white horses thundered past, churning the snow upwards and covering the front line of the Still in great clods of ice and sludge. They streaked like a single bolt of pure white lightning, aiming irrevocably for Ethanril, Sufi and Peter.

Astervarn sped at the helm, with Ratavarn and Jessavarn close behind him. Lockavarn cantered as fast as he could behind them. They moved as one, cutting a violent path straight through any wailing Still that separated them from the trapped group.

The Still, all on the brink of pouncing, fell away in surprise as the horses steamed past. Their brilliant white coats shining in sharp contrast to the ash covered creatures beside them. The horses eased from a gallop straight into a canter as they formed a protective circle around the three companions. They never broke formation, or stopped running, gradually increasing their speed again, until they were galloping in a continuous circle directly around Ethanril, Sufi and Peter. Like horses being led around a big top at a circus, they circled and circled the trapped friends, forming an almost invisible barrier between them and the enemy. Ethanril slowly opened his eyes; he had to blink harshly to adjust his vision to the blur of thunderous muscle that swept past them. The wind whipped in frenzy about them, almost bowling the three companions over as Ethanril released his grip first on Peter, and then Sufi. With an audible gasp, the two opened their eyes. They were utterly disorientated by the sight that now greeted them and in surprise they almost staggered into Ethanril.

"*What's happening?*" Peter breathed. Sufi was almost crying with delight.

"It's the white horses Peter. They're here to *rescue us.*" She sounded overjoyed.

The Lord of the Now looked on in anger, as Peter Bettany and his two companions disappeared completely from his view. All that remained was a blur of shimmering white. He growled like a caged tiger and dug his heels harshly into the flank of the Still-Rider. The great beast reared up on its hind legs and expelled a thick cloud from its nostrils. He attempted to spur it forward into the ring of white, but the beast just reared again, its hind legs backing unsteadily away and trampling on any Still directly behind it. The wounded beasts leapt at the legs of the Still-Rider, biting into the flesh deeply, more in shock than in rage. The demonic horse whinnied in agony, and before the Lord of the Now could take full control of the reins again, it had turned completely around and plunged itself in fury into the panicking mass Of Still.

"*STOP!*"

he bellowed, but the scent of fear was palpable in the air, the horse spurred onwards as he desperately yanked at the reins.

On all sides the Still were utterly panic-stricken. Some fought with each other while others, seeing their master retreating, or so it seemed, followed suit. A large percentage remained close to the white horses, who were now galloping so fast it was almost as if they were not moving at all. The Still stared at this archaeol circle in front of them, and tried to find a weak point to attack. The scent of the Sacred Mother and the Mist Children still permeated from within the impenetrable ring. Still were dropping from the twisting branches of the Oak tree, released finally from the imprisonment bestowed on them by the Lord of the Now. They expelled horrific cracking noises as they exercised their aching brittle bodies. Their minds filled with the circle of white, they knew they had to penetrate it to atone for past failures.

One Still, maddened with panic and frustration, launched itself at the thundering troop of horses. A violent noise erupted as it collided with the barrier. It was torn in half by the speed of the horses, and the other Still watched in fear as its body was dragged continually round in a sweeping arc, trampled under the heavy hooves of the white horses. Eventually it remerged like a tattered and torn rag doll, thrown clear of the ring, and sent crashing into several other Still who had moved too close to the front. The wounded Still lay shaking on the ground for several minutes, as slowly and painfully its limbs knitted together as though an invisible seamstress where performing a delicate operation on a shredded mannequin.

The weather had once again altered to match this new turn of events. The wind intensified, bringing a heavy sleet pelting down from the sky, dampening the flames, which had consumed Myfanwy. The blizzard battered down upon the Still driving them further together for protection against nature's own formidable fury.

The Lord of the Now flailed his hands, trying desperately to stop the Still-Rider's furious retreat. The driving sleet was blistering the beast's skin, causing it to panic even more and hurtle forward at an unstoppable pace. The Lord of the Now hissed in rage as the sleet became torrential, his vision blurred with the motion of the horse's violent galloping.

Ethanril was moving like he'd just been electrocuted. His whole body seemed jerky and unstable, as he first squatted, and then paced and finally dropped into a crouch on the snow-covered ground like an Olympic sprinter. Sufi and Peter watched him, their bodies gently being rocked backwards by the wind caused by the constant motion of the white horses.

"What's he doing?" Peter yelled at Sufi. She was right next to him, but the thunderous noise of the horses' hooves had made normal conversation impossible. The blockade of horses made the whole nightmare of the Still army seem unreal now. The group couldn't even see Myfanwy from where they stood; it seemed as though they had all been taken out of time and placed in a safe house until the danger had passed. Sufi, who had lived by her instincts for as long as she could remember, knew that this feeling was a fallacy. The Still wouldn't have abandoned them, even if their attacks were failing. The Lord of the Now did not give up that easily.

"He's looking for an escape," Sufi called back, her own body becoming agitated with excitement.

Peter had no idea what the next move could possibly be. In his own mind it made no logical sense that they were all still alive at this point. At that moment an image of Lucy Doran scribbling her phone number on a piece of paper filled his mind. That had happened only hours before. He couldn't clear the image from his head; it caused his brain to whirl in unhelpful directions as he tried to dispel the image of his home. He had to sit down, but just as he did so, Ethanril appeared at his side.

"Are you ready to run Peter?" he asked matter-of-factly. Ethanril's face was flushed with adrenaline; his deep chocolate-brown eyes studied Peter's confused countenance. "You're thinking too much, it's not good to lose track of the present Peter. Lets run free, then I'm sure we can all help each other," Ethanril said wisely. Before Peter could raise an objection, he had continued. "Do you ride Peter?" he questioned.

Peter hesitated in his answer; a fresh image had flashed across his mind, replacing Lucy. This time he was five years old, sitting mortified astride a donkey at Great Wick Holm beach. The donkey appeared equally disgruntled to be carrying Peter. Cyril and Jayne were standing a few feet away from him, all smiles. Peter had sat wrapped tightly in his small brown coat. He had been freezing in the wind chill from the sea and utterly incapable of moving his body for fear the donkey might rear upwards.

"*Smile for the camera!*" Jayne said enthusiastically. At this point the donkey had shuffled slightly, adjusting its weight on its stumpy legs. The unexpected movement had caused the already petrified Peter to burst into tears. It was that image that his Mother had captured on camera. And it was that image that now shined down on him when Ethanril asked his question.

"Not professionally," Peter admitted, shaking away the memory. Ethanril was trying desperately to read him.

"But you have been on a horse before?" he asked again, fearing the lack of experience Peter had. Peter cleared his throat nervously.

"*Sure!*" he said with unexpected confidence. Sufi smiled at him.

"He can't be any worse than Fess and Pigeon are!" she said to Ethanril, who quickly nodded agreement.

"Then get ready you two. We have one chance at this," he announced. He motioned for them to do as he did, and quickly he crouched down on the floor again. "I'm going to go first…" Ethanril began.

"*I don't think so!*" Sufi suddenly interrupted. "I can't defend Peter the way you can," she scolded her brother. "Besides, I'm a much faster rider than you are!" she said with feeling. Ethanril smiled at his sister.

"You're so *fiery* today!" he laughed. "Very well… *Sufi* will go first; take Lockavarn and ride as fast as you can. Make for the Tarn River, and do not wait for us. We will all regroup at Kilfanfyn as soon as we can. Remember that Sufi. *Don't hesitate.*" he insisted. "Are you ready Peter?" Sufi asked, glancing back at him.

Peter still looked troubled. The image of the donkey had stubbornly refused to budge. He stared first at the blurring horses, and then back towards Sufi.

"*Yep!*" he said, in a slightly strangled tone. Sufi smiled encouragingly, she knew he was petrified. Without a word she turned and squatted down in the snow, she moved her arms between her legs so she took on the position of a sphinx. The movement of the white horses transfixed her; it took all her instincts to detect Lockavarn amongst the others. To the untrained eye it would have been impossible, but Sufi could tell immediately that Lockavarn was slightly out of synchronisation with the other horses. She hesitated for a couple of seconds, and then shifting all her weight onto her ankles, she leapt forward. Her bare feet slipped slightly in the snow, and she cried out with exertion as she reached Lockavarn, grabbing him painfully by his mane. Her legs were dangling outwards, and her whole body was in danger of being ripped in half, like the Still had been before her. The horses sped in their eternal circle like a possessed merry-go-round, never letting up, even after Sufi's arrival. She screamed in pain, as she felt her slender frame buck and twirl in the whipping wind. With a final effort she pinioned her body around, and straddled Lockavarn's back. The second she was upon him Lockavarn galloped straight out of the circle and into the paddock of Myfanwy. The action appeared seamless to Ethanril and Peter, as in the same instant, the other three horses bunched closer together forming a slightly decreased circle around the two remaining companions.

The Still were utterly bewildered by the sudden appearance of Sufi and Lockavarn, free at last from the circle of horses. For a second they remained immobile, confused as to this new twist of events.

That second was all Sufi required.

She spurred Lockavarn onwards, darting amongst the confused Still that had strayed from the pack to examine the circle. Sufi stared about her, seeking the boys or any sign of the Lord of the Now. She could see neither. Remembering Ethanril's warning, she steered Lockavarn towards the Tarn River.

"Are you ready Peter?" Ethanril queried. He was still crouched on the ground, every muscle of his body seemed to have tensed in anticipation.

Peter's muscles had failed to follow suit. Anything but in fact, he felt as though they had all turned to jelly. He was finding it very difficult to balance his own weight on his wobbling legs.

"Now?" Peter tried to ask calmly, though it came out more like a demand. Ethanril glanced back from the horses to Peter, and for the first time he seemed to notice the look of abject terror on his companion's face. He quickly rushed to Peter's side, just as his legs seemed to be failing him completely. Peter went into an ungraceful slide, but Ethanril grabbed him, slipping his arm around his waist and hoisting him back to his feet.

"Breathe," Ethanril said calmly, though his voice carried such power in its tone that Peter immediately gulped in air. "*Slowly.*" Ethanril was insistent. Peter's chest palpitated as though he had just run a marathon; his own breath hurt his windpipe as it exhaled from his mouth. But gradually he began to calm down, his breathing becoming deeper and more regular.

"I'm not sure I'm up to this…" Peter stammered as Ethanril let him go. "I get travel sick even in a car on long journeys!" he pointlessly confessed. Ethanril seemed confused by the words Peter was using, but he stared him straight in the eye and said, "you have come so far Sacred Mother, been through so much. My sister tells me you rescued her from your own world. That takes great courage. Believe me; I know Sufi is not the sort of woman who requires rescuing unless a situation has gone beyond her control. You have an inner strength Peter, I see it blazing behind your eyes. Find it for me now? Let us ride out of here together… *to freedom.*" Before the enormity of this speech had fully sunk into Peter's struggling consciousness Ethanril tugged at the straps of Peter's bag. The action propelled him towards the centre of the circle of horses. He looked at the expectant face of Ethanril. It was clear that the time for talking had now passed.

"I'll never make the jump," Peter felt it his duty to point out, but as the words left his mouth Ethanril jumped into the cavalcade. Peter just stood, rooted to the spot with his mouth hanging open. Heavy sleet rained down upon him from the unrelenting sky, but all he could do was watch Ethanril fly through the air and land perfectly on one of the white horses.

As soon as Ethanril took a firm hold of Astervarn's reins he cried out to the circle:

"Scatter." The command was short, but obeyed with alacrity by the remaining two horses; they immediately darted off in separate directions. Peter watched in horror as the white force field he had come to rely on as his sole protection from the nightmarish army that awaited him outside of it, dissolved into nothing as the powerful stallions galloped away from him. His eyes now filled with the sight of thousands upon thousands of Still, all turning to stare at their much-anticipated feast.

For a second nothing happened.

Peter stared at the gathered creatures, and the hairs on the back of his neck quivered with fear. He knew as soon as he moved they would all attack him. They had simply let the other two horses charge away. They were unimportant. To his horror Peter realised that he was the sole object of their unwanted attention. A sensation seemed to pass amongst the Still, as one by one they scented the Sacred Mother. Peter was so transfixed by the mass of darkness that confronted him he failed to hear the pounding of approaching hooves. As every Still in his field of vision opened its mouth, revealing rows of lacerating teeth, he slipped to his knees.

With a mighty tug he was hoisted upwards, propelled out of the snow and flung over the back of Astervarn. "*Sit up* and grab hold of my coat," Ethanril commanded as he deposited Peter swiftly, and resumed the reins calling out to Astervarn to pick up pace again. Peter felt the pounding rhythm of the horse's powerful legs drumming through every muscle of his body. It juddered his precariously perched frame as he tried desperately to swing himself around to face Ethanril's back. His long coat seemed to be restricting his movements, and despite the cold Peter pulled it free and let it slip over the back of the horse. He knew he dare not look back; he had already seen two Still leap at his coat and begin shredding it. He was sweating badly, a thin line of perspiration flecked his top lip, and he could feel the beginnings of a headache start to pound his temples. He felt physically sick, but managed to grab onto Ethanril's multi-coloured jacket and rest his head, shivering against his companion's back. Peter felt the cold comfort of the straps of his bag digging into his shoulder. "*I'm alive…*" he managed to whisper. Ethanril heard this pitiful cry and smiled.

"Hold tight Peter," he advised. To Peter's astonishment Astervarn began to gallop even faster. The scene around him was blurring, just like the circle of white horses had, moments before. Myfanwy, the Still and the paddock were all becoming one horrible splurge of violently shimmering colour. Peter's head felt like it was on the brink of exploding, he closed his eyes but still the image seemed burned onto his retina. The next sensation he felt was falling.

4

The Pig-Beast.

*T*he Still-Rider had not slowed in nearly four miles. Leaving behind the chaos of Myfanwy it had set out at a tremendous gallop across the empty Wastelands to the west of the farmhouse. The Lord of the Now watched in dismay as the burning building disappeared into the middle-distance. Even the screaming of his Still army sounded fainter from here.

"Curse you!"

His rage was relentless as he tugged once again with inhuman strength upon the reins trying to slow the beast's retreat. The Still-Rider seemed impassive as it continued its charge towards the horizon. The Lord of the Now abandoned all restraint and, gathering up the reins for support between his ruined fists, he lurched forward in the saddle. His twisting neck slithered left and then twisted right before finally darting forward, with his savage jaws open almost to the point of dislocation. He aimed his bite directly at the horse's jugular. The Still-Rider, despite its panic seemed to anticipate this swift attack, and tried to twist its neck away at the last minute, but the Lord of the Now just mimicked the movement, sinking his prominent fangs deep into the black horse's neck. A cloud of ash erupted from the puncture wounds, as the Lord of the Now locked his jaws around the prey. The beast gasped for air, wildly shaking his head like an untamed prairie horse. It bucked upwards but the vampiric creature that thirsted upon its neck would not be shaken off. The horse's black eyes rolled over white with fear, and slowly its maddened pace began to lessen. All grace of movement seemed to have deserted the monstrosity, as with each further bite, the Lord of the Now appeared to drain the creature of its stamina. It made strangulated protests but nothing could dislodge the parasite that fed upon it. Finally, just as it arrived at an outcrop of pine trees its front legs buckled, bringing the creature to an ungraceful halt. Its head and neck slammed into a furrow of snow, and the Lord of the Now released his hold at the last second, leaping free. He turned to look at the convulsing beast; its back was twisted at an unnatural angle and wet froth was pouring from its open mouth.

"When you revive, return to Stilfanwyn Chasm,"

the Lord of the Now commanded, slithering away from the crippled horse.

❧

Peter hit the ground a second before Ethanril realised he had slipped off Astervarn's back. He felt the sudden change in weight as he sped the horse forward. Glancing back Ethanril saw Peter lying prostrate on the snow-laden field. He pulled quickly upon Astervarn's reins, stopping the horse mid-gallop and turning to face Peter's unconscious form a few metres away. Ethanril could see several Still already bounding towards the fallen Sacred Mother. He bent low to Astervarn's neck, kicking the horse firmly to reach Peter faster than the enemy would. At that moment he heard two distinctive screams.

Ethanril had no time to think as two Still curled either side of Astervarn and launched themselves into the air. Releasing the reins Ethanril squat-jumped so he was balanced atop Astervarn and like a surfer he stretched out his arms momentarily to gain his balance. As the Still cannoned towards him he jumped off the horse, drawing his sword and twisting his body into a spin. The two Still passed over him and were sliced in half by the whirling blade of Ethanril's rotating broadsword. Seconds later his body landed heavily in the snow. Astervarn galloped onwards and Ethanril had to break into a run as soon as he landed, ignoring the pain he now felt in his legs and arms.

Peter was coughing and spluttering in the snow as he quickly regained consciousness. He felt extremely foolish that he had fallen after he had been so bravely rescued. He was on his feet in a second, as to his surprise he saw the rider-less Astervarn heading straight towards him. Peter poised himself, taking in the approaching Still who were also encircling him. He tried to block them out and concentrate only on the pounding of the horse's hooves. He breathed deeply just as Sufi had done and at the moment he instinctively knew was right, he threw himself forward. He opened his eyes fully as he felt his fingers snaring Astervarn's mane. With some exertion he was astride the white horse, his breathing calm once again. The same adrenaline rush was flowing through his veins, just as it had done when he defeated the Still outside his flat block. He heard a cry to his left, and turned to see Ethanril with seven Still bearing down upon him. Peter spurred Astervarn on, holding onto the reins with just his left hand. Ethanril sheathed his broadsword, his eyes filled with surprise as he watched the Sacred Mother riding towards him on Astervarn's back.

"The prophecy is true." Ethanril whispered as he held out his hand. Grasping its opportunity the Still leapt straight at his unprotected back, their hind claws fully extended to shred his flesh. Peter grabbed hold of Ethanril's outstretched hand and with one firm pull he hoisted him beyond the reach of the attacking Still and onto the back of the white horse. The two rode on.

∞

Lockavarn was keeping a steady pace in front of the pack of nine Still that had steamed after the horse when it first broke free of the circle. Sufi rode with her thighs slightly raised above the horse's back to allow him to gallop even faster across the paddock. Lockavarn's movements were too random for the Still to imitate, and several became entangled in shrubberies and fencing as the horse and rider spurred ever onwards.

"Stay calm boy," Sufi whispered to the horse. Even she could sense that his movements where becoming more random than usual.

Lockavarn was panicking.

Sufi had complete trust in the wild stallion but she realised that the sight of so many Still may have unnerved even him.

Something had always been wrong with Lockavarn, ever since Annabel had first introduced him to Sufi all those years ago. Ethanril had groomed and inspected the white horse often, but had never been able to satisfactorily explain the horse's disorientation. He was not lame; he was not even poor sighted.

Sufi placed a small hand on Lockavarn's neck; she could feel the strain of his muscles and the beating of his great heart. She knew in her bones the horse was always holding something back, maybe a strength that had yet to be seen. "Show me what you can do," Sufi begged as the Still gained on them.

In that instant she screamed out in terror.

Looking forwards Sufi saw the fence that had formally penned in the white horses when the Mist Children had lived peacefully at Myfanwy. It stretched straight ahead of them, a web of vicious-looking tightly woven wire, linked to ancient wooden posts. She yanked Lockavarn's reins desperate to vault him over the fence, but the panicked horse did not respond quickly enough. They torpedoed into the fence at the gallop.

The speed at which Lockavarn hit the fence, combined with the weight of the colliding pack of Still, wrenched two of the thick wooden struts straight out of the icy ground. The wire pinged free of its holdings and whipped through the air, impaling two leaping Still. The creatures screamed in agony as they hurtled into the mesh of steel. Lockavarn's front legs slammed into the fence supports, propelling the white horse forward. Sufi was tipped straight over Lockavarn's head; she fell bodily to the ground, rolling to avoid the horse's falling bulk. She had landed at the brow of the embankment that led down to the Tarn River. Lockavarn violently twisted his neck and fell awkwardly. His body was lacerated from the weaving coils of wire. Sufi choked on some of the heavy snow that lay around her as she dragged herself to her knees. She was struggling to regain her composure as she watched Lockavarn convulsing on the ground, also attempting to stand.

Something growled behind her.

One Still sat squat on the snow, looking directly at her. Immediately she stopped moving. The Still had obviously jumped in time, unlike its companions who all seemed to be entangled in the wire. Sufi struggled for breath, her arms shaking to support her weight. She saw a broken stump of wood from the fence lying beside her. She took a very deep breath.

Moving like lightning she grabbed for the wood and swung it around with both hands. The motion caused her to lose balance but it successfully connected with the Still's head as it leapt at her. Momentarily the creature fell away as though it had been stunned. Sufi scrabbled in the snow on her hunches trying to sit up, but to her horror the Still was furiously shaking its head to dismiss the effects of the recent blow. With an ear-shredding scream it launched itself at her again. She swung out with the broken fence post, but this time the Still clamped its jaws tightly around it. She pulled and the vile creature tugged back like a dog playing with a stick. Playfully it suddenly let go, allowing Sufi, who had used all her reserves of strength to try and free the wood from the creature's mouth, to fall heavily backwards. The Still leapt upon her chest, she felt its weight bearing down on her. By a miracle she had still held onto the post. She swung again.

Below her, the River Tarn beckoned to her. If she could have just reached it, she knew she would be safe.

The Still grabbed the post between its jaws once again, its screaming face only an inch from Sufi's now. She knew it was far more powerful than she was; it just wanted to torment her. Behind the Still, Lockavarn had finally managed to stand up, though the horse seemed unsure of itself, rocking unsteadily upon its badly bruised legs.

"*Oh no you don't!*" A welcome voice bellowed across the paddock; just as the Still bit clean through the wooden post, showering Sufi in ash and splinters.

Pigeon rode Ratavarn triumphantly towards the pinned Sufi. He tore at the reins, forcing the white horse to clear the remainder of the fence first time. They landed close to the impaled Still, churning snow into their screaming faces as the horse sped onwards. At the last second Pigeon jumped free of the charging mare and catapulted himself at the Still just as it bent its wicked head to tear out Sufi's throat. He hit the creature with such force that he toppled it over the embankment, wrapping his strong arms around its waist, the two enemies hurtled like a barrel straight down the hill.

Sufi was on her feet a second later, watching in horror as her newfound hero disappeared in a cloud of ash and snow. He was spinning relentlessly down the embankment towards the icy waters of the Tarn River.

"*Are you ok?*" Fess called out to her, having just arrived on the scene. He had his rapier drawn as he rode Jessavarn at a canter, pulling on her reins to clear the fence and finally slowing next to Sufi and the shuffling Lockavarn. "What the hell..." he religiously began but Sufi was just pointing down the hill in shock.

The Still wrapped in Pigeon's non too-welcome embrace had regained its senses, its jaws were snapping violently together as it tried to bite Pigeon's exposed throat. The speed they travelled made any kind of a struggle impossible, and it was all Pigeon could do to keep the Still's head pulled back away from him. If anything he was screaming louder than the monster as they finally shot over a small hillock and unceremoniously splashed down into the dark waters of the Tarn.

The second they hit the water, Pigeon felt his grip loosen on the Still. He had been grabbing on so hard that when the creature disappeared, he found he was hugging himself underwater. He blinked his eyes, swishing his hands through the dark water, which if anything seemed even blacker than the last time he was in there. He was petrified as his lungs filled with water, expecting at any second the face of the Still to loom out of the darkness like a waiting shark.

Pigeon's head broke the surface of the water just as Fess and Sufi reached the edge of the river.

"Where is it?" he screamed, kicking and splashing towards the water's edge like a drowning swimmer. Sufi grabbed his hand and hauled him up onto the bank. He collapsed to the ground panting like a beached fish. "*Kill it Fess*, kill it if it grabs for me!" he spluttered, seeing his friend standing above him rapier in hand. Slowly Fess sheathed his sword. "*What are you doing?*" Pigeon cried out, struggling to his feet and drawing his own rapier. He looked back out at the babbling waters, then back to Sufi and Fess who were just staring at him. "*You might say something?*" Pigeon accused. "I have just *rescued you!*" He sounded most put out.

"Your trousers..." Sufi began.

"*Oh...*WHAT?" Pigeon was exasperated, was that still such a big joke with everyone?

"Your shirt...your face..." Fess tried to help her out, but he too was speechless. Pigeon briefly glanced down at himself, and then he did a double take.

His clothes were covered in thick clods of matted ash. He was stained head to foot as though someone had chucked the contents of their fire grate over him. He slid his hand down the thick muck, and stared in horror at the mess on his hands. There could be no doubt what had happened.

"The waters dissolved it," Sufi said, confirming what they where all thinking.

"Serendipity!" Fess whistled in amazement.

Pigeon stared back out at the water, part of him still expecting the Still to rise like a phoenix from the depths. He wiped his hands on the snow. Then getting to the floor, he rolled over in the ice, wiping off as much of the remains of the Still as he could. The three friends had no time to dwell on this revelation as Ethanril's voice called down the embankment to them:

"*Are you all ok?*"

They looked up to see him standing next to the now stationary white horses. Pigeon and Fess glanced at each other as they both caught sight of Peter standing next to him.

"He made it then?" Pigeon asked Sufi; his tone did not sound enthusiastic.

"I knew he would. Come and meet him, Pigeon," she said, smiling at him and squeezing his hand. Pigeon's heart did a small cartwheel in his chest. He hesitated for a moment and looked back at the coagulated mess of ash and snow left behind him on the ground. He half expected to see the particles knitting back together, but nothing moved. "You're my hero, Pigeon," Sufi said genuinely, hugging him tightly as they hurried up the embankment. "You saved my life."

"When have I *ever* let you down?" Pigeon joked, trying to mask his emotions.

Peter and Ethanril were talking quietly together, as Ethanril inspected the wounds on Lockavarn's legs. Peter had his hands pressed against the sides of wounded horse's head, and the effect seemed to be calming the animal. He had fixed Peter with his charcoal black eyes, and he was breathing steadily through his flaring nostrils.

"The Still are regrouping," Ethanril suddenly announced, not turning round to face anyone. Fess and Pigeon stood either side of Sufi, book-ending her; both of them had their eyes fixed on Peter's back.

"Is Lockavarn fit to run?" Sufi asked. Ethanril had one of Lockavarn's hooves in his hands and was inspecting the horseshoe. Gently he lowered the leg and stood up.

"He's injured Sufi, quite badly by the look of him. I'm confident he can ride, but not with any excess weight. *Pigeon,* Sufi will ride with you," Ethanril declared. He glanced at the boys; they were still staring at Peter who appeared to be whispering in Lockavarn's ear. Finally he turned. "I'm afraid we have to make this quick," Ethanril declared. "Fess, Pigeon…this is the Sacred Mother. *Though he prefers Peter!*" Ethanril said, flashing his mischievous grin. Peter took in the two new companions, offering his hand in greeting. A strange atmosphere seemed to hang between the three of them. Pigeon was the first to take Peter's hand, and this appeared to be what Fess had been waiting for, he then offered his hand.

"Glad to meet you Peter," he said, and Pigeon nodded.

Sufi sensed the tension that unfolded in this meeting. She could tell immediately there was a spark of jealousy between Peter and Pigeon. She tried to suppress it, but it had made her smile. She looked to her brother, but he was already sitting on Astervarn's saddle, with his spyglass trained back towards Myfanwy.

"Where do we go Ethan?" Sufi asked. "*Back?*" She sounded fearful.

"We can't go back...Saddle up," he suddenly demanded. "*They're coming.*"

Peter, Fess and Pigeon all quickly raced for their horses. Pigeon clambered onto Ratavarn, while Fess and Peter shared Jessavarn. "We've distracted them that's all!" Ethanril confessed. "Their leader has gone and they were lost, but the scent of us is all that drives them, remember that. I can see them converging here en masse, so we ride through the coppice to the river NOW!" Ethanril commanded. Sufi leapt behind Pigeon.

"Where's Mundo?" She asked.

"He should be in that coppice if I haven't lost my skills as a tracker?" Ethanril called back, staring at the broken twigs and trampled foliage near the entrance to the riverbank copse.

"We have something to tell you about the Still..." Fess called out.

"It will have to wait!" Ethanril cut him off, digging his spurs into Astervarn. The riders darted into the trees.

✍

"*COWARD!*" Mundo screamed out into the darkness of the coppice. He was leaning against a tall Wych Elm and wheezing with exhaustion. His shirt was ripped in several places, and he was clutching his right arm which had a sever gash running from his shoulder to his elbow. The blood had seeped through the white, and knitted his shirt to the torn skin of his arm as it dried. Mundo screamed through a split lip that refused to stop steadily bleeding. His rapier hung loosely from his wounded right hand. His flowing black hair dripped with sweat, and even the eagle feather in his hat appeared to have drooped. It was clear that if he didn't have the tree for support he would have fallen over.

"WHERE ARE YOU?" Mundo screamed again. His voice sounded as brave and strong as usual, yet physically he appeared defeated.

For what seemed like an age now Krinn had left him lying blooded and bowed on the ground. He had had the opportunity to kill him in that instant, but the Servant of the Now had suddenly appeared distracted. Mundo could still see him spitting down on his bleeding face.

"Keep breathing till I return?" Krinn had suggested before vanishing into the shadows of the trees.

Mundo's body shook with fear as with a mighty effort he wrenched his legs into movement. They supported his weight, thanks partially to the adrenaline pumping through his battered body. He had no concept of time anymore, and the strange and distant noises he had heard occasionally over the rushing of the Tarn were too abstract to attribute to anything. He silently prayed his friends were alive.

Without warning Krinn stepped from the shadows and aimed a vicious kick at Mundo's ankles, toppling him backwards. The fall jarred the rapier from his hand. The next thing he felt was Krinn's black boot pressing against his windpipe. Mundo looked fearfully to his left, watching as Krinn purposefully embedded the glaive into the ground.

"I had to wait till you'd regained your strength..." Krinn began, his voice as cold as a crypt. "...I refuse to kill you unless you can stand, Mundo," He stated. There was no triumph in his words. Mundo stared into Krinn's impassively hellish face.

"You've been waiting here all this time...waiting to see if I had the strength to stand?" He couldn't believe anyone could be so callous. Krinn idly flicked his oily hair. Without confirming Mundo's suspicions he pressed firmly down on his neck. Mundo gagged, his eyes bulged in their sockets and his Adams apple felt like it was about to explode in his throat. His tongue slathered out of his mouth and his brain began to panic as its oxygen supply was cut off.

A split second later Krinn was hit in the chest by a fast moving blur.

Mundo staggered to his feet clutching his throat and gasping for air. He had just seen Ethanril take Krinn down in one movement.

"Mundo!" Fess was sprinting towards him. Everything was a little out of focus; Mundo slid to the ground again.

Ethanril rolled off Krinn the second the two hit the ground; he drew his broadsword swiftly as he sprang to his feet. Krinn was already standing. He looked back at his glaive; the long-staff was still plunged into the ground several feet away. Krinn's cold eyes registered no response to this as he looked back at Ethanril.

"Your move?" he conceded. Ethanril allowed himself a smile.

Peter, Sufi and Pigeon rode into the open circle. They had been holding back, waiting with the white horses as Ethanril and Fess had continued on foot into the coppice. It had been Sufi who had first seen the bloodstains that had soaked into the snowy ground of the coppice floor. It was as clear a warning sign as she'd needed.

Pigeon leapt down from Ratavarn and made his way towards Krinn's glaive. It stood like a solitary marker, the morning light reflecting off its skull hilt.

"*Krinn!*" Pigeon called out. "I wondered when you'd show up?" he mocked. Krinn never even turned to look in his direction. It was Ethanril that noticed Krinn's gaze; it was fixed on the trees behind him.

"You're a fool if you think I'd turn round?" Ethanril quipped, his broadsword still pointing directly at Krinn's heart. For a second no one spoke, and then Krinn broke the silence.

"Something *unstoppable* is coming this way," he said with an inscrutable smile on his lips.

Taime burst through the cover of trees behind Ethanril. His brown steed galloped directly at the two frozen enemies as though he hadn't seen them. Ethanril hurled himself at the ground to avoid being trampled to death by the frantic horse. Krinn nonchalantly stepped aside, though even his idle movements had an essence of fear about them as Taime sped past, pulling harshly at the reins of his mare.

"TAIME?" Sufi cried out in total surprise. Taime seemed to register his own name, but his eyes could not take in the sight of all his friends unexpectedly converging in this one place.

Taime looked distraught, his eyes were filled with tears and his body shook with static energy. He gripped the reins of his horse so tightly his knuckles gleamed white against the skin.

"What has *happened* to you?" Pigeon demanded. Peter was staring at the newcomer, unsure whether he was another friend or an enemy.

Ethanril was on his feet and running a minute later. He sheathed his broadsword and screamed in frustration. He barked an order to Pigeon:

"Watch Krinn."

Pigeon drew his own rapier and approached the Servant of the Now at a measured pace. Krinn was transfixed by his glaive and seemed to be muttering under his breath. He looked up to see Pigeon striding towards him and mockingly held up his hands, feigning surrender.

Ethanril was staring at Taime's frightened horse, trying to calm the beast by keeping total eye contact with him. Taime himself was making the mare even more alarmed by his constant shifting in the saddle. He was sweating a great deal, and wiping at his forehead, always his eyes darted into the woodland around him. "What has happened Taime?" Ethanril breathed, his voice as calming as an infusion of camomile. Taime glanced down at him, seeming not to recognise his old friend. He looked back at the silent trees. Fess had his arms around Mundo and was helping him onto Jessavarn, aided by Peter.

Behind them a thousand invisible eyes watched the eclectic group.

"I *couldn't* save her, Annabel!" Taime exclaimed, his eyes welling up with fresh tears. He was clearly traumatised. Mundo could hear his friend's anguished cry. Even slumped in the saddle of Jessavarn he realised what must have happened.

"He's gone into shock again Ethan," Mundo cried out. "He hadn't fully recovered from that blow Krinn dealt him on the Tarn Steps; something has pushed him into trauma again." Mundo finished, coughing in agony himself. Peter attempted to dress the gash in Mundo's arm with ripped cloth from his own clothes.

"Couldn't save who, Taime?" Ethanril pressed, keeping his voice low. Taime's horse was jolting dangerously; Ethanril feared it could throw him off its back any second.

"The little girl...she just didn't run *quickly* enough...OH ANNABEL!" He was hysterical now. "I led it away from them, but it won't give in." He sobbed as with a deft movement Ethanril leapt up and joined Taime in the saddle. On impact the brown horse rose onto its back legs as though it had been electrocuted. At the same moment a violent rustling filled their ears and a strange smell was carried across the coppice by the cold east wind.

"*Sulphur!*" Fess yelled in a panic.

The air filled with horrific screaming.

The Still surged through the coppice, penning the small group in. Their foul screaming stopped as soon as they saw Krinn's glaive glowing like a beacon in the centre of the circle.

"You will let me go," Krinn informed Pigeon, and before he could respond he had already strode away from him. Once he reached his glaive he pulled it free of the ground, and marched towards Jessavarn and the wounded Mundo.

Before he could reach him, the ground had begun to shake. Krinn did not look back as everyone else, including the vast army of Still fell silent.

"*It has found us!*" Taime screamed. The noise of heavy foot-falls had snapped him back to reality. Ethanril grabbed Taime's chin from behind and forced his head painfully round to look him directly in the eyes.

"WHAT HAS?" he demanded.

At the same instant, the blood stained Wych Elm that Mundo had leant against for support, was uprooted from its sixty-year stool and flung violently towards the River Tarn. The beast that forced its way out of the coppice to stand four metres tall in front of them sent Peter's mind reeling into the realms of absolute terror.

The Pig-Beast roared like a thousand enraged lions, stretch-ing out its powerful arms, to reveal a chest whose girth must have spanned over a metre across. Its violently quivering muscles seemed to bulge with this action. It bent its great head down, and opened its mouth that seemed infested with row upon row of gleaming teeth. Two giant tusks like mountain peaks protruded from the corners of its mouth. Its head resembled a razorback pig, with a snout that constantly belched forth clouds of angry smoke. It stood upon two legs like a mockery of mankind. Its hind legs looked as thickset as tree trunks, supported by mighty hooves that stamped the ground mercilessly. Its whole skin seemed to be constantly alive as though it had been poured in warm sticky tar. The ever-swirling black mass only added to the already terrifying demeanour of the monster. It grunted and roared again, the trees around it shaking with each fresh violent outburst.

Peter was staring mesmerised by the abomination in front of him. He failed to see the Still begin to scatter in panic around him. He completely missed Krinn sprinting towards him. All he could focus on was the swirling blackness of the creature. It had taken him a moment to realise why the skin of the Pig-Beast seemed to be constantly shifting, but now the true horror was revealed to him. It didn't have flesh; the whole gorgon was a writhing mass of one evil word; as though the creature was intent not only on rampaging its hatred through the world it now plagued, but also vilifying its name upon all those who saw it.

So no one would forget, least of all Peter.

The two words were repeated over and over again, forming layer upon layer of thick, wet, leathery skin: *Pig-Beast*.

Peter almost vomited, as with one sudden movement the Pig-Beast swung its head in his direction, its eyes seemed to be brimming over with hell's brightest fire. Then it plunged its snout forward, raking its arms through an entire mass of Still, and turning the air foul with the stench of visceral horror.

"*We Ride* NOW!" Ethanril screamed, reaching around Taime and grabbing the reins. He sensed immediately that they had been given a reprieve in the form of this monstrosity that now seemed intent on slaughtering the entire army of Still around it. The evil black creatures were sprinting away in all directions, their screams no longer of triumph, now they were fuelled with panic. The Pig-Beast was relentless in its attack, and to the amazement of the group, who were all straddling their respective horses, the wounded and crushed Still, did not recover from the attacks rained down upon them by the beast.

"It can actually kill them!" Sufi said, almost in wonder.

"HELP ME!" Mundo screamed out.

Everyone turned their horses in a panic. No one could focus immediately on the direction of his cry. The white horses were rearing and whinnying, as they tried to avoid the fleeing Still.

The Pig-Beast was hammering its fists upon the front ranks of the army who had formed into splinter groups with the intention of battering its legs from beneath it. The Still rushed forward, but the Pig-Beast tore up the ground with its hooves, crushing the charging cohorts with giant clods of earth, snow, and fallen deadwood.

It was Pigeon who saw Krinn pull the struggling Mundo free of Jessavarn's saddle. He allowed the wounded Mundo to fall bodily to the ground, then snaked his arms up and wrestled the mesmerised Peter Bettany free of the horse. Jessavarn was trotting in a small circle, trying to back away from the Servant of the Now. The jerky panic of the horse only aided Krinn in toppling Peter. While the group attempted to converge on him, Krinn dragged Peter away from the chaos and into the darkened coppice.

"Where is he?" Mundo demanded as Pigeon helped him to his feet. As if in answer Krinn tore out of the trees, riding his black horse directly through the clearing. He was too fast to be stopped by any of the confused group.

"He's aiming for the river, he has the Sacred Mother," Ethanril cried, riding after the disappearing Krinn. The group rallied themselves quickly. Sufi helped Mundo back onto Jessavarn, and then leapt up beside him, wrapping her arms around him and taking the reins. They all bent their heads low as they galloped away from the destruction in the clearing.

Still fled in all directions, so preoccupied with their own escape, they ignored the retreating group. The Pig-Beast was diving at them with squat lurching movements, as though he were foraging for food. His head would shoot forward, and then quickly pull backwards, his jaws crammed with dying Still.

Krinn was shouting commands at his thundering black steed as he urged it forwards down a short embankment and into the waters of the Tarn. The horse plunged in, the water level reaching its neck. Krinn jammed the reins in one hand, using the other to keep the gasping Peter's head above the fast moving water. As strong as his horse was, the powerful current of the river continually threatened to drag them all under its choppy waters. The horse strove for the far embankment, and by the time it reached it, Ethanril was already leading his group into the water behind them. Krinn glanced back, registering that he was still being pursued. Viciously he sank the spurs of his black boots into the horse's side, drawing blood. The dark animal galloped forwards across the icy plain.

The weather had broken now, the sleet storm having passed over, but the chill of the wind blistered Peter's face as the horse sped on. His mind was still dealing with the vision of the Pig-Beast. He seemed to be in the grip of a mental tug of war. One part of him knew he should be fighting Krinn, yet another told him to give up now, it would all be so much easier that way. He couldn't grasp the concept that the giant boar he had just seen ripping apart the Still, was the same monster that had foraged for him in the snow the first night he'd met Sufi.

The rushing of the river Tarn forced the group to match each other's pace in order to stay together. Several times the undercurrent proved too strong even for the horses, and despite their best efforts Sufi and Mundo found themselves drifting slightly away from the rest of the group. Ethanril and Taime had penned Lockavarn betwixt their horse and Ratavarn. The white horses did not fear the water, but they were all anxious to reach the riverbank. Fess rode Astervarn, and Pigeon kept one eye on Sufi, and another on Ratavarn's progress. Already they could see Krinn disappearing across the plains of Carrastorc. He was making his way back to Stilfanwyn Chasm with the Sacred Mother; if he reached it all would be lost. Behind them they could still hear the roaring of the Pig-Beast. They each silently prayed it would remain distracted by the Still for long enough to allow them all to escape.

❧

A mile upstream a black shape sat hunched on the Tarn Steps watching thoughtfully as the little group made their slow progress across the river.

✍

Krinn whistled harshly through clenched teeth as he continued his relentless drive across the plains. Behind him he could sense that Ethanril was gaining on him. He knew in his black heart that he would never make it back to Stilfanwyn Chasm, the weight of the extra body was slowing his horse, and the animal was fatigued from crossing the river. In front of him Krinn saw the lake of Carrastorc looming. A fresh idea flashed across his mind.

✍

"Wild dogs!" Sufi cried out, alerting the charging group as from the east and west of the plains six fast moving shapes could be seen. She shuddered in the saddle of Jessavarn, and Mundo felt her convulse.

"Are you ok?" he asked, concerned.

"This is just like my dream..." Sufi began in a whisper. She was working it through in her mind, and suddenly she shouted to her brother.

"*Ethan!* He's going to drown him in the lake." With a sudden tug Ethanril brought Taime's horse to a halt. The whole grouped slowed as Ethanril leapt off and turned to Taime.

"Keep a firm hold of the reins. The horse will carry you," he said. Taime's eyes looked more focused; he nodded but did not speak. Ethanril was heading in Fess's direction. Without being asked, Fess had already started dismounting Astervarn.

✍

"Come," Krinn advised, leaping down onto the thick ice of Carrastorc and gesturing to Peter.

Krinn's black horse lay dead near a large boulder at the edge of the ancient lake. The Servant of the Now had flogged the black horse to death in his haste to escape the Mist Children. He cared little and had all but forgotten the animal as he dragged Peter mercilessly away from the fallen stallion.

Peter sat on the hard ground, dabbing a finger at his bleeding lip. Without warning, Krinn swiped him across the face in exactly the same place again. The blow was even harder this time, and the already throbbing pain in Peter's skull intensified. "*Come,*" Krinn ordered again. He was determined Peter would walk like a man to his death.

Slowly Peter rallied himself, and with fear making every footfall ten times heavier than normal he began to slowly rise and follow the swaggering Krinn. Peter clawed his hair out of his eyes and stared at Krinn's swirling black cloak. He looked out at the ice of the frozen lake, desperately seeking a way to turn this situation to his advantage.

What was this place? Even in Peter's wildest dreams he had never imaged such a landscape. He searched the ground for a weapon.

"What a *disappointment* you have turned out to be, Sacred Mother," Krinn mocked. "I think Ethanril was expecting *so* much of you…I do believe he thought *you* were the saviour of the Mist Children." Krinn spun on his heel and viciously punched Peter in the stomach, so hard Peter thought his insides had exploded. He dropped to his knees gasping for air. "You wheeze like that old woman," Krinn commented. This seemed to snap Peter out of his distress. "*Ahh…*I see you know who I refer to…*Candicote?*" Krinn said emotionlessly. "She took several minutes to die Peter. I wonder how long *you'll* take?" He announced it as though it were a scientific experiment.

"The question is…*Krinn,*" Ethanril shouted, as he halted Astervarn at the lake's edge, and drew his broadsword. "…How long will it take *you?*"

∽

At mid-day Nurse Samantha Raynor finally finished her shift at Great Wick Hospital. It couldn't have ended any sooner for her. She had practically raced through the final items of paperwork she had to complete before she checked out. Normally she would have hung on and had coffee with a few other Nurses from the day shift, but not today. Her experience with Patient 143 earlier that morning had left her frightened and claustrophobic. She needed to get out of the dark wards of the hospital.

The electrics were still playing up and the lights continued to flicker like fireflies as she made her way down to the medical library situated on F-wing. She had nodded politely to Janice Speakman, the mousy looking librarian and then proceeded to find a free computer terminal from which to work.

The library was crammed with fourth year medical students desperately trying to read long journals on all manner of medical subjects, or finish essays before the Christmas holidays. Samantha found a free space near the middle of the room and pulled up a chair.

With shaking hands she inputted her personal details and password in order to gain access to patient records. She found herself surreptitiously glancing over her shoulder, for some reason fearing she was being observed.

"I'm doing *nothing* wrong," she reminded herself under her breath. After all, this kind of research into patient history was all part of her job. She coughed self-consciously as the computer asked her for the patient's file number. Her fingers gingerly pressed the relevant keys: 143

The screen filled with information concerning Samantha's coma patient. She shuddered as she glanced through the early paragraphs, and then hit the print button.

She had practically run to her car, and found that her hands were shaking uncontrollably as she turned the key in the ignition. As she hurriedly pulled out of the staff car park she paused only to wave at Doctor Kidson who was also striding towards his car. He allowed her a cursory wave back. Samantha grimaced at him through her misted windscreen; safe in the knowledge that he couldn't see her. She was soon away from the hospital and in slow moving traffic.

The storms of the previous evening had abated and the aftermath could be clearly seen as she headed home. Power lines and trees had been toppled, and traffic jams congested the main roads out of Great Wick Holm. Local radio was filled with unsubstantiated stories of multiple murders and vandalism in the local area. Samantha turned it off; she was feeling spooked enough without wanting to listen to speculation. It was always the same at this time of year, she thought. The dark nights draw in, the weather vents its spleen and everyone starts to hallucinate. "Hog wash!" she said, resting her head on the steering wheel as she tugged at the handbrake. She rubbed her bleary eyes and shivered. The morning was cool and crisp, and the clouds still hung heavy with the threat of snow. Samantha wiped her windscreen with a cloth and stared out at the line of cars in front of her.

On the back seat rested Patient 143's file. Samantha had only once been inclined to read it, and that had been about twelve months ago when she had taken over 143's care from Mary Graham.

Slowly the cars started moving and half a mile later, Samantha turned off into a cul-de-sac. She rolled her side window down; slowing her car to a crawl until she located the house number she was looking for.

A small cottage sat inconspicuously a few yards back from the road. A white picket fence hedged the prosperous wildflower front garden, and large trees kept unwanted onlookers from staring into the small windows of the cottage.

Samantha parked up, wondering why she was doing this. She reached into the back seat of the car and retrieved the file, then made her way gingerly towards the cottage. She was still feeling jumpy, even as she unlatched the gate and made her way up a slightly cobbled path to the lattice-framed front door. A knocker in the shape of a fox caught Samantha's attention and she rapped on it three times, bundling the file under her arm. She pulled her coat around her for warmth while she waited for someone to answer.

"Hold on!" called a timid voice from beyond the door. Samantha took a step back, fearing she would be seen as too presumptuous if she simply stepped inside. She took another look at the garden. The storm had broken some of the fencing away in one section.

To her left something moved very quickly amongst the bushes.

Samantha caught it out of the corner of her eye, too big to have been a cat. She motioned towards it, when the door swung open.

A stout, white-haired old lady stepped over the threshold towards her. Her figure did not match the small reedy voice with which she spoke. She was wrapped in a woollen shawl, and was holding a television remote control in her left hand as though it were a club. "*Yes?*" she said in a voice no louder than a whisper.

"Mary Graham?" Samantha asked, suddenly feeling very foolish. The old lady clearly didn't remember her.

"Yes my dear? *Are you selling something?*" she queried, eyeing the file clamped under Samantha's right arm.

"*Oh no...*no!" Samantha quickly explained. "I'd like to talk to you about patient 143." She had not planned to blurt it out like that, but the old lady was surprisingly intimidating. Mary registered no response to this.

"*Who* my dear?" she said, and then abruptly continued. "You have called at *rather* a bad time I'm afraid if you're canvassing…I'm afraid I've just had some *very* bad news…" Her voice sounded suddenly even more distant.

Samantha wished the floor would open up and swallow her away. Why had she come and disturbed this poor old woman?

"I am very sorry…" Samantha began, casting her eye in the direction of the bushes again and starting to back down the path. "I just wanted to talk to you about your time at Great Wick Holm hospital."

"Don't go dear," the old lady suddenly shouted, beckoning her back. "Time at the hospital you say?"

"Yes…you *obviously* don't remember me, but I took over the care of your patient. That's *who* I wanted to talk to you about…patient 143?" Samantha tried again. Mary cast her eyes over Samantha, taking in her slightly disturbed appearance. Something seemed to grow clearer to her. With a gentle pat on the back Mary led Samantha indoors.

"Oh…now I understand my dear…*I do*." she said, closing the door behind her. "You want to talk about Annabel."

5

The Frozen Lake.

$\mathcal{P}$eter clamoured to the edge of the lake, his breath heavy in his chest. He pulled at the wavy-haired grass that grew in tufts by the water's edge. They came away in his hands and he fell back a short distance wincing in pain. He reached upwards again but this time a soft hand grabbed his wrist. He was pulled upwards by Sufi, and the minute he realised it was her he threw his arms around her in delight.

Mundo was sitting a few yards away atop Jessavarn; he managed a wave in Peter's direction. Close by him stood Lockavarn, Astervarn and Taime's brown mare.

"Thank *Annabel* we found you Peter…I thought you were lost to us!" Sufi said, squeezing him tightly. Peter was smiling like a maniac; the warmth of Sufi's skin seemed to be reviving his spirits. She allowed him to pull away from her, as he seemed to be collecting his thoughts. Quickly he turned back to stare at the duel that played out across the lake.

"Ethan…" he began.

"Don't *worry* Peter," Sufi said. Peter stared back at her. He had suddenly become aware of the absence of the rest of the group.

"Fess…Pigeon…Taime?" he asked.

"They're having a small dog problem!" Sufi said with a knowing smile.

౿

"This is truly *unbelievable*!" Pigeon moaned. He was beating his hat against Ratavarn's head as the horse sped across the plain. In the distance he could barely make out the figures of Krinn and Ethanril duelling on the ice.

"Don't take it out on the horse!" Fess yelled from behind him. "It's your girlfriend's fault!" he commented. Pigeon attempted to turn round and start beating Fess with his hat, but the movement nearly toppled him off the horse.

"It's not Sufi's fault...and she's not my girlfriend!" Pigeon defended her. Fess suppressed a smirk. "Once is an accident... but this is the *second* time this has happened!"

"He's right though," Taime's voice called out from the back of the horse. Both Fess and Pigeon turned to look at him.

"Oh...feeling *better* now are we?" they asked. Taime, who was hanging precariously onto Fess, and trying once again to prevent himself slipping off Ratavarn altogether and into the waiting mouth of one of the pursuing wild dogs, considered this diagnosis.

"I've been *better*!" he concluded.

"No one *asked* you to come!" Pigeon called. "Or you!" he said to Fess who was in the process of pointing and laughing at Taime. He stopped, and swivelled back round.

"This is *my* horse!" he declared.

"It's *my* horse as a matter of fact, I let you borrow him after the *tragic* loss of your own; and just because Ethanril pinched Astervarn back from you, doesn't mean you had to come with me and lead the dogs away from everyone!" Pigeon was into his stride now. His voice was wobbling as Ratavarn churned up the bumpy ground.

"I THOUGHT..." Fess deliberately yelled down Pigeon's ear, causing his friend to wince in pain, "you'd never handle it on your own!"

"What?" Pigeon exploded.

"That's certainly why I came!" Taime announced.

"You've certainly recovered now *piggy's* gone!" Pigeon said. "*Here!*" He continued reaching backwards and slapping Fess roundly on the cheek.

"*Ow!* What was that for?" Fess yelled.

"*Pass it on!*" Pigeon laughed.

∽

The ice around Ethanril's boots creaked violently as he backed away from Krinn. The Servant of the Now seemed to move more surely across this terrain then he did. Neither had spoken for several minutes as they had clashed over and over again, edging further towards the centre of the lake.

Krinn swung forward with his glaive, and Ethanril managed to deflect the first strike with a swift side cut of his sword, Krinn twisted his glaive backwards in the hope of spinning Ethanril's sword out of his hands, but his opponent held on tightly to the weapon, jarring his wrist badly. With a cry, Krinn lunged forward again, this time grabbing the glaive with both hands and violently slamming the length of the staff into Ethanril's face. The blow jarred Ethanril's head backwards, and blood erupted from his nose. It wasn't broken, but his head was swimming from the attack. As Ethanril dropped forwards, Krinn spun the glaive again, thrusting downwards like an Eskimo spearing a fish. Ethanril rolled to his left, and then quickly back-flipped to avoid the razor sharp tip of Krinn's evil staff. The metal glaive chipped away at the hard surface of the lake, sending splinters of sharp ice into the air. Ethanril stood up quickly, but he felt the tread of his boots sliding on the deadly ice. If he fell over uncontrollably he was in danger of breaking his neck.

"You *can't* save him," Krinn stated, gesturing with his head, back towards Peter. "You're only delaying the *inevitable*." He struck forward again, whirling the glaive towards Ethanril's head. It didn't leave Ethanril much time to react; he was forced to crouch again, which left his balance unstable. The glaive whipped through the air just above his head, but before Ethanril could stand again, Krinn twisted the weapon downwards, slamming the tip into the ice. Using the glaive for support he lashed out with a vicious roundhouse kick that caught Ethanril across the temples. Krinn's boot had opened up a deep gash across his forehead. Blood poured down Ethanril's face. He was wobbling as he stood and the blood was stinging his eyes, he blinked to clear them just as Krinn retrieved the glaive and sliced him across the chest with the tip. Ethanril dropped his broadsword in shock as he clutched his now bleeding chest. The heavy weapon clattered onto the ice and slid several feet away from him. *"You're dead,"* Krinn informed him, as without mercy he launched himself forwards.

Ethanril toppled backwards, seeing the Servant of the Now jumping at him. He landed hard, but managed to avoid slamming his already woozy head against the ice. As he watched Krinn bearing down upon him, he kicked out with both legs, hitting Krinn squarely between the eyes. Krinn fell sideways on contact, and hit the ice violently. Ethanril didn't allow himself any time for a reprieve; he was on his feet and running for his broadsword, with Krinn already pursuing him.

Ethanril fell forwards again, sliding across the ice completely off balance, but managing to reach the hilt of his broadsword. He barely had chance to spin and hold it in front of his face to deflect the blow Krinn was hammering down upon him. The two weapons sparked on contact and the mortal enemies separated for a brief instant, holding out both hands to steady themselves as they regained their balance and prepared to strike each other again.

"Surrender Krinn…" Ethanril advised. "You *can't* win. There's too many of us here. Your master has *deserted you*, you're all alone." Krinn failed to react to Ethanril's violent stance. He rolled his shoulders to loosen off the muscles and then beckoned Ethanril forward with his finger. Ethanril had one hand against his bleeding chest. The wound was not deep, as his chain mail had taken the full impact, but the cut had ripped his skin.

"I'm not the one who's *dying* here," Krinn assured him. Again he darted forward, and the two parried each other's attacks across the now blood stained ice.

The harsh winds whipped up the icy air around the two fighters, now locked in mortal combat, though neither seemed to notice the worsening conditions. The air was filled with the clash of metal against metal. Ethanril deflected every thrust that Krinn made, but he was becoming fatigued. His balance across the ice seemed to worsen. As he arched his back to avoid a particularly violent swing, his spurs struck the ice and rotated like cogs. Ethanril wildly flailed his arms like a windmill as he fell to the ground again. Krinn laughed manically and bore down on his floored victim. "You Mist Children all die *so easily*," He whispered as Ethanril struck the ice. Before he could defend himself, Krinn had slammed his right boot hard against Ethanril's wrist. The blow reverberated across the ice as Ethanril's sword once more fell from his grasp on impact. He cried out for the first time in genuine agony. "Is it broken?" Krinn sounded interested. Ethanril glowered at him, and without warning grabbed Krinn's leg with his free hand, tugging harshly with all his strength. The Servant of the Now was thrown off balance, releasing the pressure upon Ethanril's right wrist as he to crashed onto the ice. Ethanril leapt upon him, beating Krinn's face with his whirling fists. The glaive dropped from his hand as Krinn attempted to protect himself from Ethanril's attack. He grabbed for his throat, attempting to choke the life out of his enemy. Ethanril gasped for air as the pressure increased on his larynx. He gripped the material of Krinn's black clothes, and rolled over, dragging the Servant of the Now with him. The two enemies spun over and over again across the ice, attempting to dislodge each other. The frozen lake seemed to moan in protest with each fresh impact.

⟡

Peter was on his feet, his body tensed to breaking point as he watched the pair wrestle across the icy lake; gradually they were heading closer towards the bank.

"He's *killing* Ethan," was all he kept repeating under his breath. Sufi and Mundo were looking on in horror as the battle continued. "He saved my life today...I can't just *stand here* and let him die," Peter suddenly announced. His voice sounded strong and decisive, and Mundo and Sufi seemed unsure as to whether they'd just been berated.

"You *can't* help him Peter," Sufi implored as she watched the Sacred Mother striding towards her. Peter's face looked sterner than she'd ever seen it before. He ignored her words, and stopped his pacing just in front of Jessavarn and the resting Mundo. Without asking, he grabbed the hilt of Mundo's rapier which he could see hanging at the wounded boy's side. He drew the sword with a flourish.

"Hey!" Mundo yelled in anger and alarm, too weak to actually prevent Peter from taking the weapon. Peter stared at the sword in his hand; he clenched and unclenched his fingers around the hilt, feeling the weight of it for the first time.

Something inside him told him he already knew how to use it.

"*You'll* end up killing Ethan yourself if you try to join in," Sufi admonished him. She was scrabbling on the snowy ground, searching for something.

"That thing out there...*Krinn?* He told me *he'd* killed Old Mrs Candicote before he found us, Sufi," Peter said. His voice had lost all the apprehension and excitement it normally carried, and his eyes fixed upon the young wild girl, brimming with tears.

"*Jean Candicote?*" Sufi couldn't comprehend the words that Peter was saying. She stopped her search immediately. "*She's dead?*" Sufi reiterated, hoping that Peter was playing a very sick joke.

"Krinn *murdered* her...or so he tells me," Peter growled. He sliced the air viciously with Mundo's rapier. The action rallied Mundo into life.

"You will do this lady no favours by putting yourself at risk Peter. We've only just met...*I know*. But I think you're just starting to realise how *important* you are to all of us. Think of the risks everyone has taken to get you here. Jean Candicote was a wonderful old lady. The whole group will feel her loss, I *assure* you of that. But the time for revenge is not now." Mundo finished harshly, forcing Peter to look back at him. "You are *not ready* to face Krinn yet Sacred Mother, *believe me,*" he insisted, gesturing at his own wounds. "This fight is Ethanril's I'm afraid," Mundo sighed. Peter let the words sink in. Sufi had begun scrabbling through the undergrowth again, wiping away the thick snow. Her actions had become manic.

"We *can* help him Peter..." Her voice had gone light, almost as though she were singing him a lullaby. "I *dreamt* this all once.... we can help him, we just..." Her words died in her throat, replaced by a whimpered scream.

The wild dog sat hunched a metre away from her right hand; the hand she had just closed around a large flat stone. Sufi froze, staring the satanic beast straight in its glowing black eyes.

No one had seen it break free of the pack as they pursued the Mist Children across the plain. The dog's senses had picked up the Sacred Mother being carried eastwards by Krinn's horse. It set out on this course while its brothers were led away by the boys towards the west. In the chaos that had followed the great beast had stalked undetected through the bracken by the lake's edge, keeping downwind of its victims and looping them like a sheep-dog herding a flock. It had waited patiently in the snow until the moment was right to strike. The dog had been pertinacious; convinced it had also detected the scent of the Dream Blender. Its patience had finally been rewarded.

Sufi stared at the dog. Its jaws had begun to froth at the edges and its giant tongue lolled eagerly out of its mouth. The panting of the dog was only fractionally louder than the beating of Sufi's heart. She knew she'd never pull the stone free in time. The dog was already preparing to savage her.

For a moment time seemed to stand still. Then the wild dog began to violently growl, jerking its head backwards and forwards, each time producing more and more saliva in its throat as it ground its fangs viciously. It dived towards her, teeth bared, snarling and growling as though it were rabid. Sufi screamed and staggered backwards.

Peter sped at the leaping dog faster than he thought it possible he could move. As the creature tore at Sufi's clothes in a fury to reach her skin, Peter thrust out with the rapier, impaling the wild dog straight through the side of its throat. The power of the strike caused the dog to immediately topple off Sufi's chest and slide to the ground next to her. It made violent retching sounds as Peter drove the rapier deeper into the dog's skin, until it erupted in a shower of blood from the left side of the dog's neck. Peter released his hold on the rapier, stunned by what he had just managed to do. Sufi scrabbled to her feet, backing away from the dog. They both watched in horror as the black hellhound shook violently in a death spasm. Its tongue wormed out of its mouth, lathered with blood, its black eyes bulged with the violence of the strike that had speared its throat.

It died abruptly.

Mundo staggered towards them. He was clutching a large rock that he had managed to prize free of the ground in an attempt to save Sufi. He was staring awestruck at Peter. Sufi watched in wonder as Peter strode over to the dead dog. Placing one foot firmly against the creature's head he withdrew the rapier in a deft movement.

"*Thanks.*" he managed, offering Mundo the bloodied weapon. Mundo quickly handed Sufi the rock and took back his sword.

"That's *ok*," he said, looking utterly perplexed.

Sufi was staring at Peter with renewed admiration. She felt a strange sensation in her heart.

Peter's hands were shaking, but his mind felt clearer than it had since he'd arrived in this new world.

Sufi was making her cautious way towards the lake's edge again. Everyone's attention had returned to Krinn and Ethanril's duel.

"Where are you going with that?" Peter called after her.

∽

Ethanril squatted on top of Krinn; he had his hands pressed tightly around Krinn's throat. To his left he could still see his broadsword, glinting in the midday sun. Ethanril tried to turn his head to locate Krinn's glaive, but the staff must have slid further away than he remembered, as he couldn't see it. The Servant of the Now was struggling for breath, but refused to relinquish his own hold on Ethanril's throat. Finally both warriors released each other at the same time, gagging on the icy air, and shakily regaining their composure.

"You are a fool to let me go Ethan…you should have killed me while you still had the chance," Krinn said. A movement caught his eye and he appeared briefly distracted. Ethanril had learnt to ignore these tricks when in combat with his enemy.

But Krinn *had* anticipated the Pig-Beast's arrival last time.

Stubbornly Ethanril refused to look. When Krinn next met his eyes, he was smiling triumphantly. "*Time's up...*" he began, preparing once again to lash out. Ethanril bent his head forward and dove at Krinn, bringing him bodily to the ground. This time however, Krinn appeared to relish the move, it allowed him enough room to twist away on impact and kick Ethanril in the head again. The blow sent Ethanril's head swimming. Fresh blood dripped into his eyes and a sick feeling rumbled through his stomach.

He was passing out.

Krinn was the first to stand. He watched amused as Ethanril staggered upwards, like a blind man trying to locate his stick. Krinn kicked Ethanril's sword away.

"*I can't see...*" Ethanril began, panic-stricken. Krinn mocked his jerky movements, keeping just out of reach of Ethanril's grasping fingers. Blood was streaking down his face, and his whole vision flickered in and out of focus.

"*Such a pity*," Krinn laughed, preparing to throttle Ethanril to death. As he stepped towards his confused opponent, something whizzed through the air in his direction. Krinn leapt backwards to avoid the rock that had been aiming for his head. It smashed at his feet, sending a violent splash of dark water up through the small crater it had left in the ice. He shot a glance back at the bank where Sufi, Peter and Mundo stood defiantly.

"You missed," he spat.

"*I don't think so*," he heard Ethanril reply. Krinn turned to see him backing quickly away towards the bank. Ethanril's movements where still shaky, but his vision had cleared. He slipped on the ice a few times but managed to right himself without actually falling over, stopping only momentarily to retrieve his fallen broadsword.

Krinn stared in horror at the jagged crack that split through the ice in front of him like a lightning bolt. In a second a gap had erupted in front of him cutting off his escape. He couldn't make the jump across it for fear any harsh movements would cause the ice to crack even more severely. He watched mortified as Ethanril reached the Sacred Mother on the far bank. The original crack now had connecting splinters veering off in all directions around him, and Krinn felt the weight shift on the ice he was standing upon. He tried to move backwards as tiny icebergs began protruding upwards from the churning black water of the lake around him. More and more sections of ice were separating and forming miniature islands. He tried to balance out his weight, but the ice moved and tilted with every step he took. He looked imploring around him for assistance, but no one was coming to his aid.

"*This is not over,*" he screamed defiantly at Ethanril who had fixed him with a victorious stare.

"*It is for you,*" he retorted. Krinn hissed in anger, as he moved to jump onto the next section of ice. As soon as his weight shifted, the ground slid upwards from under him and the ice flow tipped him off balance. Krinn looked behind him to see nothing but swirling black waters beckoning him to an icy grave. He fell backwards, arms outstretched to save himself from the merciless ice flow. His black cloak swirled around him as he hit the water and disappeared into the all-encompassing darkness of the lake.

As Ethanril clambered onto the lake's edge, aided by Sufi and Peter he heard the final cracking of ice as the waters swallowed up Krinn's body. He looked back and saw the tremor causing more and more disruptions across the ice.

"It's breaking up completely," Mundo whispered in wide-eyed wonder. "The lake is *breathing* again Ethan...I never thought we'd live to actually see *the water.*" He was almost crying in amazement.

"Everything is changing Mundo…just as the Great Find promised it would," Ethanril said, wiping blood from his eyes.

"*Are you ok to ride?*" Peter asked him, noting all the wounds his friend was checking. Ethanril looked up with a smile.

"I thought that was usually *my* question to you Peter?" He laughed.

A cry from behind them made the whole group turn their attention away from the splintering ice. Ratavarn was speeding towards them still carrying the three boys on his aching back.

"We have to ride *quickly* Ethan!" Pigeon was calling out as he halted alongside them. "What in Annabel's name has *happened* to the lake? We could hear it cracking," Pigeon continued, staring out at the chaos of the twisting ice.

"No time to explain now!" Mundo apologised as he and Sufi struggled onto Jessavarn.

"The wild dogs are still after us. I think we lost them in the scrubland, but I doubt it'll take them long to pick up the scent again," Taime explained.

"Either that or they'll spot Pigeon's trousers from a mile away!" Fess laughed.

Ethanril, with some help from Peter, mounted Astervarn. Peter gestured towards the body of the wild dog in the snow.

"*You missed one*," he stated, climbing up behind Ethanril as the boys tried to work out what had happened.

"Do *you* think Krinn's dead, Ethan?" Sufi asked. Ethanril was staring back at the churning lake.

"*I don't know*," he sighed truthfully. "Come!" he suddenly announced to the group. "It look's like we have granted ourselves a reprieve. Let's take Peter back to Kilfanfyn Forest. We all have *so much* to discuss, and *so much* to prepare." His voice sounded refreshed; once again it was tinged with hope.

"I don't think I've had chance to say thank you," Peter managed. He felt stupefied by all that had happened and he knew that no words could truly express his gratitude. "You've all risked so much to rescue me," Peter said, cursing himself for sounding so pathetic.

Fess and Pigeon were both smiling at him, very aware that a strange feeling had passed between them as they watched Peter struggling to find the right words. They feared that they might actually like him.

"Well, *Peter* Bettany," Mundo announced, "we are the Mist Children. And you…" he deliberately paused, "…are our last hope." Peter felt a shudder of responsibility pass through him as the group spurred on their respective horses, heading out across the desolate plains of Carrastorc.

❧

The dark shape watched them gallop away. It gripped Krinn's glaive in one of its ruined fists. With stealth it had tracked the group this far. It was waiting for a suitable moment to continue pursuing them.

It had only one goal in mind.

With Myfanwy burning to the ground, it needed only to find the second hiding place of its enemies, and then the real destruction would begin.

The Lord of the Now moved with alarming skill and speed. His hatred drove him forward, it was all he knew.

❧

Morquinda scattered the runes away from her, an expression of frustration creasing her already haggard face.

"What vision do you see now sister?" Elyse asked, crouching next to her. The noise of gargling snores echoed through the caves as Felicia and Isabella slept soundly near the crackling fire.

Morquinda coughed in announce, trying to dislodge the phlegm clogging her throat.

"I see the truth that everyone awaits," she rasped at her sister, turning awkwardly to observe Elyse's reaction. The firelight danced hellishly across her eyes.

"Time is running out then?" Elyse questioned, fear cracking her voice. Morquinda laughed horribly and nodded.

"Who will be the next to die?" Elyse morbidly asked. Morquinda reached up with her withered right hand and pulled her sister closer, whispering a name in her ear. Elyse sat bolt upright, her expression one of utter dismay.

"How very sad," she managed with a woeful cry.

6

Mary Graham.

"*B*e careful dear...it's hot!" Mary Graham advised, gingerly handing Samantha Raynor the steaming cup of tea. Samantha had to awkwardly retrieve the hospital file from under her arm and then find a resting place for it, before she could actually take the cup. The little sitting room was extremely orderly and Samantha felt as though she were upsetting the karma of the entire cottage just by sitting there. Mary was still holding out the teacup, seemingly oblivious to the nurse's discomfort. Finally Samantha precariously balanced the file on the edge of the armchair and accepted the tea. She smiled, noting the manufacturer's stamp on the base of the saucer. It explained why Mary had taken so long to return from the kitchen. She must have been trying to find the best china for her guest.

"Thank you," Samantha said gratefully. The old lady smiled kindly at her, but instead of returning to her seat, she hovered, her eyes searching the room for something. Samantha followed her gaze, guessing she was now looking for a coaster.

The sitting room looked spotless. The highly polished mantelpiece displayed only two neatly framed family portraits. The walls exhibited a couple of paintings by a local artist, and a certificate from the Wick Holm Poppy Brigade, congratulating Mary Graham on twenty years of service.

A large and inviting sofa dominated the far wall; book-ended by two matching armchairs upholstered in a patchwork weave. The armchair which Samantha currently occupied felt as though one of the springs had actually snapped inside it, she had to keep adjusting her weight in the chair for fear of actually ripping through the bottom lining.

Mary was clearly a collector of glass, as her sideboard contained an impressive array of hand-sculpted pieces. A small open fire crackled happily in the hearth and even with the curtains half-drawn to block out the drizzly morning, the room still looked bright and inviting. The thick cream carpet covered a slightly uneven floor. Two incongruous lumps protruded from the centre of the room, as though the carpet fitter had forgotten to remove a couple of small rocks before he fitted the underlay. The lumps, as Mary had explained to Samantha immediately upon entering the sitting room, were in fact tree roots, belonging to an oak tree, which had only recently been felled from her front garden. The tree had obviously been of some considerable age, but Mary confessed she was *'glad to see the back of it!'* The tree had been blocking the light from her windows all the time she had lived in the cottage. Samantha struggled to imagine the cottage cast in shadows; it was appalling to think that this picturesque view from Mary's front window had once been completely obscured.

"It was Annabel who kept suggesting I cut it down…" Mary unexpectedly began. She had just found a three-week-old magazine that would double as a coaster. She placed it down in front of Samantha and with a nod of thanks; the nurse placed her teacup upon it. "…Oh and I'm going back years now, before she even came to the hospital, poor girl. She used to sit…right where you're sitting now and say 'Mary, that tree is *jealous* you know?" Mary raised her eyebrows, which caused the wrinkles on her forehead to furrow like a ploughed field. Samantha was unsure if the pause here was dramatic, or whether she was expected to react to this news. She bent to pick up her teacup, knocking the file off the arm of the chair as she did so.

"I'm sorry!" Samantha apologised, hastily retrieving the file, her face flushed with embarrassment.

"Please don't worry yourself. I drop things all the time; you wait till you reach my age miss...err *miss...*?" The old lady had obviously forgotten her name already.

"Raynor...Samantha Raynor, but please...call me Sam."

"Sam...what a lovely name. I once had a Border Collie called Sam!" the old lady announced, in a tone that suggested she was paying Samantha a complement.

"That's very...*sweet*!" Samantha managed. She gave up trying to balance the file, and just placed it on the floor by her feet. Mary was now sipping her own tea quite contentedly; the air was thick with an awful empty silence.

"You were saying about the tree?" Samantha prompted, reaching for her cup again. For a second Mary didn't react, and then suddenly she seemed to bluster into life once more.

"That tree's jealous! That's what she said. *'Jealous?'* I asked her. And she looked at me; you know, in that way she always used to?" Mary questioned. Samantha looked frustrated but kept her impatience in check, remembering why she had come to visit the old lady in the first place.

"I'm sorry, I *don't*...I thought I'd said before? I never knew Annabel before she became a patient. In fact I've only known her for twelve months...since I took over her care after you retired." Samantha cursed herself, she could hear the strain in her voice, it made her sound unfriendly and that wasn't her intention. Mary seemed not to have noticed and carried on without changing her approach.

"Of course dear...you will have to excuse my memory. It really isn't up to the standards it used to be. Well anyway...

Annabel had this way of looking...you see? Oh! She was such a pretty little thing. A *real* heartbreaker in the making. I tell you that girl had a smile that could fetch *ducks off water!* But it was her eyes that got to you...I don't suppose you've ever seen them open...such a pity." There was a definite pause for a sip of tea; Samantha didn't dare interrupt for fear of throwing her completely off track again.

"Deep green eyes they were, just like emeralds," Mary continued, swallowing her tea with a polite gulp. "I know that sounds tacky...even from an old *biddy* like me, but I swear as sure as you're sitting there, they were the most extraordinary colour. Almost..." she laughed, but it was a nervous reaction, "...almost, as though they weren't a part of her at all!" Samantha felt a chill creep across her shoulders. In her mind she was back in Patient 143's tiny room, the sound of her regulated breathing filling her ears. She briefly closed her eyes, shivering slightly.

"Are you cold dear?" Mary asked, making to stoke up the fire. "I've kept it burning low today after the weather turned. Still..." she tailed off, looking out her cottage window at the turbulent skyline, "makes a change from all the snow," Mary chirped. Samantha leaned forward, with her elbows resting on her knees. She had both hands wrapped around the teacup.

"I'm fine Mary...just shivered that's all. Tell me more about this tree?" It was almost a plea.

"She *hated it!*" Mary continued as though she'd never deviated from the topic. "Couldn't stand it," she reiterated. "Kept on saying it was *jealous! Jealous* of the warmth and happiness of my living room and that's why it was trying to invade it!" She gestured with her finger to the bulging lumps in the carpet. "She used to talk about it as though it were actually capable of thought! Jean and I would sit here for hours listening to her go on...such an *imagination*. She drew me a picture of the oak tree once; *uhh!* You should have seen it! It would put you off gardening for life. Looked nothing like my tree...*no...not at all!* It was all brittle and horrible with these things hanging from the branches like baubles on a Christmas tree..." Samantha finally managed to cut her off.

"*Jean?*"

"Jean Candicote."

"You say it as if I should know her?" Samantha tried again to be polite. Mary looked offended for the first time in the whole conversation. The teacup in her hand shook ever so slightly. For some reason Samantha tensed herself, as though she were expecting the old lady to suddenly hurl the cup at her. Mary breathed unsteadily for a moment, then, as though she had been sedated, she smiled at Samantha.

"Once again, I beg your forgiveness. Just because she was a close friend of mine doesn't mean you'd know her...I just thought you might have heard the news that's all?" Again Samantha looked perplexed.

"*News?*" she cued.

"I had a call from Winnie Bloomer...she works at Wick Holm library. She only phoned a few moments before you came...I guess that's why I'm so uptight with you, it's just *not* sinking in..." The old lady's eyes had moistened, and with shaky movements she ferreted up the sleeve of her gingham blouse for a tissue. Samantha felt even more agitated. A sense of guilt now pressed down upon her, it was clear she should never have come round. Mary had retrieved her tissue and was wiping a stray tear from her eye. "Look at me *blubbering* here." She half smiled. "Apparently there has been a murder...or at least that's how it seems at the moment, possibly more than one." She sniffed.

"*Good lord!*" Samantha exclaimed. "Was your friend...*Jean Candicote*, was she...*" She had no intention of finishing the sentence, but Mary nodded sadly.

"I'm so sorry."

The awkward silence that followed felt like a pressing weight on both their shoulders. Samantha bent to pick up the file, not knowing what to say next but managing: "I should go Mary... please *forgive* my intrusion I had no idea it was such a bad time." The redness of embarrassment flushed her cheeks with gusto. Mary blew her nose like a whistle, and waved her hand.

"No, no! Please don't. Of course you had *no idea*, and I have no wish to be left alone waiting for the next phone call. Please, *stay awhile*. You obviously came here to talk...let's do just that." She was insistent. Despite every instinct in her body telling her to go, somehow Samantha resettled herself in the armchair.

"I did hear something on the radio as I was driving here from work, but I must confess I thought it was a *hoax*."

"Well...*tragically* it appears they have got it right, though there is no official announcement yet. Winnie was saying quite a few names, I couldn't catch them all because that *blooming* Ivy Meredith was prattling on in the background, but I think Trevor Crispin has been injured, possibly killed."

That was a name that did register with Samantha; in her twenty years living in the area she had made frequent visits to confession at Wick Holm church. She knew all about Trevor Crispin, and his war of attrition with Father Deane.

"The whole town's gone crazy in the storm." Samantha stumbled over the words as though they were hurdles.

"It would seem so...it's just *not* possible," Mary accused. "Who would have a grudge against Jean Candicote?" She looked at Samantha as though she were holding the truth in her hands.

Self-consciously Samantha alternated her teacup from one hand to the other.

"I can't begin to tell you how awkward I'm feeling right now Mrs Graham..."

"Mary, please," the old lady corrected.

"Mary...*sorry*. I was just driving home from work, and I'd had such a bad night at the hospital, what with the storm and everything, I just *needed* to talk to someone. It had been on my mind for a long time to come and see you, but I *swear* I had no idea I would be calling at such an awful time...." She paused, nervously sipping her tea as though it might contain poison.

"Please dear...*calm yourself*, you're getting in such a state. Of course you couldn't know. Honestly, your coming round here is the *best* thing that could have happened on a day like today. The very last thing I needed was to be on my own, and a little conversation is exactly what the doctor ordered this morning!" Mary reassured her, stooping forward to pick up the teapot and refill Samantha's half empty cup. As she leaned across towards her, Samantha looked up, ready to shake her head and refuse a second cup. It was then that she experienced the power behind Mary Graham's stare. It was as though the old lady were burrowing into her skin with those dazzling grey eyes. Samantha felt her heart momentarily race in her chest, and then, incomprehensibly a feeling of incredible calm flooded her system, as though the old lady had just mentally massaged her anxious heart. Samantha fixed on Mary's smiling face, and in that instant she felt her whole body relax as though she had just fallen victim of a hypnotist. Her breathing softened and her jumbled train of thought seemed to spread out across her mind, forming an almost primitive spider diagram of sub-headings. In that instant she knew exactly what she wanted to ask the old lady, and the order in which the questions would be most coherent.

She blinked for a second.

When she re-opened her eyes Mary was sitting down again, stirring her tea. She had one foot resting on a small pouffe.

"My arthritis is bad this morning; the doctor tells me I have to keep elevating this leg. That's easy enough for him to say, but at my age it's a little difficult to can-can!" Samantha smiled warmly at this. She took a fresh sip of tea, allowing it to roll over her tongue as though it were wine. The effect cleared her throat without the need to cough and she was able to speak softly and calmly:

"I'm *too* old to believe in fairy tales Mary." she unexpectedly began, and Mary lowered her cup, immediately interested. Samantha paused, realising that she had just randomly changed the direction of the conversation she had just been having with the old lady. It startled her, but only momentarily. Feeling her face begin to flush again under the full scrutiny of Mary's gaze, she continued quickly: "I've spent my whole life realising that the dreams of youth just don't come true. When I was a little girl I always wanted to be the princess trapped in the tower, waiting for the prince to rescue me. But the prince *never* came, the tower became a mortgage around my neck, and that little princess went into hiding. But I must confess, ever since I've looked after Patient 143...*Annabel*, sorry. I can feel that little princess growing stronger inside me. She *wants* to come out again. Does that make any sense?" Samantha gestured. Mary was already on the brink of interrupting:

"Annabel has a way of making people feel younger Sam, that was one of her many gifts. When I used to sit with her, before and indeed *after* the accident I would never feel like the vulnerable old woman I've become. My blood seemed cleaner in my veins, my mind seemed clearer, I felt like I actually could have *can-canned!* I really did! I wasn't old with Annabel; I was always young, especially if I held her hand. It makes me sad to hear that you don't believe in fairy tales anymore. With Annabel there was never any question about whether they existed or not. That wasn't the issue, only *where* they existed." Mary pointed a bony finger directly at Samantha's heart. Samantha felt her hand slip to her chest, almost in reassurance to feel her heart still beating there. "That's where fairy tales live, and that's where they should *always* stay. It's what comforts us the most when we need it, the thrill of what might be if only it *were* real life. But the fairy tale should *never* be committed to paper. Not ever. That's when it changes. That's when it becomes *corruptible*. Nothing can ever be altered, not if you keep it in your heart. Not if you keep it to yourself. But if you read the words of someone else's fantasy…well, then it's loose in your own mind, and it's impossible to stop it spreading." Mary spoke like a venerable sage, and somehow it didn't matter to Samantha the order in which she said things, or the content. It was the way she delivered her speeches, the rhythm of her voice that filled the room up like fresh oxygen. Somehow the words all made perfect sense, if only while the two of them were sitting in that room. Mary's talk of fairy tales had taken Samantha back to her experience at the hospital earlier. Once again she saw the majesty of Khynous Morf. If ever there had been a fortress built to contain a princess that must surely have been it. Samantha rested her teacup on the floor and brushed her hair nervously out of her eyes. She knew she hadn't come to visit Mary Graham to talk about fairy tales, yet it somehow made perfect sense that the old lady wanted to discuss the nature of childhood fantasies. Somehow the whole topic had altered Samantha's feelings towards Patient 143. No longer was she viewing the comatose girl as an unnerving entity, now Annabel was finally coming to life in front of her; a living, breathing person with thoughts, ideas and beliefs all her own. Samantha could almost see her, almost…

But she still needed to replace the mental image she had of a young girl with all her vital signs supported by whirring, humming, constantly droning machines; the only non-metallic sound being that of her breath expelling into a plastic coiled tube, accompanied by the rhythmic hiss of a compressor to chaperone the air into her lungs.

"Don't we *all* need fairy tales?" Samantha forced herself to ask. She was fighting to suppress the image of Annabel lying comatose in her hospital room. "I mean, without them what would we have? Nothing to dream about...that's for sure. Simple stories really, good versus evil. They're really all the same when you break them down. You have heroes to cheer for, princesses to save and villains to despise. That's *it* really." Mary was nodding her head in agreement.

"I agree in part dear, truly I do. As Annabel used to tell me, there is no need to over complicate things. Why try and tell such a simple story in a convoluted, difficult fashion? That's when fairy tales get out of control you know? Ten pages of heroism suddenly become five hundred! And what have you achieved by the end of it? Probably the same story you had in your head right from the start. Good triumphing, while evil fails. Annabel always said...don't *try* to be clever. Don't write anything down. Keep the story *short. Simple,* and above all else.... keep it *locked in your own heart.* Why share it with the world? Why give it a fresh chance to escape?" Mary winced from a slight twinge of pain in her leg. Samantha was stirring her tea; creating swirling eddies in the liquid.

"It sounds like Annabel was scared of something..." Samantha deduced, but before she could complete the sentence Mary Graham was on her feet.

"My God what was that?"

Samantha rose up, more in shock by the old lady's stance than anything else. Mary seemed very unsteady on her legs and Samantha was terrified that she was going to suddenly collapse and injure herself. Mary's eyes were fixed upon the half drawn curtains.

"What's the matter?" Samantha asked in total bafflement. She eased herself past the coffee table to get closer to Mary, but the old lady bustled past her, shaking off any offers of help. She shuffled towards the lounge windows and opened the curtains fully. For a moment she just stood there, bathed in the morning light, squinting out of the lattice windows. Finally, with shaky movements she unfastened the windows and opened them with a flourish, as though she were shooing something off her lawn.

"What's out there?" Samantha demanded, making her way to join Mary at the window.

Outside the weather had taken a turn for the worse in the half hour they had been talking. The drizzle of rain, which had been left over from the previous evening's storm, had now abated and the first flakes of thick snow had begun to fall again. Samantha stared out at the deserted garden; automatically she was focusing on the bushes where she had seen movement when she arrived.

"What did you see?" Samantha asked, desperately wanting to put a comforting arm around the old lady, she hated to see anyone distressed.

"I swear to you Sam…I swear I just saw a *face* at this window," Mary confessed, shivering slightly. Samantha looked out into the garden again. The gate by which she had entered remained firmly closed, and there were no obvious signs of footprints in the flowerbed beneath the window.

"I think I saw a dog earlier or maybe a fox…" Samantha began, helping Mary to close the windows. "When I first got here, as I was walking up the path…I think, it was in the bushes, by the fence." She took Mary's arm, and this time the retired nurse did not protest as she helped her back to the armchair. "I only caught a brief look at it before you opened the door, but it could have run past the window…" She let the sentence tail off, realising it sounded a little implausible, but she wanted Mary to relax a little. The old lady was clearly upset about the death of her friend, and she was probably suffering delayed shock. Samantha's nursing instinct was showing itself plainly as she made to check Mary's pulse as the old lady sat down.

"I'm *not* in shock!" Mary vehemently informed her, surprising Samantha as she accurately pre-empted her thoughts. "I was a nurse myself for forty-seven years!" Mary reminded her as Samantha groaned with embarrassment.

"I am sorry Mary, I forgot," she almost cursed. Gingerly she let go of Mary's wrist and retreated back to her chair. She felt sure Mary was smiling at her, but the many wrinkles on her face made it difficult to distinguish a smile from a frown.

"It was far too big for an animal," Mary assured her, adjusting her dress across her legs, and repositioning her foot on the pouffe. "Now...what were we talking about?" Samantha couldn't recall the end of the conversation, so she posed a fresh question.

"Mary...can you tell me everything you remember about Annabel? I just need a clear picture in my mind. I feel I *should* explain myself to you...*I don't know why?* You must be sitting there wondering why this middle-aged woman is so incapable of saying what's on her mind. The fact is Mary; I had an experience this morning that's just left me a little unnerved..." Samantha gestured with her hands, and almost spilt her tea in doing so. Mary breathed deeply, collecting her thoughts.

"If I had to guess my dear..." she began, looking first at Samantha, and then back to her throbbing leg, "I'd say you've been to the Dark Realm."

ு

The atmosphere within the police car felt claustrophobic despite the fact there were only three people occupying it. With the windows closed tight shut and the air conditioning rattling away, desperately trying to dehumidify the interior of the car, the heat was unbearable.

Outside the snow was falling as thick as possible, seemingly trying to make up for the previous night's respite. Cyril Bettany wrapped a strong arm tightly around Jayne, and pulled her closer to him. It wasn't for warmth, just comfort.

"Sorry if it's a bit hot!" Superintendent Toland apologised from the driver's seat of the car. He was fiddling desperately with the air conditioner knob, while trying to keep his eyes on the road ahead. "*Bloody thing* broke a couple of weeks ago, I've tried to fix it but I think I've actually made it *worse!* Doesn't matter which way I turn this thing now…" he said, indicating the knob. "It just seems to want to blast out the heat of a small nuclear furnace!" As if to back up this argument the temperature subtly increased.

"It's fine," Cyril assured him from the backseat, and with his free hand he loosened his shirt collar. Droplets of sweat stood out across his temple. He glared out the car window, estimating how much longer it would be till they reached home. The underlying tensions within the car were making him more edgy than he felt comfortable with.

Jayne hadn't spoken since they'd left the police station fifteen minutes before. She had her head pressed firmly against the side window. The running condensation from the glass had wet her hair and forehead. Cyril made to pull her head away, but she angrily shook him off. He hesitated to try again, but decided against it. He glanced around the police car. It smelt heavily of an unhealthy blend of body odour and stale nicotine. The previous occupant of the back seat had left a small collage of sweet wrappers strewn across the foot well. Cyril exhaled heavily. He rubbed his brow and squeezed Jayne's shoulder. When they'd left the flat last night to attend the Carol Service, neither of them had any inkling they would be returning in the back of a police car.

Toland indicated right and gently turned the vehicle into the side road adjacent to their flat block. The main car park was a hive of activity. An ambulance was still parked directly in front of Jean Candicote's window, and several police cars were haphazardly stationed around the area to keep onlookers away. As Toland drove up he waved to several officers he recognised.

"Now you two, I'll be about an hour here, so please take your time," he informed Jayne and Cyril, easing the car into a free space. They jolted slightly as he applied the handbrake, and this seemed to rally Jayne back into life.

"You're sure we can go up to our flat?" she said. Her voice came out half-choked and she coughed harshly to clear it. Toland was in the process of switching on a portable radio. He turned away from the couple, speaking quietly into the microphone, as another officer confirmed that forensic had finished in flat twenty-six.

"How are you feeling?" Cyril whispered to his wife. Jayne looked at him through bloodshot eyes. She looked inconsolable.

"I want to see him," was all she managed before a heart-breaking cry escaped her lips. Cyril had her gathered up in his arms quicker than she could have asked him. Jayne buried her head in his chest, her body heaving with sobs.

"We will, we will," Cyril kept repeating as Toland ended his radio conversation.

"Forensic has finished," he informed them. Despite his personal connection to the couple he was desperately trying to maintain a professional air. He stepped out of the car and opened the passenger door, helping Jayne out first. "An officer will have to go in there with you I'm afraid, and everything you take out of the flat will have to be itemised and recorded," he half apologised.

"Why?" Jayne asked; wiping her eyes as Cyril stepped free of the car. Toland coughed in slight embarrassment.

"They haven't ruled out aggravated burglary yet as the cause of Jean Candicote's murder." He couldn't look at them while he explained, instead he watched two forensic experts, dressed in white jumpsuits, exiting the building with two black holdalls.

Jayne almost laughed at this revelation, but the action just caused an ever-deepening ache to pulverise her heart. She reached for Cyril's hand.

"I hope you don't expect us to start searching for missing furniture?" Cyril sounded angry. Toland reached back into the front seat of the car and retrieved his helmet.

"Of *course not* Cyril! Not today, good Lord! You two haven't had any sleep or anything yet. Look...I apologise. I've known you both for a long time, and I know this all seems a bit slap-dash here..." He gestured at the circus of people coming and going through the front doors of the flat block, "...but it's standard procedure and it has to be done. That's all there is to it. We need evidence, and we need to interview people, and I'm afraid the next few days are going to be a constant cycle of questions and disturbance. But I can promise you that we will know the truth by the end of it. *Now!* The best thing you two could possible do is go and get yourself a suitcase of clothes each, and then I'll drive you over to the Village Inn. I called Tony Simpson and he's preparing the spare room for you. You can stay there until we've finished up here," he offered. Jayne stared at him, ashen-faced.

"We're never coming back here." She sounded final on this point. Her voice edged just enough to prevent Cyril protesting.

"What about Peter and Lucy?" Cyril managed. Toland had started to follow them towards the main entrance. He brushed snow from his jacket and held the door open for them.

"We're doing all we can, I *assure* you. As soon as there's any news..." He let the sentence trail away. He'd been expecting this next reaction ever since they'd all left the police station.

Cyril and Jayne were frozen in shock, just staring at the devastation of the flat block. All other concerns were momentarily forgotten.

It looked as though the entrance hall had been consumed by conflagration. The carpet and walls were covered in thickly congealed soot. It had turned the usually homely atmosphere of the flat block, into one of dereliction.

Four police officers stood on the stairs, examining a series of deep scratches that had left such a complex configuration in the brickwork of the walls that it looked as though someone had uncovered ancient hieroglyphics beneath the plaster. The grooves had to have been caused by an extremely large knife of some kind. The initial line taken by the police was that the random patterns were the result of potential bayonet lacerations.

The doorway to Jean Candicote's apartment hung limply from its hinges. The open frame was plastered with yellow hazard tape to keep out the public.

No one spoke for a long time.

Finally Toland broke the silence.

"Harris?" He was addressing one of the policemen on the stairs. A young man turned around, he couldn't have been above twenty years old. He looked too small for the uniform he was wearing and the desperate expression he wore revealed his inexperience in these situations.

"Yes sir?" he answered, in a voice filled with trepidation.

"Harris, this is Mr and Mrs Bettany, they live in twenty-six. They're here to collect a few personal items. I'd like you to accompany them to their flat and keep a record of everything they choose to take. Do you understand?" Toland seemed adamant he should receive confirmation of this before he let them all go. Harris nodded sharply, and with a slight sigh of panic, he stood aside allowing Cyril and Jayne to pass him on the stairs. Toland watched the small party reach the next landing and disappear from view. With his heart weighing heavy in his chest he turned to consult the forensic team outside.

❧

The bathroom smelt of lavender and sterility. The combination was both intoxicating and upsetting, like fresh flowers in a hospital ward.

Samantha Raynor gripped the toilet bowl firmly with both hands, and bent her head fully over the rim. She had been certain she would be sick, but the nausea was passing. She heard a gentle knock on the door, accompanied by:

"Are you ok in there dear?"

She raised her head up slowly, not wanting her reply to resonate with the echo of the porcelain bowl.

"I'm fine Mary thank you...just washing my hands," she lied. She waited a moment for the sound of the old lady's shuffling footsteps to recede, and then made her unsteady way over to the sink. Her stomach did a slight cartwheel enroute, and the sound of churning gastric juices rumbled deeply within her stomach. She put her hand to her mouth to suppress a belch. She could feel how dry her lips were, and her forehead was sticky with sweat. She filled the sink and splashed a healthy measure of cold water on her face. She blinked uncontrollably for a few seconds, but the action appeared to have calmed her slightly. She stared hazily into the mirror of the bathroom cabinet. She was shocked by how pale she looked.

A few minutes later she was once again sitting in the living room opposite Mary Graham. Her teacup had gone; in its place she found a slice of Victoria sponge cake presented on a small sliver plate.

"I thought a little sugar would help you dear," Mary said kindly. "It's homemade," she added, in case Samantha needed more of an incentive. Mary needn't have worried. Samantha had already reached for the cake, taking a healthy bite and spilling crumbs down her blouse.

"Lovely," she managed, brushing at the crumbs.

"You're sure you're alright?" Mary persisted. "I thought you were going to faint back there." She was pressing for an answer; Samantha could feel her eyes searching out her face. She wiped at her cheek, feeling a droplet of perspiration there, or perhaps it was still the left over residue of the water she'd used to calm herself down.

"Really…I'm fine. I just got a little disorientated." She waved her arms emphatically as though she were swatting a swarm of flies. "Too much information in one go…" The excuses continued.

Mary was distinctly smiling now; two prominent creases had appeared at the corners of her mouth. As if to dispel any further doubt, the old lady suddenly let out a shrill laugh. The sound acted like an alarm. All noise ceased in that one instant and something about the cosy living room suddenly became very claustrophobic for Samantha. She had never heard laughter like that before. It was almost a cackle.

"You sounded just like Morquinda then." Mary laughed, wiping at her moist eyes with her now grubby handkerchief. She was sitting with both hands clawing the edges of her armrests, and to Samantha she looked slightly demonic.

"Who?" she managed.

"An old friend dear, no one *you'd* know. I'm so sorry, just experienced a little bit of déjà vu then. It just tickled me that's all. Morquinda was just like you; always wanting to believe in fairy tales, yet when one actually started happening around her she panicked, went completely into denial for a time. Of course Annabel finally persuaded her…now there was a mistake! Still, she wasn't to know. And now Morquinda's as caught up in all this as the rest of us."

"What do you mean *the rest of us?* Caught up in what?"

"We *all* have a part to play in this story child…you must know that after what happened to you last night…No? You don't have to tell me, I can see it in your eyes. Annabel has chosen you. That is not something to be scared of, I promise you. I was too old to take on the burden of responsibility. She'd already seen the mistake she made with the old ones from Lambert House, there was no chance she'd try that again on me. For all her faults, at least the poor girl always *tried* to learn from her mistakes. Not like that other one. Evil little child." Mary shook with rage as she uttered this last sentence.

Samantha sat dumbfounded. Her head whirled even faster than before. She almost wanted the old lady to have gone senile, yet something in the tone of her voice convinced Samantha that however convoluted this story was, she was being told the absolute truth. She knew she was confused, but before backtracking, she wanted the old lady to conclude this portion of the tale.

"Some people are just born jealous. I think that's what Annabel was trying to imply about my old oak tree. My word she had a game with that young brat! He hated the ground she walked on for years and years...until he grew up a bit. Well I guess that kind of behaviour is forgivable in some people's eyes? I know Father Deane and Jean Candicote had a lot of time for him, but I didn't. Never spoke to the lad if I could help it. Not even after Annabel's accident. That must sound harsh...and I know us old dears aren't meant to talk like that..." She paused and breathed uneasily. "But I've lived through some harder times than he'll ever know, times when all you've got is one another to get you through something; you haven't got time to be jealous or vindictive about anything. I lost my husband just after the war. He survived all that horror, all that hardship only to come home and pass away in his sleep one October night. I ask you for justice there? I still look up sometimes when I'm dozing here by the fire, thinking I've heard his boots on the mat outside. I expect him to open this door and give me a hug. But he *isn't* coming home anymore. I've had to accept that, and the best bit of comfort is my memories of him and of all the times when we were together. He had his hopes and dreams and I never interfered with them, I just supported him the only way I knew how. You see child, that's what I'm talking about, right there. Nothing should be left unresolved and nothing should be left unfinished. You interfere with someone's dreams, for whatever reason, and goodness knows what *damage* you can cause." Mary was looking increasingly agitated as her soliloquy touched on personal secrets she would not have normally chosen to reveal.

"Who is this boy you're talking about?" Samantha hadn't intended to interrupt but she couldn't sit quiet any longer. Mary looked as though she'd just been slapped across the face.

"Peter Bettany of course!"

7

Secrets and Tea Cups.

$\mathcal{T}$he Still crept across the rocky shoreline, moving with the tenderness of a lilting breeze. It seemed as if the creature wouldn't even touch the pebble-strewn ground with its feet. As though it were walking across hot coals, it leapt and glided faster than the human eye could follow, making for the cave opening, and not hesitating in one spot for too long.

Something however, was watching its progress.

Not a human eye, but one that never blinked day or night. It watched, almost with amusement, as the Still leapt onto a jagged rock, and twisted its head to see if it was being followed.

It saw nothing.

Relaxing for a split second, it raced into the blackness of the waiting cave. Once inside, the babbling of the Tarn River was immediately diminished by the vastness of the cavern it now found itself in.

The hollow provided its own music. Water dripped incessantly down the cold walls, deadened in places by tufts of moss, which grew thickly in a random configuration down the dark stone, catching and absorbing the crystal clear water that ran so freely. Bats and other nocturnal creatures could be heard flying overhead, returning to their roosts in the crevices high above, their cawing and screeching creating a cacophony that drowned out all other noises.

As the Still continued further into the cave, the noise of the Tarn River faded completely, leaving it alone with only the screeching of the birdsong, and its own rhythmic breathing for company.

A thick slime clung to the rocks in places where the river had risen and broke its banks at times of high rainfall. The Still grew increasingly more uncomfortable with the geology of the cave as it tried to avoid touching the damper rocks, or accidentally stepping into the pools of icy water that had congregated in the grooves of some of the larger stones. It loped across the rocks, pausing every few hundred yards to sniff the air.

It could smell fresh meat.

It moved more slowly, seeking out the carrion. A few hundred yards further it located the source of the scent. The dismembered remains of an owl lay strewn across a perfectly smoothed boulder. It had been plucked of all feathers by an unseen predator, and most of its tender meat had already been devoured. Strips of still bleeding flesh clung to its shattered ribcage. Mangled bones and gore had been flung in frenzy across the stone.

The Still did not hesitate; it drove its head into the mess and began stripping the raw meat from the bones. It was engulfed in a bloodlust and remained utterly unaware of the other occupant of the cave who had tracked it so perniciously since it had fled from the coppice several hours previously.

The Pig-Beast crouched against the cave wall, its ever-swirling leathery skin blending in with the total blackness of the cave. The only reason it had not slaughtered the abomination it saw before it now, was due entirely to its appetite being sated by the carnage it had wreaked upon both the Mist Children and the Still army the previous evening. To devour this Still would have been pure avarice on the Pig-Beast's part. The monster had hoped the Still would lead it to further meals, but instead this solitary escapee had sought only to conceal itself from the wrath of its master. The Pig-Beast watched the Still masticate the owl's bones between its teeth, ripping playfully at the stone with its sharp back claws. Despite its own animalistic tendencies, this action seemed to enrage the Pig-Beast. It had grown tired of this cowardly creature, and any further time spent in its company was a waste. The Pig-Beast couldn't remember how long now it had had to share its lands with these demons. Something inside it told it that a wind of change was blowing across the Dark Realm. Soon these unwanted visitors would all be gone. The lands would once again belong to nature and the Pig-Beast.

It was inevitable.

The Still was now picking at the final morsels of meat that the carcass had to offer. Like a connoisseur it sniffed, chewed and rejected certain putrefied offal, in favour of more tender meat near the belly of the owl. It tore a particularly thick shred of meat free of the corpse and swallowed it with a flick of its head. It stepped back from the mutilated remains and screamed its approval. It felt nourished and from the scent of the bird's carcass it could tell that the cave would provide enough sustenance for it to live on while it remained in hiding here. Even the Still knew it could never go home. The Lord of the Now would have it put to death for daring to flee the rest of the army. The Still had no intention of becoming another addition to the already full branches of the dead oak tree at Myfanwy. It screamed again more swiftly, and this time its cry was echoed by the bats that swirled amongst the stalactites high above it.

Something else also returned the Still's call.

This new noise rumbled through the cave like a seismic tremor. It shook the walls with its intensity, dislodging a small shower of rock from the higher ledges within the cave.

The Still quivered slightly as a sweet smelling steam blasted the ash across its body. It rotated its head to face the east wall of the cave. Two more thick rings of steam expelled from the nostrils of the Pig-Beast as though it had released a pressure valve. The air turned white hot around the Still as the enormous monster placed one cloven hoof upon the rock it was perching on, and bent its leathery back low enough to bring its giant face closer to the trembling Still.

Two blazing red eyes glared down at the cowering creature as though a bush fire were spreading out across the cave towards it. The Pig-Beast's expression was one of total malevolence, as its slavering mouth opened and a monstrous roar escaped its throat. The Still made to sprint free off the rock, but the second it moved the Pig-Beast had trapped it in one of its mighty fists. It squeezed the life out of the screaming creature, raising it off the ground and dragging it slowly towards its cavernous maw. With a violent tug the Pig-Beast bit the Still's screaming head off.

Darkness engulfed the cave.

❧

"I'll wait outside for a minute," Constable Harris gingerly announced. He excused himself and brushed past Cyril in his stumbling haste to leave the flat. He didn't want to make eye contact with Jayne, because he wouldn't have known what to say to her. Cyril managed to mumble a response, but he wasn't really aware that the policeman had even been speaking to him.

It all seemed like a dream now.

Everything had drifted into surrealism since they'd entered the flat a few minutes previously. He turned now and distractedly watched Harris attempting to disentangle himself from the sticky police tape that had blocked the front door to their home. In other circumstances this sight might have amused Cyril, but not tonight.

Looking at the wreckage of the flat for the second time in eight hours, there really wasn't anything remotely humorous about it.

Jayne was moving quickly from room to room as though she'd lost something. Her eyes were full of stinging tears. Cyril hurried after her, finding her sobbing over the kitchen sink. He had to manoeuvre carefully through the wreckage of the kitchen table, and the upturned fridge, which had spilled its contents all across the floor. He'd nearly slipped over the steadily defrosting mess twice as he raced to be at her side.

"It's ok…its ok baby I'm right here," he offered, squeezing her tightly in his arms. Jayne sobbed even harder; her knuckles had turned white from the grip she had on the sink. Slowly her sobs began to subside, and Cyril turned her around so he could cuddle her properly. She hugged him as though her life depended on it.

"Where is he?" she managed. "I can't go through this again."

Cyril hugged back even harder, muffling his own cry in her shoulder.

"He'll be home soon, I promise you," he said, with more conviction than he felt.

༄

"Annabel had this gift you see. I don't understand why, and I'm certain she didn't, but all I can tell you truthfully, is that she was the girl who dreamed. That's the easiest way of describing it. She was just born with this wonderful gift. Nothing profound I might add. She couldn't see into the future, she didn't have premonitions. She could just conjure up the most magical of places when she fell asleep. Are you listening dear?" Mary suddenly asked. The question surprised Samantha, who had admittedly been looking at the photograph held in her hands, but she was gripped by every word the old lady was saying.

"Of course I am…please continue," she said, tearing herself away from the picture. The old lady eyed her suspiciously, and then began again.

"Most of us dream, but not in the way Annabel could. That girl could remember everything that had happened during her dreams and tell you about it in exact detail. I'm not joking; it was a gift I tell you! And she used to dream every single night!" Mary seemed to stress this last point.

"Well, aren't we all supposed to dream every night, it's just that we can't always remember what we dreamt about?" Samantha decided to play devil's advocate.

"You're not listening to me. Annabel could remember every dream she'd ever had. I doubt you could even remember every dream you had last week, let alone two years ago?" she argued fiercely, once again adjusting her position in the armchair as though she were in some mild discomfort. "She would come and visit Jean Candicote every weekend while she was growing up and tell her about these magical dreams that she'd had. Have you ever had a recurring dream?" Again the question was directed back at Samantha. With a sigh of resentment that once again the dialogue had been interrupted, Samantha nodded her head.

"I used to occasionally dream that I was suspended at the highest point inside a big top...a circus big top. There was this witch on a broomstick..." She smiled at the absurdity of her confession, but Mary urged her to continue. "She would fly round and around me; continually until I became so disorientated I would lose my grip and start to fall. The sensation of falling was so real, that I would jolt myself awake just before I hit the ground. I had this irrational fear that if I didn't wake up I would die from the fall in real life as well." She let out a nervous laugh. Mary was looking keenly at her; she dismissed Samantha's fears with a sentence.

"That's not irrational child. Believe me; people do die in their dreams, all the time." Mary rubbed her throbbing leg. "How many times would you say you had that dream...on average?"

"Not every night, but on and off for about twelve months I guess. I'm sure it was just a phase I was going through…"

"Very well, but you can at least identify with the concept of a recurring dream?"

Samantha nodded.

"Then try and imagine visiting the same place every night in your dream. Every night. And it's your world, your realm. The only person living there is you, and you can manipulate this world in anyway you like, because you created it in your own head. Like a fairy tale…yes? You didn't write it down; you didn't sketch pictures of it, no! All you did was dream about it. You made it all it was. What would you do with it?" Mary held out her hand. Samantha stared at her open palm for a long time, as though she expected a spinning globe to appear there. Finally she cleared her throat.

"I'd make it perfect…I'd be God," she breathed. The sudden realization of having such hierarchical power seemed to flood her brain, and her voice grew stronger. "I'd create a paradise and then…and then…"

Mary was leaning forward now, her eyes fixed on Samantha. The younger woman licked her lips to free them of perspiration and confessed.

"I'd want to show other people what I'd achieved."

"Exactly!" Mary exclaimed, clicking her fingers in triumph.

"This is what I said to Jean all along. It's human nature to want to gloat, to boast and brag about what you've achieved. And after all, Annabel was only human. She was special, certainly. But her emotions were human. She'd spent years creating this world in her dreams, the world she called the Dark Realm. Every single night she'd add something new. Tweaking, changing, and perfecting the landscape until, so I'm told, it was breathtaking. She'd filled it with fortresses, fields, open plains, rivers, forests and deep caverns, all lovingly forged by this young child's untainted mind."

As Mary described this dream world, Samantha looked down at the picture she was holding. Mary had handed it to her minutes previously. Annabel smiled out of the frame at her. She looked every inch a fifteen-year-old princess resplendent in her school uniform. A mane of tousled auburn curls flowed down past her shoulders. Her skin showed no signs of the trials of adolescence. Instead it was as pale and smooth as cream. She had a bewitching smile that seemed to radiate a power all its own, and enchanting emerald eyes that stared straight out at Samantha. The quality of the picture was so clear that if Annabel had suddenly winked, Samantha wouldn't have been surprised.

She looked so alive on the canvas.

"I've seen that world…" Samantha began, but Mary quickly interrupted her.

"No you haven't. You've seen the Dark Realm the way it's become since her accident." Mary's voice had changed. Her words were harsher, and a chill seemed to have descended on the room. Samantha shivered as though someone abhorrent had just traced his fingers right up her spine. "This goes back to our original conversation. The minute you start to tell people your fairy tale, that's when the corruption begins. She did well to keep it to herself for so long. But she was just like any other normal teenager; she knew that secrets are for sharing," Mary admonished.

"Who did she tell?" Samantha couldn't bear this suspense any longer.

"Only people she could trust. Her close friends and family. People like Jean Candicote, and Father Deane. Good people, people who already knew she was a very special girl. But that wasn't the real problem. Oh no! Annabel began to bring her dream world to life in the real world. She'd draw it, and map it and invent histories for the different areas she'd created. She would sit on my rug here, and list off names for all the different places within this Dark Realm of hers. Jean and I would sit placidly listening. Not taking her imagination too seriously, yet feeling awed in her presence all the same. Like I told you earlier, everyone wants to believe in fairy tales. When you reach our age, they'll become even more of a necessity, because without them, you're only left with inevitability, and depending on your faith, that can be a very frightening prospect." Mary allowed her arthritic leg to gently slide off the pouffe and she rested it once again on the floor. "So we let her talk about this mythical place, it seemed to make her so happy. That was the other amazing quality Annabel had. She was always such a happy child. Nothing ever seemed to depress her. Her Mother and Father used to be worried to death about her dreaming. I think really they were more concerned that the rumours would spread through the village that their little girl was different. Wick Holm is seeped in gossip; you must know that? If you lifted up the first layer of tranquillity here, you'd find a quagmire of intrigue festering beneath it."

"Of course you would, but that's the same in most parochial little villages though surely?" Samantha argued.

"I don't disagree dear. What I'm saying is that for Annabel's parents it was a worry. All that unwanted attention. It's difficult for any parent raising a child who's born a little different to the norm. I guess they didn't want her branded a heretic in the parish that's all. So they tried to keep her contained in her own thoughts. They were lucky because Annabel didn't have any desire to mix with anyone her own age. For some strange reason she seemed to prefer the company of us old ones instead. When she turned sixteen she started to do voluntary work on weekends at Lambert House nursing home. That's where she first met Morquinda," Mary explained.

"You've mentioned her name before. Was she someone you knew, Mary?"

"She was once a great friend of both mine and Jean's. We also knew her sister, Elyse very well. Spinsters through and through but they both absolutely adored Annabel. I guess she became the daughter they'd never had. They were both residents in Lambert House at more or less the same time. I think Morquinda was admitted first but Elyse just pined without her. She couldn't look after herself anymore. I remember Father Deane had to make the phone call to the nursing home one afternoon after he'd been to visit her." Mary paused as though it pained her to remember the events. "Elyse was just sitting in her armchair apparently. She hadn't moved for at least a couple of days…not even to go to the lavatory." Samantha looked up sadly. There was nothing she could say to that. "It tortured him to make that phone call. But what else could he do? And of course after they disappeared and all that stuff came out about the nursing home, well…"

"Were they part of the four then?" Samantha suddenly saw a connection she'd never imagined making.

"Oh yes. Morquinda, Elyse, Isabella and Felicia. They were the four old ladies who vanished from Lambert House." Mary made a sudden gesture with her hand as though she were casting a spell. "When the police investigated the nursing home after that, the full truth of the malpractice taking place there was finally exposed. Well! We all thanked God they had vanished. Father Deane never forgave himself for being instrumental in having Elyse admitted there. I so wish Annabel had been able to tell him the truth." Mary sniffed again. She seemed on the verge of tears.

"What truth?" Samantha felt she had to press.

"That she was responsible for their disappearance of course."

"What?"

"Oh my child, I do wish you'd keep up with all this. You're acting just like me when Jean Candicote first told me what Annabel could do. And you've got no excuse, because she's actually done this to you! Yet still you deny it!"

"Done what?" Samantha pleaded.

"Taken you to the Dark Realm." Mary's voice trembled with suppressed anger. "That is what happened to you last night? At least that's what you described to me!" She sounded indignant, as if there was now doubt as to whether Samantha had told her the truth. The younger nurse seemed on the verge of saying something to the contrary, but instead turned away from Mary's vehement stare and nodded her head in agreement.

"Well then! Don't sound so surprised in the future!" she admonished. "Annabel had already told Jean and myself about this Dark Realm, just as I told you. We believed her as far as it is possible to believe in something you haven't actually seen for yourself. But I think Annabel wanted to take it that one step further. So she decided, against her better judgement, to take the four ladies she'd become such friends with at Lambert House, to visit it"

"Yes, but how? Did they all just hold hands with her like I did, or what?" Samantha had so many questions inside of her now that it was a struggle to stay in her seat with the building excitement.

"She took them all while they slept. That was how powerful she was." Mary's voice had calmed somewhat, but her words still seemed a little frayed at the edges.

"What are you saying? That she was a shaman of some kind?" Samantha sounded unconvinced.

"No, that's not what she called herself." Mary dismissed this accusation. A pause followed as Samantha waited for an explanation. It didn't seem forthcoming.

"So what then? What did she call herself?" she finally demanded.

"She said she was a Dream Blender."

❧

8

Caged Rats.

*T*he ice didn't break the first time Taime slammed his left foot down on it. He grunted with pain as the shock of the impact travelled up his already throbbing leg.

The little band of friends had been riding for nearly two hours now. Ethanril had been determined to throw off any trace of their scent in case the wild dogs were still pursing them. Finally after many swift changes of terrain and direction, he had led them all back across the majestic plain of Carrastorc, to the outskirts of Kilfanfyn Forest.

Taime stomped down on the ice again. He was trying to break the surface of a small rock pool that had gathered in one of the hollow trunks of a willow tree near the bank of the river Tarn. This time his anger paid off, the ice cracked and a small splash of water covered his leather boot. He knelt down quickly, his long coat flowing out behind him in the snow.

"Come here Peter." He called to his companion, who moved with alacrity to kneel beside him. Taime had his hands in the icy water, and was splashing cupped handfuls onto his face, smearing back his long hair. "Try some of this," he said, fixing Peter with a steely glance. His companion looked back nervously at the young, ferocious looking boy. Before he could reply, Taime had thrown a handful of water all over Peter's startled face.

The effect was immediate.

Peter was on his feet, shaking his long hair to free the ice cold water that clung to every strand. His tired eyes blinked harshly on impact, but somehow, despite his panicked reaction the water had refreshed him. He stopped gesticulating, realising that Taime was smiling up at him. Peter hesitated. "Feel better?" Taime asked, rising to his feet. Peter rubbed the residue into his skin and smiled back.

"Thanks," he said, and meant it. He stretched upwards to alleviate the tension in his back. His legs had never felt this sore before. The constant chaffing from the saddle had left him in severe doubt he would ever be able to sit down again. He looked back towards the others. Ethanril and Sufi were tending to the horses, while Pigeon, Fess and Mundo were all slumped on the ground in various states of exhaustion.

"Are you feeling calmer yet Peter?" Taime asked, walking a little way past Peter to lean against the trunk of the willow tree. The morning was cool and crisp, and the snow fell lighter than it had done for a long time. Peter also moved under the shade of the willow canopy before answering.

"I can't believe I'm finally here," he confessed, raking back his dripping hair with both his hands. He rubbed his palms across his face, almost to confirm he still had one. The ice water had woken his senses, and made his skin prickle. He felt the light stubble that now graced his chin, and rubbed his still bleary eyes. The dust of riding still clung to his clothes, but at least his face was cleaner. "I'm shaking," Peter said. It came out as though he were talking to himself. He was looking at his hands, which shook from tension. He could see the strap marks across his palms where the reins had dug into his skin.

It was all so real.

"Believe me Peter; this is as strange for us as it is for you. It's been along time since we had any visitors to our world. And no one was really expecting you…" He turned his head to gesture towards Ethanril and Sufi. "Apart from them." Taime adjusted his position against the tree, so he could rub his shoulder blades against the rough trunk.

Peter seemed to be taking in the whole world with every sense he possessed. He was breathing deeply the morning air, while occasionally crouching down to run his hand over the snowy ground. Each time a bird cawed overhead he was back on his feet trying to identify the breed. He felt like Adam in the Garden of Eden, he had to experience every new sensation, yet he was conflicted by this strange feeling of familiarity that confronted him with every fresh discovery.

"I'm a long way from home," Peter concluded, his eyes watching the flowing currents of the Tarn. Taime moved away from the tree to stand next to him.

"Listen Peter…" he began, his expression hardening from one of sympathy to a look of concern. "Things are going to be very strange for you at first…I understand that. You've only just arrived here really and all we've been doing since we met you is running…" He started brushing dust from his coat nervously, glancing back at the others in case they were making a move towards them. "Hopefully you can rest awhile now, but there's going to be a lot of questions Peter…Ethanril seems to be convinced you can help us in some way…though I don't really understand how? There's even talk that you know what's happened to us here? Again I can't begin to imagine how you could? Sufi tells me you're the second Sacred Mother?" He stared Peter directly in the eyes. It was a glance that instantly made Peter uncomfortable. He could tell that a question was brewing in Taime's mind, one he didn't wish to answer. "The thing is Peter, I knew the Sacred Mother. She was the most incredible thing to ever happen to these lands…and more than that…" He paused again; the words seemed to have become uncomfortable in his dry mouth.

Peter wanted to silence him. With every bone in his body he suddenly saw himself pinning Taime to the ground and beating him unconscious to make him stop talking. He shook slightly with revulsion at his own irrationality.

"Annabel was the most important person in my whole life." Taime spoke clearly and resolvedly. "I loved her Peter. I know I wasn't alone in this…" Again he glanced at Ethanril, who was now crouching down to examine Astervarn's hooves. "I can't explain how she made me feel. Not the way it sounds in my heart." Taime was moving now, pacing round in a small circle as though he were trapped in a confined space. "Before she came to us Peter, we were nothing. We didn't even have any names, not that I remember. This place you see all around you…" he gestured with his arms, "this was all a mystery to us. Annabel called it the Dark Realm…I think because some of it was still a puzzle even to her. But she helped us Peter. She was like a mother to the Mist Children. Oh I'm rambling!" Taime stopped his pacing. He eyed Peter, half expecting a sympathetic reaction, but Peter was just staring straight at him, his expression as rigid as granite. "There'll be time for all these explanations later I'm sure…the point is Peter, that before the others start taking you away and bombarding you with questions…"

"Yes?"

It was a harsh response, but Taime appeared not to have noticed the tension in his new friend's voice.

"I have one," he said. He was looking at Peter now with an expression that didn't sit easily on Taime's face. His eyes had softened, and he appeared more vulnerable than he had intended.

Peter was practically shaking with discomfort. He glanced behind Taime, wishing someone would interrupt them. He hated to talk about the girl.

"I'm told by Sufi that you knew Annabel?" Taime probed gently. Peter wouldn't meet his gaze, but he nodded despondently. "I don't know if you can understand how I'm feeling Peter? I know so little about you. Are you in love?" The four words hit Peter like a bolt of lightning. He realised he was watching Sufi intently; she was kneeling beside Ethanril, tugging her long hair behind her ears to keep it out of her face. As she did so she looked up, meeting Peter's gaze even from that distance. She smiled at him. Peter tore his gaze away as at the same moment Lucy Doran flashed before his eyes. She was leaning on her elbows staring at him across the bar of the Village Inn.

Peter rubbed the bridge of his nose in turmoil for a second, then glanced distractedly back at Taime who was still waiting for a response.

"Yes I am," Peter said quietly.

"Then you do understand how it feels to miss someone as much as I do," Taime stated. Peter had sat down with his back to the rest of the group. If anything he looked more agitated than ever as he stared out at the Tarn River. Taime sat down expectant. "When is she coming back to us Peter?" he blurted out.

"What?" Peter asked, mortified.

"When is Annabel coming back to us Peter…I mean…rather…how is she? What happened to her? Was it something I did?" The questions were falling from his lips like rain. Peter stared dangerously at him, his own mind full to capacity with the madness of his current situation. Despite all the trials he had already endured, this young man's questions were as terrifying to Peter as the morning he had first discovered Annabel's name etched across his car windscreen.

"Stop!"

The cry had escaped his throat before Peter had chance to stifle it. Everyone looked up in surprise at that moment. The four white horses pricked up their ears in agitation. Both Peter and Taime suddenly felt very self-conscious. An awkward moment followed with no one sure if they should approach the pair. Peter shot to his feet in anger. "I can't talk about this now," he said, his tone absolutely final. He stormed away from Taime, who was looking completely stunned. He watched Peter walk down to the very edge of the river and slump down. He hesitated for a moment, unsure whether to walk over and apologise, though he wasn't quite sure why. Instead he turned, and with a slight shrug, he walked up the embankment towards Mundo, Fess and Pigeon.

"What was that all about?" Mundo struggled to ask. He was gripping a shredded length of cloth between his teeth and trying to wrap the rest around a deep cut on his left arm using only his free right hand. He was obviously having immense difficulty with the task. Pigeon and Fess were sitting a little way off from him, watching enraptured. They both wore expressions of complete admiration as they studied the incredible skill going on before them as Mundo struggled to dress his wounds.

"You could help him!" Taime pointed out, crouching next to Mundo and taking hold of the bandage.

"Wherrr...what?" Fess and Pigeon managed, looking as though they had just snapped out of a trance.

"I said you could have offered to help him!" Taime said even more angrily, tying off Mundo's makeshift bandage so aggressively that Mundo screamed in pain. "Sorry." Taime hastily apologised, calming down.

"He seemed to be doing so well on his own," Pigeon offered.

"Yeah! Really well, and he was obviously in pain! Marvellous skill!" Fess commended.

"You pair!" Mundo snarled through gritted teeth. He checked the bandage over, and flexed his hand.

"How'd you feel?" Taime asked, sitting cross-legged next to him. Mundo gave a slight smile.

"I'm better now we've stopped riding. I thought my insides were going to be pulverised. There's being cautious and then there's being over cautious." Mundo moaned.

"You fought with Krinn?" Taime asked. Peter had told him snatches of the events. Mundo nodded.

"Just about!" He modestly dismissed his efforts. Taime rubbed his bruised forehead.

"Believe me, you must have fought well. I don't even remember my encounter with him."

"I do!" Fess suddenly announced, cocking a wink at Pigeon. "Pigge's trousers will act as a constant reminder!" He laughed, pretending to shield his eyes from the sun. "Ahh my eyes!" he cried, rocking backwards with mock laughter. Pigeon quietly fumed.

"So what was that all about?" Mundo repeated, gesturing down the embankment towards the solitary figure of Peter. Taime briefly followed his gaze and then turned back. He ferreted in the snow for something to mess with, finally having to make do with retrieving handfuls of cold stones. He idly flicked them one at a time back at the ground as though he were dealing out cards.

"It's my fault...I guess. I didn't mean to upset him; I just wanted to ask him a few questions before Ethanril did..." he broke off. Mundo was looking sadly at his old friend. Fess and Pigeon were grinning roguishly at him.

"Annabel?" they both said.

"Partly!" Taime retaliated, trying to make it sound as though he'd had a whole list of questions for Peter.

Pigeon quizzically raised one eyebrow.

"All right, entirely!" Taime confessed, hurling the last stone away. "I just need to know that she's ok that's all...you understand?" He pleaded to all three of them. They all nodded.

"We understand Taime. Honestly we do," Mundo reassured him. He lowered his voice so Ethanril wouldn't hear him. "Did he say anything?" Mundo pressed. Taime glanced at Peter's defiant back. Slowly he shook his head.

"He went very defensive. Said he didn't want to talk about her. What do you make of that…in fact, what do you make of him?"

"I haven't really talked to him yet." Mundo answered for everyone. "Understandably I think he feels a little out of his depth, and let's face it Taime, goodness only knows what he's dealing with mentally at the moment. This is a whole new world to him, and ever since we arrived here, all we've done is run, fight and bombard him with questions, it's bound to make him a little edgy!" Mundo justified. Taime nodded in agreement.

"I'm not arguing with that. All I'm saying is…it was just a question. That's all. He didn't have to fly off the handle like that." It was clear the whole experience had deeply upset Taime.

"Well I don't trust him!" Pigeon unexpectedly butted in, passing his own judgement on Peter's character. Fess twisted round to look at him.

"What a surprise!"

"And what's that supposed to mean?" Pigeon demanded to know. Fess stared calmly back, while Taime completed the question for him.

"You don't trust him because Sufi fancies him."

"WHAT?" It came out much louder than Pigeon had intended.

"Don't pretend to be surprised." Fess laughed.

"That is just not true. I don't trust him for a whole host of reasons…private reasons that I must keep to myself until the time's right to share them with you guys," Pigeon woefully mislead himself.

"Oh really? Name one?" Fess dared, but Pigeon had gripped his arm in shock. "What's the matter?" Fess asked a look of agony on his face. Pigeon was squeezing his arm quite painfully now.

"You did say Peter fancies Sufi didn't you?" He looked as though he desperately needed conformation of this. Mundo was glad to oblige.

"Nope!" he said, shattering quite a substantial number of Pigeon's dreams with one simple word.

"WHAT?" This time, Pigeon felt, it hadn't come out even half loud enough!

"Sufi fancies Peter; come on Pigeon, even you must have noticed how she's been looking at him."

"I thought she was worried about him!" Pigeon moaned piteously. Fess suppressed a laugh, not altogether convincingly.

"So now that's me, Taime, Mundo and Peter she fancies! You've moved even further down the list!" Fess cajoled.

"You've probably fallen right off it!" Taime laughed.

"Was he ever even on it?" Mundo chipped in.

Pigeon looked mortified for a few minutes. Then suddenly he brightened. He pointed at each one individually.

"You're all kidding me? Right?"

The others nodded, knowing that if they didn't they would never hear the end of it. Pigeon seemed immediately happier. He looked back towards Sufi, who was grooming Lockavarn and talking hurriedly with her brother. Pigeon sighed.

"We'll all feel better once we're back at the Warren." Mundo suddenly realised what he'd said. He looked concernedly at Taime. "It will be fine when we get home Taime, I promise you. You've nothing to fear, you did all you could. You led the Pig-Beast away from the others..." Taime was already shaking his head. His troubled expression revealed his true fear of returning home.

"I failed them," he said simply. Fess and Pigeon looked at him sadly. Their hearts reached out to their friend, but words failed them.

"I wasn't fast enough. I'm sure Ethan would have saved them all..." His voice was edged with a bitter resentment. Mundo offered a hand in sympathy, but Taime ignored it. "She'd spoken to me you know...the little girl who died." He was on his feet now, the anger welling up inside him like a balloon. "Before the Pig-beast attacked, she'd grabbed hold of my hand and asked me if it was 'going to be alright?'" The first hot tear streaked down his cheek. He couldn't understand how he'd managed to hide these emotions for so long. "She was just like the others you know? Nameless…featureless. So prematurely old, but…but…" The memory was too painful. He sucked a tear back angrily. "She was a real person, individual, unique…different. I never knew her name; I guess no one ever will…oh this is all so messed up." He collapsed to the ground; the sobs flowed as uncontrollably as a river. His breathing sounded strained as he fought to control it, waving away the others' offers of assistance and reassurance. "Don't help me," Taime finally managed, wiping his eyes and sitting up. "There must be a reason for all this," he concluded. "And he had better know what it is?" he accused, angrily pointing at the oblivious Peter. "Why do we have names and identities and they don't? What in Annabel's name is the Pig-Beast? What happened to our world that night she disappeared?" Mundo grabbed Taime's shoulders, before he could push him away. He'd had to do something to stop the rising panic that threatened to consume his friend.

"Calm down." He breathed out as if instructing Taime in what to do next. Although he refused to make eye contact, Taime did breathe out a shaky long breath. "That's better…" Mundo continued his voice still soft and soothing. "You did all you could Taime. You led the Pig-Beast away from the Warren before it could kill anyone else. You put your own life at risk to save all the others. You have nothing to be ashamed of. You're not to blame." He was insistent. Taime looked downcast, but nodded gently. "Ethanril could not have done any more. He left you in charge of them Taime, and you didn't let him down. You're wounded from your fight with Krinn, that's why you're not at your best, yet still you saved them all," Mundo stressed.

"I wish she hadn't died." Taime let out a cry, and Mundo hugged him.

"I know," he confessed. "But you did all you could," Mundo assured him.

Peter Bettany heard the sobs of Taime even above the churning river. He looked back over his shoulder feeling an incredible mixture of guilt and foreboding. Since he had killed the wild dog his whole body seemed to have changed. He couldn't explain it, but his muscles felt bigger than his skin, as though an inner strength were inflating him like a pump. His mind had cleared so much during the ride from the lake of Carrastorc. He had accepted his situation entirely; he knew he was finally in Annabel's Dark Realm. He knew that despite spending most of his youth ridiculing her for claiming she had created this world, that all a long he had only been fooling himself.

When he'd started to dream regularly, he'd finally felt vindicated. For so many years he had pretended he could dream just the way she could, but he knew he was lying. One lie led to more and more deceit. Annabel was so careful whom she told about her dreams, but Peter had told everyone. Within a month he had achieved notoriety. Every child in Wick Holm knew Peter was the 'boy who dreamed'. Annabel would have been disgusted by his behaviour, but still she would have found it in her heart to forgive him. Peter had never been able to understand that. He had been so cruel and manipulative towards her, yet she was always so willing to except him for all his faults, and offer him her forgiveness.

It had taken Peter ten long years of growing up to fully reach that level of humility, and it was only now, as a grown man that he could look back on this time with eyes full of shame.

"I'm so sorry," he quietly apologised to the river, the trees, the air and the matrix of the Dark Realm. He wiped at a discreet tear that slid freely down his face. He stood up to stretch his weary legs, again looking back at the small eclectic group he now found himself with.

He knew who they all were.

They were right to call him the Sacred Mother. He knew that clearly. He cursed himself for not yet being man enough to tell Sufi the truth. He stared back at the distraught Taime, knowing full well that the secrets he had to reveal to him would cause him more pain than he could yet imagine. Peter breathed out heavily. He was utterly resigned to what he must do. With the dawning realisation that he had been handed a second chance, he felt a growing sense of clarity and commitment. "Whatever it takes…" he whispered under his breath. "I won't fail them again."

Sufi knew when her brother was shocked. Ethanril was notoriously difficult to read at the best of times; he had the kind of face that most poker players dreamt of. But Sufi was one of the few people who could read him, and from the way his shoulders tensed, ever so slightly, Sufi knew he was momentarily surprised. She nervously ran her small hands through Lockavarn's mane. Ethanril stared for a moment in the direction of the other Mist Children. Taime seemed distressed and he was unsure whether he should offer some assistance. He saw Mundo, Fess and Pigeon crowding around him, and thought it best to leave it to them. He returned to examining Lockavarn's hind fetlocks.

"So Peter prevented you from returning through the void?" he idly asked, seeking confirmation that he'd heard Sufi correctly. His sister crouched beside him, resting her hands on her knees. She was unsure how to continue the story. For the last half an hour she had been telling Ethanril exactly what had happened to her since she'd left him the previous evening. For the most part he had been quite happy to listen while he continued inspecting the white horses. Even when she had explained what had happened to the Still that Pigeon battled into the river, he had seemed less surprised than he was about this one point, which he now kept bringing up. It had clearly unnerved him.

"I think he'd just panicked…" Sufi began, once she was sure she had the whole thing clear in her own mind. She worried sometimes when Ethan asked her direct questions. It always felt like an interrogation. "He was having a lot of trouble coming to terms with the reality of everything, and I guess he just did what he thought was best?" Sufi offered. Ethanril was rubbing Lockavarn's leg muscle as if to ease it.

"Indeed," he managed, finishing the inspection and raising up, very slowly.

"You're hurt!" Sufi accused, noticing her brother's discomfort.

"I'm very sore!" Ethanril admitted, rubbing his shoulder. "Don't worry about me," he pleaded, knowing it was falling on deaf ears. "Tell me more about your escape. What happened outside Peter's dwelling again?"

"Krinn was manipulating the void…I've told you all this once!"

"It's all in the little details…" Ethanril pushed. He was wincing slightly.

"Never mind what happened to us, what was going on here? How did you end up inside Myfanwy?" Sufi pressed.

Ethanril thought about pushing for an answer to his question, but seeing the expression on his sister's face he decided against it. He leant against Lockavarn, who easily supported his weight and quickly filled Sufi in on the events leading up to the storm.

"…Once it had calmed down, and we realised you weren't coming back, we made our way to Myfanwy. I thought that was the one place you were most likely to make for if the void reopened. You see we had seen it open over Stilfanwyn Chasm… course with hindsight that must have been caused by Peter keeping you in his world. It opened up a gap large enough for a battalion to travel through. I couldn't understand why no Still had been sighted anywhere? We arrived at Myfanwy and unlike the previous time we'd rode through there, the paddocks and fields were empty. The only Still we saw where those executed ones that hang from the branches of the dead oak. I decided to take a look inside Myfanwy, just to see if there was any trace of you. I left the boys with the horses, as a contingency if anything went wrong. I said I'd signal them. Course I could never have anticipated what did happen…" Sufi interrupted him.

"They forgot the signal?"

"No! I always knew they'd forget the signal…no, once I was inside Myfanwy…and I honestly can't have been in there more than a few minutes, cohorts of Still arrived. I just watched from the downstairs window, utterly horrified. There must have been thousands of them. I prayed to Annabel for the safety of the Mist Children…I was just trapped in there, I had no idea if they'd already been captured or what was going on outside…"

"You must have been terrified?" Sufi asked, shuddering from her own memories at the sight of the vastness of the army that had awaited her and Peter.

"I'd be lying if I said I wasn't. They surrounded the building in one perpetual circle. There was just no way of escape from the farmhouse, and there would have been no way for anyone to have rescued me. They just stayed outside encamped for what seemed like hours. I daren't have moved. I just sat in the hallway with my back against the grandfather clock, watching the front door, expecting them to come charging in…in the early hours of the morning I heard movement outside. Cautiously I crawled to the kitchen window. Looking out, I could see the Still moving in agitation. The sky had turned blood red, and there were sporadic torches burning at intervals throughout the ranks of Still. In the flickering light I saw the Lord of the Now standing at the front of his army, lighting another torch. I nearly cried out in fear, and a second later I heard a thunderous commotion from upstairs…well, I certainly didn't think it was you two. I had to assume the Still had gained entry to the house and were on their way down. I scrambled about looking for an escape route; I was just running on pure adrenalin and not thinking straight. This lasted several minutes until I suddenly realised nothing had tried to get down the stairs. I could hear shuffling feet upstairs, but not the tell tale screaming of the Still. Cautiously I crept up the stairs; I'd only gotten to the first landing when the sky erupted outside. I saw the void open, blazing light onto the fields of Myfanwy. I just remember staring with a mixture of awe and revulsion as I witnessed the Still army return from Peter's world. Krinn was at the helm; with a bloated Still carrying two bundles…which again I had to assume must be Peter and yourself. I felt sick to the pit of my stomach…" He broke off for a second, clearing his throat. "…And then I heard your voice!" He smiled at her. "I almost cried in relief…you were shouting something to Peter…I couldn't hear the actual words, but I knew it was you. I raced up the stairs to the partition, and pressed my ear against the brickwork. I could hear Peter calling out of the window, I almost shouted out myself but I realised we didn't have time for any conversation…"

"So that's when you went downstairs to get the clock?" Sufi was smiling as the missing pieces slotted into place.

"It was the only thing that stood any chance of breaking down the wall. I knew the brickwork wouldn't hold too many knocks…" Ethanril tailed off with a smile of relief. He stretched out his sore arms. "So here we all are again!" He hugged Sufi tightly. "I'm very proud of you…don't ever forget that." His voice was an insistent whisper in her ear.

Unexpectedly Lockavarn became restless.

His ears had once again pricked up as though he'd heard something. Ethanril, who was hugging Sufi tightly, slyly moved his eyes to follow the horse's movements, detecting immediately something was wrong. He gently detached himself from Sufi's embrace saying: "Well...I think it's probably time we were moving on."

Lockavarn tipped backwards, rising onto his hind legs and whinnying in panic. The other three horses also began to snort with fear. Ethanril quickly moved Sufi away from the distressed animals as they shied and began to tiltup. Their alarmed movements caused everyone to turn in the direction of the tethered horses.

"What's happening?" Taime asked. He was the first to reach them. Sufi was desperately trying to calm the erratic animals, as they circled each other causing their reins to become more and more entangled round the trunk of the beech tree they were tied to.

"Something's disturbing them." Ethanril quickly stated the obvious; he was scanning the trees for any sign of movement. "Call Peter back, I think it's time we moved on and got ourselves back to the Warren."

Fess and Pigeon had joined them, and they quickly aided Sufi with the fidgeting mares.

Peter was already making his slow way towards the group when he heard Taime's call. He involuntarily broke into a run, as he could immediately detect the fear in the tone. He reached the top of the embankment in time to see everyone saddling up.

"We're riding for home Peter," Sufi called to him, fighting to keep Lockavarn from bolting. She forced him to trot towards Peter and reached her hand down. "Come on," she said with a smile. Peter could tell that something had clearly happened in his absence, but he grasped her hand, and hoisted himself onto Lockavarn's back. His hands slid round her slender waist, and Sufi tilted her head towards him. "Don't let me go," she coyly informed him. Peter was suddenly overwhelmed that he could feel her blonde hair rubbing against his face.

"I won't," he managed.

"Let's ride!" Ethanril commanded, and the party galloped into the woodland.

∽

Several hundred yards behind them, the Lord of the Now dropped to the ground with a wood splintering crash. He had been nestling in the bows of a thick ash tree, hanging from a branch like a giant fruit bat. He scented the air, slavering at the mouth with the excitement of the chase.

"So close..."

he whispered, watching the party disappearing into the trees.

Still clutching Krinn's glaive, he raced after them, his movements so fast and graceful that he appeared as nothing more than a blur against the landscape.

∽

"A Dream Blender?" Samantha repeated. The phrase just didn't sit right in her mind. Mary was watching her from the opposite end of the room. The young nurse was obviously having difficulty with the story she was being told. Mary's heart fluttered with remembrance, and for a brief moment she saw Morquinda sitting opposite her denying everything that was happening around her.

"That's what she called it. She had a way of sliding into other people's dreams...well, at least a few people anyhow. In order to not scare them to death initially she would linger in the background and just observe the dream. She tried it on Jean Candicote first. Poor old Jean, she was mightily disturbed I can tell you! Just imagine having someone else sitting in front of you telling

140

you exactly what you dreamt the previous night? Enough to scare anybody!" Mary admonished. Samantha wanted to laugh out loud at the absurdity of this story, but she knew she couldn't. In her own mind all she could think of was Khynous Morf. "Anyway, once she'd established enough trust with Jean she decided to try and bring her into the Dark Realm. Well that was extremely foolish, and so dangerous. The silly girl was so absorbed in what she was doing; I don't think she stopped for one minute to examine the consequences. Fancy taking an old woman into a world so powerful and tempting, that it would seem as real as the one she already lived in? I thank the good lord she never took me there. She chose wisely with Jean Candicote. She was an exceptionally strong-minded woman. I'm not saying the experience didn't disturb her, because it did…without doubt it had a profound effect upon her life. But she was able to recognise that she didn't belong there…that it wasn't her home."

"But did Annabel ever take her back?" Samantha asked, inwardly worried that as soon as she fell asleep she would be pulled back to Khynous Morf.

"Oh certainly…but at Jean's own request I might add. You see, by the time Jean visited the Dark Realm, Annabel was no longer alone there…" A look of widening horror had spread across Samantha's face. "There were other children living with her. Jean never really explained where they'd come from, but she used to call them the Missed Children."

"Mist?"

"No dear…*Missed* Children, like orphans I suppose or those who have run away from broken homes. Strays of the world…or maybe even from somewhere else? The explanation was always so vague. Anyway, whoever they were, Annabel had taken it upon herself to rescue them, and she decided to make the Dark Realm their new home…" Mary looked quite moved by the story, but Samantha stared back in stunned incredulity.

"She was playing God again…" She barely managed to pronounce the words. "When she pulled me into her dreams last night, she wasn't trying to show me what she'd achieved…not like with Jean Candicote, she was showing me what she'd done. I think she's regretful." Samantha surprised herself with this revelation.

"I agree." Mary didn't doubt her words for an instant. "Because you see, although she promised Jean that she'd never take anyone else into the Dark Realm…the foolish girl just couldn't resist…" Mary didn't have time to finish her sentence before Samantha sat bolt upright, staring at her in horror.

"The old women from Lambert House…the ones that disappeared…" Mary was looking downcast as she nodded agreement.

"It was an accident waiting to happen. But that was the start of the end for her, like an apocalypse element. One event that triggers another, then another and finally…" Mary trailed off. She began the long process of standing up. Samantha was on her feet with an offer of help before she had time to stop herself. However, for once the old lady accepted gratefully. "I must just move about a little…I've been sitting still too long. Would you care to join me for a short walk around my garden?"

Moments later they were outside. The chill of the morning air struck Samantha immediately. Her cheeks gave off a rosy glow, and her nose began to run. She sneezed as her body adjusted to the temperature change. Mary Graham seemed less affected. She had a warm shawl wrapped tightly across her shoulders, but her manner revealed that she was happier to be outdoors than cooped up in that tiny living room. "You can't beat the fresh air," Mary wisely said, breathing in a good lungful of the crisp winter breeze. "Little walks, nice company and plenty of cups of tea…yes! That's the key to a long and happy life." Mary chuckled. Samantha smiled back, finding some comfort in these words; she took the old lady's arm, and allowed Mary to gently lead her around the front garden. "I'm sorry if my story is coming out all convoluted dear. If I'm honest you're the first person I've told it all to since Father Deane sat with me a few years back; *full* of questions he was. You know how he gets? Suddenly has a big zest for knowledge and then just as quickly he's forgotten the lot! I can tell from your face you're trying to put all the facts in some kind of order," Mary observantly noted. Samantha was nodding; she was finding it extremely difficult to put everything in its rightful place. "Let me try..." Mary began. "Annabel invented the Dark Realm, all by herself. She dreamt of it, wrote of it and even drew it, in all innocence to amuse herself. Then she confided in Jean Candicote and myself. Naturally we assumed it was all just the work of a teenager's over active imagination. Then, sadly, an event caused Annabel a great deal of distress...I'll have to get to *that* later. By then she was already thinking of taking Jean Candicote with her to this Dark Realm. As I said, something else must have happened in the meantime because when Jean arrived, there were others already there...are you following it all ok?" she asked, as though she were proposing a script and pitching it to Samantha. The younger nurse nodded more defiantly this time.

"Yes...I think I'm getting to grips with it now. What happened next though? Did she confide in the four ladies at Lambert House?" Mary smiled brightly as Samantha correctly deduced the next element of her tale.

"Annabel took a weekend job at Lambert House; while she was still studying...I think I may have already said that?" Samantha was smiling at her. "Oh...you must say dear if I over run my tale, I'm a perishing nuisance for doing that. When Father Deane comes for a chat, I end up keeping him most of the afternoon. He doesn't seem to mind though, as long as I've made a fresh supply of my mince pies, he's quite happy. Anyway, I digress! She was always torn about the best possible career path she should choose. She was studying psychology at college, and I think that's why she became so interested in some of the ladies at Lambert House. Many were suffering from Senile Dementia and I think Annabel wanted to get closer to some of the residents there so she could study the effects of the disease first hand…"

"So strange…" Samantha interrupted, her voice almost breathless. Mary looked puzzled. "Sorry, I was just free talking then. It's curious how so often other people's lives mirror your own. I studied psychology when I was at college, I always felt I was destined to go into counselling…but circumstances changed…" Samantha curtailed her rambling, realising she shouldn't have interrupted Mary's flow. Already the elderly lady was looking mildly confused by the interruption.

"That's nice dear…" she began, her elderly mind trying to pick up the thread once again.

"So did Morquinda suffer from Senile Dementia?" Samantha prompted. Mary's expression suddenly cleared.

"Oh no dear! Not as such. She certainly had flights of fancy, and she had had to be admitted into care, but that was more for her own protection than anything else. Her and Elyse were becoming incapable of looking after one another. They just weren't eating properly, or taking care of themselves. When Annabel met Morquinda, she was in perfect mental health; she was just a very old woman sitting alone in her chair. It's so cruel the effects of time on the human body. I can feel it in every bone of mine, but I thank the lord for the time that I've been allowed," Mary said resolvedly. She shivered, but Samantha knew instinctively it wasn't the cool air that caused the motion. "That place…. that house. I can't tell you what the atmosphere was like there. It's as close to true evil as I think I've ever wanted to come!" Mary stopped walking momentarily and bent to dead-head her winter cyclamen. "It was a sprawling mess of corridors, most of them badly lit. Took Jean and I several visits to even begin to know our way around! Sometimes, Peter would come with us, to visit Annabel on her weekends working there. You could almost see the wheels of his little mind working as he walked those corridors. He once told me he actually relished his visits to Lambert House! Sent me cold I can tell you, evil little child. He kept on saying it was a place to 'let your imagination run wild!' Can you believe it?" Mary finished her clipping, which had become more severe as she continued her story. Samantha looked nonplussed.

"It's impossible for me to comment. I never saw Lambert House before it was shut down. I read all the newspaper reports of negligence and I was naturally horrified, but as to the extent of the validity of them…I really couldn't say. It sounds like this Peter had just as much imagination as Annabel, albeit a little more on the dark side," Samantha commented, hoping to at least throw a fragment of an opinion into the conversation.

"You've hit the nail on the head there!" Mary commended her; Samantha allowed herself an inward smile. "He might not have had the dreams that she had, but he could tell a story in exactly the same way. Annabel would come back from her weekends at Lambert House, and each time she did, she seemed to have grown a little more disturbed by what she was witnessing around her. She once told us, in full earshot of Peter, that she believed the house was a living organism, that it was responsible for sucking all the life out of the residents! I've never heard a young woman so adamant about something in all my life. Jean Candicote tried and tried to explain to her, that most of the residents of Lambert House were no longer mentally fit enough to deal with the outside world, and that as a result of this, they would be taking medication to ease their condition. Annabel wouldn't hear of it. She said she understood all of that perfectly, but her own experiences within the nursing home were proving to her that there was something else askew there." Mary seemed to be struggling for breath again. She lent against her garden fence and composed herself. "We realise now of course that a lot of what she was being told by the likes of Morquinda, were stories of real abuse happening to other patients. But the residents who were confiding in Annabel were only fuelling her already overactive imagination."

"What sort of stories were they telling her?" Samantha could barely hide her intrigue now. The winter wind was blowing even stronger, but somehow the cold seemed to have stopped bothering her.

"They filled her head with fantasy stories, telling her the place was haunted. People claimed to have seen strange unexplainable sightings of faceless monsters waking them in the night by screaming into their faces. The very fact that Annabel had never once seen the nursing home director, led Morquinda to tell her he was one of these creatures...it's almost laughable, if it hadn't been so upsetting for the young girl."

"Yes but surely...as a student of psychology, Annabel could see what was happening in these stories, surely she could interpret the distortion?" Samantha pressed for answers.

"She was only sixteen Sam remember? The girl was only starting out on her studies, and her head was so full of this Dark Realm she had created for herself, well what else was likely to happen? If she knew for certain that her own dream world was real then why not the tales of these old ladies? Let's face it, *no one* believed Annabel's stories until she *proved* to Jean Candicote they existed." Mary was making her way back to the house now; she had been slightly perturbed by the argument she had just had with Samantha. "So in utter desperation to help Morquinda and her friends escape the horrors of Lambert House, Annabel offered to work a night shift at the nursing home..."

"And while they slept...she pulled the four of them into the Dark Realm." Samantha finished the revelation. Mary paused by her front door. She turned with a startled look of pain on her face and gripped Samantha's arm tightly.

"We all knew what she'd done the minute we saw Morquinda. I had gone with Jean to visit her on a Saturday afternoon. She was different, somehow..." Mary appeared to have forgotten what she was talking about, but before Samantha could prompt her she had continued. "Younger both mind and body. Elyse was the same. Felicia and Isabella were actually babbling at one point in the afternoon. Salivating like dogs in their armchairs, hungry to go back. It was a horrible sight watching the orderlies restraining them, big strapping young lads trying to hold down these apparently frail old ladies while trying to force some green gunk down their throats at the same time. Yes, it sedated them, but not before they'd told us they were all leaving; leaving Lambert House for both a new world and a fresh chance at life." Mary fumbled for her house key. "Absolutely terrifying I can tell you. Jean and I didn't know where to put ourselves, and Annabel just sat quietly watching the chaos she'd begun. That's the one time I almost slapped her. Even though she was doing this all with the very best of intentions, she was sending them insane. As the weeks went on they became incapable of knowing which 'reality' was real. Their medication had been upped to ridiculous levels. I feared they'd all die of heart failure they were becoming so agitated. And then it happened. One night they all travelled in their dreams to the Dark Realm with Annabel...and they just didn't come back." Mary announced, unlocking the door. Samantha was staring at her in amazement.

"You mean Annabel left them in the Dark Realm?" she asked incredulously.

"I don't think she had much choice in the matter. From what Jean told me they refused to come back. By now they were claiming that the Dark Realm was the true reality and that it was our world that existed only in dreams! Many nights Jean would go back to that world and try to persuade them to return with her, but all to no avail. So sad to think how it all went wrong, and she was only trying to help them. If only she hadn't believed those stories of Lambert House or taken them so literally." Mary sighed, hobbling into the cottage.

The younger nurse walked quickly after her, closing the front door behind them.

In the dimly lit hallway, Mary Graham removed her shawl, hanging it on a peg near the door. As Samantha stamped her feet on the mat to clear her boots of snow, she asked:

"What about Peter? What did he make of these stories?" reaching down she unzipped her boots. Mary sighed heavily.

"Come through to the kitchen," she said amiably.

Samantha followed the retreating old lady, pausing briefly to examine some of the family portraits that adorned the hall walls. By the time she reached the kitchen door, Mary was already busy raiding the fridge for ingredients.

"You'll stay for some lunch?" It was a question, but it sounded more like an announcement. Until Mary mentioned it, Samantha hadn't noticed how hungry she felt. "I'm making sausage sandwiches…" Mary goaded, unwrapping a bundle of large Cumberland sausages. "Fresh from Randy Roberts yesterday!" Mary laughed. The local butcher had earned this amorous nickname for reasons best kept to himself.

Within a few minutes the sausages were sizzling away in the tiny frying pan. Mary's kitchen was extremely homely. The work surfaces were covered with oak veneer, and the walls were painted a rich cream, giving the room a soft warm glow all its own. A small electric fire kept the temperature just right, and Samantha settled herself down on one of the many kitchen chairs, a wooden, high backed affair, with a surprisingly comfortable cushion. Mary lingered near the stove, occasionally turning the sausages. The need for her to be active clearly helped her to take her mind off the morning's news. But she continued with her story despite the circumstances.

"Peter Bettany was the strangest young man I've ever met," Mary said, prodding the sausages with a fork. "He had a nasty streak in him, very selfish; as I'm sure I've already told you. He was unnaturally jealous of Annabel's gift and always wanted to be the centre of attention. I swear he thought it was his God-given right to be the one with the talent. I'm surprised the two of them ever got on…but they did." Mary was now buttering two crusty cobs. "He really came into his own after Annabel's accident you know?" Samantha raised her eyebrows, indicating that she did not know. "*Oh yes!* Started claiming it was him all along that had had the dreams, and that Annabel had made the whole thing up! *What a pack of lies!* Of course he was *apparently* a changed boy by then, growing up and all that jazz! Well! All I know is I *never* trusted him. Even when he used to come to the hospital to visit her, I would do my level best to avoid speaking to him for too long. Did you ever meet him?" Mary asked, turning her attention back to the sausages.

"He doesn't come in very often. I must confess I've never noticed him to be particularly arrogant or nasty. I find him very quiet…and if I may say so, very polite. I appreciate the delicacy of the situation so I try to give him some privacy with her when he does come. But he always says 'goodbye' before he leaves. I find it very difficult to imagine him as this nasty little boy," Samantha confessed. Mary tutted and turned the stove off.

"Well…you may be seeing a very different side to him now he's *all grown up*. I know he takes himself very seriously these days, and a lot of my close friends speak very highly of him. But there are those of us round here that don't have the short-term memory problems some villagers seem to be prone to. I loved Annabel with all my heart, and I always will. Peter Bettany would have to do something very dramatic to get me to change my opinion of him. I hear he's gone back to University now? That didn't surprise me. He was always unfocused. Never knew in what direction his career lay. I don't think I've ever known a young lad have so many different jobs. Last time I spoke to Jean…" Mary's voice wavered; she was dividing the sausages between the two cobs, "she told me he wanted to be a professional writer! I could almost have laughed. *There you go dear.*" Mary handed Samantha a plate. The smell of freshly cooked sausage made Samantha even more ravenous, she gratefully accepted the plate.

"Can I have some brown sauce?" Samantha asked cheekily.

"You're just as bad as me!" Mary laughed, rummaging in a lower cupboard for the sauce bottle.

When the two were finally sitting at the kitchen table, munching on their sandwiches, Samantha asked, between mouthfuls,

"So you don't think he'd make a very good writer then?" She quickly covered her mouth with her hand, suppressing an unladylike belch. Mary chewed thoughtfully on her sandwich for a good minute before finally swallowing and answering:

"The trouble with writers…especially fiction writers, which I'm sure is the type of writing he intends to do; is that they're always the sort of people who are so lost in their own lives…in the real world," Mary indicated the kitchen, "that they have to invent fantasy just to keep themselves sane, which wouldn't be so bad if they just kept it to themselves. But instead of that they have to write it all down and inflict it upon everyone else." Mary resumed her eating. Samantha was looking shocked.

"Goodness Mary, you talk about writing as though it can seriously do some damage to the reader." Once again Mary chewed for a painfully long minute.

"That's because I believe it *can*. Annabel was quite happy in her own little world until Peter Bettany started to interfere. Even those stories of demons that the old dears at Lambert House were filling her head with would have stayed at arm's length if he hadn't decided to take it all a step further..." Mary looked momentarily distraught again, but like a thundercloud, it quickly passed over and her pained expression eased.

"What on earth could he have done?" Samantha asked. She was holding her half eaten sandwich in both hands, unsure whether she would want to continue eating it. Mary didn't even look up from her plate as she answered.

"He wrote a story about it...and that changed everything."

⁘

It was the rat that woke Father Deane.

He had been drifting in and out of consciousness for a good thirty minutes, but it was the rat that finally brought him reeling to his senses.

He felt the pressure of its tiny claws as it gingerly made its way across his prone back. He flickered his eyes, his brain telling him that something alien was resting on his shoulder, sniffing at his ear. He heard a screech, so loud that the first thing he thought of were the demons that had invaded his church.

There was one right now sitting on his back.

He had to get away.

Leaping upwards and flailing his arms around like a demented scarecrow he managed to dislodge the rat. He had been expecting to see a Still sitting next to him, but instead the small but feisty rodent fell to the floor of the cage, screeching at him as though it had been wounded. It raced around the circumference of the cage, utterly gripped in frenzy. Father Deane struggled to avoid the fast moving creature, trying desperately to pull himself upright by gripping onto the bars of the cage and hoisting himself up with his arms.

He had read that rats would leap for your throat if cornered. Horrific visions of the struggling vermin clamping its tiny jaws on his neck filled his already traumatised mind. He knew rats carried disease, and he was horribly aware that if he became infected, he would find no help in this prison.

Unexpectedly, the rat suddenly scurried up one of the bars of the cage. Father Deane felt it run across his knuckles as it escaped. He let out a cry and dropped down to the filth-ridden floor of the cage. He looked up expecting to see the rat pouncing down upon his face, but the vile creature was scurrying up the supporting chain that held the cage. Father Deane watched it disappear into total blackness.

He took a moment to collect his thoughts. He breathed slowly in and out, squeezing his eyes tight shut and then opening them again, hoping to clear his still blurry vision. He almost panicked again when he realised his vision wasn't getting any better. His hands trembled as he rubbed his eyes; suddenly he understood what was happening to him, and a strange calm enveloped him. He laughed in nervous exhaustion, his shaking hands searching his pockets for his spare glasses. By some miracle they were still intact. The frames looked a little bent out of shape from where he had fallen on them in the church, but the lenses were unbroken. He put them on and gingerly got to his feet. As he did so he became aware of the motion of the cage as he moved. It was slowly spinning on its chain, the floor turning a hundred and eighty degrees if he walked too quickly. The motion made him feel seasick. He gripped the bars of the cage, and pressed his temples against them to stave off the headache that was throbbing inside his brain. Gradually the cage slowed down. He looked downwards, but could see only blackness beneath him. He was obviously a very long way up. Looking to his left he could make out several other cages, each suspended by heavy coils of chain. They were all juxtaposed with each other, hanging at different levels, making it impossible to see if there were any other occupants.

The air he was slowly breathing was so cold it stung the back of his throat as he inhaled it. The damp chill all around him, led him to suspect he was being held within a cavern of some kind. In the dim distance he felt sure he could vaguely make out the rough walls of the cavern's sides. Above him he could hear constant movement, the flapping of leathery wings which he had to assume were bats. He was almost certain he could hear distant rumbles and echoes, but he couldn't be certain from which direction those were coming. He gripped the cage bars, as a shudder ran through him.

In that instant he was back in the church.

Trevor Crispin lay dead and bleeding in his arms, two wild dogs advanced on him with slavering jaws, and all around him those creatures stood immobile, watching his every move. He was crying for them to stop. Pleading for his life and begging the murderer of Trevor Crispin to stop this madness.

Father Deane threw up right there and then. His vomit spun down into the darkness like a dying star. Adrenaline flooded his nervous system; he was finding it difficult to breathe, his grip tightened on the bars of the cage. He hated being sick, it was a fear that had been with him since childhood. He tried to control his stomach palpitations and his breathing, but his own rising fear that he was going to be uncontrollably sick caused his whole body to shake with panic.

He threw up again.

This time it was less solid and only sprayed a fine liquid against the bars of the cage, making a horribly striking contrast of vivid colour against the blackness of the dark world around him. He sank to his knees, clutching his mouth in the hope of keeping the bile down. Gradually his breathing slowed, he could feel his racing heartbeat begin to slow. The cage was spinning round on its axis and the motion disorientated him. The damp cave air chilled his feverish brow, and the sweat that clung to his body made him feel unclean. He looked at his torn and battered trousers, his pride and confidence felt as broken as shattered glass.

He thought of Louise.

The first flood of tears poured from him, his whole body was racked with sobs. The noise of his despair acted like music in the acoustics of the cave. The bleak melancholy bounced from wall to wall and cage to cage. The circling bats echoed the cries, creating a cacophony of sadness that rose to an almighty crescendo.

Suddenly a noise that sounded like the rushing of tidal water drowned out this orchestra of woe. Father Deane fell silent immediately, a final embarrassed cry meekly leaving his throat.

The noise was deafening now, as though something monstrous was moving behind the very walls of the cave. It lasted at least ten minutes, with Father Deane kneeling as though in prayer as the noise finally abated.

"That's twice that's happened now."

The voice drifted down to him, a husky feminine voice that pricked at Father Deane's memory, desperate for recognition.

For a second he didn't respond, remaining perfectly still, trying to ascertain where the voice was coming from.

"Are you ok down there?"

The voice suddenly sprang into life again. It sounded concerned, but more importantly it sounded friendly.

"I'm ok!" Father Deane shouted back, overjoyed to hear another human voice. "Where are you?" he continued, standing up.

"I'm just above your cage. Get as close to the bars on the right-hand side as you can and look up; be careful though, the faster you move the more likely you are to spin the cage again, then you'll never be able to see me," the voice helpfully informed him.

Moving with deliberate slowness Father Deane crossed to the right side of the cage; he gripped the bars again, and tilted his head awkwardly to look straight upwards.

To his surprise he was staring straight into the equally startled face of Lucy Doran.

"Oh my goodness...Lucy?" Father Deane's voice was brimming over with joy. Lucy was crouching on the floor of her cage, craning her neck forward to stare down at the cage beneath her. She was proud of how calm she had been since she had recovered consciousness an hour previously, but the sight of seeing the village priest made her limbs shake, and tears flowed down her cheeks. In desperation she stretched her arm downwards out of the cage, trying to bridge the gap of darkness between the two prisons. Father Deane reached upwards, standing on tiptoe to attempt to reach her, their fingers entwined around cold air as they realised they were inches away from being able to touch each other.

A swarm of black bats suddenly erupted from the darkness towards them, like a plague of flying rats. They both screamed at the same instant and withdraw their arms like lightning. The bats collided with the cages in their fury to taste the proffered meat. Screaming and screeching they circled round the two separate prisons, some landing on the cage bars and stretching their leathery wings in defiance. They seemed unwilling to actually penetrate the cages, but the display of hostility was enough to force both Father Deane and Lucy to retreat into the centre of their cages again. The bats tormented them for several more minutes before finally flying off into the blackness.

For a second the only noise was Father Deane's breathing.

He calmed himself quickly, shouting up to Lucy:

"Are you alright?"

A muffled sob could be faintly heard in response.

Father Deane rose shakily to his feet. With deliberate caution he made his way once again to the bars of the cage, craning upwards to catch a glimpse of Lucy. He could plainly hear her crying now, but she seemed reluctant to venture back into view. "They've gone Lucy I promise you," Father Deane said as assuredly as he could manage.

"Are you s..s..sure?" Lucy stammered, desperately trying to control her tears of fright. Father Deane was squinting into the blackness again; he took off his glasses and cleaned them on his sweater. When he replaced them he discovered that the small specks in the far corner of his vision, that he had momentarily feared were the bats returning, had in fact turned out to be just speckles of grit.

"I'm sure," he announced with a fresh air of confidence that carried his words up to her. Lucy smiled through the tears, hearing the optimism in Father Deane's voice, even under such bleak circumstances.

"I'm glad you're here Father," she blurted out, shuffling towards the left side of the cage. Father Deane considered this last sentence; both pleased and a little shocked that Lucy was so enthusiastic he was suspended hundreds of feet in the air in a cage. "I mean…" she continued, taking hold of the bars and looking down at him, "I'm glad I'm not alone anymore, I really thought I was…" She sounded almost ecstatic, but Father Deane sensed her mania was verging on a total breakdown.

"I'm very glad you're here too Lucy, though I would much prefer it if we weren't in these cages!" he had to admit. Father Deane suppressed a cough and smiled at Lucy. She was dabbing her watering eyes with her sleeve. Hurriedly she tucked her long brown hair behind her ears so she could clearly see the kind face of the old priest. He looked almost mole-like with his little round face and blinking eyes trying to focus on her in the darkness.

"How on earth did we get here?" she asked him, hoping to find divine inspiration in the priest's response. Father Deane almost laughed out loud, but he managed to keep his own nervousness in check.

"Well Lucy, if you haven't got any plans for the next half an hour…I'll tell you all I know," he said, settling himself down again.

9

Tarnwaters and the Warren.

"You know Annabel's case history don't you? I mean you know about the fire?"

Samantha was helping Mary to clean the kitchen, and was just in the process of trying to squeeze two plates underneath an already teetering mound of crockery. The question distracted her, and a subsequent disaster was only just averted by surprisingly fast reactions on Mary's part. As the crockery tilted forward she reached up and eased it back with her spindly arm, allowing Samantha the room to slide in the two plates. "Sheer idleness you know? Not taking the other plates out first...oh! Don't worry dear I'm not scolding you, I do it all the time!" She quickly shut the cupboard door before any other items fell out.

Samantha returned to the sink, retrieving a soapy mug, she methodically began to dry it using a rather gaudy dishcloth depicting a holiday resort Mary had once visited.

"I feel like I've just spent the whole day on a fairground ride," Samantha confessed. She rested the mug back down on the sideboard, and pressed a sopping hand to her forehead as though wiping away sweat. "I don't think I can deal with much more of this story, not today anyway. I'm still trying to come to terms with the idea that Annabel could transport someone physically...not just mentally...to another world, and then leave them there!" Samantha laughed at the madness of it all. "I mean...Mary?

Where does that leave me? Am I likely to just suddenly vanish mysteriously in the night like one of those old dears up at Lambert House?" By now she was close to hysteria, and Mary was swift to comfort her. She wrapped her up in a frail embrace, and eased her out of the kitchen one baby step at a time, through into the living room.

A few minutes later Samantha was sobbing uncontrollably on Mary's shoulder. She felt as though she were fifteen, crying to her Gran to save her from the unceasing horrors of the world.

"There, there dear. Calm yourself. I know this has all been a huge shock for you, and a great deal for one person to take in all at once!" She pulled a fresh handkerchief from a box next to the chair and handed it to Samantha. Her sobs had eased a little and she gratefully accepted the handkerchief, first blowing and then rubbing her sore nose. She dried her eyes slowly, careful not to smudge her mascara too much. Samantha drew in a long breath, and breathed out slowly.

"I'm sorry Mary, really very sorry. Sorry I just arrived here unannounced this morning, sorry I've bombarded you with all these questions, and most of all I am truly sorry that you've lost such a dear friend in Jean Candicote..." The old lady was holding up her hand.

"I won't hear any more of that young lady! You couldn't have possibly known about Jean, and you came to see me in good faith this morning because you needed help, and you needed answers. At my age one ceases to be of much help to anyone! It has been extremely refreshing to be useful again. No! If anyone ought to be sorry, it's me. As usual I have gone on far too long with my tale and probably told you more detail than you needed to hear anyway! Add to that the fact that my memory lets me down left right and centre these days, to the point that I can't even tell you a simple story in a concise order. So it's no wonder you feel like you've been on a merry-go-round of some description! I tell you what..." Mary tapped her hand on Samantha's knee, "I'll wrap the story up for you now, and then you can get yourself home and get some rest. You're no doubt shattered from your shift at the hospital last night, and all these confusing tales can't be helping! I remember when I used to work nights...Oh! There was no talking to me the next day, I'd sleep in till around two o'clock in the afternoon and even then I'd wake up cranky and irritable." Samantha smiled at this; she wiped her nose again, feeling a lot better for her cry. She had to admit she was mentally exhausted, and the thought of curling up in her own bed seemed so appealing right now, but she just had to hear the end of the story. Mary seemed to divine this in her companion and almost without hesitation she continued her account:

"There's so much I don't understand about all of this either, and the only person who has all the answers is lying comatose in Great Wick Holm hospital. However, I can make a few educated guesses here and there. Annabel was unique, of that I am in no doubt. She had developed this gift of hers...Dream Blending. With it she was able to walk in two worlds, our own and that of the Dark Realm. I know she had other hidden talents as well. Jean Candicote believed that she was in the process of passing on these powers to someone else when disaster struck. That part of Annabel's story ended that night, and I'm afraid I have no answers for you as to what those powers could have been or to whom they were being passed. I don't believe Annabel took the old ones away that night without some help. I always felt there was something more to their disappearance, after all Annabel had only ever taken Jean Candicote to the Dark Realm through her dreams, never physically transported her there." Mary looked perplexed.

"It would have to have been a physical force, presumably emanating from somewhere within this Dark Realm..." Samantha offered a suggestion but Mary interrupted her hastily.

"Or someone. I truly believe in my old heart that that is what happened." Mary nestled back into the sofa and momentarily closed her eyes. "There is only one more element to this whole affair I feel I must tell you before you go..." she began, but Samantha's response was demurral.

"No Mary, I think I've heard enough for today, really I do. I could always come back to visit you at a better time..." Mary was shaking her head vehemently.

"You must hear this Sam. Then you will know all that I know, at least that way you can prepare yourself," Mary wisely intoned.

"Prepare myself for what?" Samantha suddenly looked panicked again.

"For what's to come."

❧

"And what is to come?" Lucy Doran asked. Father Deane didn't reply for a good few minutes. He was sitting uncomfortably on the rancid floor of the cage. He was focusing on the bars, as they spun in perpetual motion, twisting round and round on their axis. He had made the fatal mistake of becoming highly animated during his retelling of the events that had led up to his capture. The resulting movements had caused the cage to spin once again. To avoid further motion sickness Father Deane attempted to focus on a fixed point on the cage, he had once read somewhere that this was meant to deter the onset of stomach cramps. Although it appeared to be working, insomuch as he felt no sickness, he had given himself a blinding headache from staring so hard and his eyes were streaming. He took his glasses off and wiped them on his trousers.

"Sadly Lucy I don't know!" he confessed, shouting up into the darkness again. He knew those words would offer the young girl no comfort, so to swiftly lift the conversation he added: "I'm sure it can't get any worse than this."

At that very moment the thunderous noise of movement began again from deep inside the cave. It sounded as though something was squeezing itself through a particularly enclosed space. Whatever it was, it must have been enormous because the noise was almost deafening for a few moments. Some rubble dislodged itself from the cave walls and fell with a clatter into the blackness beneath them. The ensuing noise only added to the devastation that was clearly being wrought elsewhere behind the walls.

Lucy screamed, and Father Deane leapt to his feet, ignoring the violent movement of his cage as it pitched to one side with the sudden shift of his weight.

"My God Father, what is that?" Lucy sounded petrified.

"It's alright Lucy," Father Deane reassured her, his voice at its most calming level. "It's only subsidence deep inside this cave. Goodness knows how far under the earth we are, the slightest vibration could be causing vast quantities of earth and sand to shift. That's what's making all that noise." As he said it he realised he was also trying to reassure himself.

The noise abated once again, and Lucy stepped towards the edge of her cage to stare down at the priest again. Her face was flushed with tears but her expression was shining with hope.

"We will get out of here Father, wherever we are." Lucy kneeled down again. Her legs were aching now. She remembered how hard and fast she'd had to run as she raced through Peter's flat trying desperately to escape that monster that had pursued her.

Peter.

She just couldn't comprehend all that Father Deane had just told her. His story seemed so incredulous that if she hadn't had first hand experience of one of those creatures herself, then she would have just laughed at what she was being told. Her thoughts drifted back to Peter now, as she wrapped her coat around herself for warmth.

Was she in love with him?

It was the one question that despite the precariousness of the predicament she found herself in; stubbornly refused to go away. Her heart raced to think of him in danger. She believed without doubt that he was not far away. She almost giggled, feeling like a schoolgirl. Something inside her had conjured up an image of Peter riding to her rescue on a shimmering white horse. She tried to dismiss the image, it was so important to keep herself grounded. Peter was sadly not her knight in shining armour. She doubted that he could even ride a horse. However, if he knew they were trapped here, she was certain he would make some sort of an attempt to rescue them.

Lucy rubbed her legs to ease the tension in her muscles. Father Deane had gone quiet after his animated retelling of his part in all this. Lucy still couldn't believe that Trevor Crispin was dead. True she'd never had much time for the man when he was alive, but she'd never wished him any ill. Something was gnawing at the back of her mind. Even now she could sense a chill in her bones as she remembered entering Peter's flat block. That strange scratching sound she'd heard coming from behind Old Mrs Candicote's door. Lucy shivered.

"Did you ever meet Annabel?" Father Deane suddenly called up to her. The question interrupted her chain of thought, and for a moment Lucy couldn't respond as her mind cleared.

"No. I told you that earlier, before my time in Wick Holm I'm afraid," Lucy called back. She looked down at the priest who was shaking his head slightly.

"Forgive me Lucy. People do keep telling me what a bad memory I've got! You can take it as a compliment if you'd like to? After all you've settled into our little village so well, it seems like you've been there forever."

"I wish I was there now Father. I wouldn't even mind putting up with a whole night of Ivy Meredith's gossiping, rather that then this," Lucy said, her mood lightening.

"Let's not be too hasty!" Father Deane teased. Lucy smiled at this. She could feel her whole body had calmed down from the nervous tension she'd felt immediately upon awakening.

"It's your turn anyway Lucy."

"My turn for what?" Lucy called back.

"Tell me what happened to you? How did you get here?" Father Deane prompted her.

And so Lucy began to recount the events that had led up to her capture. Unlike Father Deane who had appeared to be quite concise on what was relevant and what was not in his story; Lucy didn't even know where to begin. So she started from meeting Peter in Ruff's Diner. She inwardly sighed, trying to comprehend that that had only been yesterday. Then again, it could have been a million years ago. The darkness of the cave was total. It made it utterly impossible to tell day from night. Lucy could only assume that only twenty-four hours had gone by.

Father Deane sat listening intently. He focused on the lock of his cage door. He was trying desperately to come up with a plan of escape but everything seemed so fruitless. If they managed to unlock the cage doors, they then had to face the prospect of a vast drop that would certainly break their legs if it didn't kill them outright. He stretched out a hand and traced the curve of the keyhole with his finger. He knew there was no point even beginning to try to undo it. The lock looked rusted and ancient but retained a quality in the harshness of its design to appear threateningly strong. Father Deane sighed, bristling slightly as Lucy described her own meeting with Krinn. He waited patiently for her to finish.

The act of remembering had caused Lucy more pain than she'd realised. Halfway through her tale she began to be assailed with nightmarish images of her attackers. Looking out of her cage into the velvet darkness of her prison she shuddered. She clasped the bars of the cage with both hands. The sensation of cold that bit into her hands as she did so stopped the hysteria that was rising inside her again. She bit her lip painfully, and remembered her earlier resolve that Peter would find her.

"It's so weird Father," Lucy breathed. The chill in her voice was not lost on the priest and he eagerly moved to the bars of his own cage to hear her more clearly.

"What is Lucy?" he prompted. The young girl was staring straight at him, as she might if they were now seated in a confession box.

"I seem to have spent the last twelve months or so trying to learn as much about Peter Bettany as I possibly could. But listening to your story just now, I realise that there is so much of his life that still remains a mystery to me. He is so dark Father. It's almost scary. I just wanted to get inside his head, all those times he was so quiet in the Village Inn. I mean all of this..." She indicated the darkness. "This is worryingly how I imagined his mind would be. It almost explains his strange mood swings, his depressive tendencies. Don't you think? I'm the one doing the psychology degree, and I tell you now Father, this sure scares the hell out of me. I'm too sensible a girl to doubt what's happened to us. I'm not like Peter; I don't feel I have to question everything. He lacks confidence. Call it women's intuition but I've always sensed that about him. I wouldn't have questioned everything as much as he did. Oh why didn't he tell me what he was going through? I could have helped him. I want to help him...Oh God, I want him to come and help us, but is that asking too much of someone in Peter's mental state? Aren't you worried about him Father? Aren't you scared to bloody death that we will be left hanging in these cages forever? Is Peter Bettany a hero or a villain? Or is he just utterly mixed up? Because the latter doesn't help us!" Lucy broke down in tears, her throat sore from yelling. She violently choked back a cry; the action caused her to cough.

"Lucy." Father Deane's voice sounded kindly even though he was brimming over with concern. Lucy didn't respond, she was too intent on not letting herself cry anymore. "Lucy please listen to me. You must calm down, if you don't we won't be able to get through this. Do you understand me?" he softly enquired. The words of wisdom seemed to cut through Lucy's traumatised mind. She nodded her head very slowly. "Peter Bettany is a true friend to me. I'm speaking entirely from the heart now." Father Deane clarified. "He has stood by his family through a very difficult time, for which they will be eternally grateful to him. He has faced his own inner demons head on, and believe me Lucy he is more of a man than most people you or I have ever met. For a start he is always the first to admit when he was wrong. He's more than paid the price for any of his faults as young boy, and although there will always be people within our little insular community who won't ever give him the chance to change, as his priest and his friend I can tell you he has finally become the man he was always intended to be. I don't know what he means to you Lucy? But I can tell you that you mean a great deal to him. I believe he will find us here. That thought comforts me even at this dark time; I pray it comforts you as well."

Father Deane had barely finished speaking when the noise began. This time it echoed down to them from far above. Inches, meters, even miles above; it was impossible to say.

"What is that?" Lucy asked, looking upwards with an expression of horror on her face. Unlike the previous disturbance this sounded as though it comprised hundreds upon hundreds of fast moving objects, or bodies.

It sounded like the noise of an army returning.

The louder the noise became, the more the circling bats became agitated. Father Deane stared up at the connecting pin, which held his prison taut to the chain from which it was suspended.

Very slowly the coupling began to turn. It was almost unnoticeable at first, but as the vibrations from above grew in intensity, the twisting chain rotated ever faster.

It was then that Lucy and Father Deane first heard the other occupants of the cages.

In all the time they had been talking, neither of them had heard or seen a stir of movement from any of the other suspension cages.

Now in one deafening moment the cavern filled with the cries and screams of a hundred tortured souls.

Lucy and Father Deane desperately began moving from one side of their cages to the other, trying feverishly to catch a glimpse of any of their fellow captives. It was no good. The darkness was still impenetrable.

Suddenly the noise changed.

If anything, it intensified.

"They're running now," Father Deane managed, staring up at Lucy's petrified face.

"Father Deane?" Lucy managed. "Something is going to be horrid."

∽

Samantha Raynor turned off the car radio with an angry twist of the dial. It was no point trying to drown everything out with pop music. Some things just don't go away.

On the seat next to her rested the Annabel file, and now on top of it, paper-clipped to the front like a police rap sheet, was the picture that had been Mary Graham's parting gift to her.

It was the picture of Annabel that she had looked at in Mary's living room.

Annabel.

Why had this innocent looking girl suddenly begun to torment Samantha's every waking thought?

Samantha had been in such a hurry to leave Mary's cottage that she had almost forgotten to pick up the file. It wasn't until she'd reached the latch gate that she suddenly realised, but by that time Mary was already making her doddery way down the path, the file and picture clasped in her hand.

"Something to help you remember what she was really like," Mary said, handing over the picture and clasping Samantha's hands firmly in both of hers. "You mustn't fear her Sam. She means you no harm. That girl didn't have an ounce of malice in her entire body. She needs your help, that's all. Her time is not yet over. Like you said to me earlier, she is trying to correct a mistake. Believe me, Annabel was a garrulous girl in life, she will not keep you in the dark for long, if she does need you. Please try not to worry. She will protect you from any harm. But be careful…" Mary's grip tightened. "Be careful of Peter Bettany. His mind is more dangerous than anyone knows."

Driving through the unnaturally silent streets of Wick Holm now, Mary's final words seemed to linger in the air. Samantha searched the side streets as she passed them, desperate for any sign of life. She couldn't even see a glimmer of movement in a shop window, or at the very least a passer-by hurrying to get home as the snow belted mercilessly down from the pendulous clouds.

Wick Holm appeared to be deserted.

'That was ridiculous!' Samantha admonished herself. The traumatic events of the storm the previous evening had obviously taken their toll on the inhabitants of the little village. It was only natural that people would want to stay indoors under such circumstances. Samantha reasoned that even Ivy Meredith's tearoom was likely to be closed. She allowed herself a wry smile, realising that it was even more likely that the tearoom would be in full swing. It was entirely possible that Ivy's takings had in fact gone through the roof in the last few hours.

Samantha drove on, putting aside the sudden urge she had to sit in a crowded room. She must get home. She knew she was only delaying the ever-growing sensation of lethargy that no amount of coffee could put away indefinitely.

She was only a couple of miles from home now, and to keep her mind active she thought back to the final conversation she had had with Mary. Even now she could almost feel the intensity of the fire that Mary had described to her.

"They don't know exactly how it started. But my goodness did it spread quickly. Possibly an electrical fault, no one can tell but once it ignited, the whole house was in flames in minutes; it was so very sad. Cyril and Jayne were distraught afterwards. They had lost such a lovely home. It grieved the family to move into that flat block. I'll say this for Peter, and only this mind! He was the one who raised the alarm. If it hadn't been for him I'm certain the whole family would have perished. Anyway, as usual I over run…the memory of that night was a lasting one in Wick Holm. I mean we all knew about it, those who lived closest were amongst the first on the scene. I know Father Deane was there that night, doing all he could. He's a good priest you know? A real brick in a crisis, always seems to know what to say. The flames could be seen for miles they say. I remember seeing them in the distance, foolishly thinking it was someone's bonfire. I was so ashamed when I found out the truth; I probably could have done something." Even now Mary was clearly affected by the whole disaster. "As I said, we were all unnerved by that night. But it was Annabel who showed the greatest signs of trauma. Something deeply unsettled that girl. She became jumpy at the slightest thing, and suffered some terrible nightmares according to Jean Candicote. Thinking the house was burning down. She used to describe horrible images of running through endless corridors wreathed in lakes of flame. Her moods began to swing like a metronome. Fire seemed to be her only topic of conversation for a good while." Mary paused, sipping from a small glass of water she'd poured herself. "Then out of the blue the nightmares appeared to stop, and all of a sudden she began dreaming of this." Mary indicated the glass.

"Water?" Samantha queried.

"Tons of it by the sound of things! She told Jean she was sleeping better because every time she'd imagine the fire, she'd conjure up an image of water to put out the flames. We didn't question it, because after all it appeared to be working for her, and gradually she began to dream of her Dark Realm again. At least then we knew everything was returning to some kind of normality."

"So where does Peter Bettany fit into all this?" Samantha felt she was rushing the old lady, but a sense of urgency was required to spur her along.

"I was just getting to that!" Mary sounded indignant. "As I said, things were getting back on track so to speak. That's when Peter told her his story." Mary paused dramatically. Samantha quashed a laugh; she knew Mary was doing this deliberately to build tension and so for once she didn't attempt to interrupt. "From what I can recall now, it was called 'The Last Moments of Forget-Me-House' I think? Or something like that anyway."

"And what's the significance?" Samantha couldn't help herself.

"Oh Sam! You'd be no good at a murder mystery night! Question, question, question!" Mary berated. "The story was a fiction about a house which traps children, making them grow prematurely old..."

"Oh I see! Like a satirical slant on the nursing home that Annabel was working at? I must admit I never took Peter for being a social satirist..." Mary was shaking her head in astonishment.

"Please Sam. You're going in completely the wrong direction with this. Admittedly Lambert House was no doubt an influence for the story, but that wasn't what upset Annabel so much when she read it. It was the ending that disturbed her. He wrote of an uncontrollable fire that spread throughout the house, burning everything and everyone it touched. Oh my! Even now I shudder when I think about that ending. It was a horrible little story even before that, peppered with all kinds of nasty creatures, again no doubt fuelled by Annabel's stories of the demons that were reported to stalk the corridors of Lambert House. But it was the description of the fire that brought back all those nightmares for Annabel. Really that was the beginning of the end for her, and the start of a very short chain of events that finished that fatal night in December five years after the cottage fire." Mary looked tearful as she began to conclude her story. "Those last few years she went downhill fast. She began so positively at first, if anything reading Peter's story seemed to give her some sort of boost…"

"Was this after she'd started taking people to the Dark Realm?" Samantha questioned. In her own mind she was still trying to piece together Mary's story, although it was clearly making complete sense to the old lady, Samantha was feeling a little lost. Mary seemed to hesitate momentarily, and a sense of embarrassment passed between them.

"Oh child! What a useless old fool! Here I am telling you off for questioning everything, while I'm prattling on with my own story in completely the wrong order. Goodness what a mess!" Mary was clearly struggling with all the information she had to impart to Samantha. She stayed silent for a few minutes collecting her thoughts. "The fire happened when Annabel was only fourteen; you can well imagine the kind of trauma she would all ready be going through…"

"Good God yes! Puberty is a hair-raising experience enough without any added shocks to the system," Samantha sympathised. Mary nodded in agreement.

"It's funny you know, you'd think someone of my age would have forgotten all that business, but it stays with you forever, I can promise you that! Prior to puberty she'd been obsessed with her tales of this Dark Realm, but as I said, the aftermath of the fire put an end to all that."

"So Peter Bettany read her his story...when?" Samantha gestured with her hands in the hope of speeding Mary along.

"Must have been the same year, she may have turned fifteen soon afterwards. How old is she now?" Mary enquired. Samantha didn't even need to consult her file, the more personal details about her patient seemed to have somehow wormed their way into her long term memory.

"She's twenty-nine," Samantha answered with confidence. The announcement gave Mary pause.

"So it's been nine years since she was admitted." Mary looked incredulous. She appeared to be looking at her shaking pale hands. In places the skin had become almost translucent enough to show the blood moving through her veins. "I have become a tired old lady in that time, and that poor young girl has become a woman. So sad...all those things she'll never have the chance to achieve." Mary shed a bitter tear. "Yes Sam...I am sorry. Forgive the ramblings of an old fool!" Mary smiled as she wiped her eyes and Samantha looked kindly at her.

"You're no fool Mrs Graham. There aren't many people who could remember all the details that you've given me."

"Oh I don't know about that!" Mary dismissed the praise. "It was those last five years that Annabel seemed to go into a frenzy. Her college work became abandoned in favour of spending more and more time at Lambert House. It was during all of that brief period that she introduced Jean and the other old ones to her Dark Realm. But nightmares seemed to overshadow everything she was doing. Her mother became so angry with Peter after she discovered his story was the source of all this turmoil, that she ripped it to shreds right in front of him. Told him straight he was never to read it to her again. Good riddance to bad rubbish I say! Goodness knows what goes on in his imagination to conjure up something like that? Father Deane and Jean Candicote both read it. I don't think Peter knows to this day, but Annabel was so disturbed by it, she took it to them so they'd understand what she meant."

"Did you read it Mary?" Samantha was eager to know. Self-consciously she tried to hide her excitement. If the truth were known, she was keen to read this controversial story herself.

"No I never did, but Jean told me the bare bones of it. Just horrible!" Jean fell silent.

For a long time neither of them spoke.

Now, as Samantha slowed to a halt at Wick Holm crossroads, she questioned whether she should ever have even called upon Mary. The whole conversation had obviously left her in a worse state of unrest than before Samantha arrived. The heavy feeling of guilt was not a sensation Samantha was comfortable with. She justified that she had not been aware of Jean Candicote's death before she'd called round.

"Oh Sam!" She cursed herself, burying her head into the steering wheel. She could have just picked up the phone and called Mary. Why hadn't she just done that? Checked to see if she could drop in to see her sometime this week? At least if Mary had been pre-warned about the nature of the conversation Samantha wanted to have with her, then she may have had time to collect her thoughts more concisely. As it was, although the story had undoubtedly been the truth, the facts were a little confusing because of the erratic way Mary had tried to explain them. However, Samantha did think she finally grasped the events. Her next course of action, after a much needed sleep, would be to draw a timeline. It was something she hadn't done since her schooldays, but logic told her it was an ideal way of getting the facts clear in her mind. Samantha was determined to have done this before she took any further steps.

Before she confronted Annabel's parents.

And before she went to see Peter Bettany.

The noise of the siren snapped her bolt upright from her slumped position over the steering wheel. It also sent her train of thought whirling round her mind like the sails of a windmill.

It had been a short burst of noise, and looking dizzily into her rear view mirror, she could see a stationary police car behind her. Its lights weren't flashing. Her eyelids felt unnaturally heavy, and she fought to keep them open.

The siren burst through the silence of the afternoon once again. Samantha could now see at least one of the two occupants of the police car making bizarre hand gestures, as though they were repelling her by sheer will power alone.

Suddenly it all clicked into place.

The lights were now on green, and groggily Samantha forced her body to respond. She pulled unsteadily away, hoping the police weren't now going to follow her home. She breathed an audible sigh of relief when they indicated left and disappeared off in the direction of Great Wick Holm.

As unwelcome as the police had been, at least it proved to Samantha she wasn't the only person left outdoors in Wick Holm. She sped on towards her home, and the sleep she so desperately required.

The crippled creature, which had so deftly pursued her since she had left the hospital car park that morning, broke cover momentarily to dart after the car. It was driven by an over-whelming sense of inhuman vengeance that no amount of bloodshed could ever possibly hope to sate. Its senses were continually assaulted by a scent it had not picked up for many years.

It was the unmistakable scent of the first Sacred Mother.

∽

After miles of claustrophobic woodland, riding endlessly through a dense coppice of conifer and pine trees in almost total shade, it was no wonder that Tarnwaters took Peter's breath away.

The small band of friends burst through the final cordon of entwining fir branches, and following Ethanril's hand signals, slowed to a trot before halting entirely.

The clearing they now found themselves in was unlike any place Peter had ever seen in his whole lifetime.

"This is like something out of a dream," he couldn't help but say, squeezing Sufi's shoulders in surprise as he dismounted. Sufi smiled at the irony, but instead of quipping back, she just watched the ever-changing expressions on the Sacred Mother's face. Peter looked the way Sufi imagined he would as a child. His wide eyes were brimming over with wonder at the world around him.

"This is Tarnwaters," Mundo announced, stepping up to Peter and putting a friendly arm around his shoulders. "It's the furthest point we ever travel to, and although it might seem as though we've been riding for miles, we actually aren't that far from the Lake of Carrastorc. I think Ethan has got a bit jumpy in his old age, he just wanted to make sure no one was following us."

Ethanril was crouching at the waters edge, cupping his hands into the fast flowing river and splashing some of the water onto his face. He had heard Mundo perfectly.

"What my equally senile friend is trying to tell you Peter is that this is where our journey ends…at least for the moment. He stood up, slightly unbuttoning his white shirt. The material was sticking to his skin, melded there by the sweat of the day's exertions. He was talking all the time he approached the pair, gesturing emphatically to the south. "That way leads to the unknown places, often called the Wasteland. It is where we believe the Pig-Beast originated. No one has ever travelled into those lands; they are uncharted on any map we have seen of our realm. The only consolation is that the enemy have not breached those borders either. Their collective fear of the Pig-Beast rivals our own, as you will have seen from today's events." Peter quelled slightly at the memory of the Pig-Beast's timely arrival. "We don't know what it is?" Ethanril continued, seemingly divining Peter's thoughts. "All I can tell you is that it arrived here some years ago, around the same time as the Lord of the Now first made his presence known. If anything, it is more dangerous than the Still. It has certainly killed more Mist Children then they have so far managed." Ethanril spoke bitterly. "We're not even sure if it can be killed...but, before I scare you to death Peter!" Ethanril suddenly changed tack, spotting the horrified look in his friend's eyes. "We have learnt how to hide from it, and the white horses are more than a match for it in speed."

Peter felt slightly more reassured by this news. He watched Mundo leading Jessavarn by her reins to the lapping waters. The white horse bent his head and drank heartily from the flow.

"They are the purest waters you will ever taste Peter," Sufi explained, stepping up beside him. Peter turned from Ethanril to look at her. "This is the meeting point of two rivers. The Tarn which we have followed all the way here and another..." She broke off almost embarrassedly. Peter looked quizzical. "We don't know its name Peter, and none of us here have much imagination for christening it. You see, we're not even sure how far it stretches...or from where." Now Peter was following her gaze, tracing for himself the interception of the Tarn to this point. It suddenly opened out into a basin of low water. Small waterfalls and masses of upturned boulders provided a dizzying landscape of sound and colour. The water was so low over the stones that it gave the false impression that you could walk straight over the river without fear of drowning. But there was clearly a correct path, and as Peter watched, Taime, Fess and Pigeon began leading their horses across in a zigzag movement. Occasionally they would stop and start as they waited for validation that they had chosen the right path.

The second river was clearly flowing down through the opening of a valley. The water did indeed appear crystal clear as it flowed over the rocks near Peter's feet. He was still hesitant to drink any, his own memory of the water content of rivers back in Wick Holm had somewhat blighted his initial desire to rush headlong in and drink his fill.

Tarnwaters was the most peaceful sight Peter had ever seen. Following the terrors of the morning it was like a blessing to now cast his eyes upon such beauty.

The afternoon wind brought less of a chill than they had all become accustomed to, and although the snow still consistently fell, it was clear that the weather had improved greatly since Peter's arrival in the Dark Realm. The light was starting to fade; it seemed to cling just above the treetops like a reluctant child who didn't want to go to sleep just yet. The stillness of the forest around them gave the whole party an expectant feel.

Something was changing.

Ethanril could feel it in the patches and corridors of landscape they had traversed already that morning. Something about the sweetness of the air told him his prayers were finally being answered.

Soon the running would be over.

Peter was slowly turning around, taking in the whole landscape as though he intended to make considerable changes to it. He followed the fast flowing waters of the Tarn from the furthest point he could see, through the centre of Tarnwaters and away towards…

Nothing.

It was this that had given him the chill in his bones. Sufi saw him shake as he saw the outskirts of the Wasteland.

It was as though an artist had painted Tarnwaters in such an energetic frenzy that they hadn't noticed how faint the brush strokes were becoming on the far side of the canvas.

It was true that a second river was indeed flowing into the Tarn, but it was travelling down from a valley that simply ended at the corner of Peter's peripheral vision. The trees, boulders and scrubland that would normally make up the geology of such an area, ended. Some of the trees were half finished. Not as though they had been high pruned, or cropped; more that they simply had no more branches to grow. As though the creator of this landscape intended to continue it, but had run out of time.

Or time had run out for her.

Peter shuddered again, and Sufi took his hand, her blue eyes full of concern.

"You ok?" she asked simply. Peter took a second to glance back at her, and then he smiled, as though dismissing something. In surprise he found himself gripping his bag, as though checking it was still there. The familiarity of the coarse material of his bag seemed to bring him back to reality.

"I'm doing alright Sufi, don't you think…so far?" He needed her to reassure him, and Sufi was quick to do so. Her earlier aggressive attitude towards him had diminished in stages since he had taken his first steps towards believing her story.

"You're fine Peter, trust me. No one else would have handled all this as well as you have. I think we need to get you back to the Warren now though." She turned to Ethanril who was tending to Astervarn. "I think we all need to get home now Ethan. Peter is going very low, and I think some food would do us all good, you as well!" Sufi emphasized, watching as Ethanril turned from Astervarn to smile at her. He gave her a mocking salute and then whistled to the boys who had just crossed the river.

"Fess, Pigeon! Come back across, we'll need your help. Taime, stay with the horses," Ethanril called to them.

Pigeon looked annoyed.

"We just crossed this thing once!" he whined, not relishing a second trip.

"Oh stop your moaning and get over there!" Taime snarled, turning back to stroke Ratavarn. He wasn't comfortable being left alone on this side of the river. Kilfanfyn forest no longer offered him a sense of safety. Even now as he stared into the thick block of black poplar trees that dominated this edge of the forest, he shuddered. Anything could be hiding in there.

Sufi and Peter stepped towards the edge of the basin of water. Like the Tarn Steps, there were outbreaks of jagged rocks sporadically dotted across the river.

"At times the water is so low you can just walk across the shale on the bottom," Sufi explained, watching as Fess and Pigeon gingerly began to cross back towards them. "At best you'll have wet feet, which is enough to keep the Still from ever coming this far, but you have to be careful Peter. Tarnwaters is deceptive. There are patches of deep water, which unless you really know where to step, you can easily fall into. So stay close." She smiled mischievously. Peter felt a tremor inside him. He held Sufi's hand as she hopped onto the first rock. She was watching him as well, enjoying his eyes on her body.

"Do you want me to hold your hand all the way home?" She was flirting now, and Peter immediately released her hand in a panic. Embarrassment flushed his cheeks, mingling with the conflicting emotions he already had for Sufi. The young girl turned away with a flick of her hair as if dismissing the moment, she began calling playful insults to Fess and Pigeon. Peter was left standing there staring at her in utter bewilderment.

"You've survived Carrastorc Peter; Tarnwaters should be a walk in the park for an old veteran like you!" Mundo joked as he now led Astervarn down to the water's edge to join Jessavarn. Peter was too flummoxed to reply, and Mundo began his journey across the basin wondering if he had offended Peter in some way.

Ethanril stood a little way behind them. His instinct told him something was wrong. He knew they had been tracked, for at least most of their journey here. Even now he could almost feel the presence of something else. He worried that his own paranoia was acting against his usually keen mind. Was he imagining it? They had ridden for miles out of their way to arrive here, through some of the worst terrain the Dark Realm had to offer. Not even the most pernicious Still could have kept up with the white horses.

He glanced at Lockavarn. If nature had been cruel to the white horse's body it had compensated by enhancing his instincts. Lockavarn was always sensitive to any changes, and instinctively knew minutes before his three brothers if the enemy was close to hand.

Lockavarn was fidgeting, adjusting his great bulk from his back legs to his front, as though he were suddenly uncomfortable in one position.

But perhaps it was just the discomfort of the wound the horse had suffered on the fence back at Myfanwy. Ethanril hissed through his teeth in frustration.

"Let's get you home," he concluded, taking Lockavarn's reins. He led the stallion down to where Peter was standing. For a moment he thought about calling to Peter to help him, but Ethanril stopped himself.

He was observing for the first time the relationship between his sister and Peter. Sufi was mockingly unbalancing herself on the rocks, and Peter was reaching out to steady her every time. Ethanril smiled. He knew Sufi was more sure-footed than anyone he'd ever met. She was teasing Peter. For a second he thought of Annabel, and how she had mocked him so playfully when they had first crossed Tarnwaters. In fact, as Ethanril remembered, it was Annabel who had knocked him into this very basin when she had stumbled for real on one of the rocks. The memory warmed him, and it was with a happy heart that Ethanril finally spoke to Peter.

"Shall I take that bag you carry Peter? It can be tricky crossing Tarnwaters for the first time, any excess weight might be against you," he said offering his hand to take the bag. Peter hesitated, startled from his thoughts at first by Ethanril's voice, and then alarmed by the request.

"I'll keep it if it's all the same to you?" Peter tried to say casually, but both Sufi and Ethanril picked up on the tension in his voice. "Might not make much sense to you, but it reminds me of home," Peter said, hoping his excuse didn't make him sound pathetic. On the contrary, Ethanril seemed to perfectly understand the situation.

"If it gives you comfort Peter, you must keep it." He apologised, leading Lockavarn across the waters. "Be careful Peter, many a worthy man has fallen at Tarnwaters!" he called back, hiding his smile from both of them.

Sufi raised her eyebrow at Peter.

"You can't hide Annabel's letter from my brother Peter. He will know!" Sufi insisted, indicating Peter's bag. Peter nodded his agreement.

"Thank you for not saying anything..." he began, catching her off guard. "There's so much I have to explain to you Sufi. I know you must be going over everything that Old Mrs Candicote said to us but I just need time alone to read this letter. Can't you understand that?" Peter implored. Before Sufi had time to answer, Fess and Pigeon had boisterously arrived on the scene.

"Did you see the size of that trout?" Pigeon was demanding of his friend.

"Shut up she's here now!" Fess mocked, smiling cheekily at Sufi who just glowered at him.

"No be serious!" Pigeon interrupted.

"Oh you two!" Sufi snapped. "Why do you have to talk so loudly? You're standing right next to each other? Are you both going deaf?" she yelled. Fess and Pigeon froze in surprise at the aggressiveness of this outburst, they meekly shook their heads. "Well you ought to be! I don't know? Boys!" Sufi accused. She indicated towards Jessavarn, whom Mundo had left grazing by the water's edge. "Take the horse and lead the way!" Fess and Pigeon looked dumbfounded. Fess excused himself from the group and walked over to the horse, leaving Pigeon feeling as though he were suddenly the unwelcome centre of attention in their little triumvirate. He was about to attempt a surreptitious whistle, but seeing Sufi's troubled expression he thought better of it.

"Ready?" Fess managed, at almost a whisper, when he returned with Jessavarn. Sufi indicated that they should go first. Without a word, Fess and Pigeon set off, Jessavarn between them. Sufi turned to Peter. "Just promise me one thing Peter." Her voice sounded deadly serious. Observing the telling off she'd just given the boys, Peter knew better than to mess her around.

"Anything," he said.

"No more secrets," Sufi said in a controlled whisper. Peter nodded.

"I promise you." Sufi turned away and began following the boys. Peter very gingerly attempted to step on every inch of shale that she had stepped on. His feet were damp in seconds, but it felt good to be finally making their way towards comparative safety.

Sufi was scowling, her arms were folded firmly under her breasts, and she was almost stomping from one stone to the next. The water splashing her legs didn't affect her in anyway, and the feeling of serenity she normally had from crossing the Tarn to her homeland was all but lost on her. She was angry with herself more than anyone else. She had struck out at Fess and Pigeon, but only because they were such easy targets. It was her own emotions that irritated her. Sufi had always been a very level headed girl. When she'd first met Peter Bettany she had understood that he was the second Sacred Mother, and as such he would be able to help them in their plight. It was foreseen in the drawings they had found during the Great Find. But Peter had been completely different to the person she had expected to find. He was in denial as to his role in all these events from the outset, and even though Sufi had sensed he was lying to her, she had trusted him enough to explain his actions. As time had gone on, Peter had changed. He was growing and becoming the man she had always assumed he would be. But still he kept things back from her. Even now after all they'd been through, he was hiding something. Sufi hated that feeling. Lies and deceit seemed to be second nature to this man, just like Krinn. Yet there was something about Peter Bettany that drew her ever closer to him. She had noticed that she no longer liked to be too far away from him, and she hated that. She rolled her eyes, feeling her heart flutter. She knew what she felt for him, and she hated that too.

She was falling in love with him.

Pigeon almost hated Peter.

He was certainly blaming him for the telling off he'd just received from the love of his life. He glanced back, turning round immediately as he made eye contact with Sufi. She glared back at him. He couldn't think what he could do to make it up to her. He was very aware that they were moving extremely slowly because of Jessavarn.

"Can we speed up?" he asked. Fess, who was leading the horse, glanced round quickly.

"I can't go any faster than this old bugger here!" he accused, venting his own spleen on the innocent stallion. Jessavarn seemed to sense this and snorted, picking up speed until she passed Fess, who dropped the reins in utter bewilderment and watched the white horse dart across the open basin, reaching Kilfanfyn Forest moments later. "Well I'll be..." Fess began.

"Move on you two!" Sufi demanded, almost catching them up. "Even Jessavarn's got bored with this geriatric pace!"

Pigeon, in sheer desperation to make her happier, decided to let her pass him and go on ahead.

Fess was already striding carefully for shore and Peter was too wrapped up in his own thoughts to notice the problems ahead of him.

"Allow me *my lady*," Pigeon said gracefully, almost bowing like a courtier as he sidestepped to allow Sufi to pass. He hadn't thought this manoeuvre through at all, and he stepped straight from the shallow pathway into deep water.

The grace and speed with which Pigeon vanished from sight was such that absolutely no one noticed it had happened. His body weight and rigid poise propelled him straight down to the riverbed as though he had been fired from a cannon. Sufi blundered on, head down, not even bothering to thank him for his courtesy, and Peter followed on quickly, nervously fingering the strap of his bag. It was only Fess who actually heard the splash. Turning immediately, fearing they had just lost Peter. Sufi almost walked right into the now stationary Fess.

"*What's the matter now?*" she asked in surprise. Fess was just dealing with the fact that Peter was in fact right behind her.

"*Where's* Pigeon?" he asked in alarm.

"*I'm alright!*" a breathless voice called out a little way behind them. They all turned to see Pigeon pulling himself limply out of the river. His clothes were dripping wet, and his expression bore all the hallmarks of total embarrassment. He coughed several times, as he turned to pick up his hat, which was floating in the water near his feet. He rung it out with both hands and put it pitifully back on his head.

For a minute no one was able to speak. Pigeon stood stock still, though he was desperately trying to act casual. He manfully ignored the water dripping down his face.

It was Fess who finally broke the silence. His laughter was akin to the noise a male baboon might make if it had sat down on a particular thistly shrub. The indigenous bird life in the immediate vicinity took to the sky cawing in alarm.

Peter tried to hide his smile by squeezing his lips tightly shut, but this couldn't fight the rising belly laugh that threatened to explode him where he stood.

Sufi was smiling too, but something about the expression on Pigeon's face, as he stood there dripping with river water, pulled at her heartstrings. Her soft spot for her would-be suitor could not allow her to do nothing. Watched by Peter and Fess, who was by now in danger of giving their exact location away to the enemy by sheer volume alone, Sufi trudged back to him.

"Did you slip?" she asked sweetly, turning the full effect of her doe-like eyes on Pigeon. He took his hat off and raked his pink tinged hair backwards.

"I *may* have done!" he admitted, flashing Sufi his cheekiest smile. Sufi hesitated for a second before taking his hand. She was very aware how much Pigeon read into her every action with him, and although there was a time before Peter had arrived when she had been sensing a change in her own feelings towards the roguish boy, she knew that her emotions were now in turmoil.

Pigeon squeezed her hand, and their eyes met briefly. Although nothing was said, Sufi felt sure Pigeon sensed the change as well.

By the time they had weaved their careful path across Tarn-waters to the edge of Kilfanfyn Forest, only Mundo remained waiting to greet them.

"Enjoy your swim?" he asked. Pigeon refused to bite, and Sufi was thankful that for once even Fess failed to pass a comment. "Taime and Ethan have carried on, just to be certain all's safe," Mundo explained. Sufi looked surprised.

"Whose idea was that?" she asked, fearing her brother may have pushed Taime into confronting his fear head on. Mundo understood the question.

"It was Taime's actually. I think it's his way of dealing with what's happened. He's convinced the Warren is secure. The Pig-Beast caused some grievous damage above ground, but it couldn't reach them once Taime had moved everyone underground. That's when he went back up to lead the Pig-Beast away. I keep telling him what a hero he was, but he won't have it," Mundo sighed.

"It's because of my brother isn't it?" Sufi almost apologised. "Taime is always competing with him. I keep telling him Ethan isn't flawless." Sufi turned to Peter who looked on the brink of making a comment.

"You keep saying Warren? Are you telling me you live underground?" To Peter it sounded absurd. Even from this position he could tell that Kilfanfyn Forest was obviously vast. Why, with all those trees to make homes in, would they choose to live below ground? He was on the verge of mentioning the tales of Robin Hood to them, when he noticed they were all looking very offended. Peter winced.

"I know it might sound strange to you pal! But believe me, this place is the reason we're all still alive," Fess answered sharply. Mundo could feel the tension rising, and quickly tried to mediate:

"I know it does sound unusual to you. Naturally you would think only wild animals would choose to live in a Warren. But believe me, it sounded just as strange to us when Annabel first suggested we build a second camp."

Fess and Pigeon were nodding, while Sufi continued the story:

"We were very content to stay put at Myfanwy. I know you never saw it at its prime, but I'm sure you could tell what an amazingly snug house it was for us. We all crammed together in those rooms…this was before the snows came; I mean many of the others would just sleep out in the fields because the nights were so warm. But Annabel was never entirely at ease there. It was almost as if she could sense something was wrong. Well, you know how she can be, Peter?" Sufi stressed this last question, almost as though the whole world hinged on Peter's answer. She stared intensely into his eyes, underlining the importance of his response to quell the tension that was building up around him.

For the first time since Sufi had met Peter, he did not shy away at the mention of Annabel's name. In fact he made eye contact with each and every one of them before answering:

"Yes. Of course I do."

It was as though a great weight had been lifted from their shoulders. Even Sufi felt the relief of Peter's words. She had been tense with worry about him, ever since Jean Candicote had begun to reveal some of his secrets the night before. But to hear him actually admit that he knew how Annabel could be was a greater boost to her confidence in him, than when he had slain the wild dog at Carrastorc.

Fess, almost in embarrassment of his early harsh rebuke of Peter, continued from where Sufi had left off. He explained how they had all worked, day and night to build the Warren. As he talked the little group began to make their meandering way through the trees, and into Kilfanfyn Forest.

∽

The Lord of the Now watched them go. He stood on the opposite bank, where only moments before they had all gathered to cross Tarnwaters. His very presence there seemed to bring with it a smothering freeze to the air, as though a pestilence were sweeping across the banks of the Tarn. The scrubland upon which he stood, so recently flush and blooming with flowers beneath the thin cover of snow, had now withered and died under his touch. The snow had cleared where his fraying bandages had swept through it, leaving a broken trail that led down from the coppice where he had been hiding. It was pebble-dashed with ash as though someone was trying to grit the pathway to prevent the ice settling there.

He felt the glaive glow white hot under his cruel touch. The eyes of the hilt blazed an unearthly fury.

He had found them.

The day had been salvaged from the brink of failure. It now marked the destruction of Myfanwy, and soon the massacre of the Mist Children would begin in earnest.

For so long they had eluded his Still, always managing somehow to disappear without trace. The Lord of the Now had always known they must hide out in Kilfanfyn Forest. It was impenetrable to the Still as the river Tarn surrounded it.

But now…

A hideous rasping noise echoed from deep inside his wasted lungs. The Lord of the Now crouched down, clearing away the blackened shrubs, and brittle earth. He pressed himself down low to the earth, as though he were listening for something.

Something deep under the surface.

His hearing was absolutely acute. Even now he could still hear Fess's voice explaining to the Sacred Mother how the Warren was constructed.

The Lord of the Now rose majestically to his feet, a triumphant leer playing across his wicked lips. Once again he watched the flow of the river through Tarnwaters, observing carefully the lowest points of the water. If he had been human he would have walked straight across it to resume his hunt. He hissed momentarily like an enraged serpent. The water would burn him alive in seconds. His annoyance lasted only seconds.

"Soon,"

he whispered, before darting back into the coppice.

⁑

They had only been walking for a few moments when Peter noticed the change. It was subtle, but only because he was so used to woodlands back in his own world.

Kilfanfyn Forest was like something out of a fairy tale. It was crammed to capacity with such a rigorous display of different species of tree, flora and fauna. A strong yield of Black Poplar, Mountain Ash, Oak, Kilmarnock Willow, Maple, Beech and Horse Chestnut trees grew from healthy stools. The under-scrub was rich with Nettles, Brambles, Ragwort and numerous shrubs. Dotted here and there, and dripping in melting snow were Palms, Ferns and the odd Monkey Tree. Occasionally the dense scrub would give way to open grassed areas, thick with flowering plants that gave striking colour against the winter backdrop. Peter walked through these open spaces, noting all the varieties of plants that he remembered from biology. He was aware that most of them should only be flowering during the summer months.

It was ridiculous that such a mixture of plants could exist in one forest, and thrive even during the bleakest winter. Many of these trees were deciduous, yet they all retained their rich canopy of leaves.

Walking through Kilfanfyn, Peter almost forgot the myriad snow-scapes he had travelled through since his arrival in Sufi's world. Here, under the dense canopy of trees, the ground was damp underfoot, but virtually free in places of any sign of snow. The air seemed altogether warmer inside Kilfanfyn. So much so that Peter observed the others removing various jackets, and hats as they proceeded through the trees. It was almost humid in here, which seemed impossible.

Fess had all but finished explaining the construction of the Warren to him, when Mundo suddenly held up his hand. The group stopped on what appeared to be the outskirts of another clearing. Mundo whistled three times sharply, and then appeared to wait for a reply. As no one was talking Peter felt it would be inappropriate for him to ask any one of the hundreds of burning questions he had about the area.

After a brief moment, the whistle was returned.

"It's safe," Mundo declared, releasing his hold on Jessavarn's reins. The white horse whinnied with excitement and bolted through the perimeter cordon of pine trees. The speed of his gallop caused the pine trees to sway and dislodge a multitude of glittering needles, spiralling down around their feet as though forming a welcome carpet. Sufi hurried past Mundo and held back a curtain of branches, allowing a small entrance through the canopy.

"Come on Peter, you go next." She was almost dizzy with excitement for him to see their home. Peter felt all eyes turn towards him, and not for the first time since he'd arrived there, he felt very self-conscious. He picked nervously at the strap of his bag, and then, bowing his head slightly to avoid the higher branches, he stepped through the gap in the trees.

He breathed out in awe and wonder.

It was something about the way the late afternoon sunshine caught the pine trees at that moment, with a soft glare that made Peter shield his eyes and turn almost in a half-circle to take in the whole clearing. The snow fell steadily around him as he watched the four white horses gently trotting around the almost perfect circle of open ground. It reminded him at once of his first encounter with them, when he had watched Lockavarn and his brothers performing for him in the peaceful fields of Myfanwy.

This was how these horses were born to live. Like wild prairie stallions, they seemed almost to blend into the background, as though the landscape they lived in was more important than the people who inhabited it.

This was Annabel's vision. This was a scene of total peace.

Behind him he could hear the others making their way towards him, but none of them spoke, allowing him the precious few seconds he needed to enjoy this. A rook darted from its nest in one of the taller pines, casting snow from the branches as it departed. Peter followed the snow, which landed close to Taime who was removing his own horse's saddle, so he could join the others at play.

"What do you think Peter?" Ethanril asked, approaching him quietly from his left. Peter was still taking in the sheer beauty of the moment.

The clearing contained the remains of a campfire, with several tree trunks arranged around it to form seats. It was to these that Sufi and the other boys made their way. They had noticed much more about the clearing than Peter. To him the occasional fallen tree, or cleared patch of snow depicted nothing more than the normal passage of time and geology. To the Mist Children, it depicted invasion, danger and now death.

Taime showed Sufi were he had first seen the Pig-Beast. The monster's penetration of the clearing was clear. Two oak trees had been uprooted close to where the campfire usually burned. The trees were bowed in the centre as though they had been forced apart like sliding doors. They lay side by side now, like fallen sentries. As Taime proceeded out of the clearing, the trail of the Pig-Beast's destruction became more and more evident. Vast areas of scrub had been trampled under its pounding feet. Many of the trees hung limply on one side where their trunks had been snapped in two. Close to Sufi a beech tree was leaking a thick yellow sap from two giant grooves embedded in its bark.

"That's where it went for my head," Taime explained, reliving the terror of the moment for her. "I spurred my horse on just in time. The poor thing was more petrified than me! I remember ducking low over the saddle and literally feeling the rush of wind from the swipe it aimed at me. It would have taken my head off, instead that tree took the impact, and the Pig-Beast just slashed it as though it were wallpaper." Sufi was looking horrified.

"How does it move so quickly?" she questioned. "It's enormous." Taime shook his head equally baffled.

"It has an extraordinary grace, for something that, like you say, should be so cumbersome; its stature almost works for it, not against it." They gradually made their way back to the clearing.

"Peter?" Ethanril said again, aware that as yet the Sacred Mother had not answered his first question.

"Sorry!" Peter said, slowly coming out of a trance. "What was the question?" He looked sheepish and Ethanril had to smile.

"It can take you like that sometimes, this place. I was wondering what you thought of it, but on second thoughts I think I'd rather you kept it to yourself. There's something profane about actually talking about the beauty of Kilfanfyn Forest. I think it's a very personal experience. Your smile says it all." He clasped his hand on Peter's shoulder in friendship, and then walked off towards the others. Peter watched him go. He was envious of Ethanril's presence. He had never met anyone like him before. He just oozed self-confidence yet totally lacked arrogance. He was everything Peter had ever wanted to be.

He was a hero.

Ethanril arrived at the campfire just as Sufi and Taime did. They all huddled down on the log benches for a few moments. It was the first time the group had been together since Peter had arrived.

"How is he?" Taime asked, nodding in Peter's direction.

"He's overwhelmed, which is to be expected…" Ethanril began, lowering his voice so Peter wouldn't hear. "I think he may even be suffering from mild shock," he continued, his tone clearly revealing his worry. "The upshot is, although we all have so many questions for him, I think to just bombard him with them all at once would be crazy. He will just break. You can see in his eyes he's on the verge of it already," Ethanril said sympathetically.

"So what's the best thing to do?" Mundo asked the question on everyone's lips. Ethanril hugged himself for warmth.

"We try to have a normal night here. I know we haven't got a lot of time to play with. We've dealt the enemy a significant blow today, but the retribution will be terrible. I have no doubt of that. The Lord of the Now is preparing to make his final assault on us, do not kid yourselves that everything will be better now Peter has arrived. We don't even know at this stage if Peter can help us. All we know for certain is that the enemy knows we have him, and that places us all in even greater danger than before," Ethanril emphasized, suddenly aware that everyone was looking slightly panic-stricken. "I believe the end is very near now…" he continued quickly. "These last few years we have been playing the same cat and mouse game with them, always we have escaped. That indicates that we are either extremely lucky…" at this Fess and Pigeon clasped each other's hands and Ethanril hid a smile, "or they've been letting us," he finished. He watched Fess and Pigeon release each other and stare at him.

"What do you mean?" Pigeon asked. "It never felt like they were letting us escape. Whenever the Still have pursued us we've been running for our lives," he argued, and Fess nodded agreement to everything he said. Ethanril was shaking his head.

"You misunderstand me. It's not that they haven't been hunting us with the intention of killing us, or capturing us. I just feel like they've been using us." Sufi nodded her agreement.

"I feel that too. I'm glad you've said it." She looked imploring at the others, but the boys had obviously not shared her premonitions. "Don't you feel like they've been waiting for something? Waiting for us to get in touch with Peter? Just like they waited for Annabel to leave us before they revealed they had been here all the time?" Sufi was getting louder and Ethanril quickly defused the situation by interrupting.

"Peter is as vital to the Lord of the Now as he is to us. With him the link between our world and Peter's stays open, and until Annabel returns, he is the only one who has all the answers..." Ethanril tailed off as Mundo asked a question:

"But the writings, the ones we uncovered during the Great Find? You must surely still believe the prophecy, Ethan? I know Morquinda has the books now, but the words are still true? Aren't they? He will lead us?" Mundo looked desperate, but Ethanril did not contradict him. If anything his answer was more confident than it had ever been.

"He will lead us Mundo, into whatever comes next. We just have to give him a little time that's all. Taime; will you take Peter down into the Warren? The other Mist Children are desperate to see him." Taime nodded in agreement and rose up without question to join Peter. "The rest of us should leave them alone for a few minutes, and start preparing some food..." Ethanril suggested, but Fess interrupted.

"The last time we did that, they fell out!" He indicated Taime and Peter. "You should have let me and Pigeon show him around down there," he continued. Ethanril was already rising.

"No thanks boys. I haven't got time to come looking for the pair of you when you get lost down there." He playfully shoved Fess as though by accident. "Sorry," he half-heartedly apologised. "Pigeon, you should get into some clean clothes after your swimming lesson," he continued. Pigeon looked briefly excited.

"I don't suppose..." he began, but Ethanril had already continued.

"There is a spare shirt in my trunk, but sadly those are the only trousers, so I would dry them by the fire later if I were you." Fess was already laughing as Pigeon looked crestfallen.

"Can we trust you two to light the fire while we go off hunting for dinner?" Sufi asked, looking warily at the two boys.

"Not unless you want to come back and find them fanning the flames away from the pine trees!" Mundo laughed. "I'll stay and baby-sit! You two carry on." With that Ethanril and Sufi disappeared into the forest.

∞

The fire had all but extinguished itself at the ruins of Myfanwy. But even now, as the Lord of the Now stood watching, the dying embers slowly crackled and sparked as they licked at the blackened husk which had once been this proud and beautiful farmhouse. The heat from the furnace was still blisteringly hot. The flames had ravaged the house, scorching the white paintwork until it blistered and flaked away, eventually turning the whole structure to an inky black. Despite the aggressive changes in the weather, which had contributed to the Mist Children's escape before the fire grew too intense, the aftermath of the arson was still hideous to observe.

The twisted smile on the Lord of the Now's lips revealed his almost tusk-like incisors. A slow trickle of ash dribbled from the left side of his mouth like warm spittle. He stared at the smouldering ruin and breathed deeply of the acrid gases belching forth from the burning timbers. He didn't hesitate a moment longer.

In two steps he had crossed the threshold of the front door, and entered the blackened interior of the house.

In that instant the flames seemed to ignite afresh, almost as though they were merely waiting for something new to burn.

The blaze engulfed him as though he had stepped up to a funeral pyre.

∞

"Watch your head on this!" Taime indicated the supporting beam, which dipped just below ground level at the entrance to the Warren. Peter warily watched Taime descending the stairs. He looked back towards Fess and Pigeon who were huddled around the now blazing campfire. Mundo was returning with fresh logs and Peter wished he could just go and help them with that, but Taime was already picking at his sleeve. "Come on Peter. It's perfectly safe I assure you." He turned and disappeared into the tunnel. Peter sighed and followed him down.

The Warren entrance, which was built into the side of a small hillock, appeared to Peter as though he were on the brink of descending into a disused mine shaft. A rough entranceway was designed using three supporting blocks of thick oak to take the weight of the roof of dirt and prevent it from giving way. He had braced himself for a journey through unrelenting darkness, and was therefore surprised by how light it was inside the tunnel. Small gas fire lanterns hung sporadically from hooks along the tunnel wall, casting eerie shadows over the two visitors, but providing healthy illumination. Peter proceeded for a few moments almost bent double as he tried to avoid banging his head against the roof, which was lined in places with timbers. The tunnel appeared to be dipping sharply and he called out to Taime in some alarm:

"How far down do we have to go?" The fingers of claustrophobia were reaching for his sweating neck. Taime turned awkwardly in the tunnel. His hat scraped the ceiling and he took it off in frustration.

"It's not far Peter I promise you! This is just one of four connecting tunnels. The plan was to dig numerous entrances and exits to the main Warren, to allow us enough variety of escape routes if the enemy should ever find us here. But as you can imagine, it was backbreaking work. So we settled for four tunnels in the end. They all lead back up to Kilfanfyn Forest, but this is the main tunnel we use," Taime helpfully explained, turning back to continue his descent.

"Sufi was telling me that the Lord of the Now has a similar lair near Carrastorc," Peter said. He found that he had to crouch even lower now as the tunnel curved around a corner. The ground was lined with straw for warmth, and at intervals he noticed there were dugouts in the tunnel walls. He had stopped to examine one as Taime carried on explaining:

"Stilfanwyn Chasm. I doubt very much it's like the Warren though," Taime scoffed, turning back to look at Peter. "Ours is man made. They say his lair was built on a fault in the ground near the Lake of Carrastorc."

"Caused by what? A landslide?" Peter thought that sounded unlikely judging by the terrain they had crossed that day already. Taime was smiling.

"No. They say a giant creature carved those tunnels out itself thousands of years before we came here. It burrowed all across the Dark Realm before finally settling in a vast chasm, the one that the Lord of the Now has taken residence in. In order to appease the beast he has to make a human sacrifice to it every few months when it wakes from its slumber." Taime could tell by this point he had Peter's full attention. "It's called the Gak Worm, and no one has ever lived to describe it," he finished ominously. The flickering light was making Peter blink, but it was Taime's horror story which had caused his hands to tremble.

"Do you believe that?" he asked. Taime paused for a second.

"No! Course not Peter! It's a fairy story, one that Annabel used to tell the other Mist Children when they wouldn't behave themselves or go to sleep. Put it this way. Stilfanwyn Chasm is one place no one goes to, if they have a choice." Taime continued down the tunnel, and Peter sighed with relief. He turned back to look at the dugout. It contained a sleeping bag and a few assorted sticks.

"Someone sleeps here!" Peter whispered incredulously.

"Come on Peter!" Taime yelled back from further along the tunnel. Peter quickly abandoned the dugout and caught up with his guide. The pace quickened and up ahead of them Peter could just make out the entrance to a chamber of some kind. He was intrigued to see what it was and had to keep looking around Taime's back to catch a glimpse of it. The action of bobbing up and down on the balls of his feet caused him to continually bump his head on the ceiling.

"What's that noise?" Peter asked, just before they entered the main chamber. Taime seemed to know immediately what he meant. Very faintly an intermittent sound was penetrating the walls of the tunnel. It was too deep beneath them to clearly ascertain what it was, but Taime seemed to already know:

"We hear it a lot. It's because the tunnel is quite deep here. It's just water, Peter." He was turning away but Peter looked less than convinced.

"It sounds too intermittent to be flowing water," Peter pressed. Taime flashed him a wicked grin.

"Perhaps it's the worm!" He laughed and entered the next chamber. Peter half-smiled and then ducked through the low doorway.

"We call this the Nest," Taime announced. Peter looked up as he stepped through and was startled by the sheer size of the chamber he now found himself in.

His surprise turned to abject terror as the waiting throng of Mist Children rose up as though they were all one consciousness from the floor and surrounded him, tugging at his clothes in their desperation to touch him.

※

10

Children of the Mist.

Samantha Raynor stirred beneath her bed sheets.

Her ex-boyfriend had told her once that she was an extremely restless sleeper.

To this day Samantha remained unsure as to whether it was that which had eventually caused him to leave her without a word one April morning, or whether it was his allergy to her cat Mrs Primly?

"That damn cat!" he had repeated over and over again between fits of frenzied sneezing. "It's always on our bed in a morning!" he would whine.

Samantha didn't miss him anymore.

If it had ever come down to a choice between the two of them, Mrs Primly would have won every time.

Again her sleeping body turned over, twisting the bedsheets round her legs as though they were restraints. She was drifting in and out of consciousness and she seemed only mildly aware that she was causing so much distress to her duvet.

The bedsheets felt unnaturally cold.

She always made a point of warming the bed before she got into it, and last night had been no exception. Even now she could stretch her left foot out and feel for her hot water bottle. It had somehow slipped down between the mattress and the bedsheets at the foot of her double bed. The bed should have been pleasantly warm from her own body.

Yet it felt damp.

She murmured as her eyes briefly fluttered open registering this temperature change. Lethargy quickly consumed her again and she was bordering on deep sleep in seconds. She did not panic about the dampness. She would have known if she had had an accident in bed, it would have woken her. The damp was from her nightmare; her body was probably wreathed in sweat. She coughed for an instant and then twisted her right arm, snaking it across the mattress and burying it firmly under her pillow.

Samantha had been so tired when she had eventually returned home. She had barely allowed herself time to dump her clothes over a chair, before collapsing into the comfort of her bed. She had rallied herself after a few moments and while the kettle boiled for her hot water bottle, she'd taken off her makeup. She had even contemplated re-reading the Annabel file, but the minute her head touched the pillow, she had dropped into the deepest sleep of her life.

She felt a pressure on the duvet, close to her chest. Mrs Primly had obviously just leapt onto her bed, hoping to secure an early breakfast.

Samantha playfully swiped at the duvet. The action was not heartfelt, but she hoped it would convey the message to the cat that she was not welcome.

The pressure increased, and something splashed onto Samantha's face. Her eyelids fluttered briefly again as she tried to wipe the saliva off her face.

"Mrs Primly!" she breathed softly, admonishing the cat. "We must get you house trained!" Samantha moaned, turning her back on the cat. She closed her eyes again, briefly wondering if Mrs Primly would begin to purr continually now until she was forced to get up.

She felt a breeze close to her exposed right ear, as though the cat was leaning in close to her. She brushed her hand over her lobe to deter her.

That was when she first heard the words.

It was the softest voice Samantha had ever heard, and yet it contained so much power. She almost groaned, believing for a split second the television was switched on.

"Your death will be exquisite. Like a thousand speared angels tumbling from a louring sky."

Samantha's eyes snapped open. Her body temperature had dropped considerably and a panic swept through her. She wanted to turn over but she had physically frozen to the spot. The voice was continuous, as though a demonic fortuneteller were sitting opposite her, dripping the sweetest malice into her ear.

Using all her willpower she finally twisted over in bed to see who was whispering such callous thoughts into her ear.

Her screams would have woken the dead.

There was a young man perched directly over her. His legs were tucked up underneath him and his black cloak was wrapped around them giving him the uncanny resemblance of a hooded crow. The light from Samantha's larva lamp cast swirling purple shadows over his angelic face. His cold blue eyes never left hers, as though they were two lovers caught in the final moments of eternal separation.

His clothes were dripping wet, and it was from him that the water was leeching onto her mattress.

In a fury Krinn tore at the duvet, ripping it upwards as though he intended to smother her with it.

Samantha's reactions came flooding back to her and she pulled away at the last moment. Her tangled legs caught on her bedsheets, and as she struggled furiously to free herself she became evermore distraught with panic. Her final effort wrenched her free of the bed, but in the darkness of the bedroom she lost all sense of direction and collided firmly with the bedside cabinet. It caught her a glancing blow across the temple.

Everything went black.

She was unconscious for only a minute.

When she woke the room was deserted. She waited for several minutes, breathing like an asthmatic, her legs tucked firmly against her chest as though she were trying to blend in with the furniture of the room. The shadows from her larva lamp were terrifying her, and she was shaking uncontrollably when she peeled back the duvet to check under the bed.

There was nothing there.

She rose shakily to her feet, her hands ferreting across the wall behind her for the light switch. In seconds the room was bathed in bright light and the shadows of the night vanished like a bad dream.

Samantha spent the next few minutes checking the house. As time wore on she became more and more convinced that she had imagined her intruder.

She wandered back through the bedroom and checked her alarm clock. Surprised to discover it had frozen at four-twenty am. She flipped the television on, and was equally shocked to find the eleven o'clock news bulletin greeting her.

Totally fuddled by the events of the day Samantha opted to take a sleeping pill. In the morning she needed to be fresh and alert to go over the events that Mary Graham had described to her.

She also knew that she had to meet with Annabel's parents.

She still wasn't sure how she could help that poor girl, but she was determined to try.

The sleeping pill worked wonders and she was snoring rhythmically in minutes. So deep was her sleep that she failed to notice the dark shape that crept from her closet and concealed itself beneath her bed.

༾

The questions were relentless.

'Are you coming to save us?' 'Where is Annabel?' 'Did she mean to leave us for this long?' 'Will you be staying Peter?' 'Do you know who we are?' 'Are you really the second Sacred Mother?'...

It was all too much for Peter. His initial panic at the clamouring group of ragged children, who had encircled him as though he were a Maypole, had now turned into something akin to revulsion.

He tried to pull away and disentangle himself from the rabble. So many tiny, grubby little hands were reaching for his clothes, trying to touch him; and in that one moment the very thought of their skin upon his abhorred him. The cacophony of questions had reached fever pitch and Taime found himself unable to control the melee. Peter was backing further away as they pulled at the straps of his bag.

There must have been a hundred children. All dressed in an assortment of rags. They looked how Peter had always imagined street urchins would look. Their faces were grubby with dirt and their hair hung lank and unwashed. None of them could have been above ten years old.

And yet...

As realisation dawned upon Peter he screamed like an animal.

That brought silence to the horde. Even Taime looked suitably stunned.

The Mist Children all looked shocked and appalled by Peter's reaction. They released him and took several steps backwards as though he were infectious.

Peter was sobbing uncontrollably. Taime remained frozen to the spot, utterly unsure of what to do.

The sound of movement could be heard from the corridor

outside and Mundo suddenly appeared in the entranceway of the Warren.

"What's happening down here?" he blurted out, trying to take in the strange sight before his eyes. Taime looked momentarily angry, and signalled for Mundo to leave. "What's going on…are you ok Peter?" Mundo continued, ignoring Taime's request. Peter slid to his knees, his body shivering with the flood of emotions he felt. He bundled his bag into his arms as though it were a comfort tool. Taime was walking towards him, his face a mask of pity.

"Mundo, please just leave us here for a few moments. Take the children up to the forest with you…Peter just needs a moment." It was rare that Taime spoke so seriously, and Mundo could tell from his tone that arguing with him at this point would be a mistake. Quickly he hurried round the children, like a shepherd herding a flock. He began to lead the children out of the Warren. As they passed him, Peter felt every single one stare at him.

Finally just Taime and Peter remained in the Warren. Peter sniffed harshly, clearing his nose, and he aggressively wiped his eyes until they looked red and blotchy. He was trying to avert his eyes from Taime as he stood up and dusted himself down.

"So many of them…" he began, feeling as though he might be able to bluff Taime into believing it was just the sight of the children that had caused this hysteria inside him.

"You know something Peter?" Taime asked casually, placing himself between Peter and the entrance of the Warren, forcing the other man to look at him. "You remind me a lot of the old ones," he stated, and Peter looked perplexed. "They have a leader called Morquinda…ah! I see you already know who I'm talking about. Anyway, she is accused of suffering from mythomania. Do you know what that means?" His body language had turned strangely aggressive, and his questions were no longer just requests.

"Yes I do," Peter whispered. Taime raised an eyebrow indicating that Peter should explain it to him. Peter coughed embarrassedly and then said: "A mythomaniac is someone who has an abnormal tendency to exaggerate..." He seemed reluctant to continue, but Taime took a step closer towards him. "...Or tell lies," Peter finished. Taime locked eyes with him.

"I know that's what you suffer from Peter. Your whole body language tells me you're in a constant conflict with yourself. Sufi senses it too; she is the most perceptive of all of us. I know you want to start telling the truth Peter, and I know you fear for your life if you do. But contrary to popular belief, I am on your side." Taime smiled at him, and in that second the tension between the two of them was temporarily broken. Peter felt the need to sit again, but this time Taime sat down next to him.

In the brief silence that followed, Peter took the opportunity to glance around the chamber he was in. He could not begin to imagine the amount of work that must have gone into its construction. The earth walls were smooth in most places where the digging had been rounded off. Occasionally there were pits and grooves in the wall where stones had been removed. A network of tree roots and wooden girders supported the ceiling. There were no chairs but the floor was covered in rugs and blankets for warmth. It was obviously also used as a stock room for clothes and equipment, and Peter could see a small annex room had been carved out in the far wall to act as a makeshift larder for storing meats and drying herbs.

"I spent a lot of time with Annabel..." Taime interrupted his thoughts. "We would sit down here and talk for hours." His eyes scoped the room as if re-living the pictures of that time in his mind. "She never spoke of you Peter. Does that surprise you?" Taime was blunt, but Peter didn't seem to mind.

"No," he confessed. "No, that doesn't surprise me in the least." Taime seemed to accept this without question. "It was Sufi who discovered your whereabouts. You see she had been given a gift by Annabel, an ability to travel through the void into your world. Sufi calls it Dream Blending. Anyway, one night she brought back some papers and drawings from your world," he explained. Peter was enthralled now. Although Sufi had described to him much of what had happened here, he found it refreshing to have the story told from a different perspective. "They called it the Great Find. You know why?" Again Taime waited, but this time Peter shook his head. "Because it led them to you Peter; Annabel wrote most of those papers, but some were in your hand-writing, Peter. All of a sudden there was excitement, the germ of an idea had been sown. Annabel had left us, but there was another. A second Sacred Mother. Someone who could fill in all the gaps that Annabel had failed to do…" Taime was well into his stride now, and Peter watched the enthusiasm flickering behind his eyes. "Our world had become an ice palace, and the Lord of the Now had us all in a choking grasp. But the answer lay in the writings of the Great Find. We could find a way to reach you, Peter Bettany. But Morquinda and the other old ones were terri-fied by this discovery. They became manic when it was suggested that you should be contacted. They were almost pleased when Annabel failed to return. So one night they too abandoned us. But they took the Great Find with them. All of those books, all of those answers. Before we had time to read them all and fully understand for ourselves what was happening." He paused, gulp-ing in the cool air of the Warren. "Months became years Peter, as we struggled to find a way to contact you. Our world grew ever more dangerous, and the Mist Children started to disappear. Ethanril explained recently how Sufi had tried for years before she perfected her gift. Because Annabel never fully explained it to her, she has had to learn the craft for herself. But she was fastidious in her studies Peter. She put herself through so much pain to make contact with you. And one night she did."

The enormity of Sufi's journey to reach him that first night in Wick Holm church suddenly registered with Peter and it left him humbled. "But you wouldn't listen to her Peter. You wouldn't come with her and worse of all...you claimed not to know what she was talking about. Ethanril has tried so hard to keep everyone's spirits up these last few days. He knows that you are without doubt our last hope against the enemy. You are the second Sacred Mother. But alas, you still deny you have the answers." Taime's words cut straight through him. Peter was about to speak, but Taime shook his head. "Now is not the time Peter. I just want you to realise that there is someone in this group who sympathises with you. I'm not like the others Peter. I'm a realist. I feared I would go as mad as Morquinda in the early days after Annabel disappeared. You see she was my rock Peter. I turned to her whenever I needed someone to talk to, someone who would understand. She never fully answered my questions, but she did keep me grounded, where I needed to be. I have no memories Peter. I know you know that. I don't believe I have a past, I don't even believe I was ever born. Look around you, where are all the mothers? Why does no one here have any memory of his or her childhood?" Taime laughed. "All a lie...a lie that only you can explain now Peter. I saw your face when the Mist Children gathered around you. It wasn't fear...it was horror. Horror because you knew they'd look like that...children with wizened old faces. And why have we few been blessed with youth, names and abilities? Why do they spend their days scrambling in the mud? Hardly able to talk or learn anything? It's been ten years now Peter since Annabel stopped teaching them, and they've not changed. We've all stayed the same. She promised them all names and identities. How can someone promise that?" Taime's voice had risen again; he suddenly turned on Peter, pointing his finger with a quivering fury. "You know. Don't lie to me anymore Peter. You know what's happened here. And if you don't tell me by tomorrow...I will kill you myself." With that he was on his feet and gone from the Warren. Peter sat looking aghast. Every word

Taime had spoken was true. A fear raced through him as he saw clearly what he must do. He understood Taime's anger, and he also believed that when he eventually sat him down and told him the truth…Taime would kill him.

∽

The Still guarding the entrance to Stilfanwyn Chasm watched awestruck by the sight that was fast approaching him. It quelled in panic as it realised this monstrosity was its Lord and master. The closer the stranger drew, the more petrified the Still became.

The Lord of the Now was stripped bare of all his bandages. The fire from Myfanwy had burnt them away as easily as the fire in the House had burnt his flesh all those years ago. He stood now glistening with renewed power. The glaive shone like a beacon in his left hand, and his muscles gleamed in the setting sun. He was a truly incredible sight to behold. His movements seemed faster and sleeker than before, and although the Still was already anticipating that his master would attack it, it had no time to avoid the first blow. The demon was upon it in seconds, clawing at its neck, and biting into its skull. The Still ripped at its master with its back claws, but the Lord of the Now simply grabbed them and pulled them off as easily as if they were paper.

He dropped the mangled remains of the Still onto the ash-strewn ground, and slammed the glaive three times against the hatchway to Stilfanwyn Chasm. Slowly it began to rise as the Lord of the Now paced impatiently across the snow.

His vengeance had begun, but his bloodlust was far from sated

∽

The next morning was clear and fresh.

Peter awoke early. If truth were told he had not slept well. He had never been a big fan of sleeping bags, even in his youth he had consistently moaned whenever it had been suggested they should have a family camping holiday. Now as he disentangled himself from the makeshift bed his body ached in protest to sleeping on the hard floor of the Warren. He missed the creature comforts of home with a burning passion. Although Peter had always been a fan of outdoor pursuits, he was not by any means a seasoned traveller. Sleeping out under the stars did not appeal to Peter, although he had to admit that the previous evening's feast around the campfire had been a highlight of his short time in the Dark Realm so far.

He had been pleasantly surprised that when he had eventually emerged from the Warren after Taime's heated rebuttal of him, the others had been busy preparing food. Peter had squeezed onto the log bench next to Sufi, and at her encouragement had enjoyed his first taste of flame-roasted rabbit. It was delicious and he had been forced to go up for more, which Mundo generously carved for him, much to the disappointment of Fess and Pigeon who had been banking on the leftovers.

All night the group had skilfully avoided any direct questions or hints to Peter's role in the days to come. Instead they had talked and laughed about old times, filling Peter in on as much history of the Dark Realm as they knew. He learnt of Annabel's earliest meetings with them at Khynous Morf. Of the time when Krinn and the Old Ones were still a part of the group and Old Mrs Candicote would visit them. Peter laughed at Fess and Pigeon's adventures with the barn owl in the hollow tree. He learnt for the first time what had happened to his Dad's Christmas tree after the void had sucked it from his flat. He also explained his own part in that accident.

All night Taime avoided eye contact with Peter, but his presence was felt throughout.

While Ethanril prepared drinks for everyone, Peter excused himself from the group and walked manfully over to the other

Mist Children who sat in a huddled cluster near the fire. To begin with they were extremely nervous that he would shout at them again, but when he sat down as inoffensively as possible and began to playfully arm wrestle with one of the young boys, he was accepted at once. For the next hour he talked and encouraged the children to try and communicate with him. He found it a more natural experience than he had expected, and they did seem to respond to him. Some were more fluent than others, while some could barely speak at all. Peter tried to avoid drawing too much attention to their disabilities, but often without realising it he would stare a beat too long at their old faces. It was with a heavy heart that he eventually came away.

By this point the group were settling down to sleep. Everyone had changed their bloodied clothes except Pigeon who was sporting a fresh shirt, but his gaudy trousers were still in place. He had been sitting as close to the fire as he reasonably could all night, trying to dry them out while ignoring the continual shouts of 'Get em'off!'

"Are you feeling more at home Peter?" Sufi had asked him, handing him a steaming cup of blackberry juice. Peter stared at the insipid red liquid.

"You wouldn't have any coffee would you?" He knew it was asking rather a lot. The blank faces that greeted this question confirmed to him that 'No' they hadn't.

"I'm sure everything will look better in the morning," he managed in response to Sufi's original question. As he said this he watched Taime saying 'goodnight' to everyone.

All night as Peter had lain in bed, he had expected to wake up to the feeling of cold steel pressed against his throat, but by some miracle he had been left alone.

He rose out of his dugout in the Warren wall, and stretched as high as he could to relieve the muscles in his back. In doing so he groaned and had to cover his mouth quickly for fear of rousing everyone else from their slumber. He had no idea what time it was, but he guessed it must be just before dawn. He stroked his thickly stubbled chin and raked his hands through his tangled hair.

"I must look a state!" he whispered, realising he had also slept in last night's clothes. He reached for his rucksack and slung it over his shoulder. He inched his way cautiously up the tunnel, careful not to wake any of the other sleepers, and quietly removed the jumble of willow branches that now covered the Warren entrance. A faint light tickled his eyes as he stumbled out into the clearing. The fire had almost completely burnt out, just a few dying embers crackled in the misty morning haze. It wasn't snowing yet but the chill of winter clung to every tree in the clearing. Peter made his way over to the first outcrop of trees, seeking a place to sit and read in peace. The thought of opening Annabel's letter filled him with trepidation.

For a moment he thought of Old Mrs Candicote, the robust old woman had been such a stable influence on his life. He still couldn't believe he would never see her again.

The direction he had taken led him through a thick belt of beech trees and out into a shady area surrounded by whispering pines. He spied a fallen beech some short way off, and was impressed by the smoothness of the bark. The angle that the tree had fallen made it easy to scale and he inched his way along the trunk until he could rest his back against one of the sturdy lower branches.

It was here that he first opened the bag. With a steady hand he pulled out the jumble of contents. His dissertation sat at the bottom of the bag, and on top of this, after quickly inspecting them, he placed the jumbled sheets of papers written in Annabel's unmistakable hand. He would study them all when he had more time; it was the letter he sought. He found it close to the bottom of the pile, and tucking it under his knee he skilfully shuffled the other papers and deposited them back in his bag. This he then dropped onto the floor. He adjusted his back against the tree, seeking a more comfortable seating position as he tore open the manila envelope which had his name written neatly across the front in black ink. The letter inside was shorter than he had expected, and written freehand on three small pieces of neat A5 writing paper. He blinked to clear the sleep from his eyes and slowly began to read:

December 12th

Peter,

If you're reading this then everything has fallen into darkness.

I must begin by apologising to you. You will no doubt have suffered much before you finally read my words and whether they will bring you any comfort at this point is debatable.

The first thing you must know is that this is my fault entirely. I know you will blame yourself, and I know that by now you will already have worked out what has happened here, so I won't patronise you by explaining it all, I just feel I should tell you that you are absolved from any blame here.

It was all my doing.

I re-read your story last night. It still disturbs me all these years later; I want you to know that. I understand why you wrote it, but I don't think you can possible understand how much it affected me.

Perhaps you do now?

I just felt such pity for those poor children Peter; I had to give them another chance. That young girl and her brother, they were so innocent. They didn't deserve to go through that experience. I know it was just a story, but it was so sad Peter.

I think it was your ending that bothered me the most; just leaving them all on that open plain. Where did they go next? How many times did I ask you that question? How many times did you tell me it was just a 'stupid' story? Well it's not a stupid story any longer Peter, because now you're as much a part of it as I was.

I brought them here, to my Dark Realm.

I wanted so badly to give them all a chance, to give them everything you never got round to in your story. You only named Krinn. Didn't you think the others deserved names?

I've done as much for them as I can Peter. I've tried to mother them in the only way I know how. I've begun by naming the close group who led the escape from the House, but there are so many more of them I've yet to name, so much more I've yet to teach them.

I don't know what's gone wrong Peter, but I feel a chill in the air these mornings. My perfect world has been corrupted in some way. I don't know if it's my fault? Have I meddled too much? I know I have. I've brought strangers into your story, who were never there at the beginning.

Morquinda has started to turn against me and we've lost Krinn to the wilderness. I feel so sad that he's gone; something just never sat right with him about all of this.

My nightmares are getting bad. I see those creatures from your story, stalking the corridors of Lambert House.

I see them here in the Dark Realm.

I cannot allow it to happen; as I sit here to write you these words I have the most palpable feeling of dread.

All these years Father Deane and Old Mrs Candicote have warned me about my dreams. Even Mary Graham once told me I should never share my fairy tales with anyone. But I have to share this with you Peter, because if anything has happened to me, you are the only hope they'll have.

These last few months the two of us have gotten along better than we ever have. I don't think I've ever enjoyed such happy times with you. I'm sitting writing this now wishing I could just tell you all about the craziness of my life, but I don't want you to worry.

Oh Peter...I'm so cold.

I've become more and more aware in the last few days of my own mortality. I'm having the strangest visions and I just don't know what to do about it.

This is a fail-safe, that's all this letter is. Hopefully when I finally hand it to Mrs Candicote later today, it will live in a draw in her living room for ever and you'll never have to sit and read it, but if something does...

Trust Sufi, Peter. Believe in her and everything she tells you.

Believe in yourself.

You're a good man, and although we may have had our rough patches, I know you love me Peter. It's just all about growing up. You will find your way and be a famous writer one day. I promise. You have a hidden talent that everyone will see, trust me on this one.

I have hidden something for you in a trunk, which Morquinda will look after until you arrive here. If you haven't already done so please go and visit her. But be careful Peter. I fear she is changing like the weather here.

I will try to spend more time with Sufi so she understands the power of the gift I've given her. She will need to learn to control the void, and I will establish a second entrance to the Dark Realm, one which only the two of you will ever be able to see, in case you need it.

Peter, so many thoughts are racing through my mind as I scrawl this down for you. I have just too much to tell you but I can't express it all in a letter.

If I'm still alive when you read this Peter then call for me to help you. If all is already darkness, then you must be the one light that shines.

I have to end this here. We're going to Laurie's party on Saturday night. Perhaps I will have chance to talk to you after that.

Please take care Peter. You must face dangers that even I cannot imagine at this stage, but I know you will succeed, if you'd only believe in yourself; the way I do.

Give all my love to Ethan. Tell him a princess is nothing...without her prince.
Annabel x

Peter's eyes were filled with tears as he read and re-read the letter. His heart felt as though it would burst and a strange emptiness filled his life in that instant, like a vacuum. The letter was dated two days before the car accident.

He sobbed thinking of Annabel wired up to her life support machine.

She had never woken up.

For ten years he had lived with the guilt that he had somehow been at fault in that accident. That he had put her into a coma. Worse still he knew that he could never apologise to her for everything he had done to her while they were still children.

The grief consumed him. He didn't even hear the footsteps approaching him.

"Who was she Peter?" Ethanril asked, kneeling down next to him. Peter was inconsolable as he managed to feebly raise his weary head and look into Ethanril's searching eyes. He had the letter scrunched up in his fist, and as he handed it to him he whispered a response:

"*She was my sister.*"

Stilfanwyn Chasm had become a hive of activity.

The Still-Pit blazed with fury, belching forth gallons of industrial waste as fresh born Still crawled free of the swirling pit, screaming for battle.

Throughout the Chasm the heat from individual furnaces burnt with nightmarish intensity and the heavy but consistent clang of hammers upon metal could be heard vibrating through the walls.

From all sides the army came.

Thousands upon thousands of Still assembled together for the first time, looping the fermenting pit, as they constantly jostled each other for the prime positions. Every few minutes they were joined by fresh additions.

In the Hold, Lucy and Father Deane hadn't dared breathe for many minutes, as they listened to the noise of the Still marching miles beneath them. As yet they had not been harmed; it was even as if they had been forgotten about. Father Deane took no comfort from this. As he mouthed silent prayers for both of them under his breath, he knew their time was coming.

Something was happening here.

He could tell from the sheer volume of noise alone that an army of epic proportions was being assembled deep within the Chasm.

He wiped at a tear.

Something told him that same army was preparing to meet Peter Bettany head on.

11

Shadows beneath the Dark Realm.

$\mathcal{T}$he Lord of the Now sat upright on his throne. He listened to the various noises that disturbed his main chamber, the clamour of feet and the roar of the fires. The endless screaming of the Still-Pit was like music to his ears. He smiled as he pinpointed the clatter of metal being wielded and bent into place.

His army was ready to finish the story now.

Deep inside himself he sensed the Sacred Mother's emotions. He knew that Peter was frightened, alone, and becoming desperate. No one would believe his story. There was nothing to fear from his rescue by the Mist Children. It was to their disadvantage that they would now have to listen to his lies. They would think him to be like Morquinda, they would think him mad.

He stretched back his shoulders, feeling the change in the muscles that now rippled there. He had only to manipulate the Sacred Mother and all would be as it once was.

He was becoming restless now, and rose to his feet, snatching up the glaive that was leaning against his throne. His mind seemed flooded with so many thoughts that he had to juggle them around his head to keep focused on the prime objective. He sensed that the void was still open, and he wondered if the Dream Blender could feel it as well?

The connection between their world and Peter's remained active because he had left one Still behind. It was a contingency plan, quite deliberate, incase something unforeseen should occur. After all, if he were forced to murder the second Sacred Mother, he would still need a way to link their two worlds. Then they could find a new lair in Peter's world from which to collect the children.

They could find a new House.

And it would all begin again.

"I wonder…"

An unexpected voice emerged like mist from the shadows.

"Just how do you plan to reach them now they're back in Kilfanfyn Forest?"

The Lord of the Now did not look surprised to hear the voice. His head slid forwards and then twisted to the left as Krinn stepped out into the flickering torch light of the cavern.

He had been resting in the shadows since his return to Stilfanwyn Chasm an hour previously. His black clothes still looked damp and cold, and in places there were dark patches where he had bled profusely. His hair was still a mass of spikes glittering like a thousand black spears above his head. His cold eyes alighted upon his glaive, which the Lord of the Now handed to him without a word.

Krinn snatched the weapon gathering it up in his aching hands, feeling once again the comfort of steel. The eyes of the glaive glimmered with a wicked green light as he ran his fingers over it. "You saw me struggling at Carrastorc," Krinn continued. It should have been an accusation, it should even have been said in anger, but in Krinn's voice it sounded like nothing more than a statement.

"You were easily beaten."

The Lord of the Now mocked him. Krinn did not react.

"As *always*…you *lie*. It was *your* Still army who fled the battle with the Pig-Beast and abandoned the chase. If it *wasn't* for me we would still be no closer to knowing the whereabouts of the

Sacred Mother," Krinn stated. To this the Lord of the Now made no reply. He would allow Krinn this moment of glory. "I was *deceived* on the ice, that much is true, but I *saw you* hiding in the undergrowth, waiting to continue the chase. I dragged myself from that wretched lake after you had all gone, bleeding my life away while the ice crumbled."

The Lord of the Now was grinning manically.

"You may mock, but you would not have survived it." Krinn silenced him. "You still *need* me if you intend to cross the Tarn River and take them by surprise."

At this the Lord of the Now began to laugh. It began as a low wheeze that shook his powerful shoulders and rasped from his ancient throat. It was the most malevolent laugh ever heard and even Krinn paused to watch this unholy sight. He seemed to notice the change in his master for the first time.

Gone were the restrictive bandages that had once clung to him as though without them he would simply peel apart. Gone too, was the unnatural gait to his stature. Instead he now stood tall, easily supporting his serpentine neck, which slithered from side to side with renewed speed. His black body gleamed with muscle, and the ash that fell from his lips as he laughed, looked darker than any pit of hell.

"Krinn, you are such a fool,"

the Lord of the Now began.

"If you honestly think that all my plans depend upon your survival I am afraid you will be highly disappointed. But here..."

At this he began striding towards the entrance of his throne room.

"There is much I must show you. Do not fear, you no longer have to hide yourself away in the shadows, the glaive will still protect you from my children."

He rasped with laughter again, and it was a more subdued Krinn that followed him across the connecting bridge.

They descended lower and lower into the heart of the Chasm. Krinn was listening keenly to the clamour of noise that erupted all around him and shook the walls as they travelled ever downwards.

"What of *my* prisoners?" he finally asked as they emerged into the Hold.

"They await my pleasure,"

the Lord of the Now proclaimed. He indicated high above them towards the suspended cages, and at this Krinn smiled. He was still preoccupied with the noise that seemed to be intensifying the deeper into the cave they strode.

The pace seemed to increase with the changes in decibel level and they moved quickly through the Hold, continuing down into a section of Stilfanwyn Chasm that Krinn was less familiar with. He was equally surprised to have not encountered a single Still enroute.

"The army awaits us in the Still-Pit,"

the Lord of the Now answered, reading Krinn's thoughts with ease.

"You will lead them over the Tarnwaters,"

he continued. Krinn looked astonished.

"They will all *perish*," he shot back, appalled that his master was thinking such suicidal thoughts.

"They will not,"

he swiftly rebuked.

For a further fifteen minutes they marched on, both lost in thought.

Eventually as the corridor ahead of them twisted away into cramped darkness, the Lord of the Now stopped, turning to his treacherous second in command.

"There is so much we have failed to capitalise upon Krinn...or so you thought. I know you think me a fool?"

He watched Krinn stare vehemently back at him. His face

gave nothing away but the Lord of the Now could divine his thoughts with ease.

"*This will prove you wrong.*"

He turned and slid between the tight gap in the rock wall ahead, disappearing around the corner.

Krinn watched him go.

He fingered the glaive nervously. Whatever lay past those rocks, he had to be ready for it. He feared a trap…or worse.

The noise was deafening him now, and the pressure on his eardrums made his head throb with pain. But he had to face his master. He simply *couldn't* back down. With a mighty effort he slipped between the rocks.

The chamber he emerged into made even Krinn gasp for breath.

Ahead of him lay the entrance to a fresh tunnel. A massive construction, which had been dug and shaped out of the sand-stone quarries deep below the Chasm. It was quite unlike the other connecting corridors and tunnels, which had been carved out thousands of years previously by the Gak Worm.

Thousands of Still were working steadily on this monstrous corridor of darkness. From where Krinn stood he couldn't even see the end of the tunnel, it just drilled miles into the earth.

Massive wooden supports lined the entranceway, built on the foundations of compacted clay and rubble left over from thousands of years of evolution.

Ancient oak trees provided the supporting struts, which the Lord of the Now explained had been dragged from the forests of the Dark Realm by his Still army over a number of years.

"*Why* have you kept this from me?" Krinn said in disbelief. The Lord of the Now was barking out orders to several Still, one of which joined him as he strode back towards Krinn.

"*There is so much you don't know Krinn. However, I am pleased you are impressed.*"

Krinn had no defence to this; his astonishment was plain to see. His attention was drawn to the Still that now crouched at his master's side. Something was different about this creature, but Krinn was at a loss to say what it was.

"Show Krinn your hands,"

the Lord of the Now commanded. The vile creature extended its arms, balancing perfectly on its back legs. It released short, harsh screams as, to Krinn's wide-eyed interest; it uncoiled its fists to reveal gleaming claws caked in sandstone. As he took a step backwards, the Lord of the Now did the same with his own hands. A brittle sound of tearing bone accompanied the action, as though he were using muscles which had lain dormant for many years.

"How?" Krinn managed.

"They are a hybrid, bred in the very heart of the Still-Pit, spliced from my own gene pool,"

the Lord of the Now announced, flexing his newly revealed talons.

"The fire in the House destroyed my body; it is only fitting that the fire from Myfanwy should restore it."

"But the other Still…" Krinn was unable to comprehend this. The Lord of the Now shook with laughter once again.

"That is your army now Krinn. I admit that they are weaker and more docile than this new breed of savages. But they will still provide a powerful distraction over land to drive the Mist Children down into their Warren."

"*Warren?*" Krinn struggled to keep up with all these new revelations.

"We have been wrong Krinn, for so long we suspected the Mist Children lived in the trees at Kilfanfyn Forest. Working on that assumption I began breeding Still capable of digging to great depths. I would create an army of tireless, unstoppable workers who could shift vast quantities of soil and earth without collapsing from exhaus-

tion. *Thus the construction of this tunnel began. We cannot cross the waters of the Tarn River that is true. Therefore it is logical to bypass the waters, and go beneath it."*

Krinn almost applauded this logic, while his admiration for his ancient master grew by the minute.

"The truth Krinn has come so much sweeter to my ears today, and this is why construction has begun again with renewed vigour."

Krinn waited with baited breath.

"I tracked them to the Tarnwaters and learnt that they live, just as we do…under ground."

His triumph was complete as Krinn's eyes blazed with comprehension. The Lord of the Now turned to the assembled Still, and above the noise of excavation he screamed:

"Dig them out my children…and let the slaughter begin."

12

Consequences.

*T*here is a moment just before tears fall, when the whole world appears to wait with anticipation.

In the stillness of dawn, deep in the heart of Kilfanfyn Forest, the world waited.

The first chorus of birdsong had finished on a sustained note of winter sadness. The many nocturnal birds and wildlife of the ancient forest were curled protectively in their various nests, steadily breathing in the fresh smells of morning.

Peter Bettany perched despondently on a boulder. His cheeks were stained with drying tears, and his head felt woozy and thick with depression. He was wishing he could just go home. Home to his solitary room in the flat and close the door on all of this.

He had his dissertation to finish.

That was the most important thing after all, and then he had to find a new direction for his life. He knew he didn't want to become lost in a career. That path just did not appeal to him. He hated structure and routine. He knew he had no flare for team-work or any enthusiasm for goals and targets.

He just wanted to write stories.

He almost laughed at this last thought. In light of the current circumstances, writing stories should have been the last thing on his mind.

After all, this particular one had turned into a living nightmare.

Ethanril had not spoken for almost twenty minutes, and Peter had neither the courage, nor the desire to try and engage him.

The young warrior just sat cross-legged on the fallen beech tree, constantly re-reading Annabel's letter. His expression was a total mask of concentration, which Peter found impossible to decipher.

In his own mind Peter was trying desperately to assemble his thoughts. He knew that at any moment the questions would begin. The Mist Children had been relatively kind to him yesterday. Only Taime had pressured him for any answers. But today, everything would be different.

A twig snapped behind him, and he glanced around fearing one of the group had snuck up on him, ready to begin the inquisition. To his relief he saw only a solitary fox, returning to the safety of the dense forest after a night's feeding.

When Peter turned back, Ethanril was standing over him, the letter folded neatly in his outstretched hand.

"Keep it safe Peter; I'm sure the others will want to read it," he said simply. Peter was utterly flummoxed for words, but nodded and hesitantly reached for the letter. He almost didn't want to take it back. He was consumed with the irrational fear that just as he reached for it, Ethanril would make a grab for his arm in anger. This did not happen, and Peter retrieved the letter easily. The sensation of holding it in his hand, made the whole thing feel once again horribly real.

"Is there anything..." Peter began, not even sure himself, where he was going with this sentence. He needn't have worried, as Ethanril was quick to interrupt him.

"Shall we walk Peter?"

The request took Peter completely by surprise and it was all he could do to stand up straight on his wobbling legs. Ethanril noted with some concern his companion's struggle, and held out his hand to steady him. "Please Peter," he whispered, "you must relax." With that he turned and began leading the way back through the belt of beech trees.

All the time they hiked, Ethanril talked.

It was as though he were frightened of the silence of the early morning and felt he had to fill it up with sound. He spoke of the past a great deal, going over and over different events that he felt Peter would find relevant.

Not once did he mention Annabel's letter.

Peter walked alongside him, somewhat relieved by Ethanril's manner. He had been expecting a strong display of anger and harsh questioning from the young warrior, but he had received neither. As he listened to the stories of the Dark Realm, he began to feel more and more at home in his sister's world.

The walk took them around the outskirts of the main clearing, and through into the very heart of Kilfanfyn Forest. They clambered up hillocks, and trudged over grassy rides. At times Ethanril would simply veer directly off the path and plunge them into such dense woodland that he would have to use his broadsword to cut a swath through the hanging vines and creepers.

The forest dripped and shook with melting snow. Peter found his clothes practically wet through as they ventured ever-deeper under the mist-laden canopy. At one point when they emerged into a bluebell-filled pasture that flourished so richly with dazzling colour, Peter almost cried at the beauty of it all. Ethanril would fall silent only at these moments. He seemed to grow ever fonder of Peter whenever he saw him appreciating the natural environment. It reminded him of Annabel's own passion for flowering plants and trees, and her empathy with wild animals.

A low-lying mist clung to the trees of the forest like a protective kiss. Peter shivered from the damp, but already he could feel the temperature changing in the woodland. As the sun began to shimmer on the horizon his skin prickled with the first rays of heat. At one point, as they stepped into a vast clearing of open woodland, Peter stopped walking altogether and listened intently for a few minutes before whispering to Ethanril, who was a short distance away from him:

"It's not snowing."

Ethanril arched his back, enabling him to look directly upwards. He cupped a hand over his eyes to shield them from the sunlight. For a moment he didn't speak.

"The Dark Realm knows you're here Peter," he said, smiling and turning back to face him. "Annabel knows."

With that he started to walk away from him. Peter felt strangely peaceful in that instant, the full realisation of Ethanril's words sinking in.

All this time he had thought it had been Sufi who had been desperately in need of his help, but it was not.

It had been his sister.

He thought of all the times he'd visited her in hospital, sitting weeping next to her silent body all wired up in that sterile room. He had never once been able to speak to her. He had always gone alone for that very reason. He didn't want his parents to see him choking on his own remorse, his throat as dry as sawdust every time he saw her.

The guilt of the car crash haunted every single day of his life. Every night in the nine years that had followed it, he had dreamt of that crash, the same recurring dream.

Sometimes it would last only seconds and then he would dream peacefully of other things. Occasionally he would only dream of the car crash, and it would wake him up screaming and clawing at his bedclothes.

But it wasn't his fault.

He had been over and over his vague memory of events so often in the years that followed, that it was almost impossible to recall the truth. But to this day Peter was clear on one point.

Someone had stepped out in front of the car that night.

"Peter?"

Ethanril was standing right next to him, and Peter looked stunned to see him there. "Are you feeling alright? You seemed to be in a trance?" Ethanril was concerned. Peter tried to speak, to dismiss his friend's fears, but his words dried in his mouth, and as he made to step backwards, his legs gave way underneath him.

Ethanril caught him before he hit the ground. His grip was strong on Peter's back, and he pulled him upright, grabbing for his shoulders. Peter was panicking now; his breathing had become erratic and nausea swept quickly through him. He didn't want to pass out and he struggled to control his racing heartbeat. Ethanril reached down quickly and gathered up a collection of small flowering plants and herbs growing near their feet. He crushed the leaves frenziedly between his fingers and then cupped this strange concoction under Peter's nose with his right-hand. "Breathe," he whispered, as Peter took in a great lungful of the scent. Immediately he sneezed violently, and his senses seemed heightened for a brief instant. Ethanril grabbed for him again, repeating the same word over and over: "Breathe."

Gradually Peter began to calm down. His eyes were streaming with tears from his violent sneezing, but the nausea had passed. His legs began to feel like solid objects again.

"Thank you," he managed a few moments later. Ethanril tossed the crushed leaves away and rubbed his hands together with rigour, brushing off the excess.

"Nature is a very strange thing Peter, don't you think?" he began.

In his usual fashion Ethanril avoided drawing attention to Peter's moment of weakness by changing the subject; now he was talking instead of the properties of the plants he had used. "If you had eaten those plants, you would be dead now. But breathing in their fragrance seems almost to restore life, or at the very least, redress the balance." He waited to be certain Peter felt better, before moving once again across the clearing.

"Ethan? Where are we going?" Peter felt compelled to ask.

It was still early morning and the first rumblings of hunger were beginning to disturb Peter's stomach. He didn't want to stray too far from camp, and was of a mind to just go back, wake everyone up and tell them the truth. At least that way this would all be over swiftly. As soon as he'd considered this a fresh image of Taime, pinning Peter to the wall, and slashing the air with his rapier, flashed before his eyes. It was a startlingly vivid hallucination, and Peter felt his stomach twist at the thought that he might be so savagely murdered.

"Come on Peter!" Ethanril called, shattering the silence of the forest. Peter looked up to see him standing at the edge of the clearing waiting patiently for him to catch up. Peter shrugged, it seemed pointless to argue with Ethanril any more, he obviously had a destination in mind and Peter would just have to continue following him like a lost sheep.

He caught him up quickly and Ethanril turned immediately and led him deeper into a blanket of spruce trees.

The scenery began to remind Peter of Wick Holm Country Park; the trees were so neatly packed together in rows of between twenty and thirty to a block. It looked almost like a plantation as apposed to a section of forest. The deeper they walked the denser the spruce became, and Peter finally felt a chill from the darkness, which surprised him. Ethanril appeared not to have noticed the temperature change, and apart from pausing occasionally to change direction, he never hesitated.

Peter tried to match his pace, but he found the terrain difficult. Often he would stumble over bare roots, or become disorientated, as the spruce branches seemed to wrap themselves around him like the arms of a kidnapper. His clothes were smeared with sap and water, and many times, he caught his legs on low branches.

Peter was on the verge of collapsing from exhaustion when they finally broke cover. Even though the landscape remained dotted with outcrops of trees, they now crossed a plain covered in thick snow for at least half a mile. This sudden openness only increased Peter's overall nervousness. He was constantly adjusting his position, fearing he would catch sight of a Still lurking somewhere close by. He was only mildly reassured by Ethanril's lack of worry, and he kept close to him as they headed towards a broadleaf coppice that looked reassuringly safer than the snow swept plain they were currently traversing.

Once inside the coppice, Ethanril broke into a short run which quickly had Peter wheezing and complaining as he struggled to keep up. Ethanril ignored all his protests and kept increasing the pace until Peter was practically sprinting after him. The terrain was solid, but the many oak trees that crowded the tiny pathways, had deceptively low branches which Peter had to continually duck to avoid.

"Ethan…I really don't mean to be rude but…you do know where we're going don't you?" Peter tried to hide the sarcasm but it lashed from his mouth like a whip.

"We're here," Ethanril said, smiling at him. He was watching Peter carefully, amused slightly by his lack fitness, and perplexed at the same time by his sudden erratic mood swings. "I'm sorry if it was a bit of a way!" Ethanril apologised. He raised an eyebrow, as Peter's face seemed to distort momentarily with tension.

"A bit of a way?" Peter fired back, his aggressiveness muffled by his own exhaustion. His annoyance seemed to surprise him as much as it did Ethanril. He pressed his palms against his eyes and breathed a deep sigh. When he looked up Ethanril was still waiting for him to calm down.

"You shouldn't be so tense Peter," he began. "I know you're worried but I assure you, you have nothing to fear from me. Let me show you why I've brought you here," he said; leading Peter across the snow scattered clearing. As they crossed the centre Peter saw the remnants of a campfire. He was about to ask what it was, but Ethanril had already begun to explain:

"Over the last week Peter, my sister has travelled several times to meet with you. I'm sure Sufi will have already told you that she has not always been very successful with her attempts to blend into your dreams. The previous few months have seen our situation worsen and time has truly begun to run out for our little group. All these years we have managed to stay just out of reach of the Lord of the Now and his followers, but in recent times they have redoubled their efforts to capture us, and the situation is beginning to look very bleak. I'm afraid it is my fault that Sufi first appealed to you for help. I wish there had been an alternative Peter, and I hope you know I am truly sorry for the chaos we have no doubt brought to your life. It was not my intention to place you in such great danger, but as with most situations, it has very quickly gotten out of hand." He stopped in his tracks, and Peter hesitated behind him, as Ethanril gathered his thoughts.

"It was vital that the other Mist Children had no idea that we were trying to reach you Peter. It can't have escaped your attention that they look to me for all the answers. It is not a position I would wish upon anyone. I certainly never chose to become their leader, but I have and now all I can do is accept responsibility for everything that happens to them. This is a burden Peter, I have no qualms in telling you, and this is a burden I hope you will now share with me?" Ethanril watched for Peter's gut reaction. He was surprised to find that for once Peter did not flinch at the thought of this responsibility suddenly being heaped upon his shoulders.

"I promise you Ethan, no matter the outcome of the next twenty-four hours, I am prepared to do whatever it takes…to put this right." Peter's words sounded like hammer blows of certainty and Ethanril beamed with pride.

"Thank you Peter, for I confess I am struggling to know where we go from here. I have led our group this far, but clouds cover my mind, a fog that I cannot see past. I brought Sufi away with me to this clearing..." he indicated all around, "on the pretext that we were going to scout the area for a fresh base in case Kilfanfyn Forest was ever invaded. That was a lie, but a necessary one to not give the others any false hope. The Lord of the Now may outnumber us with his foul hordes of Still, but it is the honest courage of the few we leave behind us now in the Warren, which has kept us all alive and free for so long. I knew this was a gamble, one that could so easily fail. Sufi was brave enough to take the chance that it might succeed, and between the two of us we agreed to deceive the others, so they wouldn't give up hope if we couldn't reach you."

Peter nodded. His own admiration for Ethanril and Sufi growing by the minute, he could now see clearly the strength of mind they must have had in order to be able to put themselves through such an ordeal.

Ethanril explained to Peter how they had remained in the clearing until Sufi had returned to visit Peter for a second time.

As the story unfolded Peter was able to pick up the thread from various other accounts of events he had heard from the others.

It felt liberating to finally be clear on the build up to his arrival. In his own mind he could relate what Ethanril was telling him to events back in Wick Holm at that time, and often he would interrupt to fill Ethanril in on missing elements of the story.

By the time they had finished dawn was becoming a dwindling memory and a new day had fully begun.

"Can you climb Peter?"

It was not a question Peter had been expecting, and for a moment he was unsure how to reply.

"Ermm...yes! I haven't climbed for a while, but yes! I can climb...why?" he garbled. This response seemed to please Ethanril and immediately he began to move away in the direction of a belt of oak trees that formed the border of the clearing.

One in particular stood as tall as a giant, towering above its brothers and sisters. Peter followed him with a slight air of trepidation. He was silently praying that it wouldn't be this tree that Ethanril wished to climb.

∽

She could smell the new day long before the dawn.

She had felt it arrive while she slept a fetid sleep, which had in itself threatened to snatch her life away like the hands of the Grim Reaper. Her breathing had slowed during the twilight hours of early morning. She had sounded more shallow than usual, and Elyse had woken up terrified that her sister was about to leave the Dark Realm forever. She had tried to wake her, as each gasping death rattle shook her body, but Morquinda could not be roused.

She was sleeping the sleep of the dead, and she knew it.

Felicia and Isabella had gathered around her quivering body; they had also been woken by the unnatural sounds she was making.

As the first rays of dawn penetrated the entrance to their cave, the Old Ones trembled and cried like demented banshees. They hated the sunlight, and prayed that their weak eyes would never have to look upon it again.

The icy cold of the cave, always so impenetrable to the elements, was beginning to feel different.

The temperature was changing. The cold rocks and boulders, which had for so long felt only winter's touch, were gradually absorbing a mild heat from the sun's rays. Not enough to melt the ice that clung to the passageways and crevices within the cave, but enough to force the three old women to abandon Morquinda and retreat deeper into the cooler depths of their ancient tomb. An irrational fear plagued their addled minds. They believed that the sun would damage them, for it had been so very long since that golden orb had kissed their faces. Perhaps they had become Nosferatu? Perhaps if they ever tasted sunlight again, they would burn?

If Morquinda had woken at that moment, she would have laughed at their senility, and banished them into the black pit of the cave herself, maddened by the sheer folly of their worries. But she had slept on, a piteous, depraved sleep.

The dawn light came like a pious servant, grovelling across the landscape, and scrabbling over the rocks, as though seeking redemption from the very geology of the Dark Realm.

It crept into places that had long remained dark.

Morquinda had awoken with a fit of vicious, phlegm-filled wheezes. As she squinted into the hazy light that had broken through the cave entrance, she screamed with a painful declaration of destiny.

"I shall die today," she announced to the damp walls of her cave. A low, punctuated cough erupted from her frail larynx and she staggered to her feet.

Morquinda smelt of decay, it was an odour she wore like perfume. She gathered her rags around her. Her lumbago was screaming agony that morning, and yet she knew she would have to move. With a concerted effort, she dragged her aching limbs to the far wall, and touched the sandstone with her wizened right hand.

By the time Elyse had picked up enough courage to make her way back to the cave entrance, Morquinda had already finished the first of her hieroglyphics.

Elyse heard the sounds of scratching as she drew closer to the cave's barren entrance. She speeded up, fearing some predator had gained access to the cave, enticed by the scent of meat. As she rounded the last corner she gasped in surprise.

Morquinda was leaning against the wall, her right hand clawing at the sandstone as she used her long nails to scratch a crude picture into the soft surface. Elyse was about to speak when she noticed the blood dripping from Morquinda's fingers; she was deliberately digging into the rock, to make herself bleed. She would then smear this into the picture she was creating, adding a macabre colour to the design.

"What do you draw sister?" Elyse spoke as quietly as she could, hoping the sudden interruption would not alarm her sister. On the contrary, Morquinda didn't so much as flinch; she was too absorbed in her work to pay Elyse more than a passing glance.

Felicia and Isabella could be heard making their own awkward journey through the dark cave. The fear of being left alone was greater than their combined fear of sunlight.

"What is happening? I feel abandoned," Felicia complained, feeling her sightless way along the ever-changing rock wall.

"Morquinda has had another vision," Elyse hissed at them as the pair emerged behind her.

"She is not dead then?" Isabella remarked coldly.

"Yes I am."

The sound of Morquinda's voice brought a definitive silence to the cave. The three Old Ones stared at her, mesmerized by the quality of the drawing she had just completed.

Morquinda stepped away from the wall, allowing the full glory of her art to be appreciated. She smiled as the sunlight picked out the finer points of the work. Her hand was still bleeding steadily, and Morquinda knew she would have to dress the wound soon. The smell of blood would attract the Pig-Beast, and that was not the end she had foreseen.

She watched as her three companions stepped cautiously into the light to gain a better view of her picture. Several expressions passed across their faces, as though they were duelling with each other for the correct reaction. These ranged from looks of utter miscomprehension, to unmitigated horror.

"I will die today." Morquinda repeated herself, aware that the news would create pandemonium within the group. Before the questions and panics could erupt she had added a pinch of spice to the mixed emotions. "We shall all die today…but I will be first."

"The Harvester?" Elyse managed, her bloodshot eyes straining in their sockets as tears flooded her cornea. Morquinda fiercely shook her head as though she were suffering a fit.

"Then what?" Felicia demanded.

Morquinda hesitated, she seemed almost on the verge of revealing the answer but something inside her told her the prophecy had been intended only for her.

"Why spoil the surprise," she spat, giggling horribly at their anxious faces. She scrabbled at the wall, while she hurried past them, disappearing into the darkness of the cave. As she walked she muttered under her breath a single sentence, which she repeated over and over as though it were a chant.

"He is coming, he is coming, he is coming…"

The Old Ones watched her go, unsure whether to pursue her and demand to know the circumstances of their apparent execution. Their eyes were drawn back to Morquinda's picture, as though the answer were somehow hidden within the sketch.

It depicted a man, inhumanly tall, standing before the opening of a cave. He held a sword in his right hand, an unusual weapon, as though the artist had been unsure of its actual shape.

It was bowed in places were it should have been straight, and seemed to have an uncertainty about its tip. Here Morquinda had scratched over and over again, grooving the weapon until it had become a blur. Beside the man, who remained featureless, stood a singular horse. It was a childish interpretation of an animal, with far too many legs.

"Perhaps it has the appearance of so many legs, because of the speed it travels?" ventured Elyse, but the other two did not expand upon her theory.

Behind the man there was a second figure, but one who was indeterminate in both shape and gender. The scratches were slight here, as though Morquinda had wanted to blend this person into the background, making it one with the landscape.

"Whom is that meant to represent?" Isabella asked, tracing a finger over the blurred figure.

"The one who has gone..." Elyse began, wiping at a stray tear. "...But cannot let go."

∽

Sufi woke with a start.

The Warren felt different, her senses told her something had changed, and although she still felt groggy from sleep, she was on her feet in a moment, pulling her bedsheets around her to hide her naked body. She stood bolt upright, looking as though she had been recently mummified.

She had slept in the Nest, having offered to let Peter sleep in her bed. All around her, the Mist Children were slumped in various positions of lethargy. Some snored, some murmured, others breathed heavily and rhythmically. It was a wonder this cacophony hadn't woken her, but it had not.

Something just felt different about the place. She listened more carefully.

As usual she could pick out the faint noise that they all believed was running water, flowing deep below ground. That hadn't changed, nor had the dim light from the night candles, which still cast shimmers and shadows upon the walls around her.

Having made certain no one was watching her, Sufi let slip the bedclothes, and quickly pulled on her white dress. The material felt tighter than ever, and it was covered in dirt and blood stains from the previous days' adventures. She silently wished she still had her Notebook Dress. That would have survived any amount of Still attacks. Not like this pitiful thing. She stared downcast at the fraying hem of the skirt.

A few minutes later she was outside the Warren entrance, looking even more perplexed and worried than she had been when she awoke.

Peter was missing.

She hadn't meant to look for him, but curiosity had overcome her as she'd edged up the passageway. For so long she had visited Peter in his dreams, but never once had she actually seen him sleeping, in a physical sense.

She had crouched down, to look into the dugout, and was horrified to find her bed empty.

Now, as she ran her fingers through her tousled mane of hair, she was in two minds whether to sound the alarm, and send out a search party.

Had he abandoned them while they slept?

Did he intend to leave them just as Annabel had done?

So many doubts assailed her, but something inside her heart told her that this was simply not the case.

Peter would never leave them. Not now, not after all they had been through together.

She decided she would wait, and not tell the others yet. Maybe he had just needed sometime on his own? After all, that was understandable.

She began to stretch, rolling her shoulders to release her tension. The quiet of the clearing was liberating after a night in the noise of the Warren. The air up here smelt clean and fresh, but there was something else about this morning which was different.

"It's not snowing."

The voice startled her and Sufi whipped around as though she had been stung.

Pigeon stood a short distance behind her, his arms laden down with firewood. His eyes still looked sleepy and his features had softened with the vulnerability that comes only at dawn. He wore his usual odd assortment of clothes; his school blazer and white shirt, with his multi-coloured trousers shining like a series of bright constellations burning away in a turbulent sky. His hat was pulled down firmly over his hair, and he had to cock his head at a slight angle in order to look at Sufi directly.

"I'm sorry if I scared you Sufi...I really didn't mean to," he apologised. "Unusual for me to be able to sneak up on someone...not that I was sneaking up on you while you were exercising or anything..." He quickly broke off his garbled excuses, realising he was just digging himself an enormous hole. He looked embarrassed now, and seemed unsure what to do with all the firewood he was carrying.

An awkward silence passed between the two of them, one born from friendship turning to unrequited love. It was a silence that made Sufi's heart tremble, and Pigeon want to be swallowed up by the ground. Eventually the wild girl broke the tension.

"I felt there was something different when I woke up, but I couldn't place it...you're right though, the air doesn't feel full and oppressive anymore, not like when it snows. The weather is changing," Sufi managed, hoping that if they talked about practical issues Pigeon wouldn't feel as awkward. Or was it that she didn't want to feel ashamed? Ashamed that she was breaking his heart with every look she gave him?

"The world is changing...that's how it feels to me anyway," Pigeon confessed. He looked unusually thoughtful as he gazed out at the trees. Sufi watched him for a moment, her eyes darting over his face.

This was Pigeon, her best friend for as long as she could remember.

He had always stood apart from the other Mist Children in Sufi's eyes. He didn't possess the calm studious air of Mundo, or the intensity of Taime. He lacked Fess's caustic wit, and yet together they had made her laugh over and over again. But Pigeon had something else, a vulnerability that she had not seen in many men...until she'd met Peter Bettany.

"Shall I help you with those?" Sufi asked indicating the logs; her sentence shattered the claustrophobic silence as she ran up to him. Pigeon had a momentary panic as she held out her arms to take some of the logs from him. In the fumbling moments that ensued Pigeon attempted to ease a few of the brittle branches into Sufi's hands. At times they brushed against each other as they became entangled in the act, this only panicked Pigeon further and his movements became erratic. After a couple of minutes it became clear that all they had managed to do was push the logs backwards and forwards and Pigeon had in fact ended up with all of them in his hands once again.

"Oh dear!" Sufi giggled, and Pigeon frowned, offering her a: 'How did that happen?' expression.

"Guess I'll carry them then!" Pigeon said, moving past her to begin making the fire. Sufi stopped him in his tracks by resting her hand for a second on his arm.

He felt the warmth of her touch, and he hesitated, unsure how to proceed. He looked at her, and saw that she was hesitating as well, as though she hadn't meant to touch him.

"Pigeon..." she began, and an atmosphere of blistering tension settled upon both of them. It was the tone of her voice, he could tell immediately that she intended to talk about his affection for her; he had learnt to tell because her voice became more subtle, as though she were whispering advice to an errant child. He hated that change, and yet he always waited in the vain hope that she was about to tell him that she loved him too.

She took a step away from him, wishing he would interrupt her now and change the subject she had so pathetically started, but all he was doing was waiting.

Waiting for her to hurt him again.

"Pigeon, I just want to tell you that things have.... well! Things have changed for me in the last few days, and I don't want you to be hurt by anything that might happen in the future..." She was woefully rambling, and the more she tripped over her words the more wretched she felt. In front of her, Pigeon's whole world was crumbling to dust.

He knew what she was saying, in fact he could have interrupted her at any moment and finished the sentence for her, yet something masochistic in his nature wanted her to deal him this final blow. He was staring at her face, watching as her blue eyes moistened with emotion and she was unable to look back into his own equally expressive eyes. He could have drawn her face from memory with ease. He knew every line, and every perfect curve of her body. For as long as he could remember Sufi had been his girl. While the others had focused on Annabel, he had never altered his devotion for Sufi. He loved that they were best friends, and it did mean more to him than anyone would ever know. But he loved her. He wasn't afraid of his feelings; they were simple and honest. Today she was going to hurt him with one sentence, more than the Lord of the Now could do with a thousand Still. Yet he almost welcomed the pain. At least the very fact that she was struggling to tell him meant that she did care for him on some level. In many ways all that mattered was that he loved her, even if it remained unrequited forever, at least he would have the comfort of having loved someone.

"...This is so difficult Pigge," Sufi was saying, almost as if she were talking to someone else. Pigeon looked imploring at her.

"Please, just say it Sufi," he suddenly begged her in an almost inaudible whisper.

In that moment their eyes met and a thousand emotions flashed in front of them. With a glance she told him that she was in love with him, and that they were always meant to be together but someone had stepped into her life and pulled her emotions to the furthest corners of the compass of her heart.

All Pigeon heard however, was her apology:

"I'm sorry Pigge. I'm so sorry."

He felt his stomach empty as though he had been winded, and his heart seemed to drain away into the forest floor. She was crying so much, that his own anger and sadness seemed nothing by comparison. He dropped the bundle of firewood, and embraced her, gathering her little frame up in his arms and squeezing her so tightly.

"I love you Sufi, with all my heart. Please never forget that," he begged her, knowing that his life was now forfeit to destiny. She hugged him back, apologising over and over again.

Their tears joined the forest's orchestra of birdsong, signalling the dawn of a new day, and for some, the final calling they would ever hear.

෴

As Peter rested his foot against the next branch, he felt it wobble under his weight. The action panicked him and he scrabbled upwards, grabbing onto any branch he could find with his hands in order to secure a better position. In the chaos he suddenly gripped Ethanril's strong right hand and found himself being pulled upwards into a cluster of branches. His feet found a firmer footing, and Ethanril let him go as Peter took hold of a strong, thick branch.

"You're walking too close to the middle of each branch," Ethanril explained as though he were a seasoned expert. "You must stay close to the trunk; it is the heart of the tree and your lifeline." He was beginning his ascent again and shouted back to the petrified Peter. "You'll only fall if you don't respect the tree. Don't look down, the height will just distract you, focus on something else." With that he had vanished into the thicker canopy of the treetop.

Peter hesitated a while. He knew that this was a test. Ethanril had told him before they'd even begun to climb, that this was his tree. A magnificent spiralling oak with more branches than Peter had ever seen look comfortable on a forest tree before. The ancient oak stood proud and tall, standing out from the various other trees in Kilfanfyn as though it were royalty in exile. It had such a mystical presence that it appeared not just to simply grow out of the ground, more that the ground grew around the tree to accommodate its needs.

As they first scrabbled upwards into the lower branches, Peter sensed that Ethanril wanted him to make this ascent alone. It wasn't that it was some kind of test of manhood, more that if he did the climb unaided, Peter would somehow share in the same spiritual bond that Ethanril felt with the tree.

It was a test of faith.

Now, as Peter watched Ethanril disappear from view, he felt his own fragile faith abandon him where he stood. The climb had made his arms and legs ache, and at this stage it was now impossible to tell whether he was weak from either exhaustion or fright. Something beating deep inside him told him that he had to carry on.

He glanced down at the needle-like lower branches far below him. He could vaguely make out a hazy blur, which must by now be the forest floor. This just made his stomach feel very strange indeed. Ethanril was right; looking down just wasn't helping. He chose instead to follow the second piece of advice and focus solely on one fixed point. Choosing the thick matted bark of the trunk as his focal point, Peter stepped onto the next branch along, and swiftly stood upright in order to reach the upper canopy.

In that same second he saw and felt white light, like the aftermath of an explosive flash in front of his eyes.

In standing upright he had slammed the top of his head into a particularly thick branch, and the effect had been like receiving a head butt from a giant. Peter crouched down low upon the branch he was balancing on, clutching the top of his head and stifling a cry of immense pain.

"Are you alright down there Peter?" Ethanril called to him from the pinnacle of the tree. "It's not much further I promise."

Peter was rubbing his head vigorously to try and deaden the pain, and muttering obscenities under his breath. Despite the blow to his head he couldn't help but smile at his situation and that in itself made him feel a great deal better.

"Everything's fine!" Peter managed, although he felt like howling in pain for a good hour or two.

"Trust in the tree Peter." Ethanril's voice called down to him, "if you respect it with all your heart, it won't let you fall."

Peter looked daggers at the offending branch that had nearly knocked him unconscious. The very last thing he felt like at that moment was showing this particular tree any respect.

An image of himself approaching the oak tree nonchalantly carrying a gleaming axe over his shoulder suddenly popped into his mind at that moment.

"You'd better not let me fall pal!" he whispered to the ancient branches, a wicked glint in his eye. The wind whistled through the upper canopy at that moment and the boughs creaked and protested against the interference of nature. The branch Peter was standing upon made a particularly fearsome noise, as though it were finally surrendering its life to a mortal enemy.

Peter was certain the branch was about to snap, and he scurried upwards into the highest branches like a man possessed.

Ethanril was quite taken aback when Peter suddenly joined him on the highest branch, as though he had been fired up there by a cannon.

"That wasn't so difficult!" he said, watching half amused, as Peter seemed finally to register just how high up he actually was. The realisation made his legs temporarily wobble and Ethanril had to quickly catch hold of him so he didn't lose his footing. "Just sit down, slowly," he advised, keeping a firm hand on Peter's arm as they both began to squat down.

Very soon they were sitting facing each other, legs dangling recklessly over either side of the thick branch.

Peter was surprised by how comfortable this unconventional seat actually was. He soon learnt not to look downwards too often as that only led to him experiencing slight stomach palpitations, and strange brain signals which would tell him that it would be 'ok' to simply fall off the branch.

He tried to remove the look of abject terror from his face by slow degrees. He was currently sporting a slightly more relaxed expression, albeit with a hint of moderate concern; much like a person who is ninety-nine percent certain their car keys are tucked safely in their jacket pocket, but know they will have to check before too long.

Ethanril was simply staring out at the view.

Peter finally calmed himself enough to take his eyes off the crisscross stitching of branches and look out across the far horizon.

"Oh my God!" he managed, gasping at the full beauty of the Dark Realm, which unravelled before him like a tapestry woven by the perfect hands of love itself.

He could see forests, and rivers, patches and corridors all of which formed an interwoven landscape that looked as though it had been dipped in a perfect dye of virgin white.

He saw nesting birds taking to the clear blue sky of morning and fanning out like stencil lines across a blank canvas. He watched as the sun's warm rays picked out certain features and contours of the scenery as though it were a spotlight on a snow covered stage. He even spied a ruined fortress sitting defiantly atop a ridge of crimson white, and as he craned his neck painfully to see all about him, he shuddered at the sudden empty skyline to the west as the world emptied outwards into nothingness.

It was beauty beyond beauty.

And Annabel had created this herself.

Despite the corruption that both she and Peter had brought into this fairy tale kingdom, the sheer divinity of this sight remained unspoilt, even on a day like today.

"Tell me why Peter?"

Ethanril was staring back at him, his eyes red with tears, and Peter found the words came more easily than he had ever dreamed possible in this, the most difficult of times.

"I hated my sister..." Peter began. He had been uncertain where to start, but he quickly realised that once he had begun talking freely, it would all fall into place. "She was exceptionally gifted as a child. From my earliest memories of her she just had this incredible talent for writing and drawing. We would sit together in our kitchen, Annabel, Mom and I, and we would have a go at drawing pictures. I don't know if you've ever done that? But anyway...by the end of an hour I would have a series of blobs and smears of colour, which I would probably announce, was a cow or something! Mom would always smile sympathetically, and then Annabel would show us what she had drawn. It would be something extraordinary...a castle or a landscape or a person...and we were only young at this time remember...maybe five or six, and she would be drawing as though she were some sort of child prodigy. It was the same with her writing; although she never actually wrote stories, she was strangely superstitious about it, as if she feared releasing her imagination onto paper. Instead her writings focused more on snippets of ideas, or descriptive passages about someone she knew, or something she had invented."

Ethanril was listening intently; Peter had expected him to bristle at his harsh early memories of Annabel, yet Ethanril seemed utterly enthralled to learn even the smallest thing about her childhood.

"I can understand your jealousy Peter," he unexpectedly announced, immediately humbling Peter with the honesty of his confession. "I have had a similar envy of my own sister as we grew up together, we are both very competitive and we tend to try to outdo each other with feats of agility...sibling rivalry is very common." At this juncture Peter held up his hand.

"I'm afraid my jealousy ran rather deeper than sibling rivalry Ethan," Peter confessed, watching as Ethanril turned his full stare upon him.

"Go on..." he whispered.

"I was the eldest and naturally I expected to set a certain precedent over my younger sister as we grew up...but I just couldn't. Whereas I spent my youth searching for who I was and where I was going, Annabel just knew instantly. Her talents were so natural, yet any academic signs that I was showing in English, I had to work tooth and nail to achieve. I struggled with spelling and grammar, to the point where I feared I was partially dyslexic..."

"Dyslexic?" Ethanril looked confused; this word was unfamiliar to him.

"It's a condition of the brain..." Peter was trying to simplify it for him. "It means that you struggle to read and write." This seemed to clarify it for Ethanril who nodded his thanks. "Yet Annabel was always so encouraging towards me. She would take the time to come into my room and sit with me, going over and over essays I was writing, helping me with my punctuation, and all I could do was resent her for it. I was such a selfish little brat in those days Ethan, I can't tell you how ashamed I am of it all now. It's so difficult to have to admit your own faults, but I do. I was wrong to hate her the way I did, she was my sister…she thought the world of me." He wiped at a tear, but he didn't stop talking. "It must be hard enough to grow up with prodigious parents, but to have such a multi-talented sister whom everyone remarked upon was just too much to bear some days. I would sit in my room cursing my parents, cursing Annabel, cursing God as to why I had been born so talentless. It was so stupid, so selfish. I measured everything I did by comparing it with Annabel's achievements, instead of accepting them, and then branching off in my own way. But I couldn't, I just had to do something better." Peter's face was flushed red with despair and personal anger; Ethanril sat rigidly still, as though he had become an abnormal branch of the tree. He waited for Peter to continue.

"I should have been grateful to have such a wonderful sister. She wasn't arrogant or selfish; she never boasted about her own ability…that was always done for her by other people. If anything, she would rather see what I was doing, before she even felt comfortable telling me anything that was happening to her. I know that she trusted me, despite my hostility towards her, because I was the first person she confided in about the dreams."

At this Ethanril seemed to perk up. For a long time he had been sitting rather listlessly, not with an air of disinterest, more an impression of melancholy that hung about him like a heavy coat. Now however, he sat forward on the branch, as though he were some wild animal sensing that his prey had just hoved into view. Peter also sensed the change in his companion. If anything it made him slightly more self-conscious and he began to feel under threat.

"My sister always dreamt, every single night of her life. I know that probably doesn't sound all that spectacular, but believe me Ethan, there are very few people who can recall their dreams with the same vivid accuracy which Annabel could. She wasn't like any of her school friends, she was different.... special."

Throughout this speech Ethanril stared into Peter's eyes, almost as though he were challenging him to begin talking about a girl that he didn't know so well. He quickly relaxed however; the Annabel that Peter described to him now, was the same girl he had fallen so deeply in love with.

"Even as children it was obvious to me that she stood apart from the crowd...there was just something otherworldly about her, as though she were on loan to us for a while from somewhere we could never go. She was the sort of girl who attracted attention...in equal parts, boys loved her, and girls hated her. But not for the obvious reasons that this normally happens. I know you will disagree, but she wasn't strikingly beautiful, or outwardly dazzling. If anything Annabel used to dress quite frumpily, as though she wished nothing more than to blend into the background and not be noticed by anyone. But she couldn't just fade away, no matter how hard she tried. There was almost a glow about her, like a beacon attracting people to her wherever she went. She earned herself the nickname of 'Witch' from the local girls, and any boys whose amorous advances she rejected. My Mother and Father became worried about her, we were both being bullied at school because of it, and they seemed to have to forever come up to the school and sort out problems with the headmaster. I didn't lift a finger to help her Ethan...that was the kind of brother I was, I just resented all the unwanted attention she got, and grew ever more jealous of her..."

"And that's why you started pretending the dreams were yours?" Ethanril guessed. His face showed true pity as Peter sadly nodded.

"Sufi has told you...Annabel confessed to me that she had this unique gift, one which enabled her to recall all her dreams every single night. Well! I just seized upon it. She had told me that no one was to know about it at school, although she did also confide in Jean Candicote, and a local priest of ours by the name of Father Deane."

"Jean Candicote..." Ethanril whispered. "I cannot believe she is gone."

Peter looked at him in surprise.

"You know?" he said.

"The Dark Realm feels her loss. Can't you sense it in the wind? It is weeping her name through these trees. The rivers are full of our tears. We have lost another child."

To hear Old Mrs Candicote described as a child was disorientating enough, but Peter was still unsure of how Ethanril could have known of her death. Did he sense everything?

"Sufi has told me all that happened in your world Peter. I just wish I could have been there to help you both. I wish I could have stopped Krinn earlier. Jean Candicote was precious to us."

Ethanril was still clearly distraught at her murder, and Peter hastily pressed on with his own story in order to alleviate the tension:

"It seemed as though I had been handed some sort of a reprieve from my life of normality. I finally had something, which my sister was afraid to tell anyone about, so I claimed it as my own. Within weeks I had become known as the 'boy who dreamed.' My newfound fame came at a savage price. Apart from the betrayal of my sister, which took years for her to forgive, I had presented myself as an easy target for the malicious bullies at my school. I was constantly taunted, and soon I grew to hate school, and hate myself for the lies I'd made up. But once you start something like that, it is impossible to stop it, unless you are prepared to face the dire consequences of your actions, and believe me Ethanril, I was never man enough to be able to do that. Lies after lies spewed from my mouth like poison. It's no wonder so many people in my hometown still despise me to this day. I was like some sort of enfant terrible at home as well, always moody, and Machiavellian in my scheming against my sister. I was in danger of becoming like some demented 'Richard the Third'..."

"Who?"

"Sorry...it's not important right now...let's just say if Annabel personified sweetness itself, then in comparison I was the epitome of sourness," Peter said, trying desperately to find an analogy Ethanril could relate to. "And at the very apex of all this, an accident occurred that tipped the scales right over." By now Peter was struggling desperately to keep a check on his emotions. The psychological trauma of recalling all this was both exhilarating and cathartic in its release. "Did Annabel ever tell you about the fire at our old home?" Peter asked tentatively. His face was flushed a deep red, and his nerves were dancing like an addict in need of narcotics.

Ethanril leant back against the tree trunk. He picked at his sleeve idly for a moment, as though he were considering whether he should tell Peter anything at this point.

Very slowly he raised his world-weary head, and stared at Peter through his deep brown eyes.

"I love Annabel with all my heart Peter. You must be aware of that before we continue." It was said so softly, yet with such conviction that Peter almost thought he briefly felt that extraordinary bond that comes from unconditional love. It reached out and circled him for a moment, before drifting away on the morning breeze. Peter brushed his hair away from his eyes, and tried to meet Ethanril's gaze. "In the unfairly short time we knew each other Peter…we lived a thousand lifetimes," he explained. Peter shivered as the words sank deep into him. He felt privileged to be hearing such honesty from the one person he had grown to admire more than all others. "To sit and hear your story Peter is both an extraordinary experience, and a deeply tragic one. I was undoubtedly closer to your sister than you or indeed anyone could ever possibly be. We shared every secret we both had to tell. Many days we would sit beneath the shade of this great oak and talk of countless things…but sadly never of you Peter." Ethanril sighed, but was surprised by Peter's lack of emotion at this point.

"Taime told me last night that she never spoke of me…I guess that's why you never knew she was my sister?" Peter reasoned.

"I'm not shocked that you're her brother Peter, we all assumed you were close to her as she had passed her gift onto you, but as I've said, for a sister to not talk of her only brother, the rift between the two of you must have been substantial."

"Yet despite that, you have trusted me to come here and help you." Peter sounded amazed.

"I believe there is good to be found in everyone. That is a character trait I share with your sister Peter. I also believe in you, if that means anything? People change Peter…boys grow up," Ethanril said. Not for the first time in Ethanril's company Peter felt very humbled, and unable to speak. "You have proved yourself already Peter by your own acts of courage against the enemy. You only add to that by your actions today."

"Taime has said he will kill me if I don't tell him the truth…" Peter began, but his nerves engulfed him. Ethanril lent across and placed a strong hand on his shoulder. "You will not face your destiny alone," he assured him. Peter looked doubtful. A small part of him had hoped that Ethanril would offer to fight that particular duel for him.

"Tell me about the fire Peter…forget what you think I already know," Ethanril persisted, once again leaning back and giving Peter his full attention.

"It was an accident. That is what you must remember above everything else," Peter practically pleaded. Ethanril nodded softly. "Before we had to move to live in a flat block in Wick Holm…that's my home town incidentally, we used to live on the outskirts of the village in a cottage…not dissimilar to Myfanwy in many respects. It's strange, but I knew the minute I entered that farmhouse that I had been there before, almost like a feeling of déjà vu. I could never quite put my finger on it, but now as I sit here telling you all of this, it becomes quite clear. Not in appearance, but in essence Myfanwy is very like our old home and I'm sure that's what Annabel intended to achieve when she created it." Peter had become quite wistful as he mused on this discovery. "My Father bought the cottage as a pet project, his business is associated with building work and architecture, and he put his heart and soul into repairing and renovating that old cottage. It had something so cosy about it; the ceilings were very low in every room so you always felt as though someone was patting you on the head in reassurance that all would be well. We used to run home from school just to feel the embrace of that cottage again. No matter how bad the day had been, the welcome you could expect from a building such as that is beyond words…it just made everything seem a million miles away, and at times for both Annabel and I that was all we wanted." Peter stared up at the brightening sky, and breathed heavily. "My Father used to smoke in his youth…quite heavily I believe, much to my Mother's displeasure. It was a vice he soon had to give up upon marrying her, but the one reminder he kept from this era of his life was a silver Zippo lighter…" Already Ethanril was holding up his hand to stop Peter in midflow.

"I'm sorry Peter…I follow most of what you're saying, but you must explain about the smoke?" He was obviously struggling to comprehend, and Peter was quick to clarify it for him. Using a series of elaborate mimes, Peter demonstrated the art of smoking a cigarette, and then tried the rather more complicated task of translating what he had meant by the term Zippo lighter. He noticed that during this later discussion Ethanril became uncomfortable with the subject matter. It was as though a long repressed memory were slowly and painfully returning to him. As Peter rapidly rubbed his thumb across the top of his clenched fist to indicate the igniting of a flame, Ethanril suddenly drew back in alarm.

"I know what that is now," he said in a response so definite that Peter didn't dare press for reasons as to how he knew. He inwardly shuddered, wondering how much of the 'Final days of Forget-Me-House' Ethanril could recall if pushed hard enough?

"I came home from school one night as though the Devil himself were inside me. I had been mercilessly picked on at school all day and not one single teacher had lifted a finger to help me. When I arrived home Annabel came into my room to talk to me. I was in such a foul mood that I really didn't want to spend any time with her, but she seemed so disturbed herself, that I allowed her to stay. I pretended to be distracted by some writing I was doing for school, and while I sat with my back towards her, hunched over my desk in the pretence of writing…all I was really doing was scribbling meaningless words onto a piece of paper…she sat on the edge of my bed and began to tell me about the Dark Realm for the first time." Peter paused to steady himself on the branch, as a sudden chilly wind picked up around them. It lasted only seconds but Peter seemed to understand its meaning at once, and he continued without further pause. "I wasn't the first she had confided in by this time. Both Jean Candicote and Father Deane, a priest from our village, had already heard of this place. Also another woman...a friend of Jean's called Mary Graham whom I used to see in the village sometimes when I would go shopping with my Mother. She was a nurse and Annabel would often talk to her if she happened to be visiting Old Mrs Candicote. She was very like Mrs Candicote, and we always ended up sitting by her when we called into Ivy Meredith's Tea Shop...that's like a meeting place in our village, a little like the Warren...somewhere people go to tell all kinds of stories. This Mary Graham had a real dislike for me, that much was obvious. She was always outwardly pleasant towards me, but you just got the feeling she would much rather have not been talking to me. Of course now I can completely understand why, but at the time it was horrible. Anyway, as usual I digress..." Peter paused before continuing.

"I just sat listening as my sister began to tell me this fantastical story of how she had invented the Dark Realm. It was basically an amalgamation of all her favourite places she'd visited as a child. We were very lucky where we lived in Wick Holm, I don't know if Annabel ever told you about it?" He paused briefly; Ethanril tensed his lips and nodded, indicating that she had.

"We bordered some wonderful countryside, and my parents were never much into going abroad for summer holidays. Instead we were taken to visit various parts of our own country, like the Welsh Mountains, Devon and Shropshire. Incredible places, all with unique landscapes, which you could just lose yourself in. For someone as imaginative as Annabel, they were the most stimulating of times. It's no wonder that she has based so much of all this..." He indicated the surrounding landscape, and was about to carry on, but Ethanril suddenly clasped his hands on his head as though he were in insufferable pain. "Are you ok?" Peter was terrified by this sudden action, he reached across the branch towards his companion, but Ethanril drew backwards as though Peter intended to harm him.

"It just can't be true?" The words escaped him like a cry of anguish. Immediately Peter felt sick to the pit of his stomach. All the time he had talked it had not really sunk in how painful this story was going to become. He had thought only of himself, and how difficult it would be for him to recount it. He cursed himself, staring now in true horror at the emotionally crippled warrior.

He was killing him.

"I read Annabel's letter and just went numb Peter," Ethanril began. He had huddled himself against the trunk, in a foetal position which just did not sit right with Ethanril's usual demeanour. He looked broken and defeated. "I understood what I was reading but I just shut it out…hoping you would explain it all so differently…hoping it wasn't really true." He was beginning to cry now, his shoulders shaking from the effort of holding all this pain inside. "I had suspected for so long that something was wrong with this world…you only have to take a careful look. But Annabel was always with me, always explaining my questions, telling me what everything was called and why. She had all the answers Peter, and then one night she just vanished, leaving us all in darkness. This," he briefly nodded towards the horizon, "is all I know…This is home; only now it isn't my home…it's all in the imagination of a young girl whom I still love with all my heart. So what am I Peter?" He was fierce with anger now, his face contorted in pain. "What am I then? Just another figment of her overactive imagination…is that it?" He was acting menacing, his whole body shaking with hostility towards Peter. Everything that he had promised suddenly evaporated, and Peter realised the threat of Taime was insignificant in comparison to the fact that Ethanril could kill him right now.

"No Ethan…" Peter began, resigning himself to his fate. "No you're not. Annabel did not invent you…she isn't the reason you're here now, and she isn't the reason everything has gone so wrong." Peter's words seemed to shock Ethanril out of his rage like a breaking storm.

"I am. I invented you."

The world seemed to hold its breath. For a sustained moment nothing stirred in the forest. Even the breeze blew softly, like a Mother singing a lullaby to her restless children.

Peter awaited his destiny, staring fixedly at Ethanril across the branch. He welcomed the thought of his own death. In this most tranquil of places his death would be almost exquisite. For some bizarre reason all he could think of was his A'level English lecturer Mr Doug reading the final passages of Mary Shelley's Frankenstein to an attentive class.

Was that what he had become... Victor Frankenstein? Would his own monster now exact its revenge upon him?

"You must finish your story Peter."

The tone of Ethanril's voice had softened. He seemed to have calmed himself and was now looking expectantly at Peter.

"Are you sure?"

This had not been the request Peter was expecting. He had prepared himself for the worst, and yet he was suddenly being granted a reprieve.

"I must understand it all Peter. Please... go on."

Peter hesitated for a further minute, shuffling nervously before continuing:

"The night that Annabel described the Dark Realm to me was a turning point in our lives. She was both excited and fearful of her own powers. She knew that this went far beyond anything she had achieved before. She was dreaming of this place every single night. It was as though she had some Shamanistic power to just travel to a specific place in her subconscious and build this world out of everything she'd known as a child. I mean look around us Ethan. I can prove I'm telling the truth so easily. If you look at this world's topography, nothing fits. All these varying landscapes don't make any geographical sense. How, for example, can Carrastorc remain frozen while the Tarn River flows on unaffected just a few miles away? How can Kilfanfyn Forest contain so many varieties of trees, some of which would never survive in such a cold climate? In fact the temperature is the killer point. It is so inhumanly cold here, yet none of you have frozen to death? Instead you are able to live reasonably normal lives in such sub-zero temperatures." Peter was becoming quite animated, and Ethanril seemed to understand what he was saying, despite his looks of confusion at certain terms Peter employed. "Every animal, every tree...geology as a whole is all interlinked, in such complex symbiotic ways that most human beings don't even fully understand their importance. My own grasp on the subject is very vague, but all I do know is that we all form a link in an ecosystem of life," he stressed. "If you remove certain elements from the chain...it all breaks down. And those elements can be as minute as bacteria. I doubt any of you have ever even been ill?" Peter questioned. He had become tactless and harsh, but Ethanril allowed him this moment. In some ways he needed to hear it.

"All I'm saying Ethan, is that this world is a paradise. And that's only wonderful if it remains a personal dream or fantasy for the person who created it. When my sister first described the Dark Realm to me, she was the only one who had ever visited it. But after that night it was all to change." Peter sighed heavily as he continued to describe the events of that night. Ethanril didn't dare to interrupt.

"After she left my room I was in turmoil. I hadn't even spoken that much in the whole time she was there, just grunted the odd syllable at her, hoping she would believe I was utterly uninterested. Eventually she took the hint, and made her excuses and retired to her own room. I nearly burst into tears after she'd gone. I'd been holding my amazement and disbelief clenched inside me like a fist. I knew immediately that she was telling me the truth. Annabel never lied. It was that simple. I was full of such vicious jealousy. As if it wasn't enough that she was the one with the real ability to dream so vividly, she'd now taken it a step further and actually dreamt a world into existence. To an unstable sixteen-year-old boy the injustice of it was just too much to bear. I staggered down the stairs in a haze, searching for a way to channel my anger. My parents were already in bed asleep, and I doubted very much if Annabel would venture out of her room again all night, so I was left alone downstairs...alone and full of hatred. Honestly Ethan, it kills me to think back to all this now, I am so utterly ashamed, but that was how I felt at that time." Peter's honesty seemed to strike a cord with Ethanril, and although he was unsure how this story would conclude, he encouraged him to continue, struggling to conceal his own inner emotions so as not to panic Peter further.

"I searched for something, anything to take my mind off all the pain. My Father always kept his Zippo lighter in a glass cabinet in the lounge...sorry, ermm...main room in the cottage. I was slumped in a chair staring listlessly about me when I spotted it. I couldn't tell you to this day what drew my attention to it; it just stood out above all the other little trinkets he kept in there. I can remember retrieving it from the cupboard, this ultimate symbol of my Father's rebellion against his own parents and even my own Mother. There was just something so cathartic about it. I shook it next to my ear..." he paused to mime the action, "...and to my astonishment there was still oil inside it, it hadn't evaporated. When I flicked open the top, the wheel of the igniter was all rusted, and I never imagined for a second that it would still work. My Father hadn't smoked in the whole time I'd grown up. It had only been since my sister and I had turned thirteen that he had even shown us his lighter. I stood thinking about all that had happened, holding his old Zippo in my left hand. I was so angry with the world in that moment; I just didn't know what to do with myself…" Peter broke off to wipe a bead of sweat from his brow. "Do you understand the term 'ignis fatuus'?" Ethanril stared blankly at him, and Peter felt a little foolish for even mentioning it, he hadn't meant to sound arrogant. "Will-o'-the-wisp?" At this Ethanril smiled.

"You mean foolish fire," he translated, and Peter was suitably impressed.

"That's right! Well the second I ignited that old lighter, that's the closest I've ever come to understanding that term. The thing probably hadn't been cleaned in over sixteen years. It was so full of rust that the minute I struck it, the fuel just lit like a bomb. The whole top of the lighter flared up as the gas expelled from the blocked innards, and burnt my hand in an instant. My gut reaction was to drop the burning lighter on the floor, in shock and pain. I should have just shut the cap quickly and extinguished the flame, but I was so startled by what had happened that my reactions were all askew. Well, I don't have to tell you how quickly fire spreads?" Peter knew Ethanril would understand after their experience at Myfanwy the previous day. "It was out of control in seconds. The carpet and curtains were ablaze before I'd even begun to try and stamp out the flames. The shock of seeing the fire seemed to stir some sense inside me, and I raced upstairs, raising the alarm that the cottage was on fire. We were all able to escape unharmed, but to this day I've never told anyone what really happened. My parents still think it was an electrical fault…ermm, electricity is like a source of power inside the house…it, provides light and heat, stuff like that." Peter attempted to explain, but Ethanril didn't seem interested in this last point.

"You saved everyone's life Peter." It was a statement, not a question. Peter looked away in shame, so many times he'd heard those words said to him, but they brought him no comfort.

"It was my fault that it started in the first place." Peter confessed. "Only you know the truth." Again Ethanril seemed uninterested in excuses.

"Peter, you just told me that the 'Devil himself' was inside you that night? That you were more angry and jealous of the world and your sister than you had ever been in your life? Yet you saved her life, and the lives of your parents? That doesn't strike me as the actions of a demon?" he pressed. Peter shook his head.

"That's not the point. I started that fire," Peter snapped back.

"It was an accident," Ethanril clarified.

"It was my fault…"

"It was an accident and nothing more." He seemed final on this point, and for the first time Peter realised what the young warrior was doing for him. It was something which he had needed for such a long time, but thought he could never possibly receive.

He was being forgiven.

"I keep that horrible night locked deep inside me," Peter continued, shivering with tension. "I never wanted to admit my guilt; it would have caused my family too much pain. Instead I was forced to sit back and watch them all try and re-adjust to a new life. We were forced to move into a flat block, which is like a collection of smaller houses; all built one on top of the other. It was a horrible time for my parents who missed the freedom of their garden, and the cosiness of their old home. Annabel was probably the worst affected. She began to have these nightmares. She would wake up screaming in terror at all hours of the night. Mom and Dad were seriously worried about her; they just didn't know what to do to make the dreams stop. Even I realised that something was different about her. In the twelve months that followed the fire, she had begun to talk less and less about the Dark Realm. If anything she tried to avoid the subject of dreams altogether. It had ceased to become a pleasant experience for her, she actually feared going to bed. It was all made doubly worse by the fairy stories she was being fed by the residents of a local nursing home...Lambert House. It was somewhere that Annabel had to visit on a work experience placement from school, and she eventually ended up working there on her weekends. It was a strange place Ethan, even when I used to go I have to admit I felt uneasy about it. But do you know what's weird?" His expression had darkened, but Ethanril unexpectedly answered for him.

"It inspired you."

Peter raised an eyebrow in surprise.

"Many times we talked about Lambert House. She was so worried for some of the elderly ladies there, that's why she brought the four Old Ones to us," Ethanril explained. Peter raked his hands through his hair, exhaling loudly.

"Then that's all true as well." He thought back to his sister's letter and her message for him: Seek out Morquinda.

"For the first time in our short lives, Annabel's creativity had stalled. She wasn't painting, or writing or inventing anything anymore. She used to be this whirlwind of activity, ideas and enthusiasm flowing from her like wine. Then suddenly, she seemed to have dried up, and finally it was my turn to shine. Sitting in my room one day after college, I began writing my first serious short story." At this Peter opened his bag. He searched through the papers within and finally pulled his dissertation free of the jumble. He went to hand it to Ethanril, but his companion stopped him.

"I fear to read it Peter. It is the story they spoke of in the prophecy is it not? The one the Old Ones keep locked in their trunk of secrets?" He was looking agitated, and Peter feared he could accidentally lose his grip on the branch.

"I don't know Ethanril," he honestly confessed. "This Great Find that Sufi always speaks of...Taime told me it was a collection of my papers and..." Peter didn't know how to continue, but Ethanril finished it for him.

"The Great Find happened long after Annabel had vanished from our world. It was one of the first times Sufi successfully travelled through the void into your world. She arrived in a bedroom, which she later discovered belonged to the first Sacred Mother. Sufi panicked, and grabbed for the first pile of papers that she found and brought them back through the void with her. She was only gone minutes but when she returned some of the papers were already burnt and ruined, while others miraculously survived the journey and remained quite readable. But Morquinda stole some papers from us. It is said that after she read them she went insane." Ethanril swallowed, his mouth was as dry as desert sand. "Sufi was the only one swift enough to snatch a glance at the title page. She said it was a story written by Peter Bettany." Peter stared incredulous, making a horrible connection he had never made before.

"My parents have always kept Annabel's room exactly as she liked it, even to the point of not disturbing the clutter of papers on her desk; amongst them must have been some of my own work which I always assumed had been destroyed in the cottage fire. I had made two copies of this story…" He brandished the dissertation again. "I had to tear one up to appease the wrath of my Mother, but I kept a second copy, which I, again, assumed I'd lost somewhere. Annabel must have taken it. When Sufi gave me her Notebook Dress, I was amazed that all my early work still existed. There is more here as well," he said, looking through the other papers that Annabel had returned to him with her letter. "It's heartbreaking to think all those times I thought Annabel was too caught up in her own work, she had actually been secretly stealing mine to read for herself. She knew if she'd asked I would have said 'No' out of spite. But she was still interested."

During this speech Ethanril had begun to look even more alarmed, and Peter had to continue swiftly before the inevitable question was asked. "I originally wrote with one purpose in mind. That was to frighten my sister. My jealousy towards her had altered very little even after the fire, and I seized upon the nightmares she described and moulded a story which would fit all of the elements that terrified her the most." Peter once again offered Ethanril the papers. Ethanril stared at them as though he were being handed a poisonous snake.

"Why should I read it Peter?" he demanded. "It sent Morquinda mad."

"I'm certain she was well on the way before she ever read this story," Peter harshly snapped back. "You have to read it Ethan. If you want to know the whole truth, you have to read it. It's your history," he finished; the sound of his own heartbeat threatening to burst his eardrums. He waited, holding out the dissertation as though it were a peace offering.

Finally Ethanril took it from him, and in the silence of Kilfanfyn Forest he read for the first time 'The Final Days of Forget-Me-House'.

∽

Krinn had flitted through the darkened passageways of Stilfan-wyn Chasm like a malignant infestation.

Since being shown the full extent of the Lord of the Now's plans, he had made it his business to seek out and discover every hidden inch of the Chasm. He spied into the darkest corners where no human eye had ever looked, demanding answers from the very rocks and stones. He must know everything; he had been kept in the dark for too long. The final solution was at hand, but he feared his master was still keeping secrets from him.

He now stood upon a raised platform over looking the disgorged Still-Pit.

Beneath him stood legions of Still, fresh born and ready to do battle with an enemy they had been bred to kill. The Still-Pit had emptied for the final time and now simply blazed content-edly, like a cesspool of pure evil.

Krinn's eyes filled with the sight of such an army. He watched the creatures swarming over each other in their eagerness to begin the hunt for the enemy. The air was filled with the clamour of reeking bodies and their screams of vengeance for lost comrades.

It would be a massacre.

Krinn allowed himself a smile. This was the day he had antic-ipated all those years ago when Ethanril first expelled him from the group.

This was their day. The day, which would see the end of the Sacred Mother and everything that threatened them, would be gone.

He thought of the consequences.

The Lord of the Now intended to create a permanent link with the Sacred Mother's world. He intended to build a second House.

It would all begin again. Krinn would be sent to lure fresh children away, and this time it would never stop. Never stop until the Sacred Mother's world feared to have any more children.

Childless worlds, grieving like bloated, pathetic mothers. That was what the Lord of the Now most desired.

It would mean the end to all possible futures and a complete termination of the past.

There would be only now.

"The time of vengeance is upon us," Krinn screamed to the assembled troops. The Still roared in triumph.

"We will soon leave here and march for Kilfanfyn Forest. That is where the enemy is hiding," he continued, as the rabble of noise gradually subsided. The Still were all fidgeting in their eagerness for battle. Some beat their fists upon their chests like apes, while others brawled with their nearest companions, jostling for supremacy.

Krinn had never seen them so agitated. They were like a lynch mob, lawless and without mercy. It excited him intensely to think he would soon be commanding such a vile collective.

"We will bring nothing but death to their homes. I want no survivors," Krinn bellowed at the top of his lungs. This final announcement practically incited a riot in front of him.

Still stood upon the shoulders of their comrades as they each began to scream out a war chant that echoed for miles around the walls of the Chasm. They shook with anger and they surged forward to gather closer to Krinn's podium.

Krinn twitched for a second, as if a glimmer of nervous tension was firing behind his cold eyes like a faulty ignition. He stood his ground, watching as the Still drew ever closer to him like an unstoppable black ocean. He spun the glaive in his right hand and then slammed the spike down hard upon the platform floor, the noise of which seemed to shock the unruly Still into total silence.

They all stared up, halting where they stood to examine the glowing eyes of Krinn's glaive. It had them all enraptured in a moment, like animals caught in the headlights of an approaching vehicle.

"Be silent," Krinn demanded as the last echoes of the war chant finally ceased. He was filled with personal anger at his own moment of weakness, and his words expelled like shrapnel from an explosion.

"The Sacred Mother is to be captured alive. He is the only one who must survive this massacre. Drive them into their Warren underground, track down and pick off any who flee the battleground, but leave the Sacred Mother to your master. He wishes to break him…" Krinn paused, savouring the moment. "…and burn him alive," he screamed, unable to resist eliciting a final clamorous cry from his troops. He turned his back on them in that instant, swirling his black cloak around him as he stormed out of the Still-Pit. The roaring of the Still provided a constant drone of hellish music as he descended the passageways of the Chasm.

He was making for the Hold. He had kept his prisoners waiting far too long.

∽

Peter sat in silence as Ethanril read through his dissertation. The young warrior would only occasionally speak, but usually just to clarify the meaning of a phrase or a word within the text.

Peter watched him as he read. Ethanril took a long time, as though he were not content to simply read the words once, he had to fully understand what it was he was reading. The paper, the style of print and the amount of words contained on each page all seemed to captivate him, and he would often ask Peter why he had chosen to include certain elements, and leave out others.

Finally he reached the end, and for a few moments he seemed preoccupied with just turning the pages, he was clearly deliberating whether he was expected to read any further.

"You don't have to read on…" Peter finally broke the silence. Ethanril looked up from his reading. He held the book the way a new parent might first hold a baby. Both hesitant and nervous, as though he was frightened he might break it.

"There are more words to follow though Peter," he explained, as though Peter hadn't noticed the remainder of his work. Peter shuffled forward along the branch, suddenly eager to retrieve the work.

"Have you read the two stori…pieces?" He tactfully corrected himself. Ethanril flipped a page leisurely, trying to mask his own discomfort.

"You write extremely well Peter…" he began, but found he was unable to continue. Instead he closed the paper, hesitating only for a second, as though it had crossed his mind not to give the papers back to Peter. He leant forward, and Peter gratefully accepted his work. As he did so, he placed his hand on Ethanril's shoulder.

"I am truly sorry," he managed, drawing back quickly for fear of a rebuttal. None came. Ethanril seemed suddenly lost in the horizon again, and unwilling to speak. Peter folded the dissertation back into his bag, and as he flipped the flap down to close it, he realised that Ethanril was asking him a question.

"The Pig-Beast has no flesh because you never describe it? That is why it can kill the Still, because it is not subject to the same natural laws as the rest of us? Does that sound good Peter? I never was that intelligent, but does that sound like a good use of reasoning, from a fictitious character like me?" The anger that Ethanril had fought so hard to repress was finally boiling the blood in his veins. "You have both been so kind!" he sarcastically continued, not allowing Peter even the smallest chance to explain himself. "You and your sister...I mean...my biggest thanks must go to you of course Peter. Thank you so much for writing such an enchanting fairy tale. Thank you for not granting any of your characters names...oh! Except Krinn! And he was always so important wasn't he? I mean forgive me if I've got this all wrong in my imaginary head...but the girl and her brother in your story, that's Sufi and myself right?" Peter was only able to nod in shame. "The other four boys...I take it that would be Fess, Pigeon, Mundo and Taime? Am I right?" Again Peter nodded in silence. "I must confess Peter, you had very little imagination for names, I don't blame you for waiting till your sister could think of such good ones. I love the touch about the four white ponies. Who would ever guess what they would grow up to be? Forget-Me-House, with the Silent guarding all those children...that's what the Lord of the Now meant when he spoke to you outside Myfanwy? You created him, and by burning Forget-Me-House you mutated them into the Still. What a genius you are...you fool!"

Ethanril was across the branch in a swift movement. He twisted Peter painfully around, dislodging his position from the tree and pushing him backwards off his perch. Bracing himself against the strong branch, Ethanril swung Peter outwards, leaving him clinging desperately from Ethanril's wrist, swinging his legs backwards and forwards and floundering like a fish caught on a line. Only Ethanril's grip on his wrist was preventing him from falling.

"Tell me why I shouldn't let you fall Peter? Tell me why I should forgive you for what you've done?" Ethanril demanded. He appeared to have lost his capacity for patience and tolerance, the full rage of his feelings finally venting themselves against the one person he could completely blame.

"Let me fall Ethan. You would be doing everyone a favour," Peter screamed back in defiance. "How can I justify my actions to you? I'm a writer. I write stories to entertain people...that's all there is to it. I'm not the second Sacred Mother...I don't have the powers that my sister possessed. I just write. It's all I can do with my life. I had no idea I'd done this...I swear to you. This was just a stupid story I wrote which I only recently rewrote properly. I never thought about the consequences of it...it was just a fairy tale," Peter begged. He could feel Ethanril's grip weakening; he was becoming too heavy for him. Below, the branches of the oak billowed out beneath his swinging feet, like an intricate spider's web, caught in a storm. If he fell, he would certainly break his back.

Ethanril tensed his arm, trying to hold Peter steadier. He was sweating profusely and, as his rage began to subside, he realised that he had over stepped the mark by tipping Peter off the branch.

He didn't think he had the strength left to pull him back.

"That fairy tale is my life Peter." Ethanril practically screamed with the effort of supporting Peter's weight.

"It was my mistake. All I can do is admit that, and explain what happened. Kill me if you wish Ethan. You're only prolonging my death if you don't. Taime will do it for you when we get back to camp," Peter declared, he cast his eyes downwards once again, and braced himself for the fall.

This last sentence seemed to have struck a cord with Ethanril. It was as though he had momentarily passed out and now woke to find himself dangling Peter out of the oak tree. It was exactly the kind of impulsive behaviour he would have expected from Taime.

But he wasn't like that. That was why he was the leader. He was always in control.

"Hold on!" he managed, almost laughing at this unintended pun. Peter appeared to have lost all hope, and was hanging like a dead weight from his arm, no longer thrashing about.

Ethanril jerked him upwards, using his stomach muscles to haul him closer to the branch.

The movement snapped Peter back to reality, and he looked up to see Ethanril struggling to lift him back onto the branch. Peter reached up quickly, trying to find a handhold on the impossibly smooth branch so he could balance out the weight for Ethanril.

"I've got no grip!" Peter cried out in desperation, scrabbling to hold on to anything. Ethanril looked contorted by the pain of his own efforts, but he stubbornly refused to let go, wrenching so hard that Peter felt certain his arm was about to pop out of its socket.

In that instant his back collided heavily with the branch, and as he braced himself against it, it appeared to have allowed Ethanril the pivot point he was trying to achieve. He felt himself being dragged over the branch like a box on a conveyor belt. He howled with pain, twisting around and finally releasing himself from Ethanril's grip and grabbing a firm hold on the branch for himself.

Ethanril collapsed backwards against the trunk wheezing from his exertions, while Peter remained half on and half off the branch, floundering like a beached turtle.

It was many minutes before he felt capable of speech.

"Why didn't you let me go?" he gasped, struggling to regain his former composure before the attack. Ethanril was watching him through half closed eyes. He looked as though the very effort of speaking had become all too much for him. He breathed heavily for a moment.

"I'm sorry Peter," he managed, choosing not to explain why he had saved him. Peter watched him for a moment, seeing the calm return to Ethanril's eyes. Very slowly he edged along the branch towards him and soon they were sitting, as they had been moments previously.

"I wrote it for Annabel. Not for anyone else. I wrote it to upset her, to shock her. And I did. The first time she read it she looked at me as though I was the Devil incarnate. I'll never forget that look. She then asked me exactly the same question that you just did: Why did I write it? But how could I answer a question like that? For so many years I had struggled to piece together even the simplest story. I would either start something, but never have the time or inclination to finish it, or I would simply just give up halfway through. I never seemed to have any decent ideas. So one day when the basic story for Forget-Me-House popped into my head, well I had no real choice but to run with it. I wrote it in four hours straight. It was the weirdest sensation, as though the story was actually just writing itself; I was simply the conduit to carry it from the pen onto the paper. I hadn't even proof read it when I handed it to Annabel; I just wanted to see her reaction. I knew it would disturb her...for

God's sake it had scared me, but it was only a story. I didn't want to get bogged down with names and places because I liked the simplistic approach. One of the dangers for any writer is to allow your plot to become too pedestrian and I never wanted that. So I openly admit I didn't give one iota of thought to the histories or names of any of my characters, except for Krinn." Peter held out his hands, as though he were surrendering himself for arrest.

"Why Krinn?" Ethanril still struggled to say his name.

"He fascinated me, I have to admit. I was pretty certain right from that early draft that I intended to make him one of the principle villains of the story. But sadly in the version that Annabel read I hadn't clarified this…"

"…And that's why he was with us at the beginning, when we first met Annabel." Ethanril suddenly understood. Peter coughed nervously before continuing:

"He was a natural betrayer, and linked to the Lord of the House so strongly that he was destined to return to his master as soon as he heard him call. That's why he acts the way he does. Krinn was never intended to have any emotions, I wrote him as a completely nondescript character, just like all the others. The difference is that Annabel helped you all to realise your potential. The only thing I granted him was a name. That's all Ethan…I promise you." Peter looked imploringly at his companion, wanting Ethanril to believe him as he once had. He was almost overcome with emotion when Ethanril looked back at him with eyes full of trust.

"I do believe you Peter. I understand Krinn more now than I ever did while he was alive. It is no wonder he never showed any fear to us, you'd never given him that capacity."

"I wish to God I had," Peter said with feeling, recalling Krinn's cold-hearted stare as he had battled with them both across the ice of Carrastorc.

"I do have one question Peter, a question which I must insist you answer honestly," Ethanril commanded. Peter raised his head, and nodded, slightly fearful of what the question could be.

"Why, if you realised how much pain this story caused... why did you rewrite it?"

It was the one question, which Peter had asked himself time and time again:

Thinking back now he could remember sitting in Bob Streatham's English class as they were all read out the proposal for their final year dissertations. A cold, clammy feeling had crept over him. The fact that it was to centre on two creative writing pieces both thrilled him and sent him into a panic.

It had been years since he had written anything of any substance. Occasionally he had been able to begin stories, usually they would feature imagery from his dreams as a starting point; but he was never able to finish them. His attention span seemed to have been diluted by years of working at jobs which did nothing to excite his brain. To actually sit and write a full length original piece just seemed an impossible task.

He spent two months planning stories.

Each time he would begin in earnest, writing fluently for a while, but gradually the thread of the story would begin to unravel itself. As the days wore on he would become less and less interested in his subject matter until finally he would find himself staring at a blank computer screen.

His mind an empty canvas once again.

Following the car crash, his creativity seemed to have deserted him altogether.

He had always known this day would come. His sole intention when he had returned to education was to find himself, find his creativity once again. It had been a success, if only in terms of forcing him to go out and collect resource material for his essays, and then sit and piece them all together, but it hadn't stirred him back into any of his own creative writing. He didn't write any new poetry or any more stories.

"I had nothing to write anymore Ethan. I was in serious danger of failing the course I was studying because I'd been asked to write these two short stories, and I couldn't even think of one. I was in despair with myself. Time was just passing me by and all I was doing was watching it stream away from me," Peter explained, using his arms to indicate a clock relentlessly ticking on, hour after hour. "Then one night it just came to me. I was sitting at my desk, staring into space and it was just as if..." He hesitated; Ethanril goaded him to carry on.

"...Just as if something were calling to me, reaching into my subconscious. All of a sudden I knew exactly what I had to do. I ferreted through my jumble of story ideas, like a man possessed. Although I'd destroyed one copy of: 'Forget-Me-House' I still had the spider diagrams and notes that I'd made when I was originally writing it. By chance I also stumbled across an idea I'd had for a series of plays I was thinking of writing. They had the working title of: 'Fresh Flesh' three independent stories with one common link..." Peter looked at Ethanril. "The Pig-Beast. It was a monster, which I'd never fully worked out in my mind. I had so many different ideas of how I could describe it that, to be fair, they were all blurring into one. So as I began to work on rewriting Forget-Me-House, I also began to work on a new story concerning the Pig-Beast."

"Did Annabel ever read about that animal?" Ethanril suddenly questioned.

Peter could tell what he was thinking immediately.

"Just because I never actually wrote of it until recently, that doesn't mean I didn't talk about it," Peter regretfully explained. "It was a labour of love...and I know that sounds sick!" He laughed nervously. "But it was the first time I'd ever come up with an original monster."

"So this was before you created the Silent?" Ethanril was interested.

"Oh yes! Long before them, I'd had the idea for the Pig-Beast while I was still at school. I remember jotting the name down on a piece of paper, looking at it. Thinking what a 'good' name that would be for a monster...and then doing nothing with it for years! I would sit and try and describe it to Annabel, just to see the look of disgust on her face. But like me, she was never entirely sure how exactly I intended it to look. So when I came to write: 'The Morning Star' I thought it was an opportunity to put that right."

"But you don't describe it, even in that?" Ethanril reminded him. Peter looked a little sheepish.

"I know, once again, the more I pressed myself to describe this creature, the less I was able to do so. Finally I just gave up, and the Pig-Beast became, just a name on a blank page."

For a while they were both silent.

It was an awkward silence as though there was so much to be said, it was almost impossible to know where to begin again, like a meeting between two old friends after years of absence.

"I knew it was wrong to rewrite them, but at the same time Ethan you have to understand I knew nothing of what Annabel had done. Not until I read it in her own handwriting just now," Peter pleaded. Ethanril was still calm; he seemed to accept all of this part of Peter's story.

"Then you no longer see her?" he questioned. Peter swallowed.

"Yes I do see her." he said truthfully. "We just don't talk anymore."

Again Ethanril seemed to accept this answer. To Peter's great relief he did not press for reasons.

"So tell me what happened after Annabel read your story?" Ethanril asked. Peter studied him for a moment.

"It was just horrible," he said, but the words did little justice to sum up the state of panic his sister had entered into as a direct result of reading his story. He described to Ethanril how she had changed almost overnight, becoming reclusive and agitated. He explained how her dreams had ceased to revolve around the Dark Realm and had instead become plagued with nightmares.

"It took a long time for her to calm down. Mom wanted to send her to a psychologist, but Annabel bluntly refused. Once again Jean Candicote and Father Deane were her rocks in a crisis. They would always stop by to visit her, as though she were convalescing from some terrible illness. I was never allowed into her room when they were there. But I wanted to be, Ethan. For the first time in my life, I wanted to go and visit my sister." He wiped at his eyes slightly as the relief of having finally let go of his emotions overwhelmed him. "I felt such unequivocal guilt. The idea that I was the sole cause of all the misery she was now suffering was just too much to bear. I had never considered anyone else's feelings other than my own. But as I sat one day in the confessional box, pouring my heart out to Father Deane, I finally realised the sort of person that I had become. I was horrified with myself. Father Deane was wonderful. He just sat and listened, without judging me once. At the end of my speech he forgave me, saying how proud he was that I could admit such sin so openly and have the strength to seek forgiveness. It was my epiphany. Sitting weeping in the arms of a priest, it was as if I was being re-born. I was being given the chance to put right all that I had done so wrong. That night I returned home, and without asking anyone I walked into Annabel's room. I'll never forget her face. She was sitting up in bed, reading a book. Before she could say anything I had embraced her. I held her so tightly, and just sobbed in her arms…" Peter had to regain his composure, and Ethanril averted his eyes, feeling embarrassed that he had ever questioned Peter's true loyalty.

"From that day on, I never hurt her again."

Peter slowly adjusted his position on the branch, swinging his right leg back over so he could sit with his legs crossed under himself.

Ethanril observed how assuredly he moved, as though Peter no longer feared the height of the tree. He seemed so much more at peace with his surroundings.

"I would be lying if I told you our relationship improved over night. It did not. After so many years of jealousy and tension existing between us, it would have been a virtual impossibility to deal with that over night. But in the next few years we built a strong friendship, and began to trust each other more and more."

"But what about us?" Ethanril pleaded without much hope. "Did she tell you anything about us?"

Peter shook his head.

"In all honesty Ethan, Annabel told me very little about the Dark Realm after she'd read my story. I knew that her nightmares had finally been cured. She did at least tell me that!"

"How?"

Once again Ethanril surprised Peter; he had thought Annabel would have told him this herself. He shrugged and began:

"She had started to dream of water…oceans of water which would wash away all the fire in her dreams and I think…"

"…That's why the Still fear to cross open water!" Ethanril suddenly interjected, throwing Peter completely off track. For a moment he couldn't fully understand where Ethanril's logic was taking him.

"You see that really makes no sense!" Peter argued. "The Still can't be harmed by water that easily…snow is made from frozen water, they walk freely across that...and it falls from the sky readily enough yet they are quite at home out in the elements." Peter argued, but Ethanril was just smiling at him as though he had finally found the missing piece to an age-old jigsaw puzzle.

"It's not just water Peter...it's fast flowing water, anything that brings with it a power and volume that will dissolve them. Think about it? The Still that Pigeon wrestled into the Tarn River died instantly. Why? If not because of the sheer volume of water that drowned it...you said yourself just a moment ago that Annabel began to dream of oceans of water to combat the fires of her nightmares. Well...this is her world Peter..."

Peter was looking dumbfounded. It seemed so simplistic, yet it had clearly never occurred to either of them. Ethanril could see the look of distress passing over Peter's eyes.

"Sometimes when one of the elements is missing, the problem remains impossible until..." Ethanril reassured, "...a solution finally presents itself." Peter nodded, still subdued by his own lack of reasoning. He rubbed his eyes, and stretched his limbs. The branch was finally beginning to become uncomfortable and he idly wondered how long they had been sitting up there.

"So Annabel never told you of us?" Ethanril asked again, though his tone still sounded probing as if he were seeking further conformation of this.

"Those words in her letter are the first acknowledgement from her, to me, of what she has done. But I can see why, Ethan. I know how difficult this will be for you and the other Mist Children, but I truly believe her intentions were honourable. She was trying to give you all the chance that my story never had..."

"She gave us life Peter," Ethanril unexpectedly interrupted. Peter had been expecting further anger from him, maybe even denial of what had truly happened to them, but instead Ethanril seemed resigned to his fate.

"There has been much talk over the years Peter. Many questions to which we have struggled to find answers. This is the only life we have all ever known. Yet sometimes we have nightmares. Nightmares like those described in your story. Of having once had parents…and then lost them almost over night. Of a House that called to us while we slept and would even have held the other end of the skipping rope as we played if it thought it would help to lure us in. That's the kind of House you created Peter," Ethanril whispered sadly. "Annabel would tell me it was just bad dreams. She kept reassuring us over and over again, despite the fact that we could all clearly remember our arrival in the Dark Realm…"

"…We had been standing looking lost and bewildered on a ridge leading to a ruin which we now know as Khynous Morf. How we got there was anybody's guess, yet at the time none of us questioned it, besides which, Annabel was already there, waiting for us, ready to take over from the House and hold our hands like a mother. Ready to tell us there was nothing to fear from this momentary lapse in our memories. Nothing was important before we arrived there. There was nothing before we came that we needed to remember. But now I know." Ethanril indicated Peter's rucksack. "Now I know where we came from. Annabel was not the first Sacred Mother…it was you Peter," he cried. Peter was nodding, out of admittance and nervous tension.

"Yes. Yes it was. And the others should know all this as well. But there is something we must do first." Peter was suddenly being more insistent than Ethanril had ever known him.

"You must finish your story Peter," Ethanril continued, just as adamantly. "You have yet to tell me the most important part," he stressed. "What has happened to Annabel?"

Peter looked straight back at him and for the first time in his life Ethanril felt his own stern gaze being beaten down. Peter had such a steely glare that he momentarily feared to keep eye contact with him.

"Khynous Morf...Is it far from here?" he asked. Ethanril seemed disorientated by the question, but finally responded with a vague answer:

"We would need horses...but..."

"Then let's fetch them now," Peter said, ignoring Ethanril's protests and beginning his descent of the tree.

13

Crossing the Line.

$\mathcal{T}$ he cutting had stalled.

The tunnel was being redirected into a curve, passing out of the softer sandstone under the Tarn River, and winding slowly at a right angle into the granite-stone base layer of earth beneath Kilfanfyn Forest.

The work had halted because a solid wall of granite had slowed the pace of digging to almost a standstill.

The Lord of the Now, who had remained in the tunnel for nearly six hours to oversee the work, had recalled the majority of the Still back thirty metres away from the wall.

It wasn't that they needed rest, more that they were beginning to hamper production as they fought with and often blocked each other in their haste to appease their master.

He had sent only forty Still back to the blockade, with instructions to dig lower, keeping in line with the tunnel floor, concentrating solely on ripping out the foundations of the wall.

They had excavated furiously for over an hour. At times it would seem as though the wall was finally giving way. Flurries of rubble would cascade down, often-burying sections of the digging party as though they had been caught in an avalanche. Other Still would then rush forward and free their comrades from the debris. The creatures were using their claws as though they had mutated them into organic rakes. They would sift and level the fallen earth; keeping the tunnel width to the exact specifications set by the Lord of the Now.

In other words, large enough to allow the army to filter through it as easily as water carried along a length of corrugated pipe.

The Lord of the Now watched the progress silently, while his mind raced over problems.

Leaving Stilfanwyn Chasm would be a risk.

Not least because the enemy could attempt to gain access during the chaos of battle and free the imprisoned Mist Children.

This thought had disturbed the Lord of the Now only briefly during the conception of his plans. It was the reason he intended to send two armies into the fray. Krinn would lead the original Still over land; trapping any Mist Children who may try to flee the battlefield and then driving them back underground. Once there they would be easy picking for the Hybrid Still who would tunnel directly into their encampment.

No, it was not this problem, which now troubled him.

It was the Gak Worm.

The creature had been silent for many days now. It had remained in hibernation far longer than usual, and the cycle of its life appeared, unexpectedly, to have been broken.

This was not an eventuality the Lord of the Now had accounted for. He feared that his own decision to create a fresh tunnel deep below ground had in some way upset the delicate balance of nature. Something which would normally have pleased him greatly, but this time, he feared it could work to his disadvantage.

The Worm was ancient. More ancient than anything else that lived within the Dark Realm; its life pattern established over centuries, never changing.

Until the Still had arrived.

Even now the Lord of the Now could remember that time. He almost shivered as the image of the flames roared in front of his eyes.

Just a memory, yet the heat was still scorching him to this day.

It had blistered his skin as though it were paper. He had watched it bubble and liquefy before finally dripping off him like thick glue.

The pain had been excruciating. He had screamed and screamed.

He shouted for Krinn, crying out his accursed name, over and over again until he was hoarse from the effort.

"You have abandoned us."

He had cried out to the flames.

"Traitor. I will find you Krinn. Your body will bleed for an eternity for this."

He had retreated down one of the blazing corridors of Forget-Me-House. All around him the Silent had begun screaming in tormented pain. The heat was rising by the minute, and most of them were turning into blackened husks where they stood.

Some cowered, hunched up like animals on the floor, their bodies a writhing mass of flames; while others raced down corridors, engulfed in fire, desperate to find a way out of the ever-changing corridors of the House.

Only the Lord of the House had known which way to go.

For a brief moment he had considered saving them all. It was in his power to do so. Even at the very zenith of this pandemonium, his voice would have restored order.

At his feet the wild dogs quickly assembled. Although they too shook with fear, they had managed to find him, and now waited patiently for instruction.

The Lord of the House respected this.

Order out of chaos.

He would save them, but *only* them. The Silent would burn. It would teach them respect. It would harden them to endure any form of pain.

It would be the making of them.

With his mind now full of future glory, he raced through the burning building. He could smell the retreating Children, and it was a scent which he clung to as closely as a wolf tracking a deer. The Children were his lifeblood. He may be on the brink of losing the House, but he would never lose them.

Around the next corner he found the water mirror.

It had always been part of the House for as long as he could remember.

Which was no time at all.

The wild dogs pawed at his heels as they raced alongside him. Even he shared their anxiety; they would be crossing through the mirror; leaving the House behind and journeying into nothing. There was no way of knowing if they would survive or where the mirror would take them. But they had to go.

Without further hesitation he plunged headlong into the cascading waters of the mirror.

All became blackness, forever.

The next time he was conscious all he could feel was agony. He was vaguely aware that he was moving, but he only knew this because every single movement caused him such exquisite pain that he lost consciousness after only a few seconds.

The roar of the Pig-Beast woke him the second time.

At first he thought his body was caught in a tumultuous storm, as the breeze whipped around his crumpled form. It took him several seconds to realise that there was in fact, no wind.

It was the breath of the monster.

The Pig-Beast stood towering above him, its flaring nostrils snorting at his ruined form. It hesitated, sensing he was still alive, but seemed unsure as to whether or not he would prove edible.

The Lord of the House had lain as quietly as he could. For the first time in his life he realised that he was in the presence of a malevolent force far greater than even himself. This thought brought a new sensation to him. One he would never forget.

Fear.

He had expected death to follow with each separate inspection the leathery creature gave him. Yet, for whatever reason, the monster suddenly grew tired of waiting for him to react to its probing, and with a final sniff, it moved off at a slow, measured pace. He watched it disappear over Bayous Ridge.

Since that day he had never seen the Pig-Beast again. He knew not from where it had come, or what its true intentions had been, but this brief glimpse of it had been enough to convince him that the world he had once known had now irrevocably changed. He was no longer the master of the House, nor was he the highest link in the chain. The fear of the Pig-Beast was to remain with him forever, and would only be cemented by the creature's subsequent attacks upon his newborn Still army.

Finally, when he was sure the creature had left him for dead, he moved. He remembered scrabbling to his knees, the pain from the burns suddenly becoming excruciating as the grass, which had acted like a cold compress, fell away from his raw skin. The sores caused by the fire were now fully exposed to the air. It was a pain beyond anything he could ever imagine.

Yet somehow he still managed to stand.

He cast a glance at his blackened body. The skin, what little there was left of it, hung from him like rancid meat from an age-old spit roast. He screamed with pain, but only for a second. The tidal wave of agony swept him up in its calming embrace and once again he passed out.

Hours must have passed before he awoke. Once again he was not alone. The wild dogs had returned to his side, and with their persistent nuzzling and barking, he finally managed to gingerly stand up. He awaited the return of the pain. He did not have to wait long.

This time it came accompanied by a wave of nausea, which saw him vomiting ash onto the grassy plain. The dogs became distressed at this sight, and took up a dreadful howling, which threatened to bring the Pig-Beast back down upon them.

"Be silent."

The Lord of the House had quelled them. The sickness was passing and once again he felt confident enough to move. Summoning all his reserves of willpower he managed to stem the sensation of pain his body was feeling. It was the darkest form of magic, one which he had perfected, in the secret depths of the House. It allowed him to release his mind to the world outside his body, granting the chance for his senses to channel outwards across this strange land and seek out anything familiar.

As he swayed in this deep trance, the dogs rested at his feet as though he were their messiah.

The Lord of the House had expected to sense traces of the Silent, feeling certain that at least a few would have survived the conflagration.

He was surprised to detect Krinn.

For a second he lost the trace, but once his surprise cleared his mind reached for the betrayer once again.

So the mirror had only one exit.

This confused him.

He had always been of the belief that the water mirror was the doorway to a myriad of worlds. Yet Krinn was here, wherever *here* was?

And if he had followed the Missing Children then surely…

As this thought began to take shape he sensed that Krinn had become aware of him. Without a word the Lord of the House summoned him back.

Back to his master.

In the days that followed Krinn was punished viciously for his crimes against them all. He took his punishment wilfully and the Lord of the House had to grudgingly respect him for his dutiful purgatory. Krinn proved useful, quickly, as the eyes and ears of the Lord of the House. He was able to steal bandages from a place called Myfanwy, which had evidently become the new home of the Children. They helped to strap up the wounds he had suffered in the fire and in a matter of weeks the Lord of the House felt strong enough to travel.

He was greatly alarmed when Krinn began to tell him stories of the achievements of a child known as Annabel, or the Sacred Mother, who was somehow able to travel between this world she was calling the Dark Realm, and another she called the Earth.

It grieved him further to hear that a great deal of time had passed since he had fled the House. It was an indeterminate amount, as Krinn had been with this renegade group every day since they had escaped the fire. It was clear that the Lord of the House had been caught between the two worlds for an unnatural length of time, left in a limbo until finally he had successfully penetrated through into the Dark Realm.

From Krinn he learnt of the Mist Children.

Some had been named while others still awaited that particular honour. They were no longer prematurely aging. It seemed as though the curse of the House could no longer reach them.

"It *has* left its mark upon them," Krinn explained. "Most of them still look like old croons, trapped in the bodies of young children, but several of them have escaped relatively unharmed."

"The final captives, the girl and her friends, they were not with us long enough for the curse to take a full hold upon them."

"That is true. They do *not* look so old, and it is this small collective who are being trained to look after the others. There are being helped by this Sacred Mother, and visitors from her own world. They are a threat to us. If they learn that you have escaped my master, they will hunt you down. You are not yet strong enough to face them."

"For once you are right Krinn. The news you bring me is both irritating and shocking, but we must be cautious. They have had far longer than us to establish themselves in this world. I must know everything there is to know about this place before we finalise any plans."

"It would be impossible for the two of us to destroy them alone, there are far too many of them..." Krinn had begun to complain but the Lord of the House silenced him with a wave of his hand.

"Fool. We will do nothing until I have assembled an army. But first we need answers. Tell me more of these visitors you mentioned? They are from the Sacred Mother's world?"

"She has brought them all with her on several occasions. Four old witches who reside in a home full of old bones...they resemble the walking dead, and also a woman who is different from them, yet *just* as ancient. Her name is Jean Candicote. She makes more sense than the other four, yet her words seem to displease them. They are convinced that this is the world in which they were born. The more often they visit, the more they refuse to accept that they have to go home."

At this the Lord of the House shivered with excitement.

"Then this place...the Dark Realm. It is like the House once was? A place where there is no past, and for those who are caught here...no future. Only now."

He breathed harshly. Krinn's eyes moistened with emotion. His own personal longing to return to the safety of the House was just as strong as his master's.

"Then we can start again?" he hesitantly asked. For a time the Lord of the House did not answer him, as though his mind were too preoccupied with the information he had been given to digest. Finally he turned to face Krinn.

"We will begin again. But make no mistakes Krinn; there is much we must do in the mean time. You will stay in the company of this group for a while, and learn all you can about this place and the Earth. If this Sacred Mother is as you say...a child, then chances are there will be more children there for us to enslave. We must establish a link between the two worlds. This home where the Old Ones live, it sounds perfect for us. You are to act as though nothing has changed when you return to them. But you must bring me back something of this Sacred Mother's. Preferably skin tissue...or a lock of her hair. We must learn how she travels between the two worlds. They still trust you Krinn; it is an advantage we cannot afford to lose."

"She does seem to have a magic about her master, one that I cannot explain. Though I am certain you can discover the properties of such a trick. What will you do first my Lord?" Krinn asked.

The wild dogs all rose up as the Lord of the House moved away from Krinn.

"It is time I journeyed. It is time we found a new home. The House is gone, Krinn. From this moment all that matters for us is now. That is what I must become, Lord of the Now. You must seek me out with any news you have. I shall travel west through that copse. Is there any water in this land?"

It was an unexpected question.

"There are two major rivers that flow freely through the neighbouring valley, why?" Krinn was intrigued.

"The water mirror has caused me more pain than the fire,"

the self-appointed Lord of the Now divulged. He looked down at his bandaged form.

*"I fear I must keep away from any more. The fire has been....
kind to me. It would be a mortal sin to undo its work."*

His cryptic answer left Krinn floundering for more information but the Lord of the Now was already walking away, the wild dogs running ahead of him like a flock of black sheep.

In the months that followed The Lord of the Now journeyed for miles across the Dark Realm. He was able to memorise his route, and often he would scratch a rough map into the soil so he could keep a constant check of where he was going. He would leave signs for Krinn to be able to follow. These would usually take the form of mutilated animals, which he would hungrily masticate and then leave their rotting corpses hanging from trees, their bodies dusted with ash from his insatiable lips.

Krinn brought regular news of the developments within the camp. He was also able to extricate a length of Annabel's hair from the pillow on which she slept.

Using this small token the Lord of the Now set to work, determined to discover the mystical properties the child had developed. His dedication to this study was inhuman. He would spend hour after hour in continuous meditation, using his own mind as a conduit to travel across the Dark Realm and seek out this magical window into Annabel's world. He had expected to discover it within weeks of beginning, but a whole month had passed and he was no closer. He had begun to doubt, fearing his own skills had deserted him, when, quite unexpectedly, he saw the void for himself.

So immersed in his studies had he been, that he hadn't left the confines of the cave he was sheltering in for thirty days. He finally abandoned the wild dogs, and crawled painfully out of the mouth of the cave, like a horribly crippled bat, seeking the moon's rays to heal him.

He rested on the cold stone ledge of a lofty promontory, hunched over, his breath shallow as though he feared to inhale too much of the fresh night air.

If he had been blessed with prescience he couldn't have chosen a more perfect spot. The cave mouth was several metres above ground level, and offered a panoramic view of over thirty miles of the Dark Realm. Although in places there was literally *nothing* to see, he was able to make out the dark shadows of the forests, and the twisting margin of the rivers, which in the moonlight looked like a prison for stars; as though the ground was jealous of the beauty of space and intended to capture the finer elements for itself. To anyone else the sight would have been nothing short of beautiful.

To the Lord of the Now it was like staring into the very heart of pestilence. The glittering river represented nothing but cold, clammy death. He turned his gaze away from it, casting a glance over to the north.

It was then that the void erupted from the leaden sky, blazing a purple ray of inhuman power directly downwards. When it reached the ground, it seemed to intensify, and then thin down to almost a needlepoint, as though it were seeking an individual, not a collective.

"So this is the magic,"

the Lord of the Now decried with a hint of admiration in his tone. He locked his mind onto the void, dazzled by the degree of power it exuded. He clenched the strands of Annabel's hair tightly in his ruined fist and felt the slightest of tugs as though the void were actually reaching for him. He let the hair fall to the ground, and watched in horror as it was pulled, fibre-by-fibre from the ledge floor. It whipped away in the wind straight back towards the void. He quickly lost sight of it but he knew instinctively that that was where it would have gone.

His mind seemed almost to liquefy as he forged a frail link between himself and the void. He felt his back claws begin to slide across the stone as the void reached for him again.

In that instant he locked minds with Annabel.

The pain was indescribable, and he had to break the connection immediately.

With a scream he realised he was now teetering on the lip of the ledge, the void had pulled him six feet from where he had been standing. He looked back at the two deep grooves his claws had gouged into the stone in an effort to resist. His breathing was rapid, and a tension rippled through him like a shockwave. He staggered back from the edge, and almost immediately his legs buckled beneath him. He crumpled to the floor like a broken puppet.

He watched the void, utterly mesmerised at its ever-swirling velocity. The sky above appeared to have darkened more than was necessary, and now the only visible sight in the Dark Realm was the pillar of light. The oppression of the night was making it difficult to breathe. In the dim distance the Lord of the Now could hear the croaking and cawing of several nocturnal birds as they took to the air in panic that their sacred trees were about to be crushed by the sky.

The effect lasted only minutes, but it held the world spellbound for hours afterwards.

With a heart-stopping crackle the light began to dim. It flickered as though suffering a power failure, and then briefly intensified, so the whole world was almost lit up like a monstrous firefly.

Then it was gone.

Normality returned like a jilted lover, seeking out everything that was familiar and pulling it close in a welcoming embrace.

The Lord of the Now was shaking as though in the grip of an apoplectic fit. The wild dogs were howling in fear and frustration; they gingerly emerged from the cave mouth and huddled round their master. They feared he had finally died as the fit suddenly ended and he keeled over.

Stillness taking his body, but joy seizing his mind.

He had seen the void. For one brief second he had been linked inexorably to it, and a part of him was now joined eternally to the Sacred Mother. A fleeting glimpse of her home world had been revealed to him.

He had seen the children of her neighbourhood, all safely at play. Rows and rows of dwellings filled to capacity with families. It was a world of parents and children all living in tranquil obliviousness to the terror that he could bring to them. It was in that brief glimpse that the seed for the germination of his master plan was sown.

The House may have been destroyed by fire, but it *could* be rebuilt, and where better than this fresh clean world he had just gazed down upon? A link would be forged between the two worlds. If this girl had some sort of power to travel between them, then surely she was not *unique* to this gift? Logic told him that *anyone* from the Sacred Mother's world would be intrinsically linked to it. He thought immediately of the four old witches whom Krinn had referred to. The ones who dwelt in the house of old bones; that house could replace the one they had lost. That way there would *always* be an open doorway. It might take years to perfect, but it could be done.

When he had originally spoken to Krinn of his plans they had been nothing more than ideas and talk. He had not wanted his second in command to think he was beaten. But now...now all was different. He was a genius. Every diabolical thought he had nurtured was now a possible reality, providing he could eliminate the threat of this Sacred Mother and her allies in this world.

He feared that they would try and interfere in his plans.

For a short while he stayed, kneeling triumphantly as though he were offering thanks to the night for its revelations.

He had seen deep inside her mind, and in doing so he had been startled to see his own image reflected back upon himself.

She feared him.

She even dreamt of him.

It was a deep-seated fear, one that had clearly been with this girl for a long time.

Yet how was that possible?

She was certainly not a captive of the House. For some inexplicable reason this young girl was linked to him, by what means he could not imagine, but it gave him a power over her beyond anything he had previously hoped. She had no doubt been aware of him, even in the split second of contact with her, but this could only add to the Lord of the Now's triumph.

"Sleep well my pretty one,"

he whispered, savouring the sweet taste of victory.

It was short-lived however, as the clouds rumbled overhead and a heavy mist began to fall in an unforgiving furore upon the Dark Realm.

The Lord of the Now hissed and spat like a viper, he began to quickly crawl his way back into the shelter of the cave as the mist continued to torment him.

He watched it falling like a thousand horrible deaths from the venomous sky.

"This world fears me."

He smirked in triumph.

"It will learn that it can't wash away my stain from this perfect picture so easily."

He scowled at the heavens.

He was eager to make acquaintance with the four Old Ones. They would have all the answers he needed about the Sacred Mother's world. Perhaps they were not so mad as Krinn suspected. After all, what did that fool know anyway? It was more likely that these ancient women were lost prophets, shamans from the other world.

"We will travel tomorrow. It is time we headed south, into the colder climbs. We need a more permanent home and I need time...to prepare,"

he told the dogs.

The next day they travelled for miles, barely stopping to rest as they crossed the craggy rocks of the South Meade Hills. From this level the Lord of the Now first gazed down upon the vast Lake of Carrastorc.

For the first time during his journey through the Dark Realm he did not feel any distress at seeing such a huge volume of water. The bright sunlight of the morning was reflecting across the Lake, making it difficult to view the waters, but something else was wrong with the ambiance of the scene, and it was this which had captured the Lord of the Now's attention.

"The lake is freezing over!"

he exclaimed, a sudden rush of excitement seizing him. He scented the air, hoping to make certain that the temperature was dropping to the south.

He inhaled deeply, picking up an all-familiar smell.

Ash.

His gaze turned to the plains of Carrastorc; he was searching like a bird of prey for any sign of movement.

The wild dogs seemed to sense that the hunting instinct, which had lain dormant inside them for so long, was finally being reawakened. They began to grow ever more agitated awaiting a command.

Finally the Lord of the Now was forced to accept defeat; he glanced down at the slavering dogs.

"One of the Silent is down there. It is crippled and alone. I cannot see it, but I know it is not far from here. Find it for me...do not spoil it until I join you,"

he advised.

As one, the dogs took off at a tremendous speed, they tore full pelt through the underbrush of the hillside, making for the plain.

The Lord of the Now rested awhile, listening to the collective barking of the dogs as they grew ever fainter into the distance.

He had remained motionless for almost an hour when he heard the sound of galloping hooves. A horse and rider was approaching him from the southwest. He grew fearful. Alone and weaponless he suddenly realised the vulnerability of his position. He was an easy target for one of the Mist Children in his current condition.

As panic gripped him and he began to scrabble around looking for a place to shelter, his instincts finally got the better of him.

When Krinn appeared moments later, sitting atop his jet-black steed, he was confronted with the sight of the Lord of the Now sitting nonchalantly on a boulder, looking as though he had anticipated his arrival all the time.

"I would have thought you would have tried to conceal yourself better my Lord," Krinn commented, stepping down with a graceful flourish from his horse. The Lord of the Now snaked his neck to view the approaching Krinn.

"I would have thought you would have learnt stealth by now, my useless hunter."

He admonished him as though he were merely wasting his breath on an unruly child. Krinn failed to react to the jibe; he was looking about him as though he had lost something.

"The wild dogs are tracking one of the Silent. They should bring it back alive before sunset,"

the Lord of the Now explained without looking up. Krinn raised an eyebrow as though he were genuinely surprised to hear this news.

"One of the Silent survived the water-mirror as well; I would have thought they had all burnt? Why did we not spy it before?" The questions rolled off his tongue. The Lord of the Now stood up, stretching to his full height and towering above Krinn. For the briefest of moments Krinn feared his master was actually going to strike him, but the mood seemed suddenly to shift and the Lord of the Now settled himself back onto the boulder.

"I ache for battle Krinn. This existence of running and hiding does not sit right with me. It is time we began preparations and...what has happened to your face?"

The Lord of the Now had ignored all of Krinn's questions, but suddenly his eyes had alighted upon the shocking spectacle of Krinn's wounds. For the first time he noticed his ragged appearance, as though he had been rolling across the ground locked in combat. Krinn's nose was bleeding steadily, his lip was split at the far edge and one of his eyes seemed to be swelling from a horrific bruise.

Krinn shifted his weight from foot to foot nervously. He wiped a gloved hand across the bottom of his nose and seemed annoyed to discover blood smears on his fingers. He clasped the bridge of his nose and sniffed back violently, attempting to stop the bleeding.

"Were you beaten?"

The Lord of the Now continued his questions, as Krinn seemed too preoccupied with his own appearance to answer him. Finally the Servant of the Now spoke.

"Ethanril fought with me, he had suspected for some time that I was working against him, trying to breed discontent within the camp. Our quarrels were becoming ever more aggressive, it was almost impossible for me to keep a check on my temper. This morning we finally came to blows...I could have killed him but that would only have led the group to hunt me down...they would have found *you*. It just seemed easier to...to..."

"Lose?"

The Lord of the Now was laughing, as Krinn stood before him, stupefied with anger.

"He bested you. This Ethanril sounds as though he is our biggest threat, a warrior good enough to defeat even Krinn? Ha! You pathetic fool. Annabel is obviously training these children well. But not well enough for the horror I will unleash upon them...what was that?"

His voice had become urgent, and before Krinn could respond to his taunts, he heard the baying of the wild dogs.

"They must have *found* it," Krinn said, spinning around to face the direction the sound was drifting from. The Lord of the now reacted with less panic; he waited upon the boulder idly scratching at the rock with his back claws.

"It will come crawling to us Krinn, it is still our servant,"

he nonchalantly reminded him. Krinn seemed less convinced.

"Time has changed my Lord; this Silent is no longer a servant of the House. You are *too* quick to trust your own powers."

"And you are too quick to question them."

The lord of the Now flew into a rage, leaping free of the boulder and slamming against Krinn. The Servant of the Now toppled forward, jarring his back against the rocky ground. He screamed in pain as the Lord of the Now twisted him round, and jabbed one of his sphere-like fists into Krinn's swollen eye.

"Mercy!" Krinn squealed, fearing his master was about to deprive him of his sight. At that moment, two wild dogs burst upon them, barking in triumph as they emerged from the surrounding shrubbery. Behind them lumbered a creature, which mirrored the Lord of the Now's own ruined appearance. The five remaining dogs herded it forwards and then circled it in order to trap it for their master.

The Lord of the Now abandoned Krinn and moved forward to examine this debilitated mess that had once been one of his Silent warriors.

It was a blackened husk of a creature, so burnt by the intensity of the flames that its skin had barbequed into ash and soot. It looked as though someone had taken the contents of a fire grate and attempted to construct a man from it, as a child might build a snowman. The Silent crouched on its back legs, looking like an abandoned statue. The Lord of the Now noted, with mild interest, that it still gripped tightly the two knives it used to attack its victims. They were now melted onto the underneath of its feet, giving the impression that they were in fact an organic part of its body, like claws.

For a while the two stood staring at each other, both seemed to be waiting for some sign of recognition. Finally, with deliberate slowness, the Lord of the Now drew back his right hand as though he were about to signal to Krinn, but instead he struck with unparalleled speed, driving his fist into the Silent's heart.

Two things happened at once.

The Lord of the Now felt his own fist drive directly beneath the Silent's ashen skin; he was immediately triumphant that he had disposed of one of his own failed warriors in such a melodramatic fashion. However, in that same instant he felt an indescribable pain in his own chest. He looked down to see that the Silent had mimicked his action exactly, driving its own fist through his ragged bandages and burying it deep into his dusty chest.

Krinn, who was by now on his feet and shaking himself free of the dirt which his cloak had accumulated during the recent scuffle, looked upon this tragedy with gleaming eyes. His usual demeanour returning to him despite his facial injuries, and he approached the dying pair with a fresh spring in his step.

The Lord of the Now had dropped to his knees, with one arm wrapped round the Silent's shoulder in almost a gesture of solidarity.

"You're dying!" Krinn sounded delighted. He looked from one to the other, while the wild dogs growled nervously around them. The Silent looked in as poor condition as its master, yet was still somehow capable of hanging on to life for a few seconds more.

"I hate to disappoint you Krinn,"

the Lord of the Now suddenly said, his voice as clear as it had ever been,

"but we are not."

As he said this he retracted his arm. The Silent mimicked him and both their fists slid cleanly out of the wounds they had just created.

Krinn watched, open mouthed as the two temporarily gaping exit wounds began to knit neatly back together. A slow but persistent flurry of ash trickled back into the wounds like grains of sand through a vacuum. The process took seconds, during which neither of the combatants spoke, transfixed by what was happening to them. Finally, as the wounds sealed over, the Lord of the Now passed his hand over the spot, tentatively prodding with his fist.

"How?" Krinn managed, as his master rose to his feet again.

"How dare I still be alive? Or how did the wound seal itself?"

he mocked, as Krinn lost his debonair swagger and stood uselessly in front of his suddenly godlike ruler. He could not summon up the courage to actually voice his question, but the Lord of the Now saved him the trouble. He was now stroking the top of the Silent's bald head as though it were a lap dog.

"I have felt a kind of strangeness since the fire. As though my body were no longer solid, and the slightest breeze could rent it asunder. I had hoped to prove my theory right, by easily killing this poor specimen here."

At this, he indicated the Silent.

"But I was to be proved thankfully wrong. The fire has healed us Krinn. It has made our bodies incapable of pain, unlike anything your putrid human flesh could endure. I can be ripped apart on a rack, and I would repair the moment the wind blew. You cannot kill, what doesn't die."

His laughter was like a banshee's wail, ripping apart the air and defiling it with pure evil. The sound chilled even Krinn's bones.

"This is dark magic indeed," Krinn declared, and the Lord of the Now turned his cadaverous face upon his servant.

"The darkest magic in any of the worlds Krinn and not of my doing for once, I assure you. This is a result of our injuries, good fortune for us, and the coming of great evil for others. But it does come at a price, my servant,"

he confessed. Krinn looked suddenly expectant, as though he were about to uncover the means by which to eliminate his master once and for all.

"I fear however, this knowledge will be of no benefit to you, my perfidious underling,"

the Lord of the Now mocked, knowing full well Krinn's desires for power. Krinn remained phlegmatic, as though the news did not affect him in any way.

"I fear that neither myself, nor any of my once Silent warriors will ever be able to enter water again. Even now the smallest amount unsettles me, but the sheer thought of a multitude of water, turns my body cold. It would be the end of us. That is why we must avoid the rivers, and find shelter beneath the ground. And that is where you and the wild dogs will prove invaluable."

Krinn gazed intently upon his master, finally seeing the full extent of the predicament he faced. He had become indestructible at the hands of man because of the flames of the fire, but nature still held a power over him, greater than any other enemy before it. Krinn's gaze moved to the Silent, and for the first time he noticed how intently it was looking at him. Although it had not moved a muscle since the attack, the blackavised creature seemed to have concentrated all its attention upon him. Krinn swallowed nervously.

"See how it watches you Krinn?"

The Lord of the Now had picked up upon Krinn's distress.

"You have the pure flesh it so desires. It is only my presence here which prevents it from attacking you. Am I not right my child?"

he asked the abomination before him.

For the first time since its arrival the Silent opened its hideous jaws, revealing gleaming fangs, and screamed violently for several seconds before closing its mouth and returning to its silent vigil of Krinn.

The sound had caused Krinn to take a step backwards and the Lord of the Now sensed the fear within his companion.

"My, it does have a fine voice,"

he understated, looking greedily upon the Silent.

"I fear we can no longer address him as Silent, what say you Krinn?"

he asked. Krinn had yet to take his eyes off the unmoving creature.

"It sits so still, why does it not move?" he demanded.

"Still is an ideal word for it Krinn. It is waiting, waiting to attack,"

he wearily explained, as though that should have been obvious.

"But there is nothing here for it to attack," Krinn pathetically pointed out.

"Now, don't underestimate yourself Krinn. This beast wants to kill anything human, which includes you! In fact, I do believe it is waiting for you to run, so it may pursue you like one of these dogs. What do you say to that? Shall we test another of my theories today; perhaps I shall be proved wrong again?"

Krinn looked appalled. He still could not draw his eye away from the creature in front of him, to see if his master was just tormenting him.

"You wouldn't kill me like that, not after all I've done for you. Besides which, you *need* me, more now than ever before."

"Do not get ideas above your station dear Krinn. You are and will always remain...expendable. However, for the moment you may rest assured I will not let it harm you. We will travel down past that lake, and venture into those colder climbs. This change in temperature pleases me greatly. I wonder if I am not in some way the cause of it."

Krinn was only half-listening; his concern for his master's apparent mercy was growing inside him.

"I will need constant protection from it, if you wish me to follow you, then you must guarantee this, because the minute you turn your back, I fear this thing will be upon me. If you cannot accept my terms, then you must kill me now," he defiantly proposed.

The Lord of the Now was impressed by Krinn's courage, and knew instinctively that he would not be an unworthy combatant if it came to it, but he did still have need of his talents for a while.

Krinn's suggestion of constant protection had flashed an idea across his mind. If he were to make Krinn a weapon of some kind, one that would contain an essence of his own mind, and therefore keep the Still hypnotised away from striking Krinn down; then perhaps it was equally possible that he could use this selfsame weapon as a conduit for the magic he had learnt from the Sacred Mother. Krinn could become the vessel by which they could cross the void and explore the Sacred Mother's world. Of course when the time was right, he could dispose of Krinn and claim the weapon back.

With these treacherous thoughts in mind he addressed Krinn.

"You are brave to make such demands of me Krinn, however…this time I concede. You shall have your protection. But for now you must rely solely upon my word and conduct me to a place of safety. Let us travel at once."

Krinn was surprised by his master's decision, and privately believed that it was a show of weakness on his behalf that he should entrust a mere servant in this fashion. However, he was undeniably relieved.

They journeyed for the best part of two days, having been forced into hiding on the first day when the scent of the Pig-Beast was detected. The monster did not emerge however, and the small band continued well into the night as they sought shelter.

The lake of Carrastorc had by now entirely frozen over, and Krinn had begun to detect further changes in the weather the closer they approached the Wastelands of the west. He was also inclined to believe that his master's presence was in no small way the reason for these changes. He also believed that their current trajectory was taking them too close to the Wastelands. He had already attempted to enter them when he had been searching for his master, but the intensity of the white light that seemed to comprise the entire landscape there had caused him to flee, and he was not keen on returning.

It was more by luck than judgement that they discovered the entrance to Stilfanwyn Chasm.

They had made their way through a circular belt of pine trees, in pursuit of one of the wild dogs who they mistakenly believed had picked up the scent of an animal. When they emerged into the clearing, the dog was nowhere to be found.

Fear swept through them, as they suspected they had walked into a trap of some kind. The Lord of the Now had strode cautiously into the centre of the clearing, and demanded that the dog's attacker reveal itself.

To their surprise they had heard a faint yelp of response from the dog, seemingly coming from below ground.

Seconds later, through a low covering of gorse the wild dog emerged barely a foot away from his master. The Still had leapt forward and hurriedly cleared away the shrubbery to reveal the opening of a dark hole leading deep underground. A heady miasma belched forth from the entrance, a sweaty smell that would have turned the stomach of any sane explorer. The Lord of the Now was the first to descend, demanding to go alone. Krinn, who was less keen than he would have openly admitted, allowed his master this display of courage.

Three hours later the Lord of the Now had returned. He described his journey deep into the labyrinthine tunnels of the Chasm. He was convinced that there was mile after mile of twisting caverns to explore, but the whole experience had been too disorientating, and it was impossible to see in places. He even confessed he had feared himself lost on several occasions.

Before they attempted a further exploration they gathered wood to make torches. Then slowly over a period of days they began to take reconnaissance of the Chasm. In under a week they were confident that they could work to make it habitable.

The Still proved a useful asset in these early days. It never tired, and was capable of making a mental map of the tunnels much faster than any of the others. The Lord of the Now used it much like a runner, and sent it backwards and forwards to the surface to fetch fuel and supplies. It was also the principal hunter, killing deer and rabbits to feed Krinn and the dogs.

During the first six months of their time within Stilfanwyn Chasm, the Lord of the Now spent all his days exploring deeper and deeper into the caverns. He had become convinced that the tunnels were the work of some organic creature, and several times during his explorations he was certain he heard unexplainable movement from even lower within those dark catacombs.

To further add weight to his theories he found the mangled remains of some unidentifiable creature, strewn across the ground in one of the passageways. It had obviously been there for some time, as the skull had completely rotted free of flesh. The Lord of the Now picked it up, hoping to recognise the victim, it looked like some sort of mutated goat, yet its body was almost human in shape. Lying next to the rotted corpse was a long black fighting staff, made of some unusual metal. It was more of a long sword than a staff as one end had been sharpened to a vicious point. The Lord of the Now was impressed by the wickedness of the weapon, and decided that master and staff should be reconciled with each other.

Over the following week he constructed Krinn's glaive. Using intense fire to blacken the goat skull and weld it onto the hilt of the staff, he then passed his hands across the length of the weapon, casting dark incantations over the melting bone, offering it the essence of his own dark soul to ward off the Still. Finally he added his pitiful knowledge of the Sacred Mother and her void.

When it was finally finished the Lord of the Now had presented it to Krinn, proving, albeit briefly, that he could keep his word. Krinn had been impressed with the weapon, and upon seizing it from his master had spun it three times in an arch in front of the Still. The creature was mesmerized by the weapon, and Krinn felt his old confidence return.

He would curse the day he had ever accepted the weapon when he was forced to enter the void for his master several months later and experience the true pain that was, Dream Blending.

It was the Old Ones who told them of the Still-Pit. Without them he would never have started to search for it.

By now Morquinda and her companions were living in a cave not far from the entrance to Stilfanwyn Chasm. Krinn had seen them there on one of his journeys, and the Lord of the Now decided it was time he made their acquaintance.

Their first meeting had been traumatic.

Morquinda had spoken at great length of her fear of being returned to a place she called the false world. She was convinced that someone was trying to take her back there at night, and she wanted assurances that this person was going to be removed from her mind.

"Of whom do you speak?"

the Lord of the Now had demanded of her.

"It is the one they are now calling the *Sacred Mother*...her name is Annabel Bettany. She is a threat to you my Lord of the twilight kingdom. She speaks of futures and she knows of history. She is a blasphemer to our creed. We want to remain here with you. We want only now." Morquinda had pleaded, scrabbling across the filthy floor of the cave and burying her weeping face into the folds of his robes. Meanwhile Elyse, Felicia and Isabella had crowded round Krinn, reaching out to him with their wasted arms, trying desperately to touch his face. Krinn stepped away from them in revulsion.

"Let us go Lord; we waste our time here amongst these wretched hags," he advised. The Lord of the Now was not so quick to abandon the hovel. He reached down and cupped Morquinda's chin with one of his burnt fists, raising her head level with his own.

"My companion believes that you are all full of lies and madness. He feels that you are false prophets and that I should punish you for it. I want you all to know that I am a very reasonable person, but to lie to me is extremely foolish. So I offer you this proposal. Tell me what is to come, and I will spare your lives. Lie to me, and I shall return here within two days and slaughter you all where you stand,"

he finished, viciously pushing the old woman away from him. He watched amused as she tumbled backwards onto the stony ground.

Krinn's mouth flickered with a smile and he made no attempt to assist Morquinda as she struggled back to her feet.

"You will allow me a moment?" the old lady asked, with as much dignity as she could muster. The Lord of the Now nodded courteously, dismissing her with a wave of his hand. They waited in silence, listening intently as Morquinda rummaged through her trunk of papers.

Twice Krinn made a move to examine what she was doing, and on both occasions the other Old Ones crowded around him, preventing him from leaving.

The Lord of the Now found it all very amusing. He had a certain admiration for Morquinda, and was impressed that she was willing to go to such elaborate lengths to try and hold on to her life. What she was searching for within the trunk he did not have the slightest curiosity to learn, he merely waited patiently, running over amusing ways he could dispose of her later.

Finally the noise of searching ceased and Morquinda sidled back to face him.

"I have consulted my books, and the runes," she began melo-dramatically. The Lord of the Now allowed her this moment in the spotlight.

"And what do they tell you Old One?"

he mockingly asked her.

For a long time Morquinda held his gaze.

"You have come from a House darker than the one we inhab-ited, a House which fire has now consumed. You seek a way of returning to this place, and you hope to find that way by using the house that we have left behind us on earth." She paused before continuing, briefly glancing at Krinn who was beginning to look uncomfortable.

"Go on."

The Lord of the Now said in a whisper.

Morquinda seemed pleased with the reaction she was having on all of them.

"You will need an army to complete this task. At the moment there are too few of you, and you know this. The answer is at hand. Look to the south, to the fires of the earth in which you live. They spawned you, and will do it again if you offer them a fresh sacrifice." At this the Lord of the Now dismissed all thought of killing Morquinda. He glowered at Krinn before coaxing the old hag to continue.

"Very little more can I tell you today, only that the runes speak of a great victory for you, soon, and I am confident that you will defeat Annabel, but I fear another is coming who will pose a larger threat…"

The Lord of the Now seized her to him, as a child might cling to a doll in terror.

"The Pig-Beast, is that of whom you refer?"

He was practically squeezing the life out of the old lady, and she coughed and spluttered in terror of his embrace. Fighting for breath Morquinda spat out her final prophesy:

"He is known as the Harvester. He will come from pain and turmoil, and he will bring peace," she managed.

The Lord of the Now brushed her away as though she were a persistent fly. He almost rounded on her again, but there was something about the old woman's words which had rung true with him. He decided instead to return to Stilfanwyn Chasm and attempt to find the 'fires of the earth' of which she had spoken.

He left with Krinn, vowing to return with a vengeance if the Old Ones proved to be wrong in their prophecies.

But they weren't.

Krinn located the Still-Pit the very next day, having spent the entire night journeying deeper into the Chasm.

When the Lord of the Now first set eyes upon the pit, he knew that the Old Ones truly were prophets. He also knew that this was the bubbling, sweating, blazing pit of hell he had been searching for since his arrival. It was the true source of the foul smells and unnatural heat that filled the tunnels and it formed the beating black heart of Stilfanwyn Chasm.

"We will build two bridges above it,"

the Lord of the Now announced, looking up into the vast recesses of the Chasm ceiling.

"One bridge will link the adjoining tunnels above us, and another will lead directly into my throne room,"

he continued, apparently lost in his own designs.

"But what purpose can such a stench sodden bog as this possibly serve?" Krinn asked, somewhat appalled that they were even discussing its merits. "Unless as you have said, as a source of heat?" The Lord of the Now slowly turned towards him.

"Krinn, you crave so much to have my power, yet you possess no imagination for it. Did you not listen to what the old woman said?"

Krinn bristled at the insult.

"The Old One spoke madness and riddles, just as I told you she would, with some facts thrown in that anyone could have guessed at," he argued.

"Fool. Your pessimistic outlook shines through as usual. The Old Ones are all prophets I tell you, and what they are foreseeing is the creation of my army of Still,"

he boomed, his voice echoing seemingly forever amongst the cavernous walls. Krinn looked unimpressed.

"How is that possible? We have only one left," he snapped back, indicating the Still which sat dutifully at his master's side. The Lord of the Now slid an arm around the Still's shoulders.

"This creature is about to make the ultimate sacrifice, for the good of the entire race,"

he intoned, gazing down upon the bubbling mass of volcanic lava.

"*Remember the House Krinn…remember how the fire made us strong, and turned my body into something beyond power. The intensity of that heat was as nothing compared to this. This will be forever known as the Still-Pit. It will be the birthing pool for all my children.*"

Without warning he propelled the unsuspecting Still forward with a blow from his arm. It had been virtually perched on the ledge above the pit, and was unable to secure a foothold in time. Krinn watched transfixed as the Still pitched forward off the ledge and somersaulted over and over, screaming for its life as it dived head first into the blazing lava.

The flames rose in welcome, swallowing up the body in one tidal wave, and illuminating the cavern so intensely that Krinn had to shield his eyes for fear of damaging them. When he finally felt comfortable enough to reopen them, he gazed down on the burning pit with relish. He turned to look at his master, and his cold black pupils reflected the burning fires of the pit.

"Nothing! You have merely rid us of that Still," Krinn mocked him. The Lord of the Now shook his head in laughter.

"*Always Krinn…always you speak too soon.*"

And with that he bowed his head in reverence and left the promontory.

For the next four days the Lord of the Now remained ensconced in his private chambers. He was deep in a trance, and often Krinn heard his voice echoing like a malevolent pestilence through the Chasm, as he muttered untranslatable chants, and summoned all manifestations of evil.

The wild dogs cowered in darkened corridors, fearing to go anywhere near their master's lair, and the very air of the Chasm seemed to have filled with a claustrophobic vapour, that clung to the lungs like glue.

It was on the final day before Krinn attempted his first foray into Dream Blending that the Lord of the Now re-emerged from his self-imposed isolation.

He was in a blinding rage, making threats and demands of Krinn that quickly backed the Servant of the Now into a corner with true fear in his eyes.

It was clear that for some reason the spells had not proven successful, and the Lord of the Now needed Krinn to attempt to cross the void into the Sacred Mother's world. If possible to capture her alive, and then force her to reveal the secrets of her control over the Dark Realm.

"Her will is unimaginably strong. She is preventing the birth of my Still army by her own strength of mind alone. But if I had her here in front of me, I could break her like a tree in a gale,"

he threatened.

Krinn had no choice; he would have to enter the void.

The aftermath of this night would live forever in the minds of all those it touched.

The very next day, the blizzard came.

It generated at Carrastorc, sweeping down across the South Meade Hills like a great white swan, covering the ground in a mat of thick feathers. The intense cold reached deep underground, and Krinn was amongst the first to step out into that first virgin fall of snow.

The impact on the scenery had little effect upon Krinn; he saw no beauty in the purity of white. From a tactical point of view, he was already calculating how much easier it would be to track the Mist Children in these conditions. He also knew that the ice would cause them difficulties in finding food and water. All things considered the coming of the winter was like sweet music to the Lord of the Now.

"I have caused this Krinn. The Dark Realm has lost its mother, and we are now its surrogate parents. It is our task to mould and change this world to fit our own desires. We will build a vast army of

Still, capable of tracking down and eradicating the surviving Mist Children; and then with Morquinda's help, we will build a bridge between our world, and that of the Sacred Mother's."

"It will take years my Lord. The Old Ones may not even survive this winter. Besides which, you have yet to encounter these Mist Children; they will adapt, you can be sure of that. Something is just not right yet...do you not feel a certain resistance in the air? See how the blizzard blows in such agitated half-circles; there is something unnatural about it. I feel a certain tightness of the air, as though a subconscious will were still repelling us." Krinn was crouching on the snow laden ground, feeling with his fingertips the texture of the ice.

The Lord of the Now looked down at him with certain revulsion.

"You miserable creature, how dare you suspect such a will could still exist? The Sacred Mother is dead; and her presence has left this world. In its place has come the snow and ice that began the day I passed close to the great lake. This is my creation, this is my winter Krinn. You will now witness my greatest triumph."

With these endorsements he led Krinn back into the Chasm, and down into its darkest depths until they eventually emerged onto the narrow ledge above the festering Still-Pit. Krinn kept his distance from his master, fearing that he would be pushed like the Still before him into the nauseous lava swamp.

There was something different about the Still-Pit that day. The flickering light cast out from the sporadically bursting flames below them, was a darker orange than Krinn previously remembered, and there seemed to be a certain anxious pressure to the air that wafted up. He was nervous to look over the lip of the edge, but his curiosity pushed him to take a step forward.

As he did so he heard the first scream.

It was almost of the same resonance as newborn baby's first cry, but mixed with a horror of masticated death that no infant would be capable of portraying through their unbroken vocal cords.

Far below Krinn, the first wave of Still were being birthed from a primordial slime that carried with it the heady scent of torrid evil.

"See how they come forth Krinn. Clones of our first sacrifice, freed at last from the spell of incarceration which the Sacred Mother was hexing them with in her lifetime. Her will has crumbled like her body, and you speak of another? Who else could hold back such an army as this? Not even this Harvester of whom Morquinda foretells could defeat such creatures,"

the Lord of the Now confidently proclaimed. Krinn was gripping his glaive, and growing ever more agitated by the increasing number of Still emerging from the pit. He was trying not to show his nervous disposition in front of his master.

"Krinn, I do believe even you are nervous of my most impassive of servants?"

The Lord of the Now laughed, as he watched with pleasure as the Still began to clamour up the sheer rock face, clinging to the stones like limpets.

In the weeks that followed the army was put to work, constructing the many chambers and fortifications that now make up Stilfanwyn Chasm.

They would be sent out on scavenging raids, seeking out Mist Children and hording them back to the lair of their dark master.

The harvesting of the children began in earnest, but it was in this initial wave of triumph that the Gak Worm first revealed its presence to them. Within days of his army beginning to emerge from the infantile Still-Pit, they had begun to disappear. At first the Lord of the Now suspected his newborn to be merely lost, struggling to find their way around the maze of tunnels.

But soon it became clear that they feared something that lived within the Chasm.

An exploration party, led by Krinn had uncovered the lair of the Gak Worm. The great beast had been sleeping with its monstrous coils woven around the ancient pillars of rock deep within the Chasm, as though it were as much a part of the organic matter of the earth, as the caves themselves. Driven to perpetual hibernation by the onset of the Lord of the Now's enforced winter.

Krinn had called the Still back, fearing the beast would awaken and devour them all. It became clear that it was the Worm which had been responsible for the depleting numbers within the Still army.

Knowing that it was inadvisable to attack such an ancient creature, and risk losing even more Still, the Lord of the Now schemed a fouler solution to his problem. He was quick to discover that the Worm sought any manner of prey, not specifically the Still.

With the first harvest of children safely caged in the Hold, like fresh meat hung in a well stocked larder; it seemed reasonable to sacrifice the odd child to appease the Worm.

The compromise had seemingly been struck, and the ritualistic sacrifice would take place every month, with the Worm emerging from its nest to feed upon the helpless children who had been selected for such a terrible fate.

But now, all these years later, something was wrong.

The Lord of the Now had hoped, albeit briefly, that the Worm had simply died, curled up in a never-ending loop of sweaty red coils, its breathing growing ever shallower as frail old age finally ended its reign of terror.

This wishful thought had quickly been dispelled. He knew the monster lived. Many times he could hear it, slithering down its own labyrinth of tunnels, often shaking the foundations of the Chasm as it passed close by.

He had even feared it might break through into his own fresh tunnel and start devouring his army as though they were ants. But although many times he had sensed it draw close, it had never appeared.

The question of why it had chosen to exile itself at this crucial time remained unanswered.

As the Lord of the Now continued to ponder this problem a sudden commotion broke out further down the tunnel causing him to turn. He twisted round in one fluid movement, his eyes glinting upon the fast-moving shape of an approaching Still.

The creature was clearly distressed, and was charging at such a sprint it swept past the other Still, brushing them aside in its haste to reach its master.

"Let it pass,"

the Lord of the Now commanded, seeing several of the Hybrids preparing to leap upon the newcomer in anger. The Still virtually skidded to a halt on the rough tunnel floor. It had to dig its sphere like hands into the dirt, and turn in a slight arc in order to stop the propulsion of its speed. It sent up a clod of dirt, which the Lord of the Now casually sidestepped.

"Speak,"

he demanded, allowing the creature no time for rest. With a series of violent throat gurgles and screams the Still conveyed its message in a language that none but the Lord of the Now could interpret. As the Still's vernacular became more heated the Lord of the Now began to look increasingly displeased. With one impossibly swift movement he had gripped the Still around the throat in one of his mighty taloned claws. It wriggled desperately in his grasp as he drew it towards him. The Still's feet dragged comically across the ground as it tried desperately to maintain a hold, but with ease the Lord of the Now propelled it into the air, until he was holding it high above his head, drawing the attention of all the gathered Hybrids.

"If you are lying to me…"

he began, eyeballing the Still with vile intent. He allowed his sentence to remain purposefully unfinished.

The gathered Still were all enraptured by this display of power by their master, and as they sat expectantly awaiting the fate of the unfortunate messenger, they failed to notice the initial sign that the wall was about to give way.

It shuddered at first; a tremor, which left several cracks, lacing outwards like spiders' webs across the dirty granite surface. The team of burrowing Still became more frantic, as they felt the foundations begin to tear free. They dug deeper, ripping out as much dirt and rubble as possible. They were uncomfortably hunched over, digging like demonic rabbits. The steady scraping of their own tunnelling was soon drowned out by the now distinct sounds of falling earth.

The Lord of the Now shuffled uncomfortably as the sound of the avalanche reached him. He hurled the virtually strangled Still away from him, screaming orders at the others to back further away.

It was a command that at first seemed to create chaos within the ranks of the Hybrids. They were still concentrating on their master's retribution of the messenger. Suddenly he was backing away from them, in a fury to distance himself from the chaos that was moments away from happening.

The fractures in the granite had now spread level across the whole circumference of the blockade. They caused the ceiling to bow slightly at the lip of the wall, and then splinter off.

The first clump of heavy earth peeled away like bark from a sawn tree trunk. It spiralled gracefully down to the floor of the tunnel and impacted like a bomb. A cloud of earth and dust mushroomed from the impact zone, and the tunnelling Still halted to stare at the devastation they had just caused.

Only a small crater in the earth remained like a permanent tattoo of destruction.

For a moment there was glorious silence, the distinctive kind that precedes immense devastation.

"Retreat,"

the Lord of the Now advised, sensing the imminent devastation.

The Still barely had chance to heed the warning as the blockade began to collapse. It folded in upon itself like a collapsing tower of cards, each layer blending perfectly into the next as though it were melting ice.

The Still backed away from the crumbling wall, clouds of brick dust and rubble pluming around them like morning mist. They were retreating in a panic, colliding with each other as they tried to escape the falling rock. One Still seemed slower than the others, and with a frightened scream it found itself trapped behind its companions as a mighty shower of debris crashed to the floor, engulfing it entirely in the wreckage.

The rumble from the moving earth echoed through the tunnel, threatening to bring down other sections of wall and ceiling. The wooden struts creaked menacingly as they shouldered the impact of the landslide. Mercifully they held, and the collapse was restricted only to the blockade.

After several minutes of almost continuous earth fall, the dirt wall was finally down and only the dust remained as an impromptu curtain covering up the devastation beyond.

The remaining Still from the digging party had reached the rest of the Hybrids. They looked filthier than ever, covered from head to foot in brick dust and soil.

They waited impatiently for the dust to clear. The air was full of choking fumes, which they inhaled as though it were the sweetest summer breeze.

Eventually the dust cleared and the Lord of the Now moved further forwards to examine the newly revealed soil bank on the opposite side of the devastated blockade. Here the earth was softer, but held together by a fibrous root system that anchored many of the ancient trees of Kilfanfyn Forest. The roots burrowed deep into the earth, often snaking back upon themselves as various stems had interwoven time and again, in a desperate search for food and water.

The Lord of the Now ran his hands across the thick roots. He knew that they would have to be ripped out in order for the tunnel to progress.

The operation would be hindered for a while, but it would be only a temporary delay. It had been accounted for, and would allow Krinn the time he required to move his army across land.

"You will continue the passage due east, remove anything… undesirable."

He indicated the tree roots.

"We are so close now…can you not smell them?"

He sniffed at the smoggy air, his mouth glistening with saliva. The Hybrids all followed suit. They began to claw at the ground as they picked up the faint smell of the Mist Children, sleeping in their Warren.

"Clear away this rubble, and load it onto the carts, it must be dispatched up to the surface. I want the ground levelled flat again. You will not stop, and you will not hesitate. This tunnel must be completed by dawn tomorrow."

The Lord of the Now barked out his orders as he turned away from the Hybrids and followed the scuttling messenger back down along the tunnel towards the entrance.

As they marched, the Hybrids, who had formed a long chain from the current excavation site, all the way along the length of the tunnel, were removing the debris of the recent rock fall. The compacted dirt and stone was passed one to another along the line until it finally reached a small team of Hybrids at the tunnel opening.

The Lord of the Now walked with his head resolutely forward, he barely glanced at the constantly working Hybrid Still as they laboured frantically to clear the tunnel for him. He thought nothing of them. They were his slaves, bred only to do his bidding. He would work them to their limits and beyond. They could not die, and even if they were capable of death by exhaustion, he would have gladly driven them to it. His mind was now so consumed with Peter Bettany that he thought of little else.

Morquinda's predictions played on his mind. The Old Ones had been right about everything to date. The *mistake had* indeed been made, and the second Sacred Mother *had been* the cause of it. Yet Peter Bettany still remained just beyond his reach, and the Dream Blender still lived.

He watched his army loading the rubble onto two giant carts which were positioned at the furthest end of the tunnel. The carts were made from tightly bound oak and ran on enormous wheels to bear the load that the Hybrids were piling into the back. They were pulled by a team of nine Still, lashed to the front like dogs pulling a sleigh. Various ramps lay positioned at the start of adjoining tunnels which would bypass the main chambers of the Chasm and allow the carts easier access to the surface.

The Harvester had still to make his presence known. The Lord of the Now had spent many nights in quiet deliberation attempting to decipher Morquinda's cryptic warnings. The ancient hag refused to show him the books from which she read, claiming he would be unable to understand the language in which they were written. Because of her continued success as a prophet, he had allowed her to continue her secrecy, but his patience was finally wearing thin.

"It must be Ethanril,"

he muttered to himself as he began to ascend one of the side passages.

"He will be coming to me soon, with the hope of killing me. I only hope that he is equally prepared to meet his own destiny."

∽

It was the turning of the weather that had drawn Fess to Tarnwaters.

He had awoken early that morning, though obviously not as early as Pigeon who was already missing from the Warren long before dawn. Fess had ventured outside into the clearing as quietly as he could, hoping to find his friend busily cooking breakfast.

The morning was crisp and dry, and a certain warmth accompanied the fresh breeze, which Fess had not felt on his face for some time.

He hid his disappointment that no one was around to make even the slightest attempt at breakfast, by cursing, loudly enough to scare a couple of woodpeckers in the neighbouring pines. He giggled to himself, pulling his blazer around him for warmth, and trudging off across the snow in the hope of finding Pigeon and goading him into some culinary action.

He had eventually walked quite a distance before he heard voices. It had taken him a while to assure himself that they were not disembodied apparitions, and then even longer to make out whom they actually belonged to.

Peter and Ethanril were sitting high above him in Ethan's favourite oak tree. For a second it crossed Fess's mind to climb up and join them, but the idea of such an enormous physical exertion, without much hope of food at the end of it, just didn't appeal to him. Besides, although he couldn't fully make out what was being said, the tone of the conversation did sound a little deep.

Deciding that he really couldn't face a philosophical discussion on an empty stomach, he abandoned this plan and continued on his quest to locate Pigeon.

As he walked he would pluck berries off a variety of bushes and pop them casually into his mouth to stave off the hunger pains.

It was stomach pains he was suffering from by the time he eventually reached Tarnwaters. He had eaten far too many berries en route. He bobbed out his tongue, crossing his eyes to see the amusing colour it had turned.

The warmth of the morning sun played across his face, and he squinted up at it through palm-shielded eyes. He pulled off his blazer and shirt, and stepped ankle deep into the cool waters of the Tarn.

"AHHHHHHH!" he exclaimed in sheer pain. The weather in general may have been improving, but it was still far from warm enough to heat up the basin or melt the surrounding snow.

He gritted his teeth, determined to prove his manliness and bending forward he scooped some of the fresh water up into his palms and splashed it over his face. He blinked several times, shivering with cold but enjoying the enlivening feeling of freedom that the water brought to him. Pretty soon he had forgotten the initial cold altogether and was washing his arms and shoulders in the fresh stream.

"There'll be celebrations in the Warren tonight!" Pigeon's voice hollered to him. He had just emerged from the forest to be confronted with the vision of Fess bathing in the Tarnwaters.

Fess rubbed his eyes and smiled back at Pigeon.

"Oh yeah! Why's that?"

"You've had a bath!" Pigeon explained, and Fess made a rude gesture in his direction.

"...And learnt to count!" Pigeon pretended to be impressed. He walked towards the river's edge and plonked himself down on a boulder.

Fess finished bathing, and then strode over to his friend, pulling on his white shirt.

"Where on earth did you get to this morning?" Fess asked, sitting down next to Pigeon and flattening his long hair with his wet hands.

"I just wanted to get up early and make the most of the day," Pigeon lied. Fess raised his eyebrows as though he had just been prodded with something extremely sharp.

"Get up early?" he sarcastically mimicked. "You? Pigge...you never get up early. Are you sure you're not sickening for something?" Fess pretended to take Pigeon's temperature by placing his palm on his companion's forehead. "Yep! You are definitely coming down with a bad case of Sufi-itous!" Fess joked. Pigeon flashed him a brief smile, and then fell instantly silent.

An awkward moment passed between them and even Fess could tell that something was wrong.

"Hey." he said urgently, giving Pigeon's shoulder a shake. "Don't you go quiet on me buddy. Talk to me?" he kindly offered, his voice now no more than a whisper.

Pigeon lowered his head for a moment, breathing deeply. When he finally looked up his eyes were moist.

"It's so hard Fess..." he began; a real sense of angst was clinging to him and making his skin itch like second-hand clothes. "So hard..."

Fess understood at once what Pigeon meant. He knew his friend was hurting, he saw it every day. He wanted to say something to make it better, but at the same time he knew the very best thing he could do was to just stay quiet and let him talk.

"I love her so much. Beyond anything anyone could ever feel for her, and I know she knows that...but she won't come running to me anymore. I'm just her clown now, like a forgotten child-hood plaything you occasionally stumble across as you grow up, and for a few brief minutes you remember how it was to be inno-cent. She loves him...Peter. I know she loves him, I've seen the way she looks at him. It's the same way I look at her, Fess. I want to hate Peter for it, but I can't even do that because...I don't know him at all, and to be honest...he seems like such a nice guy." Pigeon sniffed, and Fess had to grudgingly nod his head.

"Do you think he loves Sufi?" Fess tentatively asked. Pigeon squeezed his eyes tight shut, trying to repel the tears.

"I really don't know Fess," he managed. "I hope he does...for her sake. You see I love her that much Fess, that I can let her go...if it's what she wants." He stumbled through this final confession and then fell into fits of sobbing.

Fess cradled him like a baby, not knowing what else to do. He held him tightly until finally the sorrow seemed to peak, and Pigeon re-emerged with sore eyes and red cheeks.

"Guess you'll need another bath now, huh?" He almost laughed, as Fess looked gently at him.

"You ok?" he probed. Pigeon wiped at his eyes with the sleeve of his shirt.

"I've been better," he admitted with a smile.

"Too true!" Fess returned.

"Oh bugger it!" Pigeon said. It was a heartfelt cry of exasper-ation, and proved to be exactly the note they both needed to hear. It acted as a catalyst and they both started to laugh at the tragedy of the situation.

Peter and Ethanril burst through the trees riding Astervarn and Jessavarn at a gallop across the Tarnwaters, just as Pigeon and Fess slid unceremoniously off their boulder laughing hysterically at the hand life had dealt them once again. The two riders disap-peared in a blur before either Fess or Pigeon had even noticed their arrival.

∽

"You will answer the question again, louder this time so all these children can hear you," Krinn demanded.

He was standing over the shackled body of Father Deane, and with the softest of touches he tilted the old priest's face upwards. "Who is coming to save them?" he asked again.

Father Deane cleared his throat. He tasted blood on his tongue and that momentarily panicked him. He was unsure how wounded he was, but silently prayed his nose was not broken. He allowed himself a second's composure and then in a voice as loud and resonant as if he were delivering one of his Sunday sermons to a packed congregation, he announced once again:

"Peter and Annabel Bettany." His voice was carried far up into the vast recesses of the Hold.

Every Mist Child, held captive in his or her separate cage, looked down with eyes full of pity at the manacled priest. Each one recognised the names of the two saviours, and every time Krinn forced him to repeat it, they all glowed with an inner pride when he found the strength to say the names again and again, despite the torture it would surely bring down upon him.

Krinn released his almost tender hold on the priest's chin allowing his exhausted head to fall forward onto his chest. He took several steps away from him, breathing heavily.

Four Still stood guarding the prisoner, their gaze constantly captivated by Krinn's ever-swirling glaive.

A cold draught blew through the vast hole that housed the Gak Worm, bringing a shudder to everyone in the Hold except Krinn. His impenetrable black cloak clung to him, hiding more secrets than anyone would ever know. The temperature did not bother him, but the priest's insistence that both Sacred Mothers still lived; did.

"If you keep lying to me priest, I will be forced to hurt you even more and I know you don't want me to do that," Krinn said, idly picking his teeth with a gloved finger. The Still snarled in anticipation, their mouths salivating at the prospect of fresh meat.

"Leave him alone you coward." An angry female voice screamed down from above him. Krinn was momentarily surprised, and it took him several seconds to locate the source of the offending remark. Finally his cold eyes closed upon Lucy Doran.

"I'm a what?" he asked, in a voice so calm and yet full of menace that even Lucy's defiance momentarily evaporated and she found herself shaking with a sudden fear. She stared down at him, wishing he would look away so she could find her initial bravado again, but Krinn was waiting now, almost willing her to say something else.

"Lost your tongue?" Krinn taunted her, his head cocked to one side as he watched the terror passing over her face.

Lucy stepped backwards away from the cage bars to break eye contact with him. Her chest had tightened with nervous tension, and she felt a desperate need to breathe clean fresh air. The dampness of the hollow cave in which they were held prisoner, was seeping into her bones and making her breathing laboured. She raked her hair away from her eyes, and stepped back up to the bars again, a renewed resilience seizing her.

Krinn had not moved, and as soon as Lucy saw him again, the moment was once again shattered.

"I see that you have lost your bite. Let us try and find a way to bring it back for you." In four quick steps he was beside Father Deane again, tilting up his head and striking him three times across the face with his fist. Father Deane groaned in agony each time the blow landed, and blood flew from his split lips. Krinn seemed delighted by his own propensity to violence, and showed no sign of stopping until the priest lay dead.

"STOP!" Lucy begged, screaming in horror at the vicious-ness of the assault. She dropped to her knees, rattling the bars of her cage as though she believed she could rip the steel prison apart with her bare hands.

Krinn stopped immediately, a sinister calm descending on him in that exact instant and moments later he was acting as though the attack had had nothing to do with him.

"Lower her cage," he ordered one of the guarding Still. The creature raced forward as though suddenly animated, sliding past Krinn and making for an array of levers on the far right wall. It swung one of its arms upwards and brought its fist down upon the top of the central lever. The sound of rusted metal straining as it slid through couplings could be heard drifting down from far above, and minutes later Lucy was screaming afresh as her cage began its jolty descent. She had to cling to the bars for dear life as the prison juddered violently from side to side, the motion causing her stomach to do cartwheels and nausea threatened to claim her.

"What are you doing?" Father Deane managed to ask. He felt woozy from the attack upon him, and it was difficult for him to speak through a mouthful of blood. One of his front teeth had been loosened from the last punch and it was bleed-ing profusely. He ran his tongue over it, trying to dislodge it. He had a fear Krinn would strike him again, and he would swallow his tooth.

Krinn appeared distracted as he watched the cage descend-ing, and it was only the sound of Father Deane finally spitting out his broken tooth, that made him turn to face his elderly victim. He looked down approvingly at the small puddle of blood surrounding the tooth, and smiled at Father Deane.

"I am about to kill your girlfriend," he casually announced without a hint of emotion. Father Deane struggled for breath, his words tumbling out like barrels.

"What! Why? What possible good can that achieve?" he cried in alarm. Krinn looked immediately bored. Father Deane strained at his shackles, desperate to lunge at his tormentor and save Lucy from such a horrible fate. He cried in frustration as his ancient restraints held fast, jarring his arms as they pinned him firmly to the ground. Krinn looked clearly amused by this display, and contemplated beating the priest again, but at that moment a new voice echoed around the Hold.

"What is happening here?"

The Lord of the Now stood framed in the entranceway of the Hold, with his body visibly shaking from rage. Behind him, the petrified Still, which had warned him of Krinn's attacks upon the prisoners, sat cowering in fear of its two masters.

Krinn looked surprised to see his master, but showed no outward sign of fear. Behind him Lucy's cage reached the ground with a crash of metal. The door snapped open and Lucy teetered out of the prison, her legs shaking from the impact of the crash. Above her, all the remaining caged Mist Children began to shriek in terror. They had learnt to associate the noise of a cage opening with the arrival of the Gak Worm and they were filled with sorrow for Lucy's imminent death.

"Silence them,"

the Lord of the Now demanded of the guarding Still. At once they leapt to the walls, racing up them like rats. They sprang from cage to cage, screaming at the children until they finally fell silent, stupefied with terror.

"I will ask you again…"

he demanded, striding past Krinn and yanking Lucy to her feet by pulling roughly upon her hair.

"What is going on here?"

Lucy grasped at his wrist, trying to pull away, but the Lord of the Now ensnared her, wrapping a putrefied arm around her and tightening it across her throat. She struggled violently but he held her firm, noting the condition of Father Deane as he did so.

"These prisoners have languished for too long here, they will be in no condition to answer our questions if we leave them to rot in the Hold," Krinn explained, as the Lord of the Now bristled with rage.

"Since when has it been your decision as to what happens to my prisoners? I left you with specific orders to prepare the Still for their journey over land. The carts must be full of rubble, enough for our needs... Yet I find you here Krinn, embarking on your usual subtle approach to questioning. So tell me...what have you learnt from these pathetic humans?"

Krinn looked affronted but answered without hesitation.

"The army is prepared and awaiting your signal to march. The first cart has already left, pulled by a team of Still as you commanded. *I have broken* the spirit of both of these by my *own* methods," Krinn bragged. At this Lucy began to struggle with renewed anger and Father Deane shook his head in defiance.

"A coward like you could *never* break the human sprit, not in a thousand life times," Father Deane retaliated. Krinn's eyes blazed at the rebuttal, and he stepped forward in a rage to strike the priest again.

"Leave him,"

the Lord of the Now commanded, seeing Krinn's intentions. The Servant of the Now rounded on his master, his black clad body shaking with unmitigated rage.

"This priest *claims* that both *Annabel* and *Peter Bettany* will save them all." Krinn almost laughed. "He will not stop repeating it, and he makes *no* mention of the Harvester," Krinn revealed. This news appeared to surprise even the Lord of the Now.

"Is that so priest?"
he intoned.

"Both of the Sacred Mother's will save you…yet one is already dead and the other will join her soon. What of this girl?"

He flung Lucy to the floor.

"Do you agree with the priest?"

he demanded.

Lucy exhaled heavily, drawing herself up on her elbows. She habitually adjusted her clothes, pulling her skirt down to cover her exposed knees. She had never felt more vulnerable.

"I know very little of Annabel," she honestly began, speaking to the floor. All the strength she had once possessed seemed to have left her, and she couldn't raise up her head to face her captors. "But Peter will come for us. If he is here in this terrible place, he will come and find us." She fought back the tears.

"Lucy?" Father Deane called to her.

Hearing his voice imploring her, she found the strength to look at him. She almost wept, seeing him manacled to the floor in such a violent way, but his kindly face was seeking out her eyes, and warmth emanated steadily from behind his smile. "He *is* coming for us Lucy, *I trust him.*" Father Deane whispered to her as though they were alone in the Hold. Once again the Mist Children seemed to catch the spirit of his words and they all gazed down upon the tragic pair with renewed hope.

"Pathetic." Krinn flattened the mood immediately. "Peter Bettany doesn't even know you two are our prisoners, but I can assure you both of one thing…" Krinn broke off. "I will take great pleasure in telling him, before he dies."

Lucy was upon him before he had had time to react, and with a display of violence previously unknown to her she scratched three deep cuts across his right cheek, just below his eye. When she pulled her hand away, she was horrified to see the flimsy strips of flesh clinging underneath her fingernails. Krinn's face was awash with blood, and even he seemed uncertain of the depth of the wound dealt him, but the Lord of the Now brought

Lucy down with a vicious grappling assault before she could damage Krinn again. He clawed at her blouse with his razor sharp talons, as if demonstrating how easily he could shred her flesh. Lucy stopped struggling and looked back fearfully, she was suddenly very aware of the situation she found herself in. Her attack against Krinn had been fuelled by pure hatred and adrenaline, but now that this was passing over her, she found it difficult to explain how she had ever found the courage to attack him.

Krinn was cursing, rubbing at his bloodied cheek in a vain attempt to stem the flow.

"*Fool.*"

The Lord of the Now admonished him.

"*I will teach you how to break the human spirit Krinn. Then perhaps you will finally learn why I am master and you are only my slave.*"

With these heated words he released Lucy, leaving her curled up in a protective ball on the floor. He indicated a random cage above him, and the Still operating the levers immediately sent that prison hurtling downwards. The Lord of the Now turned upon Father Deane.

"The Old Ones have spoken of you many times priest. They claim that you were responsible for their incarceration in Lambert House. It is somehow fitting that it is now you who is held captive against your will. Morquinda will be delighted..."

"Morquinda is a very ill old lady." Father Deane daringly interrupted him. "If you have brought her to this place, then I need to warn you that she was *no* longer capable of looking after herself in our world. I was forced to take some difficult decisions to ensure that she would be comfortable. Decisions which I have had to *learn* to live with, but I carried them out with Morquinda's health and safety in mind. She had no family to support her, I was only..."

"*Be silent priest*, no one here *cares* for your excuses. You are a coward and a fool. *Remember how you begged for your life in your own church?*" Krinn hissed at him. Father Deane looked mortally offended by this remark.

"You murdered Trevor Crispin, how dare you accuse me..." But the Lord of the Now stepped between them. He was tired of Krinn's mind games, which he could see would lead them all nowhere.

"*We waste time here. Priest, I apologise for your treatment at the hands of my servant this day. I hope you realise that I had nothing to do with it? I am here only to show you the fate which awaits you once I have defeated Peter Bettany. For a time I confess I considered sparing the life of you and the girl, in case I lost my link to Peter's world, but now it all seems unnecessary. So you will die, of that you can be certain, but you have my word it will not be at Krinn's hand.*"

He spoke as though he were offering them a genuine reprieve from the greater of two evils. Father Deane found the monster's cold logic difficult to follow; he was truly astonished by the callousness with which it made such an offer.

"I hope you will forgive us if we do not *rush* to thank you for your kindness in this matter," Father Deane mocked, but his irony was lost upon the Lord of the Now. At this moment the second cage rattled to the ground.

As the door swung open, the Mist Child shot out, running free. It was a young boy of around ten. Like the others his face was lined with creases and wrinkles, but his hair still retained its natural brown colouring. He made it past the disorientated Krinn, and was within inches of the entranceway when a Still appeared blocking his retreat. It was the same messenger which had accompanied the Lord of the Now back to the Hold.

"*Bring him to me...unharmed,*"

the Lord of the Now commanded as the insatiable creature advanced upon the boy, herding him back into the centre of the room.

By now Lucy had managed to crawl her way slowly across the floor to be closer to Father Deane. The Still guards watched her approach with mild interest, but made no move to stop her. When she was within arm's length of the old priest Krinn's voiced halted her in her tracks:

"That's *far enough*," he politely advised. His face was by now streaked with drying blood and the three scratches stood out like fresh furrows across an unploughed field. Lucy looked imploring at Father Deane. She had been so desperate to make physical contact with him. The priest looked back at her, his kind eyes shining behind his, as yet, unbroken spectacles.

"*Be strong Lucy*," he whispered. As he spoke he watched the Lord of the Now snatch up the small child and carry him, kicking and screaming past them all.

"*What are you going to do with him*?" Father Deane demanded, straining to see behind him. His manacles were too tight, and try as he might he couldn't twist around. "Lucy?" he implored. "*What* is happening to that child?"

Lucy's horror-struck face spoke volumes to him, but she was unable to answer as she watched the Lord of the Now, who was dragging the screaming boy towards the vast hole in the cavern wall.

"*Do you like science, priest?*"

the Lord of the Now randomly questioned. Father Deane made no response in his confusion.

"*Because if you do, then I'm sure you will appreciate the concept of experimentation,*"

he manically continued.

"Oh please *God* no!" Lucy was on her feet, seeing the Lord of the Now pick up the boy as though he weighed no more than a snowflake. Krinn gripped her shoulders, keeping her in place while ensuring she could not look away from the atrocity she was about to bear witness to.

"I have a hypothesis priest...that says the Gak Worm has broken its cycle, and no longer returns to its lair to feed."

With that he hurled the hapless child into the darkness of the hole. His screams receded into the blackness, curtailed entirely by a horrific noise of impact. Lucy sobbed in pity, and Father Deane, who had been unable to see anything of the child's distress, hung his head in shame.

The other Mist Children wept alone in their cages.

"Now..."

the Lord of the Now continued, dusting off his hands as though he had been forced to handle something repulsive.

"Let us see if my theory is correct."

He began to untie the bonds which chained Father Deane to the ground. After a few seconds he pulled the badly beaten priest to his feet, and spun him around to face the hole.

Krinn looked on with apparent interest, as the Still began gradually to inch further away from the hole.

"I do believe *you're wrong*," he whispered under his breath.

"Is that little boy alive?" Lucy stammered, her whole body aching from the pain of her distress.

"He will be breathing,"

the Lord of the Now lazily replied, as though he had practically forgotten the boy already.

"Though I dare say his back may have broken when he slipped..."

It happened in that instant. A blistering flash of red as the head of the Gak Worm appeared briefly at the entrance of the hole. It had taken the boy away in its monstrous jaws before anyone had time to react. Only the heady scent of its foul breath remained as it darted back into the impenetrable blackness of the tunnel.

The Still had begun screaming, and the Mist Children wailed in terror from the cages, creating a cacophony of total pandemonium that lasted for several minutes.

Father Deane and Lucy, utterly unsure of what they had just witnessed, kept their eyes fixed upon the entrance of the hole, fearing that the serpent would return to finish his meal.

"How vexing it is to be wrong,"

the Lord of the Now conceded.

"You can let them go Krinn,"

he informed his servant. Already he was walking away from them.

Cautiously Krinn released his hold on Lucy. To his surprise she stayed exactly where she was, transfixed like her companion by the gaping hole.

"What was that?" Father Deane breathed.

"That."

the Lord of the Now called over his shoulder,

"is the fate which awaits you both when I return!"

Lucy and Father Deane were too shocked by the events they'd already witnessed to respond to this remark.

The Still began crowding around them, propelling them back towards the cages. Father Deane's footsteps were shaky, and after a few seconds he collapsed into Lucy's arms, his breathing laboured.

"The priest will die," Krinn proclaimed, still lingering near the two prisoners. The Lord of the Now rested for a moment, turning back towards Krinn.

"You can leave them to their destiny. The Still will herd them back into their cages. I assure you she will be unable to make any further attempts to escape. Her sprit is broken, and you have crippled the priest with your lack of patience."

His triumph over Krinn was total, and the Servant of the Now made no attempt to contradict his master. Spinning his glaive once, he marched across the Hold to join him.

"It still concerns me, this random change in the Worm's patterns. Twice now it has failed to show up for feeding, yet today it comes. Why?"

"It is the new tunnel my Lord. Perhaps the Worm believes another of its kind is burrowing deeper below ground? It has been unsettled by it," Krinn suggested. The Lord of the Now seemed to consider this.

"I have already pondered such a theory, but we cannot be sure it's correct. Either way, the Worm grows ever more of an inconvenience with each passing day. When we return here from our victory tomorrow, we will regroup and attack the Worm, using the Hybrids if we have to. I have never attempted it before because we have never had enough Still to spare, but now…now I am certain we can destroy it."

Krinn looked unconvinced; he was watching the bats flying around the higher cages.

"I don't see *why* we have to kill it? Surely it is a useful tool to reduce the amount of captives we keep?" The Lord of the Now baulked at the suggestion.

"When I was Lord of the House there was no Gak Worm, the children we imprisoned fed only my own needs. The time of the second House is soon upon us and I intend to rule it solely, without outsiders. We will have Still on every street corner, in every town in Peter's world. They will lure all the children away, until that world has no future. Parents will be too frightened to have babies. There will be only now."

Krinn caught the hint of madness in his master's words.

"But what happens when we deprive another world of its children, what then?" he tentatively asked. The Lord of the Now threw up his arms in frustration.

"Krinn…You have no imagination. Then we move on, the next world…and then the next. There will always be more and it is my destiny to rule eternal in a childless universe."

He was possessed with the insanity of his scheme, and not for the first time Krinn feared that his master's obsessions had gone beyond even his own control, but he was forced to bow his head in agreement.

"The final cart of rubble should by now have reached the surface, my Hybrid's have cut through beneath Kilfanfyn Forest, and we are only a few miles from our destination. You will start to lead the army over ground within the hour. Be cautious Krinn. Surprise will be our greatest asset,"

he advised, turning on his heel and marching away from his second in command. Krinn watched him go, his face a mask of pure hatred.

⟡

Khynous Morf still looked imposing, even when viewed from such a distance through Ethanril's spyglass.

Peter struggled to keep the image in focus as Jessavarn continually shifted her weight upon her legs.

The horses were nervous.

Bayous Ridge was cold and deserted. Although the mid-morning sun was now shining brighter than it had in many years, the warmth still failed to repel the harsh wind-torn landscape. Even Ethanril appeared to be feeling the cold, and he watched Peter from atop Astervarn, with one hand clenching his multi-coloured coat tightly shut just under his chin. He was also listening.

Listening for the wild dogs, and even more importantly, he was listening for the Still.

Ethanril feared prolonged exposure in the open countryside of the Dark Realm and normally he would not have hesitated in one spot for this length of time, but Peter had insisted they stop. He had demanded to see Khynous Morf from the same distance that the Mist Children would have first gazed upon it, yet he refused to be drawn as to why.

"It's so beautiful," Peter finally admitted, lowering the spyglass and handing it back to the practically frozen Ethanril.

"It hasn't changed since the day I first saw it," Ethanril confessed, nodding his thanks as he took back the spyglass and tucked it away in his saddlebag. "It's only the snow that makes it look so different, but then again that's something you get used to over the years." He blew on his hands and took up the reins again. With a slight clicking of his tongue he dug his heels into Astervarn's side and the two began to ride at a gentle canter up the ridge. The snow was hard and crisp here, with only a few deep flurries left from the pounding storms of the previous night. Peter enjoyed the freshness of the breeze. It was the first time in his life he had ever breathed a truly unpolluted air, and the oxygen made him giddy. He had to keep a firm focus on steering Jessavarn forward, but the white horse seemed able to second guess his desires, and without difficulty mounted the ridge to the entranceway of the ancient fort.

Before they rode into the courtyard Ethanril brought them to pause again. He was still uncomfortable with the lack of interference from the enemy. He was highly aware that he had not picked up a single trace of them since their departure from Kilfanfyn Forest an hour before.

"I don't like it Peter," Ethanril warned. "The Lord of the Now knows that we have you with us, it is a victory which he cannot allow. We should not stay here too long," he advised, dismounting Astervarn, and allowing the white horse to graze near the fort entranceway. He kicked at the snow with his boot, helping to reveal some lush grass beneath.

Peter followed suit, casting a glance all around him at the snow smeared plains. His limited vision revealed nothing but beauty, and it was almost impossible to remember the previous day's flight across this same terrain.

They walked under the portcullis and Peter whistled with astonishment as he took in the courtyard that now spread out in front of him. Despite the ruination of many of the founding pillars and towers, Khynous Morf still looked like a stronghold of peace and beauty.

"You can almost imagine the history…" he began without thinking, and Ethanril looked away from him. "I'm sorry," Peter apologised. Ethanril did not respond, instead he walked a little way further into the courtyard before resting on the ledge of an empty window.

"Tell me honestly Peter…what does this remind you of?" he asked. Peter was slowly pirouetting around, taking in every ancient brick of the fort.

"When we were children…" he began, speaking to the heavens, "my Father used to take us walking in the hills of Wick Holm, my home village. High up on one of the west cliffs, there is a ruin. Not a fort…more likely it is the remains of a brick barn of some description. It's deserted, has no doors or windows, and in places the brickwork is crumbling so badly that you can move from room to room through impromptu doors that shouldn't exist there." Peter was now looking at Ethanril; he moved to join him on the ledge. "One winter, Annabel and I went up there when it had snowed. It was one of the few times we actually did something together as kids. Anyway, we spent the day in this ruin. Having snowball fights, and telling stories of an imagined history that these ruins might have had. Annabel said that it was once the stronghold for thousands of the bravest fighting men in the whole kingdom, a sanctuary where the lost and the lonely could come if they needed to find food and shelter. She called it Khynous Morf…it was a name she invented to mean kinship and warmth." Peter smiled, his warm breath exhaling in thick clouds into the cold air as he spoke. Ethanril looked sorrowfully at him.

"And what about you Peter? What did you say the ruin was?"

Peter had never seen such an expression pass across Ethanril's face before. The young warrior seemed to age by twenty years, as though the effects of the House had finally caught up with him and he was being prematurely wasted by the ravages of time. When Peter finally began to speak, the change had passed and a light snow was beginning to fall.

"I told her that it was a ruin because a vast army had attacked it. I said that the bravest warriors of Khynous Morf lost their lives that day as they battled to protect their wives and children." Ethanril nodded, as though the news had not been unexpected. He rose up from the ledge and walked in a meandering half-circle to the centre of the courtyard. The snow was wetting his skin, plastering his hair down upon his forehead and causing him to shiver.

Peter watched him walk like a solitary actor across a vast empty amphitheatre. The courtyard lay thick with ice and he was surprised by Ethanril's grace of movement. He looked like a matador striding out alone to meet his destiny.

The sky above Khynous Morf was a blanket of white, as though all the elements had been removed from the air leaving only an empty canvas upon which a new image could be drawn.

In one florid movement Ethanril drew out his broadsword. The action almost stopped Peter's heart as he watched his companion twirl the great sword in a blistering arc of steel and bring its point to rest upon the icy floor. With a deft twist of his wrist, Ethanril dragged the blade across the ground, grooving a deep cut in a perfectly straight line in front of him. Once it was done he sheathed his sword, and turning to face Peter he placed both feet directly upon the line.

"This is how close to the edge I am Peter," Ethanril explained. His voice sounded strained as though he were struggling to keep it in check. "A few more pushes and I will be over it. Take a good look at this line my friend," he advised. "That represents my life for the last nine years. Since Annabel left us we have all been living this close to the edge of the precipice. Every day we have run, fought and just about escaped being pushed completely over it. Until we found you, we had no one to help us move away from this line of death. But now you're here Peter…and although I appreciate your honesty today, all you have done is move me those final few steps over the edge." Ethanril broke off. He was glancing down at his feet, as though contemplating taking the last step. "Look at you Peter. I'm right on this line, and you…you're watching it all from a comfortable distance. Safe at home, letting your characters do all the work…is that the true purpose of a writer? Can they do nothing for themselves? We need your help Peter…I need your help. You asked me to bring you to Khynous Morf, and I've brought you here. Now I ask you to finish your story. Tell me please, before I fall off this line forever…where is Annabel? Where did she go?" His voice cracked at that last moment, and Ethanril collapsed to his knees. He landed almost comically on his behind, but he was sobbing now, and it was all Peter could do, to not cry with him. He rose from the ledge, running to join him at the line. He sat cross legged in front of Ethanril, and the line lay between them, a physical representation of the unspoken story Peter was about to tell.

"The week she must have written me that letter…that was one of the best weeks I ever spent with Annabel. She was so excited about Christmas that year, more excited than she used to be when we were children. From the first day of December it was all she ever talked about. I think I flattered myself into thinking that it was because we were so much closer now. That maybe she was looking forward to spending Christmas like a proper family, unlike previous years when the two of us would spend the whole day practically not speaking to each other for hours at a time. I doubt in hindsight that that was the reason…" Peter allowed his sentence to tail off, hoping that Ethanril would pick up the thread. He needn't have worried.

"I'm sure that was certainly a part of it Peter," he began, his voice having found some of its former strength. "We knew nothing here of Christmas until Annabel began to explain the concept to us. The very last time she visited we had been having a mock Christmas celebration…I fear that may have been why she would have mentioned it so much." Peter was nodding but a thought had also occurred to him.

"The first time I dreamt of Myfanwy…without Sufi's help, I walked into the farmhouse and it was all decorated for a Christmas feast."

Ethanril nodded sadly.

"That is how I remember Myfanwy before we first heard the Still begin to scream. It was a truly beautiful night," Ethanril reminisced.

Peter listened quietly as Ethanril spoke of the dancing and the presents that they had all shared, and finally his parting kiss with Annabel. He seemed strangely shy to reveal these more intimate details in front of Peter, and for the first time in Peter's life he felt truly like Annabel's brother, meeting a prospective suitor. The feeling thrilled him momentarily, and then the sadness returned.

"The day after would have been December thirteenth and Annabel and I were going to a party at the house of a mutual friend in Great Wick Holm, that's the neighbouring town to ours. Her name was Laurie and she was one of the few real friends we had both made during our time at school. I think Annabel was quite nervous to go, as lots of people would be there whom neither of us had seen for a long time. We were never that popular at school to be honest, and there is nothing more difficult than having to bump into people who made your life hell while you were there, but now act as though you are all suddenly best friends. When we arrived at Laurie's house we were forty minutes late because of the weather that night. Our parents had been strongly against us even attempting the journey. I just don't know what had gone wrong with the weather that day. A storm had blown up from the coast by mid-afternoon. Howling winds and lashing rain…the whole caboodle. Weather warnings were springing up on local television and radio shows, and we honestly thought the party would be called off. I guess we should have phoned up and cancelled, but we had both been looking forward to going for so long, and I think there was an element of not wanting to back down from a challenge. In some perverse way I think we actually relished the chance of seeing those old school bullies and finally standing up to them. So against everyone's better judgement I drove us to the party."

Ethanril had been listening intently, but interrupted at this moment to ask Peter about certain elements of this story. Peter was more than happy to explain the concept of cars to a perplexed Ethanril. Eventually he seemed to have a grasp of the basics and Peter continued with a heavy heart.

"The party went surprisingly well, although to be honest we spent most of the night huddled together talking in one corner of Laurie's parents' house. The more we talked that night, the more I felt Annabel was on the cusp of telling me something very important. She had been slightly agitated all evening, but I had just put that down to nerves, but the more I thought about it in the months that followed, the more convinced I became that she was reaching out to me for help that night, help which I was unable to give her because I never found out what she had wanted to tell me…" He broke off, his throat painfully dry as though he had been walking through the sands of a vast desert.

He swallowed for several seconds, trying to lubricate his vocal cords again.

"We left Laurie's house a little after one o'clock in the morning. The storm had seemingly intensified, and driving back along dark country lanes was an absolute nightmare. We barely spoke in the car; it was all we could do to just concentrate on fighting our way home through the storm. The view through my windscreen was so limited because of the pouring rain. But I remember the sky that night, more than anything else that happened. It turned the most extraordinary colours, even Annabel commented upon it. One second it would be intensely black and overcast, and then the next it would be like a shifting mass of purple blocks. I'd never seen anything like it...we have a phenomenon on Earth called Aurora Borealis. It is series of folded bands and rays caused by solar flares and 'low-density' holes in the sun's corona. It basically causes strange colours to appear in the sky, but this kind of effect only happens close to the Northern and Southern hemisphere of the Earth. Believe me; nothing like this ever happens in Wick Holm! But it did on this night, and I have had no explanation for it until the void opened in my own living room when Sufi last came to visit me. The colours were exactly the same as the ones I saw in the sky that night." Peter broke off, caught off guard by the intensity of Ethanril's gaze at this point. It was clear that this news had startled him.

"But that was years before Sufi made her first journey into your world using the void." Ethanril whispered as though he were merely thinking out loud.

"Ethan." Peter snapped his fingers in front of his companion's face, attempting to bring him out of this trance. Ethanril looked back at him, half-distracted, before finally acknowledging him.

"Carry on Peter."

"I remember very little of the events that followed," Peter confessed. "Even though this was only nine years ago, I'm afraid my memory has blanked out crucial parts of the story. All I can tell you is we were driving so slowly down those country lanes it was almost impossible for us to have skidded off the road..." At this Ethanril shuddered. He had practically guessed the outcome of Peter's story, even in the short time he had been listening, but the shock that he was actually going to be proved right, terrified him beyond anything he had ever felt before.

"I really don't know how to tell you the rest of this," Peter said honestly. His face was creased with the pain of the memory and it seemed to mirror Ethanril's countenance at that precise moment. There was nothing Ethanril could have said to ease the situation; he merely looked imploringly at him.

"There are police records which say that we hit a patch of water or ice and skidded off the road, but although my memory of events is sketchy, I know that isn't the way it happened." He took a deep breath and then, exhaling more calmly, he continued: "Someone stepped in front of the car. Of that I am certain. We were turning a particularly tight corner; the road had narrowed so much that only one vehicle at a time could possibly have passed at that one point. On either side there were hedgerows, obscuring the views of the neighbouring fields. I don't know why one person would be out walking that late at night, in literally the middle of nowhere. But someone was...a figure; I think it was a man, stepped straight out in front of the car. All I remember is flooring the brakes and twisting the wheel to avoid him." Peter was shaking from the confession. It had been years since he had spoken of the car crash, and even now his body could still feel the impact as the car had lurched into the hedgerow and impacted against a wooden telegraph pole. Ethanril was shaking too; his own limited conception of such a crash was enough to bring harrowing scenes to his mind.

"I was knocked unconscious instantly, and I'm told I slipped into a coma within a few hours of arriving at the hospital. That's a place where sick people are taken to be looked after," he added, seeing Ethanril's confusion.

"Annabel?" It came out of Ethanril's soul, like a hopeful whisper from a child seeking news on a missing relative. Peter shook his head.

"She's dead…" Ethanril cried, his heart feeling as though a thousand spears were protruding from it. Peter looked up in alarm, seizing Ethanril as the young man's shoulders began to shake with panic.

"No…no Ethan, she isn't dead. I promise…I swear to you that she isn't dead. Annabel is alive…she hasn't left you…she is just very ill." Peter fell over the words, trying to calm his friend, but at the same time avoid lying to him any more than was necessary.

"How ill is she? Why does she not come to see us? Peter please…if she needs me you must take me to her." All Ethanril's rage and anger towards Peter had melted like the ice around Carrastorc. He was weeping uncontrollably; his usually rational sense had all but abandoned him. Even his body seemed to be out of control. He was half-sitting, half-standing with shaking legs and a desperation behind his eyes which Peter had never seen before.

"I can't take you there…" Peter said quietly, wrestling Ethanril back into a sitting position. He looked ready to bolt past Peter again, and this time a sudden strength gripped Peter.

"I can't Ethanril…calm down." Both were definite orders, and the power of Peter's tone seemed to quickly cut through Ethanril's panic. The tears still fell, but calm had descended.

For a while the only sound was Ethanril's breathing which grew ever heavier. His body slowly began to stop shaking, and he wiped at his eyes in a mixture of sorrow and anger.

"She is in a coma Ethanril. Her head was badly jarred by the impact and she lost consciousness before the ambulance arrived.

She has been stable ever since, but she hasn't opened her eyes or spoken a word in these last nine years." Peter brushed away his own tears and fought to keep control. "I have visited her every week since the accident, spoke to her, read to her and prayed that she would one day wake up. I've stayed at home and looked after my Mother and Father who needed me more than ever in these last few years, and I've been blessed to get to know my sister from her writing, and her drawing and a very special gift that was passed to me on the night of the accident." He paused shakily. "I dream now...the way I was always so envious of. Only now can I fully understand the powers my sister had, and believe me, I am truly sorry that I was so desperate for this gift. I never took the time to realise that just maybe it was as much a curse as it was a blessing. My sister was and still is an incredible human being; she had a heart that loved everything and everyone above herself. I learnt all this far too late, and I have paid and continue to pay the price for all I did against her. But I love her Ethanril, I promise you that; and I understand now that she did need my help...that she does need my help, and I don't intend to let her down again," Peter said, practically quivering with resolve.

Ethanril still looked in a state of total shock. He stared at Peter for a while, then up at the sky and finally back to the ground before he spoke:

"I have always feared she was dead. All these years without her, something in my heart told me she was dead. Because she would have come back to us...she would have come back to me. Towards the end, our conversations often touched on the idea of one of us leaving the Dark Realm. She was so adamant that it shouldn't be me. She kept on telling me I still had so much to do here. I would get angry with her, I hated to hear her talk of leaving...but I realise now that she was genuinely frightened. All the preparations that she was making towards the end Peter, writing your letter, and creating that second entrance to the Dark Realm;

she truly knew the day would come when she couldn't help us anymore…but you could. You see, all the time you were wrong Peter. Annabel didn't keep the Dark Realm from you. No. She was preparing you to save it." Ethanril rose up, he tilted his head back and roared in grief for a second, then brushed his hands through his wet hair, and messing it into a tangle of locks.

"She is still here Ethan…you know that. Despite all your gut instincts telling you she had gone from this world, you must have felt that her presence had lingered here." Peter watched his face as he stood up, and Ethanril almost smiled.

"She is the breeze that blows warm on the coldest of days. She is the little bird that sings loudest in the morning sun. She is the water I bathe my wounds in, she is the beating of my heart, she is my princess and she always will be," Ethanril said with absolute conviction, and Peter nodded his agreement.

"While she still breathes, she will always be part of this world. You say it is my presence that has affected the weather here, but I disagree. That is my sister's doing. The change in the wind that kept the fires at bay in Myfanwy while we escaped…that was Annabel. The melting of the ice at Carrastorc is my sister's work. She is reaching her mind through into this dark time, and bringing us some much needed light. She can still help us Ethanril and we must call upon her strength if we are to defeat the Lord of the Now once and for all." Peter stepped away from Ethanril's line and faced his companion with his heart and soul ablaze with hope.

"You have a plan Peter?" It was more than Ethanril could have hoped for, and Peter smiled assuredly.

"I have the beginnings of one, but there is much we must do," Peter conceded. Ethanril seemed unsure how to proceed; he didn't want Peter to just leave without resolving their dispute.

"Peter." Ethanril's voice had the same urgent quality which always caused Peter to look up. "You are a very brave man, braver than you give yourself credit for. To talk to me the way you have today, knowing how I would react to everything you had to tell me, and yet to still have the nerve to see it through to the end. I am humbled by you. I confess you are not what I expected, you are so different from Annabel, but you do yourself a great injustice to say she had such a unique loving heart. You have one as well Peter, I assure you. I am a man who believes in second chances. I can see that you made mistakes in your judgement, and that for the most part those mistakes were made unknowingly. Until you first saw Sufi, I'm sure you must have thought that all of this was just fantasy, because Annabel had kept the Dark Realm's secrets hidden from you. I hope now you can see what we have had to learn to cope with, and why your stories have become our lives. There is one thing more I must know Peter?" He looked concernedly upon his companion and Peter's open expression urged him to ask without fear. "What will you do if we survive this? Will you go home and continue your stories. Will the Dark Realm be threatened again? Or will we all simply fade away?" Ethanril looked slightly whimsical, as though he were expecting Peter to apologise to him and say his goodbyes.

"My sister created the Dark Realm on the basis that everyone who is lost deserves a place to go. Her principles are faultless, and the Dark Realm is as real now as my home on Earth. If we do survive this Ethan, if…and I make it home; I will tell this story in its entirety, so the Dark Realm will be a lesson to everyone who is careless with their thoughts. But I will write no further stories of it, or its inhabitants. The Final Days of Forget Me House has only one destination, and that is to die by fire. You will all be safe here, I promise you. Free of Annabel and myself you can rebuild this place and make it the world my sister always wanted it to be. If that is my promise to you Ethan, then you must also promise me that you will carry on after we have left you?" Peter asked. Ethanril looked at him long and hard, as though to make certain that Peter was sure of everything he had just said. Finally he pulled off one of his leather riding gloves and offered Peter his right hand. He held it across the sword line, and Peter immediately seized it. They shook firmly and then embraced. The moment lasted only seconds but when they separated both of them felt as though a great weight had been lifted from their shoulders.

"This line of yours Ethan," Peter said, indicating the sword groove. Ethanril was still standing close to the edge of it, while Peter stood several feet away.

"Are you going to pull us away from it Peter?" Ethanril challenged him, and Peter gave him a genuine smile. He shook his head, and then in four quick steps he moved to Ethanril's side of the line.

"No. I'm going to cross it!" he announced, and a thrill shot through Ethanril's nervous system. He knew immediately that Peter was now ready to face any challenge, but he was still unsure how they could proceed from this point.

"We must return to camp. I have to tell each and every one of the Mist Children the story I have just told you. I'll gather them all together and then I can answer any questions they may have." Peter sounded positive, though audibly nervous.

"We will speak to them together Peter. Believe me they will understand, though I confess it may take them by surprise, but they will trust you Peter...because I trust you."

"I'm not sure Taime will feel that way," Peter moaned. Ethanril shook his head and put his arm around Peter's shoulders in a friendly manner. They began to walk towards the two white horses.

"Taime will be very hurt Peter. He loved Annabel very much, and I hurt him inadvertently, by being the one she chose to love back. That is something which I will never be forgiven for, and I understand that. But Taime is one of the best and bravest warriors in the group. He often feels overshadowed by Mundo because I spend so much time with him, but if I'm honest Peter, Taime has the greater brain and is the finer swordsman. You must just forgive him his temperament," Ethanril apologised. Peter mounted Jessavarn, his body filled with trepidation.

"Well…if I could plagiarize one of Fess's catchphrases?" Ethanril requested, spurring Astervarn on. "What could *possibly* go wrong?" he shouted over his shoulder, as Peter bit his own lip and gingerly tugged on Jessavarn's reins.

14

The Harvester

Wick Holm looked like a ghost town.

It was eleven fifteen in the morning, and the normally bustling streets of the little coastal town remained utterly deserted.

Samantha Raynor had never known the town so quiet. She was afraid that a global disaster had struck while she'd slept, and it felt eerily as though she could be the last human being left alive.

Standing in the middle of Wick Holm village Green, there wasn't another person anywhere in sight.

Not so much as a curtain twitched.

The weather was also a cause for concern. The snow of the previous few weeks had finally abated, and been replaced by a strange inclement feel to the weather. Even now, despite the fact that Samantha was dressed for winter in walking boots, jeans and a huge furry jumper, she felt almost as if she were too hot. Yet the sun was nowhere in sight. The sky was as blank as lining paper and the only sound to break the infernal silence was the cry of a magpie in a distant field.

Samantha had left her house early that morning. She had managed to sleep for six hours thanks to the sleeping pill, but had awoken feeling groggy and ill-tempered. Her head throbbed and a strange feeling had remained with her ever since her nightmare about the intruder.

She had showered quickly, and gathered up her files on Annabel. There seemed little point in delaying her visit to Patient 143's parents. The longer she left it, the harder it would be speak with them, and Samantha was a lady who believed in seizing the moment.

She had stumbled about her badly lit flat, trying on various combinations of clothes, but nothing seemed to fit the oppressive morning. She told herself it was December, and therefore the middle of winter. No point in dressing for summer. So she had opted for the arctic look, but had begun regretting it the minute she left the house.

She was appalled at the state of her driveway that morning. The thick sludgy snow which remained strewn over her front lawn and pathway was now covered in thick soot which looked appallingly dark and foul.

As Samantha trudged her way into Wick Holm she noted various tracks of this self-same soot littering the road side. It was possible that a heavy goods vehicle or a road gritter had passed that way and deposited vast sections of its load across the streets. Either way she was already contemplating a letter to the local council by the time she reached the village green.

It was here that she first saw the poster.

In the centre of the green, attached with thick police tape to the maypole was a photocopied picture of a young woman.

It had been taken in the Village Inn on what looked to be a New Year's Eve. Despite the poor quality of the image, it was easy to tell that the girl was extremely attractive. She had long brown hair curling over her shoulders, and she was pouting mockingly for the mysterious photographer.

Beneath the picture the police had issued a short statement which named her as Lucy Doran and stated that she had been missing from Wick Holm for two days. There was a contact number underneath this, for Superintendent Toland, if anyone had any information they were to call immediately.

Samantha felt strangely uneasy seeing the poster. She vaguely recognised the young woman from seeing her around the village, but Samantha certainly couldn't claim to have known her. It wasn't this which made her feel so strange; it was the fact that the poster was up in the first place.

In all of Samantha's time in Wick Holm, she had never known anyone go missing. She harked back to Mary Graham, crying at the loss of her friend Jean Candicote. It was all suddenly horribly weird. Something sinister had happened in Wick Holm, something which no one could explain, and that was why the once bustling streets were now deserted.

A further shock lay in store for Samantha when she wandered up one of the twisting back streets that led to Ivy Meredith's Tearoom, and discovered it was shut.

The blinds were pulled down in the front windows, giving the shop an eerily derelict feel. The front door was plastered with the same police poster of Lucy Doran's smiling face, which seemed to be staring back at Samantha as though she were haunting her.

Samantha hopefully tried the door, but it was bolted tight shut, and the noise she made jarring it, echoed up and down the deserted street.

The wind was blowing harshly down the backstreet, and Samantha began to move away from the shop, huddling inside her coat as the freezing chill surrounded her.

"Samantha?"

The voice had reached her on the rush of the wind, as though carried far across distant lands. Samantha felt a pain in her chest at the exact same moment she heard the voice.

It was a girl.

Turning round in the hope of seeing someone she recognised, Samantha almost screamed when she discovered no one behind her in the street.

She tried to get a hold of her racing heartbeat and quickly turned in a complete circle to see who had called to her. As she completed her turn she saw a single figure dart from a doorway further up the street and disappear around the corner.

She was running before she could fully understand what she was doing.

"Hello?" she called, turning the corner into another deserted backstreet. The wind cut into her face, and pulled at her coat, trying to rip it from her body. Samantha ignored it, racing down the street in desperate pursuit of the figure. As she passed rows of deserted houses, she grew ever more agitated.

Up ahead she saw the figure again. It was turning sharply and darting down an alleyway. Samantha increased her pace, feeling her lungs begin to burn with adrenaline. She hadn't run like this since she had been at school and the experience was strangely exhilarating.

Before she reached the alleyway she felt something grip her shoulders. It was such an immediate physical touch that she actually stopped painfully in her tracks, twisting around to face her attacker.

There was no one there, but to her horror she could see two patches of soot on either side of her shoulders, as though someone had clamped their dirty hands there.

Then she heard screams.

They went straight through her like an abrasive scraping of metal. She called out in alarm, and was forced to clap her hand over her mouth as she saw the source of the apparent scream.

It was an old man pushing a trolley loaded with newspapers.

He had rounded the corner further up ahead, and was clearly struggling to keep his supermarket trolley in a straight line as the wheels continually clipped the cobblestones of the street. The screams turned out to be the wheels of the trolley, which desperately required oiling, and were protesting harshly against the terrain.

Samantha stood stupefied, the original stranger now totally forgotten as she watched mesmerized, the approaching trolley.

It was the most surreal sight she had ever seen. The trolley was full of newspapers, a seemingly endless amount, and each time the wind blew, it caught the top layer and sent them cascading across the street like confetti. This appeared not to affect the old man, who smiled maniacally in a horribly familiar way.

For a second she couldn't place it, and then suddenly she was turning on her heel and running.

He had the same smile as the young man who had invaded her bedroom.

She turned desperately into the alleyway, which was almost pitch black for no explainable reason.

"Hurry Samantha...the wild dogs are loose."

The female voice advised her, and Samantha rushed into the blackness as the distant sound of baying dogs drifted in on the breeze.

Almost immediately the alleyway filled with a strange phosphorescent light, which appeared to be emanating from the graffiti that littered the alley walls.

Children of the Mist

Blazed out from the dull brickwork in sudden flares of bright luminous green spray-paint. Samantha felt strangely calmed by this incongruous message, yet still she kept running.

Up ahead she saw the figure again. It was a young girl with a head of fiery auburn curls which looked brighter than any colour Samantha had ever seen in her life. As she stared into the middle distance, trying to make out the features of the girl, a howling gale rampaged through the alleyway, carrying with it a thousand newspapers, one of which plastered itself to Samantha's face. As she peeled it off with the intention of throwing it behind her, her attention was suddenly caught by the headline.

She stopped running in order to read it, and the weather appeared to oblige her. The wind died away to nothing and the alley suddenly lit with a hazy sunlight.

The newspaper, titled: 'Wick Holm Herald' was dated December 15th nine years previously and the front page carried an alarming headline:

'Brother and Sister Fatally Injured in Car Crash. Police Appeal for Witnesses.'

Samantha stared at the paper, and as she read of the car crash which she was now all too familiar with, her eye was drawn to a black and white picture taken at the scene at the time. It showed the wreckage of Peter Bettany's car, and the police gathered around the scene. In the background an ambulance stood ominously waiting with its back doors open, and two medics were hoisting a stretcher containing a young girl's body onto the ambulance.

Samantha felt her heart breaking as she saw for the first time the full horror of the events that had taken place.

In that instant she felt the wind tug at the paper, and as she desperately grabbed hold of it with both hands to prevent it being snatched away, it tore straight down the centre as though a lightning bolt had struck it and revealed the face of the young girl standing directly in front of her

Samantha screamed when she saw her horribly pale face, and puffy eyes staring directly at her. The girl was dressed from head to toe entirely in a worn hospital gown. Her arm was bleeding badly were she had torn out a feeding tube, and her mouth was dark at the edges, as though anaemia had drained her lips of all blood.

Annabel clamped her hand across Samantha's mouth to quell her screaming, and pulled her close so she could whisper in her ear.

"I'm in danger Samantha…you must help me."

Her voice was surprisingly calm and clear, and incredible warmth emanated from her touch. Samantha felt filled up with love in that one instant and her screams died to a whisper. Annabel was practically hugging her, and Samantha didn't even mind the blood which was dripping all over her clothes.

"My brother needs my help; the Unsleeping One knows that…he has left one of his servants here to kill me. You must help me Sam. You're the only one who can." At this Annabel's grip became suddenly painful, and Samantha felt herself being drawn inexorably into the swirling pools of the girl's hypnotically emerald eyes. "It will come for you too Sam, stay in company…keep close to water."

With this final cryptic warning, Annabel placed a single kiss on Samantha's cheek, and then she was gone. Samantha stood alone in the dark feeling as though she had just danced with a ghost.

The nightmarish screaming began again, and behind her Samantha felt the heavy breathing of some hellish beast. She began to run down the now collapsing alleyway, but it was never-ending, as though she were lost in a dark labyrinth with no hope of finding the exit.

Whatever was pursuing her, it matched her step for step. She daren't turn around lest fear of the sight of the beast should petrify her into submission.

Then she felt it upon her back. It collided with her like a flying barrel, knocking her to the ground and actually bowling her over on impact. She landed awkwardly, twisting her ankle painfully. She shook her hair out of her face and screamed in terror as the beast padded slowly towards her.

It was a Still.

The self-same Still that Peter and Sufi had trapped beneath the industrial bins outside his flat block, though Samantha was, of course, unaware of this.

When the void had returned for Krinn and the rest of the army, the Still had been unable to free itself in time and had been forced to remain behind. It was horrifically mutilated from the impact of the bins, and because it had never been in contact with such an alien metal before, it had been unable to repair itself. One arm hung limply from its left side causing it to lean tortuously to the left as though it had suffered a stroke. The right side of its face was horrifically staved inwards, giving it the gory appearance that it had been shot in the face at close range. But its mouth still gleamed with a ferocity Samantha had never encountered before, and its senses continually sought the Sacred Mother with all their skill.

The trembling girl in front of it reeked of Annabel.

Samantha shuddered with total panic. She felt as though her brain were actually shutting down. Death now had a physical form, and it had come in the shape of this monstrosity in front of her.

There was no escaping it.

The Still shuffled forward, dragging its arm sickeningly across the alley floor. Its sightless head leaned at a curious angle, as though it were waiting for her to make some sort of move. Behind it the walls of the alley fell away, like the ending of an era of peace, revealing a white skyline of eternal nothing.

Samantha closed her eyes, willing herself unconscious to block out the hideousness of her demise.

"Samantha?"

It was a female voice again, but she refused to open her eyes. Not even patient 143 could save her from this monster.

"Good lord you're bleeding!" The now concerned voice continued.

Samantha felt strangely groggy, and then faintly she experienced a tugging on her clothes. It was too horrible to imagine, the creature was ripping her apart.

She woke up screaming in torment, throwing off Ivy Meredith's offer of support and backing away in a maddened rage. She collided heavily with the door of a house, and this made her shout out in pain and terror.

"Goodness me Sam! It's me...Ivy Meredith...you used to treat my phlebitis leg when I came to Great Wick Holm hospital." Ivy blurted out, hoping she hadn't just antagonised a clearly delusional woman.

Samantha screamed again as she struggled to calm herself down. It took her a minute to realise she was back outside the tearoom. She stared about her, fearful that this too, was all just a dream.

Seeing Ivy rolling up her skirt to reveal the purple markings on her leg, a sight which Samantha had seen many times before in her surgery room at the hospital, brought her back to reality in an instant.

"Oh! Mrs Meredith! Do forgive me please, I must have terrified you!" From the look on Ivy's face it was clear that this was the year's biggest understatement. "I must have fallen asleep...I had no idea I was so tired." Samantha was babbling and she was very aware that none of her explanations made sense. Ivy was still looking slightly distrustful of her. She allowed the hem of her skirt to fall, and stood up straight, very slowly in case Samantha pulled a gun on her.

"I heard you trying the door...I was in the bath at the time, so I couldn't answer it, but I came down about half an hour later and you were slumped in the doorway. I thought you'd had a heart attack the way you were shivering. Your arm is bleeding by the way; I think perhaps you cut it as you fell," Ivy pointed out. "Come in for a moment and I'll get you some antiseptic and a plaster." Ivy was already turning to gingerly unlock her front door, but Samantha stopped her.

"It's ok Ivy," she hesitantly said pulling off her overcoat quickly; to her concealed horror she noticed it was also thick with soot. "It's not my blood," she helpfully clarified, looking at the arm of her coat, which had a thick stain of dried blood upon it.

Annabel's blood.

Ivy Meredith looked as though she were on the verge of screaming for the police and running as far away from Samantha as her swollen legs would carry her.

"I mean it is my blood!" Samantha tried to pacify her quickly. "Only its old blood, from when I cut myself…in the garden…yesterday…" She tailed off as her excuses dried up.

Ivy gave her a weak smile. She had begun ferreting in her bag for her keys, and appeared in a hurry to go back indoors.

"Isn't it terrible what happened here the other night?" Samantha tried desperately to change the conversation. Ivy however, for once didn't seem in a gossiping mood.

"Yes!" she said rather stiffly, turning the key in her lock. "The whole village appears to have gone quite mad!" With that she stepped inside.

Samantha rushed to the door before she could close it.

"Ivy, I am truly sorry about that. I honestly don't know what came over me. Please don't think I meant you any harm…" Her eye was suddenly caught by the poster of Lucy Doran again. "I take it you know the missing girl?" she asked tentatively.

The comment seemed to distract Ivy from closing the door, and for a second she lingered in the hallway.

"Lucy. She was, is my lodger. A lovely girl…not married yet, but…" Ivy broke off, her eyes moistening briefly. "I just want her to come home safe," she briskly added, turning to shut the door.

"Ivy…please wait. I'm sure she's safe, she may just have been frightened by the storm the other night…I need to speak to Jayne and Cyril Bettany. Do you know where I might find them?" Samantha found herself asking. Ivy looked suddenly interested.

"Well! The police think their son…Peter, has eloped with Lucy! I ask you! Lucy has much better taste than that! There's a lovely young lad…a fisherman from the village, Gerald…something…adodarwhatsit! Oh I'm worse than Father Deane for names. Anyway, he has made his intentions quite clear!" Ivy was just getting into her stride, and Samantha knew she had to curtail this.

"It's just that I have a rather urgent message for them from Dr Kidson, you know, the doctor who has been overseeing Annabel these last few years?"

This seemed to do the trick and Ivy swiftly changed tack.

"Oh! Of course!" she mumbled. "They'll be in the Village Inn I would have thought. Tony Simpson has offered to put them up for a few days while the police investigate their flat block. Obviously that isn't common knowledge but I happened to overhear…" Samantha held up her hand.

"I must rush Mrs Meredith. I do apologise again for my shocking behaviour earlier. I have to go and see them straight away though…you do understand?" Samantha explained, and with a wave she began to retreat down the side street.

Ivy watched her go, shaking her head in puzzlement. Then she quickly locked and bolted her front door, deciding to phone Winnie Bloomer in case she'd heard anything in the last few hours.

Samantha hurried back along the streets towards the Village Inn. She was at a loss to explain what was happening to her, but something instinctively told her she needed Annabel's parents to help her. To what end, she couldn't begin to explain.

∽

Krinn snapped his head upright from the desk. His eyes had glazed completely over as though a spider had netted them together with a thick web. He slid his chair backwards in anger and covered his face with his hands.

But the pain would not leave him alone.

It burrowed into his head like a parasitic tick. Nothing could have subdued it at that moment other than death itself.

"Leave me," he cried out in desperation, talking out loud to the pressure in his mind. He dug his palms deeply into his eyes, trying to blind himself.

All he could see was ice.

It moved across him, blocking his exit to the surface. He saw the shimmering reflection of Ethanril gazing down at him, his arm outstretched to save his life. But Krinn had refused the gesture, preferring death to defeat.

But he had not died.

That honour had been denied him by freak water eddies which brought him free of the compacted ice flow, and he broke the surface of Carrastorc with lungs blazing like fire.

But even that pain, the pain of total defeat, was nothing compared to this.

"*Why must I suffer so?*" he begged the darkness. His breathing quickened and he fought down the panic in his heart.

On the desk in front of him rested a steaming jug containing a foul smelling purple liquid, which he greedily guzzled down as though it were some sort of elixir of life.

The hot liquid burnt his throat on the way down but it seemed to calm his heaving chest. When he was finished he hurled the musty jug at the chamber wall, relishing the sound as it shattered into a thousand pieces.

Krinn was alone in his private chamber, an annexe room which led directly from the Lord of the Now's throne room. It was a place he rarely visited, only when he felt the need to be completely alone.

He almost laughed at himself.

He was always completely alone.

But he had the strangest dreams. Sometimes when he slept, which was a rarity in itself, he would see vast open stretches of road, similar to the kind he had seen in Peter's world, which burrowed into the distance, burning beneath a merciless alien sun. He felt like he was the last human alive at these moments, a Stranger standing alone on an open highway, awaiting his next victim. The dreams were so vivid he could feel the heat from the sun on his face, and often taste the blood of any would-be victim whom he might meet along the way. Always he dreamt of death.

Death and the Pig-Beast.

Ever since his first encounter with the monster, when it had gored his arm so badly, he had formed an inextricable link with it. He knew he was destined to face that creature once again, and he relished the challenge.

His master feared the beast...even Ethanril feared it.

But Krinn did not.

He had no capacity for fear of anything outside of the House. It was all just alien to him.

Yet he could not explain why.

He feared the Still and his master, but nothing else.

He looked around his small chamber. It was dimly lit by two burning torches which rested upon metal clasps. It had a single ash desk which he used mainly as a dining table. His clothes and weapons hung from a variety of hooks on the far walls.

It was as blank a canvas as his own soul.

He rose from the chair, his sinewy body suddenly possessed by a need to move. He was wearing only his black trousers as he had been in the process of dressing when the first wave of nausea had assailed him.

It was caused by the void.

It was still open despite Sufi having returned to the Dark Realm.

A Still had been accidentally left behind, something which seemed to thrill The Lord of the Now, but caused Krinn only more mental harm. The slightest disturbance in the void affected him.

He knew the Still was hunting Samantha Raynor.

The name meant nothing to Krinn, yet twice now he had felt himself drawn into her path. He had no conception of her connection to the original Sacred Mother, yet she did have a familiarity that disturbed him.

For the time being he ignored the pain. Dressing with a measure of pride, he pulled on his light chain mail and covered it with a jet black shirt. He then spent some time adjusting his all encompassing black cloak which concealed everything from prying eyes.

The three cuts across the right side of his face had, by now, congealed with blood. They looked raw and painful, and would leave prominent scar tissue even when they had fully healed, but Krinn ignored the throbbing pain. He removed his glaive from the rack upon which it rested and turned just as the door to his chamber swung open.

A Still sat hunched in the doorway, awaiting his command. Krinn felt his master's ever-present will spurring him forward. It was time for the army to march from Stilfanwyn Chasm.

It was time for Krinn to meet his destiny.

∽

It was the silence that Peter couldn't handle.

He had listened to the protests. He had deflected some of the criticism. He had begged them all for forgiveness and admitted his own sins. He had cried when they had cried, and he had been humbled by their comments.

But Taime had sat in absolute silence throughout.

He had become statuesque in composure, and would just sit staring straight at Peter as though he were frozen in time.

They had all been sitting around the campfire in the clearing for over two hours, as both Peter and Ethanril held council.

Everyone was present to finally hear the truth.

Peter had doubted his voice had the strength to last the entire retelling of the story, but he found an inner courage which allowed him to go beyond his shaking nerves and the tightness of his throat, and explain everything with a certain degree of clarity which had been lacking when he had originally told this story to Ethanril.

Sufi had interrupted the most. Her emotions raged during Peter's confession, and as the one member of the group who had grown closest to him, she felt she could ask the more personal questions.

Fess and Pigeon were initially surprised by the revelations, but as Peter's story wore on, like Ethanril before them, they gradually found a grudging respect for Peter's honesty and character. His mistakes were after all, understandable.

Mundo recognised the continued change in Peter's character since his first arrival in the Dark Realm. He had seen the beginnings of it the previous day, when Peter had attacked the wild dog and saved Sufi's life. He knew that the Sacred Mother's true character was finally shining through, and despite the candid confessions he was now privy to, he actually trusted Peter more than anyone else around the campfire.

The Mist Children had struggled the most with the story. They had longed for Peter to bring Annabel back to them, and many still couldn't comprehend that she would not be returning to the Dark Realm.

To his credit, Peter left the circle after his story had ended, and spent a long time sitting amongst the Mist Children, talking and explaining everything to them, while Ethanril spoke directly to Sufi and the other boys.

When Peter finally returned it was Mundo who addressed him.

"This is an extraordinary day Peter," he began, his voice slightly overwhelmed by the emotion he was feeling. Peter looked nervously from one to the other, awaiting further protests.

"I think I speak for everyone here, when I tell you this has all come as a great shock to us, and it is therefore difficult to say exactly how we feel at this time," Mundo continued.

"It is a lot for anyone to take in, even in smaller doses," Ethanril justified, and Mundo nodded agreement.

"Annabel meant the world to us Peter," Fess interjected, hoping he wasn't underemphasizing this point. "I think we've all known for a long time that something was wrong with our lives. Wrong is not the right phrase…different is probably better. But when Annabel was here, she could answer any question we posed her. I guess she had only just begun filling in the gaps when she left us. Since the Lord of the Now came, well, all our time and energy has been spent running from him and we have had very little chance to question anything else other than what to do next."

"We saw the Great Find as the answer to all our problems." Pigeon stepped in. "But before we really had time to understand the implications of those writings, Morquinda had taken them all away with her. But I think we knew then…" he paused to look at everyone, "that something was wrong," Pigeon conceded.

Peter was nodding in shame.

"The Great Find was a collection of papers...stories and poems and drawings done by my sister and I. Sufi naturally thought she had found some holy writings about the history of the Dark Realm, but I fear Morquinda knew the truth. That is why she stole the writings."

"Morquinda is a witch," Fess protested. Peter shook his head.

"Morquinda is a very old lady...we have a word back on Earth: senile. It describes someone who has reached a certain age and has begun to lose control of his or her mental facilities. In many ways they become almost childlike, unable to tell the difference between the reality of the world and the fantasy that can be happening in their own mind. When this happens they are usually placed into the care of professionals. That is what should have been happening to her at Lambert House, but sadly that particular nursing home was closed down for unethical treatment," Peter explained.

"Big word!" Pigeon whispered to Fess, who nodded in a mockingly wise manner.

Sufi folded up Annabel's letter, which had been passed around the group as Peter talked. She held it out to him, and as Peter reached forward to take it she asked:

"What happens next then Peter?"

Peter fumbled nervously with the letter, slipping it out of her fingers as though it were too hot to touch.

"What do you mean?" he asked, desperate to clarify the question as he slipped the letter back into his rucksack. Sufi looked about her, surprised that none of the boys had asked this question. They were all looking at her with expectant faces, except Taime, who hadn't taken his eyes off Peter.

"Well...I mean we are after all just characters in your story," Sufi snapped back angrily. "I'm just wondering what fates you have in store for us. Do we defeat the Lord of the Now? Or does he destroy us? And what then, do you go home and we cease to exist? And if anything should happen to Annabel, do we also die? Are we safe until your next story Peter? Tell us? You have, without doubt, finally got the attention of us all." She was practically boiling with rage. Ethanril could see the anger in his sister's eyes, and her face flushed red from trying to contain it. He was about to step in, but Peter had already begun speaking in a voice that resounded with assertiveness and a sense of calm:

"You are right of course. You are all born from one-dimensional descriptions in a feeble short story I wrote to scare my sister as a young girl. The personalities that you have developed, the situations that you have found yourself in are all drawn from Annabel and yourselves. She has every right to be known as the first Sacred Mother. She gave you something which I could never have done. She gave you all a chance at life. It is a chance that you undoubtedly seized. You talk about Annabel leaving you too soon, and I disagree. Her departure was indeed tragic, but it goes to prove that you had already developed far beyond any of her hopes. Nine years have passed, and you are all still here. The Dark Realm still thrives, despite the Lord of the Now's attempts to destroy it, and despite Annabel's reduced influence here. So if she were to leave it completely you would not die. You could carry on here as long as you believe in it all and I have already promised Ethan, and will gladly promise all of you now...there will be no further stories. If we live through this, I promise to tell only this one, so every man, woman and child on my planet can witness the dangers of storytelling. The Final Days of Forget-Me-House will be burnt. I have it in my bag right now, so that we can do it together. You should all be proud of how far you've come. Although you came to me for help I do not flatter myself. You would have found a solution without me. You don't need Annabel or myself. Everything you have ever needed is right here." At this he indicated his heart.

Everyone had fallen into an enraptured silence. They had never heard such an impassioned speech in their lives. For some considerable time no one spoke.

"Well I need her here Peter," Taime suddenly exclaimed. He was on his feet a second later and pacing away from the circle.

Peter motioned to follow him but Ethanril caught his shoulder.

"Leave him a moment Peter. He needs time alone," the warrior advised. Peter looked pained. He watched Taime disappear into the trees.

"As to the Lord of the Now…" He finally resumed his speech. "Annabel foresaw his coming, but she was unable to make enough preparations to stop his rise to power. His army is strong now, and his grip on this world grows ever more choking by the day. It is time we stood against him, but it will take all the courage we can muster…" Peter confessed. Fess and Pigeon were staring at him, unsure what he was actually suggesting, but it was Mundo who voiced the question:

"Are you saying you have a plan Peter?" he tentatively asked. Ethanril and Sufi exchanged a glance.

"I have had an idea…" Peter began. He was reluctant to say too much and wary that they were all depending on him.

"I knew you would," Sufi intoned, confirming his worst fear, "as soon as you were in the Dark Realm, I just knew you'd be able to think straight." Peter smiled at her, pleased that she had such faith in him, but he was still nervous to continue.

"Will you tell us Peter?" Ethanril requested. Peter glanced at him, suddenly aware that everyone had unreservedly appointed Peter as leader of the group. He coughed self-consciously and then shook his head.

"There is something I must do first," he confessed. "Since I first encountered the Lord of the Now at Myfanwy, I have begun to see how he can be defeated. He is a mutated form of the Lord of the House from my story, which you must all read while I'm away." Peter hurriedly continued, ferreting in his bag for his crumpled dissertation. "From this and my own recollections of Annabel's nightmares I've started to piece together a solution. But I must be sure." He retrieved it, and handed the Final Days of Forget-Me-House to Fess.

"Sure of what?" Fess asked, accepting the jumble of papers.

"That it is possible. You see we'll need the Pig-Beast..."

At this everyone froze. Peter felt himself turn crimson. He had known he wasn't ready to explain this yet.

"That's impossible!" Mundo began, and quickly Peter rose to his feet.

"I'm sorry; I shouldn't even have begun to tell you. I must go to Taime." He was already moving. Ethanril tried to calm the rabble of protests.

"You seem to be implying you are leaving us for a while," Ethanril called above the noise.

Peter, who was striding across the snowy clearing with his head down, turned sharply at this and called back.

"I have to go to the Old Ones. I must speak with Morquinda. It is clearly something Annabel wished me to do, and I don't intend to let her down."

Ethanril glowed with pride.

"You cannot go alone," he sensibly protested, but Peter cut him short.

"I don't intend to. Sufi will ride with me," he declared. His voice surprised Ethanril in its decisiveness. Sufi looked up, and Pigeon felt a deep pang of sorrow, but he did not protest.

"I'll saddle Lockavarn and Jessavarn," Sufi shouted back and Peter nodded his thanks, turning back to the line of trees through which Taime had exited.

Ethanril watched him go, unsure whether to accompany him for this confrontation. He was about to join him when he saw

Sufi moving away from the others to saddle the horses. He rose up and walked a little way with her, allowing the Mist Children to huddle together in frenzied discussion.

"You must be careful..." Ethanril began and Sufi was surprised to detect the undertone in his voice.

"You're being my big brother again," she tried to laugh off the warning, but Ethanril was insistent.

"Peter is very troubled Sufi. I know the two of you have grown very close, but you must also understand, that just like Morquinda...this is not his world. He will leave here if we all make it through this alive." Sufi looked affronted.

"I don't think you of all people are in any position to question my feelings!" she snapped back in a barely controlled whisper. "Did you ever think that Annabel didn't belong to the Dark Realm when you fell in love with her?" she questioned.

"You're in love with him?" Ethanril's voice sounded panicked. Sufi looked even more flustered.

"No!" she protested. "I don't...I don't know...I..." And in that second she lost all her usual control. Once again she was his vulnerable younger sister, crying in the darkness because the shadows on her wall were moving, and Ethanril gathered her up in his arms and let her cry for a second on his chest.

"It's okay," he whispered, stroking her hair and soothing her fears away. "I understand...honestly I do, and I apologise. I just don't want you to go through what...what I'm going through that's all," he confessed. Sufi looked imploringly into his face. She saw at once the pain and sadness which Ethanril fought so hard to keep private from everyone.

"I'm so sorry for what happened," Sufi said, as though she had in someway been responsible for the car crash. Ethanril couldn't hold her gaze, but he nodded gratefully.

"Just be safe, that's all I ask. Please remember that you are much loved...long before Peter came here," he added, surreptitiously glancing over her shoulder and watching Pigeon talking with the others. Sufi didn't even need to turn round to know of whom he referred.

"I know you understand this Ethan, just like you understand the pain Taime is now in," she coyly reminded him. At this Ethanril seemed suddenly to remember something. He looked back at Sufi.

"Are you okay now?" he asked, cupping her shoulders with his hands. She sighed heavily, and wiped her wet eyes with her hand. Finally she nodded.

"I have to saddle the horses for Peter," she said, nodding decisively as though this simple task was the answer to all their problems. Ethanril smiled fondly at her.

"Saddle them well; I want the two of you back safely. I must go and see how Peter is…" He let the sentence tail off, and Sufi nodded in agreement, secretly pleased that Ethanril did not intend to leave Taime and Peter alone for too long.

✍

"Go ahead," Peter said as defiantly as possible.

He swallowed loudly, and the action caused his Adam's apple to rub against the razor sharp tip of Taime's rapier. It drew blood instantly, opening the skin at once and allowing a curtain of blood to trickle down Peter's neck.

He had his back pressed directly against the rowan tree, and his hands were digging into the bark, peeling it away in places as though he intended to pick the tree apart and escape.

Taime was standing stock still; his back was arched slightly to allow even distribution of his weight between both feet. He was every inch the master swordsman. He casually eyed the sweat which was standing proud on Peter's brow, and listened intently to his opponent's laboured breathing, knowing it was confirmation that Peter was scared for his life.

Yet it still wasn't enough.

Taime cocked his hat with his free hand, and then held it aloft with the finesse of a trained fighter. Even Peter knew the movement was designed to draw attention away from the final sword thrust which would undoubtedly end his life.

He had barely made it through the belt of trees moments earlier, when Taime had seized him, spinning him around and pinning him against the rowan without a sound. Even Peter was surprised by the attack. He realised in that instant that this young man was practically Ethanril's equal. He had seen only the flashing of steel as the rapier had been drawn, but had immediately closed his eyes expecting death to follow.

When he opened them he saw Taime, his sword arm extended to its limit, the tip resting with pin point accuracy against his jugular. Peter had challenged him to finish his thrust, but Taime seemed unsure of how to proceed.

"You talk a lot Peter Bettany." He sounded as though the name caused him great pain to pronounce. "I wonder if you listen as well as you preach?" It was a general question and Peter was slightly flummoxed for an immediate answer. "Well that's a good start; I see you're at least listening to me now," Taime smiled sarcastically. "I wonder if it takes a sword to make you sit up and take notice," he queried. Peter was finding it hard not to blink uncontrollably, the sweat was running off his brow into his eyes and making them sting painfully, but he refused to break eye contact with Taime. He remembered reading somewhere that eye contact was essential when dealing with an armed man.

"I do listen," he whispered, coughing slightly to try and recover his voice, and then wincing as the sword dug into his neck. Taime relaxed the pressure slightly, just enough to allow Peter to talk more comfortably. "I know how much my sister meant to you, and I know how much it hurts you, that I hurt her when we were children…" Peter continued, constantly aware that his next sentence could be his last. "I also know that you resented Ethanril for getting so close to her, and believe me, I know how it feels to be in love with someone who cannot love you back," Peter emphasised. Taime raised an eyebrow mockingly.

"Do you really? The mighty Peter Bettany knows about love and heartache, is that right?" There was a nasty underlining anger to this sentence, and Peter felt the blade press slightly firmer against his already bleeding wound, but he no longer feared it. For once he did understand Taime's motivation.

"Yes I do," he said, in the same simple and distinctive tone with which he had just spoken to the group.

Taime hesitated. Something about Peter's face at that moment told him he was finally telling the truth. Instead of pursuing that line of questioning he abruptly changed tack:

"I wonder, in all your infinite wisdom, if you can actually see the damage you're causing this pathetic little group? Can you not see that you and Sufi are breaking Pigeon's heart?" The comment took Peter completely off guard. His own relationship with Sufi had undoubtedly changed over time, but he had no idea that it had become so obvious to the others. His feelings on this matter were so confused he didn't know what to say.

"Do you want so badly to be like your sister Peter, and fall in love with one of the characters from your own story?" He looked exasperated, and Peter vehemently shook his head.

"You're not giving me a chance Taime. So much has happened to me in the last week, so much that I doubt many people could have actually dealt with it. But I'm here; I have done everything you have all asked of me. I've come to the Dark Realm. I openly admit I delayed the experience because I was so frightened of what was happening to my sanity. But I came. Every question you've asked me, I've answered. You claim I don't listen to you, and yet yesterday you demanded I tell you the truth by nightfall today, and that is exactly what I have done. I am here with you now, alone and defenceless to accept your judgement of my life; but be aware of one thing Taime. Everyone is in pain here...not just you. Ethanril has also lost Annabel, so have all those Mist Children, and so have I. You're in danger of becoming like Krinn, and spreading animosity and unrest through a group that's already clinging to life by the skin of their teeth. This isn't a pathetic group...these are your friends, your family, and they need you now more than they've ever needed you before. You do yourself a great many injustices Taime. I promise you, you're no outsider to this group. Ethanril speaks very highly of you, and I guess I now have first hand experience of the kind of swordsman you are." Peter half smiled.

Taime seemed to be listening to this speech. Peter's words had finally struck a chord with him, and he suddenly felt a mixture of embarrassment and humility which combined to allow him to drop his sword and stare rather sheepishly at Peter.

"I am so sorry." He was aware how pathetic this apology sounded; especially in light of the fact that he had just tried to murder Peter. "The anger I have...it's always bottled up so tightly inside me and sometimes...sometimes I react without thinking...that's why Ethanril is by far the better man. He can control his emotions so well and...I am just so sorry Peter." He could not have been more apologetic.

Peter breathed out heavily. He wiped at the blood on his neck, but he felt nothing but pity for the deflated warrior in front of him.

He offered Taime his hand.

Taime looked as though he was unworthy to accept it, but Peter smiled again, and they shook hands warmly before embracing.

For a long time they stood talking, neither wanting the other to leave until they were certain they had cleared up their differences.

"I have done you great wrong Taime. You and everyone here, I swear that in time I will correct it," Peter vowed. Taime pulled away, sheathing his sword.

"I will be proud to be beside you, when you do," he graciously offered.

From his concealed vantage point Ethanril watched this scene with a mixture of awe and jealousy. It was the kind of reconciliation he wished he could have with Taime, yet he knew in his heart it would never take place. He moved back into the shadows as the two passed close by, shedding a single tear.

∽

The clamour of noise from the bowels of Stilfanwyn Chasm could be heard for miles. It echoed around the valley that surrounded the vast lake of Carrastorc, and reverberated through the South Meade Hills.

The wildlife nesting in close proximity, fled in agitation as the cacophony continued, seeming to grow ever louder as the mighty trapdoor rose and fell to allow the Still army to march forth.

They fanned out across the clearing, thousands of roaring Still, beating their mighty chests like enraged apes. Some launched themselves after birds and squirrels in their frenzy for blood, catching the petrified animals and shredding them in their merciless jaws.

Two vast carts stood full to capacity at the Chasm entrance. They were loaded down with rubble and slag from the tunnel dig, and their weight bore down heavily upon the great oaken wheels which supported them.

The Still lashed to the front of the carts strained against their harnesses, screaming their battle cries into the withering skies.

Deep below ground the tunnel continued at a frantic pace, with the Hybrids tearing and rending the soil apart in their insanity to be upon the Mist Children.

Amidst all the chaos the Lord of the Now stood like a conductor, barking orders to different factions of Still that filed past him, and attacking any who appeared to be slowing in their work.

His hour of triumph approached and nothing would prevent his victory once the tunnel broke through. His black heart pounded like a war drum as he watched the rubble falling from the ever expanding tunnel.

He sensed the movement of the rogue Still which had remained in Peter's world, tracking its prey and preparing the way for the Still to march upon the Earth.

"The prophesies were all lies,"

he whispered in triumph.

"The Harvester has not emerged to save them."

His laughter almost drowned out the noise of excavation.

As the final wave of Still emerged from the Chasm, Krinn strode out behind them, resplendent in his black armour. He boarded the nearest cart and spread his arms wide demanding the silence of the furious mob. Upon seeing the glaive, its skull hilt blazing with hellish light, a deep silence rested upon each and every creature.

"The hour has arrived," Krinn said, his infamously cold eyes burning with frightening intensity. "We march for Tarnwaters, and the *total annihilation* of the Mist Children. Leave none but Ethanril alive. I will face him alone," Krinn ordered. With that he spun his glaive once and brought the spear point crashing down upon the Cart.

It was the signal to march and the Still all roared as one, surging forward through the pine copse, and out into open land, the carts lurching after them.

༺ஓ༻

The Village Inn was heaving with people.

Samantha thought that Tony Simpson, with his usual shrewd

eye for business, had actually taken the trouble to remove a few rafters, and extend a couple of walls to deal with the onslaught of customers.

Whether it was a collective sense of community spirit, or a desperate need for safety in numbers; or even as Samantha reasoned, the simple fact that everyone just really needed a drink after the last twenty-four hours, the Village Inn had seemingly over night, become the centre of the world.

Samantha fought her way desperately towards the bar. In fact she was merely aiming in the general direction of where she remembered the bar to be as she couldn't actually see it due to the throng of elderly community residents who seemed intent on simply loitering there.

She stood up on tiptoe in the hope of attracting Tony's attention. She could see him moving at practically a blur in his haste to serve more customers than he could physically cope with. It was clear that he wasn't going to be able to talk to her.

Eventually she abandoned the idea of a drink, figuring that by the time she actually reached the bar it would more than likely be closing time. She prised herself free from two punters who seemed united in their unspoken plan to asphyxiate her by crushing her between them, and with a few false starts she struggled into the adjoining room of the Inn.

She had not expected to see Cyril and Jayne Bettany sitting unobtrusively in the corner. In Samantha's head she had thought she would have to ask Tony if she could be let up into their room. She really didn't imagine that they would want the company of strangers.

But there they sat. Huddled together on a corner seat, looking for all the world like two lost lovers with a whole history of pain lying between them.

If Cyril hadn't looked directly at her in that moment, Samantha would have walked straight out of the Inn.

She felt herself blush as she caught his eye, cursing under her breath as she realised she now had no choice but to go over and begin the conversation that she had been thinking about all morning. She managed a short smile as she unhurriedly traversed the cluttered room, and finally stood in front of them feeling like a little schoolgirl requesting permission to sit down.

Cyril immediately motioned to stand up, and the movement caused Jayne to stir herself. She gazed groggily at Samantha, looking for a moment as though she didn't even recognise her.

Samantha began immediately to apologise for the intrusion, and Cyril waved away her protests, stepping to an adjoining table and retrieving a free chair.

"I really don't mean to intrude, I saw Ivy Meredith in the village and she told me that Peter was missing, I realise you must be worried sick and…"

Cyril had returned with the chair, and he quickly positioned it behind her. Jayne still looked as though she had just woken from a terrible nightmare, and as Samantha eased herself down onto the chair she had a terrible feeling of déjà vu.

"Please Sam," Cyril said, sitting back down next to his wife. "A little company is exactly what we need. There is no need to apologise," he kindly explained. "I'd offer to get you a drink, but I fear you would be drawing your pension by the time I returned." He said with a smile.

The comment made Samantha giggle, and that in turn relaxed her.

"Something is troubling you."

It was the first thing Jayne had said since Samantha arrived, and it seemed to catch even Cyril off guard. "Your shoulder blades are tense and your eyes look so sad," she continued.

Samantha self-consciously adjusted her seating position, but she now found herself staring directly at Jayne Bettany. The similarity between her eyes and those of Annabel was immediate and disconcerting. They were the kind of eyes that could pierce straight through this world and look far beyond into a secret universe that only the initiated were privy to.

"No I'm fine honestly…" Samantha lied. She swallowed and tried to turn away, but Jayne seemed to be holding her, entranced.

"What have you seen?" she asked. It was the most profound question Samantha could ever recall being asked. While her mind raced through a thousand possible answers, she was horrified to hear her voice say:

"I've seen Annabel today."

The sentence hit the table like a stone pitched into a still river. Samantha could virtually see the ripples of shock resonating out over Cyril and Jayne.

They exchanged glances.

"At the hospital?" Cyril clarified. For a moment Samantha wanted to nod in agreement and let the whole conversation twist away into other areas, but in her mind's eye she could see the young girl with the emerald eyes, pleading with her for help.

"No," Samantha whimpered. "No…I saw her in a dream." She exhaled shakily, expecting to be thrown out of the door for such insolence. But Cyril and Jayne looked completely unfazed by the comment.

"I think you'd better explain," Jayne advised, tugging at her hair, and looking strangely expectant.

So Samantha started from the beginning.

She explained the strange sensations she had felt whenever she had looked in upon Patient 143. She showed them the file she had taken from the hospital, apologising for showing it to Mary Graham. She then went on to elaborate upon her visit to the retired nurse, and finally culminated her story in the two dreams she had had.

Throughout it all Cyril and Jayne sat in complete silence. They never attempted to make any kind of interruption, and their faces remained impenetrable as though they had somehow developed an emotional detachment to everything Samantha was saying.

It was several minutes after Samantha had finished speaking that they finally spoke.

"Peter is missing..." Jayne began, "so is Lucy Doran and Father Francis Deane. Did Annabel mention any of these names to you when you saw her?"

This time it was Samantha's turn to look totally impenetrable. She was completely shocked that this was Jayne's first question.

"No she didn't." Samantha almost felt as though she were apologising for this. "She seemed concerned that something was coming for her...and that I was in danger myself," Samantha continued, attempting to sound as calm as she could.

"Well I think that's probably true my dear...it doesn't take much to see the shadows closing around you," Jayne continued matter-of-factly.

The coldness of the sentence had Samantha rising to her feet.

"I'm sorry...that makes me very uncomfortable." It was an understatement and she was fumbling with the Annabel file, trying to replace it in her coat pocket.

Cyril rose up and gripped her wrist with a surprising light touch.

"Please sit down, I must apologise for my wife, she can be quite disconcerting I know. Believe me she means you no harm," he said gently. There was an undeniable honesty to Cyril's words, and despite the tension of Jayne's comment, Samantha found herself sitting back down and ignoring the strange looks other customers were giving her.

"I'm sorry," Jayne apologised. "It's very rare these days that I have feelings like that, and when I do I tend to voice them without thinking. I imagine you are now quite disturbed. That is my fault entirely and I wouldn't blame you for walking away immediately from me," she continued. Samantha caught the expression on Jayne's face; it was a mixture of desperation and apology. She realised at once that no harm had been intended by the comment.

"Are you a clairvoyant of some kind?" Samantha tentatively asked, intrigued by Jayne's apparent second sight.

"Oh good Lord no!" Jayne immediately exclaimed. "No! I'm afraid it's nothing quite so exciting." It was the first time during the whole conversation that Jayne had briefly returned to her normal demeanour, and Samantha looked greatly reassured by the smile that Jayne now greeted her with. "Occasionally, and it is very occasionally I catch a brief glimpse of the power my daughter possessed. In those moments I see a snapshot of the other world which she created with her mind." Cyril squeezed her hand, and looked distractedly through the misty window which overlooked the Village Green. "It stays with me for only seconds, and then I lose it in the hum of traffic," Jayne concluded philosophically.

Samantha was surprised by this revelation; she looked at Cyril who was still gazing out at the unsettled sky.

"Do you experience any visions?" She had to ask him. Cyril looked slowly back at her, his gentle eyes looked intensely vulnerable. He squeezed Jayne's hand again, and then reached for his half-finished pint of beer. He took a hearty gulp, and replaced the glass as though he were a judge bringing down his gavel.

"I have been blessed with normality," he said quietly. "I say blessed because I've seen what this gift can do to my wife. I've watched it devour my daughter and now I fear it has taken my son from me." He had to pause to swallow a cry. "So no, I don't have any visions. But I do have a lot of unanswered prayers." He reached for his drink again and Jayne cuddled up to him. Samantha sat in absolute silence, witnessing the love between this couple and feeling nothing but pity for their loss.

"Mary Graham was a great friend to us…" Cyril continued. "I am very glad you have taken an interest in talking to her. She nursed Annabel diligently during the first few years of her coma. She brought us a great deal of hope. We always thought it would be Mary whom Annabel might choose to make contact with…" he continued, now glancing back at Samantha. "I have never felt Annabel's presence, nor has my wife for that matter; and although Peter now possesses her gift of dreaming, she has never, to the best of our knowledge, made direct contact with him. For years we have asked Jean Candicote and Father Deane, but again they have had nothing, not even a feeling," Cyril confessed. Samantha was beginning to shuffle uncomfortably in her chair again. She was fighting to repress the feeling that something was trying to prise the skin from her bones.

"But why has she chosen me?" she blurted out. The emotions which had raged in side her for the last twenty-four hours seemed in danger of spilling out.

Jayne lent across the table and took hold of her hand. Immediately Samantha felt the same calming warmth that Annabel exuded, seeping into her skin and relaxing her fraught mind.

"I don't know Sam. You are someone she has grown close to these last few years, whether you realised it or not. She must trust you, and my daughter was always a very good judge of character. She can see that you will help her," Jayne stressed. Samantha knew she was telling the truth, but the enormity of the responsibility was crushing her.

"What can I do to help her? She was warning me against something…maybe that man in my dream or that creature? I just don't know…what shadows do you see Jayne?" Samantha asked, looking frantically around the Inn in case those self-same shadows were lurking behind the furnishings.

"They are very hazy Sam, nothing I could describe. I just sensed it the minute you sat down. Something awful has happened in Wick Holm, something which the police are unequipped to deal with, and these shadows are the reason for it. The weather is strange, don't you think? Yet everyone is ignoring it. My son has disappeared along with two others, and at least three people are dead, but they are treating it all as though it were just routine. No one can explain it, so we have been sitting here, waiting for the explanation to walk in. I know that sounds ludicrous, but you are here Samantha, and you do have a message from our daughter." Jayne raised an eyebrow as the facts thudded into Samantha like stray bullets.

"But what in God's name can we do to stop this?" she pleaded.

Cyril downed the last of his pint and began to help Jayne on with her coat.

"The first step is easy…" he began, indicating Samantha should also stand up. "We go to the hospital, and we find Annabel." He turned to assist the young nurse with her overcoat as well.

"And after that?" Samantha needed to know, the whole idea of going back to the hospital filled her with dread.

"That's anybody's guess." Cyril shrugged, offering her a smile.

The three left silently out of the main door of the Inn.

No one noticed them depart, crossing the car park looking like a small bedraggled pilgrimage.

No one even glanced out of the Inn windows, or they would have seen the Still break free of its hiding place amongst the conifer hedge and set off in rapid pursuit of Cyril's Land Rover.

An eerie darkness was creeping into the afternoon skyline; it was an unnatural warning that all was no longer how it seemed in the quiet coastal town of Wick Holm.

"You're definitely improving!" Sufi stifled a giggle. She looked down at the stunned figure of Peter, who was lying on his back rubbing his forehead rigorously with his hands.

"That!" Peter spluttered, struggling to his feet and wincing with each new action. "Was a bloody ridiculous place to put a branch!" He accused the beech tree under which they had just ridden.

Jessavarn stood a few yards away from him, looking quizzically at Peter as though he were an object of great amusement.

Sufi remained seated upon Lockavarn, she was laughing uncontrollably at the faces Peter was pulling as he struggled to remount Jessavarn.

"You can stop laughing!" he berated her. His face scowled at her briefly before he too collapsed in fits of laughter. "Bloody horses!" he joked as the two continued their journey.

They had left Kilfanfyn Forest over an hour ago, during which time they had headed east to avoid Bayous Ridge and instead approach the lake of Carrastorc from a different path across the South Meade Hills. It was a route which Sufi had specifically chosen to avoid detection from the Still.

"They rarely guard the Hills; it is not a terrain that they like. It takes them too close to the Wasteland and the threat of attack from the Pig-Beast keeps them at bay," Sufi explained as the two white horses slowly made their way through the ice and rocks that formed the base of the South Meade Hills.

Peter gazed in awe at the breathtaking scenery. The boulders that lay strewn across the ground looked as though giants might have placed them there for a game of bowls. Each boulder was glistening with snow as though it had been chalked, and the mixed vegetation and encroaching canopy of alder and willow gave the whole scene a mystical twist, like the coming of a great ice age had preserved an ancient civilisation beneath a veil of snow.

"This is just beautiful!" Peter exclaimed as they meandered through the lower valley and began their ascent of the hills.

"I remember the South Meade Hills before the snows came..." Sufi called over her shoulder. "Warm summer afternoons, Pigeon and I would climb these hills and eat a picnic at the top. You can see for miles across the Dark Realm on a clear day...not sure the view will be so spectacular today," she confessed, staring wearily at the leaden sky. The threat of snow hung unspoken on the breeze, as though the slightest stirring could set it falling in a multitude from the featureless skyline.

"Do you miss those days Sufi?" Peter asked, drawing up alongside her. The wild girl tossed her hair casually so she could see Peter more clearly. She looked troubled for a minute before answering.

"Those days will come back," she whispered. "The world has not changed beneath the snow..." she added, and then she turned her head away from Peter and whispered: "Only mine."

Peter leant backwards, pulling slightly on Jessavarn's reins to control the speed with which the white horse wanted to race away from him. He was still unused to being ridden in such a crass manner, but Peter was undoubtedly improving as a horseman.

He watched Sufi direct Lockavarn.

Despite her professionalism the white horse still veered slightly off course. Lockavarn intrigued Peter. He felt certain empathy for him, he was always trying to overcompensate for his many faults, but he just wasn't perfect like the others. Peter had often felt like that during his short lifetime. He reminisced about the day he had first met the white horses, when they had performed for him in the paddocks of Myfanwy.

"In all that I've seen here Sufi..." he announced, reining Jessavarn to halt, "nothing was more beautiful than the first time I saw these horses at play." He smiled at her, as Sufi trotted Lockavarn over to join him. Peter was glancing from her to the plains of Carrastorc, which stretched like blankets to the horizon.

"Nothing?" she questioned, fixing him with a soul-searching glance.

Peter looked at her, her angelic face cocooned by a flowing mane of blonde hair. Her flat stomach was shuddering from the exhilaration of riding, and her perfect legs were flecked with goose pimples as the cold breeze played across the hem of her skirt. She was calling to him to kiss her. He could feel the electricity of the moment catching up with him and almost demanding that he act.

"Your horse is lame Sufi...did you know?" He cringed at the stupidity of the question. He hadn't even meant to ask it but the words just tumbled out of his mouth in desperation. Sufi seemed almost as bewildered as he was by the change of conversation, but with a maturity that Peter had not expected from her, she played along.

"He isn't my horse...Annabel never actually said he was anyway. She brought Astervarn for Ethanril, and Jessavarn for Mundo, and the boys ended up arguing over Ratavarn. I just took pity on Lockavarn...he feels like he should be my horse, because I'm the only one who can successfully ride him. He's actually tipped Ethanril from his back, he can be very fickle whom he chooses to befriend," Sufi warned.

"I'd love to ride him." Peter confessed. "It's strange, but I just feel like he'll let me." Sufi looked flirtatiously as him and smiled.

"Well. If you're a good boy, I might just let you." She laughed and spurred Lockavarn onwards so that Peter had to race Jessavarn after her to keep up.

They rode across the South Meade Hills in single file as the terrain allowed for only one small track. This was littered with scree and loose stones, and many times the horses stumbled, nearly throwing the two riders.

The day had misted over, and the view over the lake of Carrastorc was limited to only a few glimpses.

The noise of the Still often drifted in on the breeze. At first Peter was frightened that they were walking into some kind of trap, but Sufi explained that they could always be heard from this distance because Stilfanwyn Chasm was so close.

Peter asked a great many questions.

Sufi was surprised at how pedantic he could be over certain points. Again and again he would question the distance of the lake in comparison to Stilfanwyn Chasm, and whether it was geologically possible that areas of the Chasm actually ran beneath it. If Sufi hesitated in her response Peter would become agitated, demanding to know answers.

By the time they began their descent of the hills, neither was speaking.

"Is it much further?" Peter was finally forced to ask. He hadn't planned on being the first to break the silence, but he couldn't bare the thought of a further few hours riding without speaking to each other.

Sufi twisted round in her saddle to look at him, her face was smiling and Peter knew instantly that she was glowing with pride that he had spoken first.

"I knew you couldn't do it!" she said, and Peter stared back placidly.

"I had to...I can't keep quiet to save my life," he said, making up an excuse for his sudden interruption.

"Oh really, and here's me thinking I was just irresistible?" she flirted, once again spurring Lockavarn onwards.

Without hesitating Peter pursued her.

Sufi loved this and began to deliberately lead Peter over increasingly difficult terrain. Several times he was practically wrenched from his saddle as Jessavarn careened down the slope, eventually reaching the west plain and spurring full pelt after

Sufi. The white horse churned up the snow with its sturdy hooves, determined to out run the weaker horse. Eventually Peter drew up along side her, and Sufi turned her head to glance at him, her hair whipping behind her in the breeze.

Suddenly she leapt free of the saddle, gambolling over into a heavy snowdrift.

Peter had passed her in seconds; he turned in a panic, not sure if Sufi had been thrown off. He tried to slow Jessavarn, but the white horse could not be shaken off from its path. Lockavarn twisted away in the distance, apparently failing to notice he was now bereft of a rider.

Peter knew he would have to jump, he had no choice. Swinging his legs across Jessavarn's back, he steadied himself for the fall. In his mind he saw himself lying horribly mangled on the snow-covered ground, having jumped into a deadly coral of rocks. He closed his eyes and with a yell he jumped free.

He landed hard, his knees jarring and his eyes watering, but he had escaped basically unharmed as he hit a patch of thick snow.

He watched Jessavarn disappear into the middle distance equally oblivious to his departure. The mist was thickening now, and he stood up feeling groggy and disorientated. He began to slowly trudge back the way he had ridden, following the hoof prints of the horses. It vaguely reminded him of the first night he had met Sufi, when he had walked the alleyway behind Wick Holm church.

He called her name into the mist, hoping she would answer him, but he heard no response.

In the distance he was certain he could hear the wild dogs, and that panicked him. He was aware that he couldn't be far from Stilfanwyn Chasm, and as he was the Lord of the Now's currently 'most desired' object, this placed him in great danger.

Then he saw her.

She was lying prostrate on the ground where she had landed. Her arms were at her side, and her legs were slightly angled as though her ankle may have been twisted.

Her eyes were closed and she didn't open them even when Peter called her name again.

He crouched down beside her, his hands fumbling to check her limbs for cuts or contusions. He cupped her head in his hands, turning it towards him to see if her eyelids flickered.

As he did so her left arm slipped around his waist, and her right gripped the back of his head, she pulled him willingly into a kiss.

As their mouths touched Peter felt elated and warmth spilled across his chapped lips, igniting the fires of his heart into a roaring flame.

His hands reached around her waist, his fingers gingerly stroking across her stomach and finally wrapping around her waist. He kissed back with a passion he didn't even know he possessed.

The moment lasted only seconds, and as they pulled apart neither knew how to react.

It was Peter who finally took the lead, pulling Sufi up from the ground and embracing her into his arms as though their two bodies were one entity. They kissed without hesitation, and Peter spun the wild girl around in his arms until she was giggling with happiness.

It was at this moment that the full implication of his actions hit Peter's conscience like a brick and he pulled quickly away, as though by distancing himself from Sufi immediately it would make everything alright again.

"What's the matter?" Sufi asked in innocence. She was self-consciously touching her lips where only moments ago his had been, in case she had done something wrong.

Peter was looking flustered, his face riddled with guilt. His movements were animated yet he seemed unclear of what to do, let alone say, next. "Are you ok Peter?" she asked with genuine concern. She moved to touch him again but he pulled away as though she were suddenly repulsive.

"What are we doing?" It was a rhetorical question, but Sufi's innocence answered it for him.

"We're falling in love Peter," she replied, her face flush with excitement. That word seemed to almost electrocute Peter; his hands were up, making wild gestures of denial before his mouth had actually started speaking.

"Love? Oh Sufi no…no we're not falling love." He seemed to run out of steam and sat down heavily. Sufi was by his side as he raked his hair out of his eyes. She tentatively rested her hand on his arm. Peter looked shocked, but resisted his initial feeling of pulling away.

"It's ok Peter…you're just nervous," she assured him. "You know how we feel about each other," she conspiratorially let on. Peter's face was still a mask of confusion. He looked at Sufi, crouching next to him in all her innocent beauty, but all he could think of was Lucy Doran handing him her phone number.

"Sufi…I….I…" He couldn't say it. The more he looked at her, the more he was aware of the impossibility of the situation. He couldn't explain what had come over him when they had kissed. The moment had carried itself before he was even aware of what he was doing. He felt a horrible guilt and hypocrisy descending upon his shoulders. All these years of telling himself he would never hurt anyone the way people always hurt him and here he was now, about to do that very thing to this beautiful young girl.

"I thought you were hurt…that Lockavarn had thrown you," he blurted out. Sufi smiled and squeezed his wrist.

"Oh Peter…you are so funny sometimes. Don't you know when a girl is trying to get your attention? I've never been thrown from a horse in my life!" she declared with a smile, but Peter looked angrily back at her, he pulled his wrist away from her touch.

"You shouldn't pretend like that...I worry," he snapped, half in anger and half in concern.

Sufi fought to control her smile. All Peter was doing in her eyes, was confirming his love for her. She was about to go to him when he suddenly said one simple sentence and instantly broke her heart.

"I don't love you Sufi."

Each individual word pounded her heart like an arrow.

She looked initially embarrassed, messing with her hair, and straightening her dress, as though she had suddenly become aware of how short it was, and now she wanted to hide her body from the prying eyes of the world. Her own eyes went suddenly tearful and then anger brought her to her feet.

"But you stare at me all the time, you walk with me, you talk with me...you laugh with me...you saved my life Peter." This last sentence lost all the fierceness of the opening and dissolved into a sob. She looked pitiful as her face suddenly broke into an expression it was never born to make.

Sorrow.

"Sufi...I am so sorry. I know we've been through a great deal together in the last few days but I...I can't love you." He tried to explain, wanting suddenly to hold her until she was happy again, but knowing that he couldn't go to her. He stood awkwardly, looking as though his arms were now an embarrassing attachment that his body no longer required.

"Am I not pretty enough Peter?" she demanded, her eyes wet from tears. "Is there something wrong with my body?" She needed answers; her initial fear that she was physically unattractive to Peter had blinded her from the truth.

"You're amazing Sufi...you know that. Anyone would say the same. But I can't love you...I'm already in love."

He'd said it. He never thought he would have the strength to, but he had actually said it.

Sufi looked as though she had been slapped. Her expression seemed to have frozen into shock. Peter felt nothing but pity for her, knowing he had just said the very sentence that he himself had heard so many times before.

"I'm truly sorry Sufi. I should have told you, but I never thought you would feel this way about me," he said honestly. "I know it's painful…"

"Pain?" Sufi suddenly yelled. "Do you want to talk about pain Peter…is that it?" she practically snarled at him. Peter was genuinely shocked by the outburst, he moved slowly towards her.

"Do you?" he asked as gently as he could. Sufi turned her head angrily away from him.

"How could I? That's your specialist subject isn't it Peter. Your pain and Annabel's pain…oh what's the point?" She broke off, crying now. She slumped down, her head drooping forward onto her knees and she pressed her aching eyes hard against her bare skin. If she closed them tight enough she felt sure she could prevent these tears.

"Sufi…please, you're scaring me." Peter tried to break-through to her. This seemed to stir a deeper anger within Sufi. Her head re-emerged from her bow, her eyes were red with pressure and her skin seemed almost painful to wear. She had an expression of utter despair plastered across her face.

"Well that's me isn't it, one scary girl!" She laughed it off, rising back to her feet. She made to walk away but the sorrow within Peter forced him to spin her around again.

"Don't say that about yourself Sufi. You're not scary…I am truly sorry for hurting you like this; I just don't know what to say. You are closer to me than anyone else here, I can't lose your friendship like this, I just can't let that happen. Please Sufi." He was begging her now. "Please let me at least explain?"

The mist clung to them now, making them look for all the world as though they were the last of their kind. Peter knew that if she turned away from him now he had lost her forever.

Out of the bleakness of the landscape there emerged two blinding flashes of white. Both Peter and Sufi turned to see Lockavarn and Jessavarn frolicking in the emptiness of the world. Like two lovers they chased, and brushed and seemingly danced together, tail to tail and nose to nose. It was the very image of love, and Peter felt a great sadness that something he had done was now threatening these wild stallions.

"Tell me Peter...tell me who she is," Sufi asked, in a voice that was strangely calm yet full of heartache.

Peter looked downcast, and without hesitation he explained his relationship with Lucy Doran.

In describing his feelings for her he knew he was mirroring Sufi's own towards him, but he kept nothing from her. He hoped she would understand.

At the end of it, she cried. It was a short private cry which Peter felt glad that he had witnessed, because now he would always know the pain he was capable of inflicting upon another person. Beyond any physical torture, nothing could ever be as painful again.

"Pigeon loves me..." Sufi suddenly announced as though it were a fact that Peter should also prepare himself for. He inwardly smiled, proud of Sufi's fast reactions of self-preservation, they made him feel small and worthless at her bare feet. "I know that I also have feelings for him, it's just that we've been friends a long time and..." She appeared to be on the verge of tears again, so Peter interrupted her.

"Pigeon is a good man Sufi. I haven't known him very long I know, but what I've seen of him I like very much. He is funny, very brave and very caring. He watches you all the time you know?" Peter added conspiratorially. Sufi seemed to brighten at this. It was of course something she knew herself, but being told by someone else, always made her blush.

"I'm very popular Peter!" she stressed with a wink. Peter smiled fully; he felt the tension of the moment had finally passed.

"I have to say Sufi…" he added, as she began to calm the two horses. "I've never been kissed like that before."

The comment caused her to smile with pride. She wasn't sure if he meant it, or if he was just placating her ego, either way it worked.

"It will always be something to remember," she whispered to him, half-longingly.

∽

The mist was thickening along the edges of the Wasteland. It moved like silent fingers, trying to unclasp a complex lock into those barren lands, but something prevented it.

There were still some natural rules in place. The order of the Dark Realm faced a final disruption, but nothing would ever change the Wasteland.

The first Sacred Mother had never told its story, and so it remained empty like a blank sheet awaiting a pen.

And at its centre, the Pig-Beast waited.

∽

They walked the last half a mile.

The two white horses had been tethered near the first belt of heavy pine trees, and the riders had proceeded on foot for fear of attracting too much attention.

The pine coppice had stolen upon them like an assassin.

One minute they were walking through a bleary mist, with nothing to obstruct them but their own fear of the unknown, and then suddenly the trees were upon them.

Thick wet branches lashed out of the mist like flailing arms, making walking virtually impossible and even the normally sure-footed Sufi was forced to crouch low to the ground, as they carefully circumnavigated the mysterious copse.

Many times branches brushed through their hair, causing them to shudder and turn as though something were making unwanted advances upon them. They were both dripping wet from the mist, and constantly tripping and stumbling over tree roots.

There was something unnatural about the place, a feeling which left them both cold and nervous as they sank deeper into the overhanging canopy.

It was a smell of decay and loss.

Peter tried not to breathe too deeply for fear his youthfulness would be sucked from his body like poison from a wound.

Despite the tension between himself and Sufi, he eagerly accepted her hand when she offered it to him as the mist grew ever thicker around them.

"Walk carefully Peter. You should begin to feel the ground change soon, we will be going up a slight incline. Then we should reach the mouth of the cave," Sufi informed him. Peter squeezed her hand in response. He was fighting the urge to run away blindly screaming his face off. Only the ever present danger that he might collide rather sharply with a tree trunk prevented him from pursuing this course of action.

Sufi felt the panic too.

It was only her second visit to the cave of the Old Ones.

She had been sent with Mundo shortly after Morquinda first abandoned them, to try and track her down. It had taken them days to find the cave, and even then neither one of them had had the courage to actually enter it and try to seize the books of the Great Find back. There had been something stifling about that cave, and it had reeked of the Lord of the Now.

She knew she couldn't let Peter sense her fear because she was absolutely certain that he too was putting on a very brave front right at that moment. She could feel his hand trembling in hers, but when she looked back at him he was smiling encouragingly at her.

They were together, and that was all that mattered.

The ground began to change beneath their feet. The soft carpet of pine needles, upon which they had been walking all this time, now gave way to a rough stone covering, and the path steepened as they began to gingerly ascend a short rise.

"We'll have to scrabble from here Peter," Sufi advised, gently letting go of his hand and beginning to clamour across the rocks. Peter followed suit though with less finesse. He wished he could at least see further in front of him. The mist was draped across the hill as though it were a vast dust sheet protecting some ancient furniture. When he glanced backwards over his shoulder all he could see was an empty white expanse, out of which he continually expected shadows to loom.

High above them he could hear the cawing of seemingly invisible birds, a sure sign that they were making more noise in their ascent than they had intended.

Suddenly Sufi froze.

Peter collided with her back and nearly slipped off the hillside as he struggled to regain his balance.

"What's the matter?" he hissed, wishing he had a sword, or anything, to protect them. Sufi was crouching like a sprinter, her legs slightly splayed and tensed with muscle. She was staring directly ahead and not moving. Even when Peter prodded her gently with his finger to elicit a response she remained perfectly still.

"Are we in danger?" Peter felt it was an extremely valid question at this point. Finally Sufi turned her head to look at him.

"Very much so," she whispered back. "We're here."

Peter tentatively moved to join her, and now he could see through the breaking mist the reason for Sufi's sudden halt.

The mouth of the Old Ones cave was barely an inch from them. It opened out of the hillside like a raw and angry sore. Jagged rocks jutted at nightmarish angles from the entranceway giving the alarming impression that the cave had grown a row of rather sharp teeth. Miasmas streamed from the opening, and Sufi and Peter tried to turn downwind to avoid the nauseous smell.

From within the cave they could faintly hear movement.

Peter drew in a long breath and exhaled very slowly. He was aware that Sufi was looking forlornly at him.

"Are you ready to go in there Peter?" Sufi asked. She was as tense as he was; the horror of that waiting cave filled her with foreboding. "We'll be safe as long as we're together," she assured him. Peter reached for her hands again, cupping both of them in his. He felt the warmth of Sufi's skin and he knew exactly what he had to do.

"I have to go in there alone Sufi," he began, and almost immediately she was shaking her head to prevent him, but he gripped her hands firmly and continued. "Sufi...you've been so patient with me, so understanding of everything that I have done, I can't begin to thank you. Without you I wouldn't even have reached this point in my life, and I know this sounds ridiculous...maybe even a little corny, but this is the first time I have ever truly felt alive," he said honestly. With a sigh he moved her hands away, and then exhaled resolutely. "My sister wants me to talk to these women. She has left something for me in that cave and I must go and claim it. I must go alone. I hope you understand?" he said, rising to his feet. He turned to depart but Sufi caught his arm.

"You are a hero Peter Bettany. In your heart, you know this to be true...I will wait for you here," she said. He was grateful to her, having expected her to protest.

To make it even easier for him, Sufi turned away and sat down with her back to him.

He never saw or heard the tears she cried.

⤳

They burrowed at a frantic pace. Hybrid after Hybrid was sent down the new tunnel to replace the front line of Still and dig at a renewed pace. It was the most cleverly orchestrated feat of excavation ever attempted, and at the very heart of it the Lord of the Now stood triumphant.

Layer upon layer of soil was torn down and cleared using only the brute strength of his army.

The fresh tunnel was less than a mile from its destination, snaking through the earth of Kilfanfyn Forest like a venomous python.

Along its filthy darkness marched the Hybrid Still.

Those who were not involved in the digging waited in perfect rows, chanting and screaming their war cries as they awaited the final breakthrough into the Mist Children's camp.

This would be their first taste of blood, and each and every creature wanted the first kill to be theirs.

"My precious children."

The Lord of the Now congratulated them as he marched up and down the ranks of Hybrid Still admiring their gleaming claws and taunt muscles. They all turned their featureless heads to follow their master, screaming in triumph at his praise.

"They are all waiting, oblivious to our coming…like lightning we will arrive, and we will slaughter them all."

He venomously spat his hatred upon them.

"I know you are all eager to bring me great glory this day."

At this he was momentarily drowned out by the roaring of his troops.

"But we must allow your brethren to herd the lambs down to the slaughter,"

he announced, suddenly more businesslike.

"The tunnel will be worked only at half capacity for the next couple of hours,"

he barked, snapping his talons to make it happen.

Immediately four lines of Hybrids retreated from the excavation site; this left only nine tunnelling at the earth.

As the muddied creatures fell back amongst the ranks, the Lord of the Now congratulated them on their diligence.

"Your master is pleased,"

he assured them, as though they were dogs.

"And soon...you will all have your reward."

♋

The second that Peter stepped into the cave he practically vomited.

A masticated rat lay festering a few feet from the cave entrance, but even that could not completely justify the pestilential smell that assaulted his nostrils.

Outside the cave had been bad enough, but the clammy low ceiling and tight walls seemed to hold the worst of the stench and then add a sweaty humidity to it.

He was sweating almost uncontrollably, his clothes already wet through from the mist.

It was virtually impossible to see his own hand in front of his face, and he did his level best to try and accustom his eyes to the darkness before he even attempted to go any further.

He was struggling to control his breathing, and with each further second he spent in the cave he was coming ever closer to a complete panic attack.

His brain was starving for oxygen and sending crazy signals to various organs in his body. He had to get a grip on the panic or he would be utterly debilitated and unable to move.

Further down in the blackness of the tunnel he could hear shuffling. It confirmed his worst fear that something was undoubtedly waiting for him beyond the veil of black.

He thought of Sufi sitting all alone at the entrance and he fought hard to repress the urge to run to her side.

His hands gripped the rough wall and the stabbing coldness of the rock seemed to bring him to his senses. Taking a firm grip on his own destiny, he edged deeper into the cave.

The ground was slippery underfoot and the walls grew gradually damper as he proceeded cautiously, waving cobwebs from his face, and praying he wasn't about to be confronted by a giant spider.

As the cave dipped slightly he stumbled, losing his footing on the rocks. His right foot submerged into a cold puddle of filthy water, which leached into his boots and caused him to cry out in alarm.

The echo from his sudden shout of terror seemed to go on forever drifting endlessly off into the distance. He scrabbled back up onto the stones and began to move quicker, realising he had just lost the element of surprise.

The cave tunnel was now twisting away and although he was about to lose the faint light of the entrance, a new more prominent illumination was reaching him from about a hundred yards away. He was practically running forward now to reach the small campfire that greeted his weary eyes.

The cave had opened out into a small rotunda cavern which was almost high enough for him to stand up straight. Peter was still cautious, constantly checking around him for any sign of movement, but the cavern appeared to be deserted.

It was squalid and smelt even worse than the adjoining tunnel. Dirty rags were strewn across the floor and in places bundles of a murky brown straw appeared to be arranged as though they were sleeping bags.

Peter edged towards the fire, noticing a few bones scattered haphazardly over the ground. It looked as though some kind of animal had occupied the cave up until recently.

Peter kicked at the bones with his feet, striking them across the floor. He had suddenly grown tired with waiting for the Old Ones to appear and attack him. He threw caution to the wind and roared: "Morquinda?"

Only the sound of the ever-dripping walls greeted him in return. He moved away from the fire in frustration, fearing for a second that he may actually have arrived too late.

They may already have died from hypothermia, he reasoned, shivering from the occasionally chilling breeze that seemed to be coming from further within the cave.

It was at this moment that he first saw the hieroglyphics.

The flicker from the campfire brought life to the pictures which Morquinda had painfully scratched into the wall. Peter looked upon them in wide eyed astonishment as they appeared momentarily animated in the shifting light.

He saw the strange image of a galloping white horse, moving from side to side at an unnatural angle.

"A lame horse?" he wondered aloud.

He began to edge his way back along the cave tunnel, realising that these pictures were all over the walls, he had just been unable to see them in the darkness.

He cursed as the light dipped away from him the further he walked from the campfire. He began to retrace his steps into the cavern again, deciding to try and remove a branch from the fire to use as a torch.

It was then that the bony hand closed around his mouth.

The grip was stronger than he could have anticipated, and it curtailed his scream easily. A second hand slipped around his throat and he felt the sharp edge of a stone press against his windpipe.

"Speech will bring only blood from your sweet lips," a hideously screechy voice informed him. He looked about with wild eyes, unable to turn his head and view his assailant. Before he could struggle free he was distracted by the sudden appearance of a ghostly old woman, leering out of the shadows in front of him. He had barely registered the madness that emanated from her grey wizened eyes when he felt the sharp point of a spear prodding into his stomach.

The second old woman was holding a sharpened stick threateningly. He froze, fearing he was about to be skewered through the heart by the strangely genteel lady who was drooling profusely onto her gown.

"Beast we have you, stealing into our home to pinch our humble possessions," a third voice excitedly accused him.

Peter looked horror struck as another elderly woman shuffled into view. She was clearly blind as she addressed all her accusations to the air, and her back was almost bent double with arthritis. "Filthy little boy, how dare you come to us…do you not know who we are?" she demanded, feeling her way over to the woman brandishing the stick.

Peter was coughing and spluttering horribly, and the stone was rubbing against the wound that Taime had dealt him, threatening to re-open it. Whoever was wielding the primitive weapon had a vice-like grip, and he could barely breathe.

"He knows who we are." A fourth and final voice brought silence to the melee. It was spoken with authority, and laced with undeniable fear.

Morquinda vacated the shadows of the cave, stepping past the campfire and staring wildly about her as though she too were unsure of her surroundings. Her wild grey hair looked like a horde of vipers attempting to battle for the supremacy of her scalp, and her viciously gaunt face appeared as bloodless as a corpse's.

"Release him Isabella and you may beg his forgiveness for laying your profanity upon him. Put down that spear my sister," she snapped, striding past Elyse who looked dumbfounded.

"But he is a thief...a Mist Child trying to steal the Holy Books," she protested in anger at Morquinda's rebuttal.

"He is not!" Morquinda snapped, spinning around and spitting a thick globule of phlegm at her sister. The old lady screamed and dropped the spear, wiping at her eyes to free them from the foul liquid. She looked menacingly at Morquinda but the old woman held her finger to her lips.

Isabella had released Peter from her grip and he tumbled forward, slipping to the floor and clutching his throat in pain.

Everyone waited expectantly as he coughed and shook, before finally rising angrily to his feet.

"Morquinda," Peter clarified. He was wiping at the blood which had spread from the wound in his neck. Morquinda attempted a curtsy but she could barely bend with the combined pain of her lumbago and her arthritis. She managed an almost comical bow instead and looked despairingly upon the young man whom she believed would kill her.

"Do you not recognise me?" Peter emphasised, horribly aware that the old woman was trembling with fear. Morquinda nodded pathetically before answering.

"You are my destroyer..." she announced. "You are the Harvester."

There was a collective gasp from the other three Old Ones. Each in turn attempted to bow or grovel while Peter looked on in total bewilderment.

"I'm Peter Bettany," he announced, hoping they hadn't been expecting someone else. "Annabel Bettany's brother."

At this Felicia hissed in disgust but the other three were quick to silence her.

"I have waited nine long years for this day." Morquinda continued as though Peter had never spoken. "Nine years since the snows came, nine years since the false girl left us..." She was speaking as though hypnotised and with each sentence she rocked slightly, pulling at the hem of her dress as though she were about to dance.

Peter was looking in mild shock at the old women who surrounded him. They were barely recognisable from their time at Lambert House. Peter had seldom visited them even then, but he had on occasion gone with his parents to see Annabel working there. He doubted they could remember him; they all seemed in the firm grip of senility now.

"Which one of us would you like to kill first?" Isabella requested, looking as though she would have been happy to write down an order. The other three Old Ones also grew animated with excitement at this suggestion. Peter held up his hands in protest.

"I'm not here to kill anyone," he cried, trying to calm the rising melee. "I'm here to talk with Morquinda...Annabel has left me a letter," he said, backing away from the group so he could keep a watchful eye on all of them. "She wanted me to come and find you...which I have done. Apparently she left something in your keeping...something for me." He locked eyes with Morquinda, and the old lady stared back at him in horror.

"The Harvester wants the Holy Books." She sounded outraged. "This was not in the prophesy." A tension settled upon the group as the Old Ones fanned out to flank Morquinda, they all stared levelly at Peter.

"You will have to slit our throats first Harvester," Elyse decreed, craning her neck upwards to reveal her throbbing jugular. Peter looked appalled.

"Who are you talking about?" he demanded. "I am not the Harvester...I am Peter Bettany, and I am here because Annabel has left something for me in your charge. You must remember, surely?" he bemoaned, staring pitiful at the ragamuffin women who all glared manically back at him as though he were speaking in riddles.

Morquinda stepped away from the others and strode towards Peter with her arms held out as though in surrender. He didn't know how to react, and so remained rigid as she drew up close to him. Her breath smelt of decay, and her rags reeked of an insipid odour, as though she had slept in faeces for a number of days.

"Did you come here on the lame horse?" she unexpectedly asked. Peter looked momentarily confused.

"Lockavarn...the white horse?" Peter assumed. Morquinda smiled revealing a mouth full of rotten yellow teeth which were flecked with the residue of a recent meal.

"The white horse *haunts* you Peter Bettany," she told him, as though revealing a hidden secret. Peter's eyes were smarting from the putrid air, and he barely managed a smile. Yet something in Morquinda's words rang true.

"It is your saviour...you must reclaim him as your own," she continued, edging even closer so that her haggard face filled Peter's vision. "Have you been tempted by the wild girl?" she demanded. This question threw Peter completely. He felt as though he were the prisoner of a sadistic inquisition, and now the killer question had been posed. He tried to avert his eyes from Morquinda's wicked stare but he found it impossible. His face flushed red with embarrassment.

"No...I haven't...I..."

All the Old Ones gasped in triumph.

"He is the Harvester, there can be no doubt," Felicia giggled, scrabbling in the dirty straw of the cave floor, trying to face the direction of Peter's words. The echoes of the cavern made the task impossible and she spun in a perpetual circle as Morquinda glared testily at Peter.

"There is one final test," she began, turning her head away for a second as though in contemplation. Peter breathed out, glad to have a chance of reprieve from the madness of the cave.

In a split second Morquinda was upon him, her lips clasped upon his and her foul tongue slipped into his mouth.

Peter nearly vomited as he felt her rough tongue sliding over his, leaving a coating of spittle like a slug's trail in his mouth. He grabbed the sides of her head like a passionate lover, but used all his strength to push her away from him. Every instinct inside him screamed that he should strike her in fury, but his morals prevented him.

Morquinda allowed him to extricate her, and she stepped back from him, wiping at her own mouth as though Peter was the one who disgusted her. She watched him pitifully spitting onto the floor, trying to free his mouth of her foul taste. He desperately needed water. "You could not strike me," she announced, and Peter stared viciously at her, scraping back his hair.

"Of course not!" he spat. "You're insane, but you're just an old woman!" he bawled at her.

At this Morquinda looked elated. She spread out her hands in triumph.

"He is indeed the Harvester," she announced, snapping her fingers. "Elyse, Isabella, bring me the trunk. Felicia!" She screamed at the still circling old crone. "You will calm down and lay still my love. The Harvester has come only for me...you will all be safe," she assured her. At this Felicia stopped her twisting circle, and lay panting upon the floor.

"Does he mean to take us home?" she asked, an almost child-like smile playing across her face.

"This is our home you foolish girl!" Morquinda berated her and the smile vanished from Felicia's face.

"This is not your home!" Peter said, finally recovered from his assault. He stormed towards Morquinda, his rage adding a brutal edge to his voice. "You are all from Earth, not the Dark Realm, and I promise you, when this is all over, we will all be going home together," he stated, as if the discussion was definitely closed.

At this Morquinda broke into peels of hysterical laughter. She virtually pulled Felicia to her feet and then pirouetted in front of a mortified Peter.

"After this is all over…we will all be dead," Morquinda announced through fits of uncontrollable cackling.

"I shall be first!" Felicia cried with joy. This brought the macabre dance to an immediate close. Morquinda was staring hatefully at her companion.

"How dare you claim that honour for yourself. Right here in front of the Harvester…he knows…" she pointed an accusing finger at Peter, "he knows it shall be me who dies first." She was adamant on this point and Peter held up his hands in exasperation.

"This is insane…you're all mad." He was almost laughing himself with the absurdity of this situation. "I'm not this Harvester whom you keep referring to…do you not remember me from Lambert House? I used to visit Annabel when she was nursing you all?" Peter turned himself around as though he were doing a catwalk twirl in the hope it would spark some inner memory. When he'd completed his half-circle he found Morquinda looking blankly at him.

"It is you who suffers with delusion. You are the Harvester of the Now; Peter Bettany. I will show you what your future holds in store."

∽

Outside the cave Sufi sat in a state of utter melancholy.

She was hugging her knees to her chest, a simple action which had always brought her a great deal of comfort in the past.

Even now she could remember some nights at Myfanwy when she would cry herself to sleep like this, trying to understand what was happening to her body as she reached maturity.

She had never asked to be a Dream Blender.

This was a gift which Annabel had given to her, and although it had seemed such an honour, and so exciting at first, without Annabel it clung to her heart like disease.

She quietly cursed the night she had first made contact with Peter.

It was that night that had sown the seeds of her love for him. If he hadn't have appeared so innocent and nervous of her, she was certain she would have kept her heart closed to him. But he had, and despite the truth of his nature which had unravelled itself in the days that followed, he had still remained her responsibility. His safety had been paramount to her, and as time had worn on, this had become a love she couldn't control.

But what now?

What was she to do now he had told her he didn't love her back?

She wiped at a tear, cursing again that she had ever allowed herself to have feelings for him. When he had been talking she had found it easier to hide how hurt she was, but now she was alone with only the mist for company, the tears came easily.

She knew he was a part of her now, and that meant he would linger inside her, making it difficult for her to move on.

"Poor Pigeon," she sighed, realising finally how it felt to love someone who could never love you back in the same way.

But she did love Pigeon. She had always loved him.

He was her safety, her protection. When the whole world was against her, Pigeon was always by her side.

"Is that love?" she questioned the mist.

Only emptiness and silence greeted her.

∽

"There is a darkness coming that will make the blackest night seem like a super nova." Morquinda wisely intoned as Isabella and Elyse dragged the trunk from the dark recesses of the cave into the dwindling campfire light.

Peter was kneeling down close to the campfire, his anxious face bathed in the soft orange glow from the flames. He was watching Morquinda, trying to catch glimpses of the sanity she would occasionally speak, amongst the riddles and the madness.

It frightened him how certain she was of her own prophecies, and at times he actually believed she was telling the truth.

His eyes widened as he caught his first glimpse of the trunk.

It was barely holding together at its tired hinges. The whole structure looked as though a number of carpenters had worked upon the project, all in complete disagreement with one another.

It slammed against the ground as the two elderly ladies finally gave up trying to lug it between them. This final impact should have been enough to burst the trunk apart, but by some miracle it held in place.

The remains of willow branches still hung from it in places, as though they had been used to hide in some way the appearance of the trunk.

"You will be at the very centre of this darkness. Your own future is uncertain Peter, but I can tell you exactly who will die?" she offered, as though this would appeal to him in some way.

Peter looked mortified, and before she could reveal any more he cut her off.

"You dare tell me such things, and I will bring torment upon you." He was trembling with fear and anger, the very thought that any of the Mist Children would die because of him made him sick to the pit of his stomach. Morquinda laughed, the corners of her mouth bubbling with warm spittle.

"You have brought me all the torment I could ever wish for simply by being here," she spat at him. "Why should I fear your threats? But…" she suddenly snapped her fingers as though casting a spell, "we will say nothing more of it…a surprise is always best unspoilt I find." She turned back to the trunk and with extremely theatrical gestures, she began to undo the various straps and clasps.

Felicia, Isabella and Elyse all gathered around the crouching Peter, nuzzling against him as though he were a source of warmth. Peter grimaced but resisted the urge to push them all away.

All eyes were on Morquinda, and she seemed to relish her moment in the spotlight.

Eventually with a final deft flourish, she opened the lid of the trunk and sent it careening over the back of the chest with a wood-splintering crash. A cloud of dust erupted from the filthy floor, threatening to engulf Morquinda as she began rummaging inside the trunk.

Reams of paper were spewing forth as she dug deep into the jumble, trying to sift through and find something relevant.

Peter made a move to pick up one of the fallen sheets, but the Old Ones penned him in.

"Only Morquinda can interpret the Holy Books correctly," Elyse informed him. Peter raised a disbelieving eyebrow.

"Why doesn't that surprise me?" he sarcastically smiled. The remark was lost upon Elyse but Morquinda had heard it.

"Foolish boy," she snapped, turning round to face him. She was wreathed in dust and the flickering light made her look almost angelic. Peter shuddered slightly at the sight. Morquinda certainly knew how to command attention. She was clutching a single sheet of paper in her withered right hand, but before she could hand it to Peter something caught her eye behind him. "Who else dares enter the cave of the Old Ones?" she suddenly screamed at such a frightening volume, that Peter nearly sprang to his feet.

He had heard no approaching footsteps, and looking in the direction Morquinda was pointing, he could see only the darkness of the cave.

"It is foolish to hide from me," Morquinda announced, stepping closer towards Peter. The Old Ones were becoming agitated, desperate to see who the intruder was.

To Peter's relief and amazement Sufi stepped out of the shadows. She had her head slightly bowed, as though she was hiding her face, and her bare feet crossed the stone floor silently.

"I'm sorry Peter, I had to come in. The mist is growing thicker and I could hear voices and screaming." She looked up, her blonde hair took on the texture of fire in the orange light, and her eyes looked dark and painfully sore.

"You've been crying," Peter said in alarm, reaching out his hand for her.

"We should kill the little beast," Felicia cried, mortified that Sufi was standing in their cave. She scrabbled around for the wooden spear, but Peter grabbed her.

"You touch her..." he threatened his face a mask of rage, "and I will end you." Felicia looked momentarily startled, and then turned sheepishly away as though she were suddenly embarrassed.

"Let the harlot sit with us," Morquinda said, trying to sound welcoming but failing miserably. Sufi looked incensed by the comment, but Peter gently guided her to sit next to him.

"Are you ok?" he whispered to her, while Morquinda busied herself stoking the pitiful fire.

Elyse, Isabella and Felicia crowded the pair like vultures around fresh meat. Sufi shivered and tried to smile at Peter.

"Are you?" She turned the question back on him. Peter also smiled.

"I will be if we get out of here!" he admitted.

"Do you not remember me Morquinda?" Sufi suddenly asked, watching the old crone gathering her dress around her as she sat down. Morquinda seemed to consider her for a moment, and then looked perplexed.

"You are not the first Sacred Mother, and you are not the one whom the Harvester loves...you are nothing," she said viciously.

The remark left Sufi cold, her hand crept to her chest as she felt her heart palpitate.

"Who is the Harvester?" she asked and Peter looked downcast.

"She keeps saying it's me...I'm the Harvester of the Now." Peter sounded embarrassed and Sufi fell silent.

"You are the Harvester," Morquinda insisted, thrusting the piece of paper towards him. "The Holy Books do not lie."

Peter gingerly accepted the sheet, studying the neatly folded paper. It was slightly weathered from exposure to the dampness of the cave, but it was undoubtedly paper ripped from a sketchbook of some kind.

With both Sufi and the Old Ones huddled around him to see, he unfolded the paper and let out a sudden cry.

∽

Through the mist they marched.

Line after line.

Their clawed feet were pounding a constant rhythm across the snow.

Each Still warrior remained pertinacious upon their solitary goal.

The Mist Children were to be slaughtered.

They screamed and they cried in unison as they pillaged the lands through which they passed. No living creature was safe from an army bred with the sole purpose of mass destruction.

They devoured birds and wildlife, uprooted trees and demolished fences as they marauded across the plains of the once glorious Myfanwy.

Krinn brought his cart to a shuddering halt as he stopped to admire the smouldering ruin of the farmhouse that had once been his home.

"Never again will you offer shelter to the lost," he whispered into the swirling mist that seemed to cling to the burnt out hulk as though it were a nurse offering comfort to the mortally wounded. "You will not be alone for long." He spoke as though the farmhouse were a living entity, a foul smile upon his lips.

"You will remain here," he addressed a Still at random, "in case they should manage to send out a scout. Go to Khynous Morf and await further instructions. If nightfall comes and no one has arrived, return to Kilfanfyn Forest." He snapped his fingers and the Still scuttled away across the plains.

Krinn herded the other Still onward, beating them with the reins to make them pull the cart faster. They roared back at him, but while he possessed the glaive they dared not attack him.

Kilfanfyn Forest lay several miles away, but already the Still had begun to scent their prey.

Krinn thought of Peter's world, so fresh and innocent, full of new children to capture and torture. His wickedness knew no bounds, and he felt certain he was yet to show his master the full extent of his malignant evil.

Perhaps he would prove himself today, when he finally killed Ethanril in combat. The thought pleased him, and he felt his tensions relax as the army marched ever onwards.

∽

"What does this mean?" Peter was asking, shaking the paper in front of Morquinda's face.

"Are you such an innocent fool?" Morquinda snapped back,

lashing out at the paper with her hands as though she intended to shred it.

Sufi moved faster, grabbing it from Peter and pulling it to her breast.

"Stop it!" she screamed authoritatively as the Old Ones attempted to snatch back the paper. She stood up angrily, and Peter rose too, desperate to see the paper again. She was staring in wonder at the pencil drawing which took up the whole page. Even in the dull light of the cave, it was easy to see whom the drawing depicted.

"This is you Peter," she said, looking up from the drawing into his face. Peter was still in denial.

"How can it be me?" he asked, looking at the drawing again. "I'm not the Harvester, I keep telling everyone," he added in despair.

The drawing showed a tall, imposing man clad in a chain mail suit of armour. He was affecting an aggressive stance and holding in his muscular right hand a sword quite unlike anything Peter had ever seen before. It was shaped almost like a scimitar, with a long curved blade that seemed to bow in places where it should have been straight. The tip of the sword was the only portion of the sketch that had been coloured in using a bright aqua blue crayon.

The man had long flowing hair, and a chin covered with thick black strokes to depict a beard. But it was the eyes that gave away the truth of this caricature. Despite the lack of colour they were strikingly wide and thoughtful.

Peter's eyes.

Above the man, in a handwriting which did not match the proficiency of the drawing was a simple title:

HArVESTEr of the NOW.

In the bottom left hand corner Annabel had scrawled her name, and a date.

The drawing was nearly twenty years old.

Sufi was staring at Peter with a joy in her eyes that he had not seen there before.

"Annabel drew this of you. All the time you were her hero Peter," she said, barely hiding her excitement. Peter was less convinced; he looked at the date on the picture.

"She was barely ten years old when she drew this!" he exclaimed. "Look at her handwriting, she's got capital and small letters all confused! This has no relevance to what's happening here in the Dark Realm, she wouldn't even have invented this world then. It's just a childish drawing." He was getting so worked up that he was struggling for breath. Sufi looked horrified, while the Old Ones laughed wickedly at Peter's angst.

"How can you say that Peter? She has depicted you as a hero...YOU. The brother who did nothing but plague her and make her life so miserable, yet she still wanted you to be her hero." Sufi was devastated that Peter was reacting so badly to this.

"I'm the only man she knew at that time! It's probably not even meant to represent me; it looks more like my Father! He would have been more of a hero to her...I was a lousy older brother. Besides which, I don't even have a beard!"

He was practically dizzy with emotion now. Everything that he had already put himself through that day was now being tested again, and this time he was certain he would finally crack under the pressure.

Sufi immediately sensed the confusion in Peter. She had been witness to so many of his tantrums now that she knew almost instinctively that he was just suffering a panic attack. In response she held up her hand, and instead of shouting back to calm him down, she just cupped his thickly stubbled chin with one small hand. Peter seemed to freeze at her touch, his breathing calming as she stroked his chin. He allowed her to lift up his own right hand and place it against his cheek. He felt the stubble under his fingers and gave a nervous laugh.

"I'm no expert Peter..." Sufi said, smiling at him and gently removing her hand, "but that feels like a beard to me! Your sister had incredible perception; she wanted you to turn into a hero, if not during her childhood then at least when you became a man. You're right, this drawing may not have been intended for the Dark Realm, but you can't deny the picture is of you. You are her hero...The Harvester," Sufi assured him.

Peter eased the drawing from her fingers and studied it in silence for a while, trying to take in all the implications of it.

All this time Morquinda and the Old Ones waited in silence. The prophecies were coming true, but in ways they had not anticipated.

"If this is me..." Peter eventually broke the silence, still gazing intently at the drawing. "I still don't believe this was the reason she wished me to see you Morquinda," he accused, lowering the paper to view the old woman. "Annabel's letter was very specific; she mentioned that you were keeping something for me? Is this what she meant?" He held up the drawing.

Morquinda stared up at it for a moment as though it were a raised sword. Then just as suddenly she cackled with madness.

It was the most disconcerting of sights, and it chilled Sufi to the bone.

"Always you question Peter Bettany...not like the other one, she only had answers," Morquinda chuckled, turning back to the trunk. "Everything I am showing you today is relevant...all of it is taken directly from the Holy Books of the Great Find..."

At this Peter shot forward and tried to grab hold of her, but the many folds of her dress made the task virtually impossible. It was lucky for Peter that the very motion of attack brought Morquinda screaming to her knees, begging him to strangle her.

Peter looked at the quivering, weak old woman, grovelling in the dirt and he shuddered.

"It's pointless to keep begging me to kill you," Peter said coldly, while Morquinda licked the grimy floor with her withered tongue. "I'm not here to fulfil any of your so called prophecies."

At this the three other Old Ones cried in alarm.

"Heresy…what can it mean?" Felicia demanded, picking at Elyse's dress in fear.

"The Great Find was nothing of the sort!" Peter wouldn't stop now; he was taking a sadistic pleasure in shattering their illusions. "Sufi took some papers from Annabel's bedroom and brought them back here to the Dark Realm. That was the Great Find. Some of those papers she sewed into a dress and the others you all stole away and horded here, in this repulsive cave of yours!" He snarled, grabbing another handful of papers. He looked through them briefly. More drawings, this time of the Still, and a half completed map of the Dark Realm. In amongst these he found the beginnings of a few short stories, featuring names that were now becoming familiar to him. He even found reference to the Harvester among them. "These aren't Holy Books!" he cried, tearing the pages up in front of the distraught Morquinda. "They're just stories…drawings, notes that my sister was making. They're not the foundations for any prophecies." He threw them into the campfire which immediately blazed hungrily. Morquinda tried to retrieve them, but Isabella held her back.

"The Harvester is right Morquinda…they are the writings of the child. All this time we have been lying to the Lord of the Now. We're not prophets," she argued, but Morquinda was shaking her head. She stabbed a finger out at Peter.

"He is a liar…a blasphemer. Everything I have told you has come to pass. The child wrote of this world, and all her stories are true, just like his. These are Holy Books." Morquinda raged, sobbing at the mental anguish she was being put through.

Peter could understand the logic of her reasoning, but he was desperate to make her see sense.

"Very well...they are relevant to the Dark Realm," he begrudgingly admitted. "But not to you Morquinda, or your friends. You're not from this world. You're from my world, Annabel's world. That's where you belong, and that's where I will take you back when all this is over." Peter tried to placate them.

"How dare you bargain with us?" Elyse suddenly snapped at him. "You wrote of an evil House where everyone is tortured daily...we've all read that story." She indicated the reams of fallen paper strewn around the trunk. "Well that's the reality I remember," she spat. Morquinda seemed to seize on this.

"You see sisters how the Harvester tries to confuse us with his lies...not like the dark one. He tells us only of now! It is the now where we belong. We are not from your world Harvester," she snarled vehemently, rising to her feet and beginning to ransack the trunk in earnest. "I will give you the gift which the false girl left in my keeping; it is my destiny to fulfil the prophecy, and then all fates rest with you." She cackled again.

Sufi was by now standing shoulder to shoulder with Peter.

"How can you call her the false girl?" she demanded. "Annabel loved you. She brought you to us because she knew that you were all being abused in her world. She saved you, and now you treat her as though she never did you a single kindness," Sufi pleaded.

Morquinda was too absorbed in her private quest to pay her any attention, but Isabella looked fondly at Sufi for a moment.

The papers were flying everywhere as Morquinda emptied the trunk. Some landed in puddles of water, smearing their secrets into an inky blue unreadable stain. Peter was trying to prevent some of the papers being lost forever, but before he could begin to gather them up, Morquinda suddenly let out a fearsome cry.

Everyone froze, and Peter was suddenly aware of a strange glow about the cave.

Its source appeared to be the now empty trunk, and as Peter approached it, Morquinda bent down and retrieved something from the depths which shimmered with an ethereal light as she drew it out of its ancient hiding place.

It was the sword from the drawing, the sword of the Harvester.

Morquinda held it out to him as though she were bearing a tray of delights, and the Old Ones all stepped away from Peter as he was bathed in the glow from the sword.

Sufi exhaled with anticipation as Peter reached out a tentative hand to clasp the hilt of the unusual blade.

"Take it Peter," she willed him under her breath. "Be our hero."

The second he grabbed it, Morquinda stepped backwards in fear. She seemed hypnotised by the weapon, which Peter moved from hand to hand, with an awestruck expression on his face.

"It's so light…" he managed, unable to think of a better way of describing the sword; he was clearly shocked to find that the drawing had a real model upon which it was based.

"It was the first thing she gave to me. She said she'd made it in a dream," Morquinda revealed, her voice now surprisingly calm. "The tip is made of ocean water," she continued, as though she were describing a perfectly ordinary item. "The chain mail is for you also," she indicated, and Peter crossed to the trunk, his eyes widening as he saw a vest of glittering gold links lying like a funeral shroud at the bottom of the trunk.

Morquinda stepped away, taking the opportunity to gather up the fallen papers while Peter, with Sufi's help, pulled on his new armour.

"It fits you perfectly," Sufi gasped in surprise, as Peter adjusted the heavy chain mail, and strapped his sword to his side. He was enchanted by the wondrous weapon, and he held the tip close to his eye to see how the water was constantly swirling from the end. It was so tempting to pass his hand over it, just like the Water Mirror in his own story, but he resisted, somehow knowing it would cut his skin like a razor.

"You are wise not to touch it Harvester. The Sword of the Ocean is more deadly than any blade in this world. It is your destiny to use it in battle against the Lord of the Now and his armies of Still," Morquinda announced, smiling a crooked smile at Peter. "You must live up to your name now Peter Bettany, you must do what Annabel always intended you to do. Put everything right." She laughed again, ferreting on the floor to gather more papers.

Peter was trying to balance out the weight of his armour, and he looked confused by Morquinda's words.

"What do you mean…live up to my name?" he asked, walking slowly towards her.

"You do know what Harvester means?" Elyse answered for her sister. Peter looked blankly. "Well…a harvest is the direct result of any action…in this case it implies your sister's vision ruined by the coming of the Lord of the Now. A harvester is a reaper…or a gatherer. Something that saves everything that is good, and gets rid of all that is corrupt or evil. That is what you have to be Peter Bettany…you must be the Harvester of the Now," the old woman wisely explained.

Peter felt as though his whole life had suddenly begun again, right there in the cave of the Old Ones. He ran his hand over the chain mail which felt so natural against his skin. This was the purpose of his coming to the Dark Realm, and although he had initially felt alone, he now realised that Annabel had walked with him every step of the way, ever since she had left him that message on his car windscreen.

She could still help him, and now he had the one thing which could help them all.

"We have lived with the darkness for so long now Peter, it is impossible to separate what was once wrong into what is now right," Felicia poignantly intoned. "We have had to help the Lord of the Now for as long as we could, while we waited for the Harvester to arrive. We have told him much that he wished to hear, but it was only Annabel's words, written in the Holy Books. He knows nothing of the Sword of the Ocean. He in turn has told us much which you now need to know, if you are to stand a chance against him," she continued, but Morquinda interrupted her.

"You are all fools if you help him now!" she squealed. "The Harvester is here with the sole purpose of killing us all. We have given him the weapon, and that is all she asked of us...now we must die at his hands," Morquinda prognosticated. Peter looked angrily at her.

"I pity you and your madness," he said honestly. The sentence seemed to enrage Morquinda even more.

With all the papers gathered up in her arms she stood looking like a caged rat, ready to fight to death if anyone should try and approach it.

"I pity you all," Morquinda said, her voice on the verge of breaking, and before anyone could stop her she had stepped into the flames of the campfire.

Her ragged dress lit like a funeral pyre and in seconds she was engulfed in flame.

The Old Ones started screaming in panic as they saw their leader writhing in agony as the fire shrivelled her skin and destroyed all the papers in her arms.

Peter reacted instantly, leaping into the heart of the fire and elbowing Morquinda viciously to tip her out of the flames. The two crashed onto the stone floor, Peter desperately trying to smother her blazing body with his own. The fire was scorching him, and in pain he had to abandon her, beating at his trousers which had started to catch fire.

Sufi looked on in despair, scrabbling in the darkness of the cave for something to help them. She managed to extract a sizable willow branch from one of the corners, and she beat at the flames to try and fan them.

"It's no good," Morquinda screamed in torment. "You must fulfil your destiny and kill me Harvester," she pleaded, as the fire blackened her face.

Peter was horrified as he realised she had purposefully done this to prove her prophecy was true.

Her violent screams for mercy were impossible to ignore, and with his eyes clamped tight shut, he drew out the Sword of the Ocean, and plunged the water blade straight into the fireball that was Morquinda's withering body.

Her screaming stopped instantly.

Peter drew back the blade with one swift movement, and he opened his eyes in time to see the flames slowly die around the blackened corpse of the once proud old lady.

Morquinda was dead.

"She was right." Elyse broke the silence, amazed by what had just happened. The shock gave way to tears, and she tried to reach for her sister but the intensity of the heat kept her at bay. She looked at Peter, but it was with a certain degree of love.

"She was in agony Harvester," she said, and Peter looked heartbroken at her words.

Sufi was next to him immediately.

"You had to Peter…she begged you," she reminded him, placing a protective arm around him.

"I've never killed anyone before." Peter was devastated. Sufi shook her head.

"You didn't kill her Peter…she was dying in great pain, you saved her…that's what the prophecy means…that's what you do," she said.

"What has happened?" Felicia asked piteously. She had been crying on the floor for the last few minutes and seemed utterly confused by what was happening. Elyse moved to her and began whispering reassurances in her ear.

"You two must go now," Isabella said kindly, holding out a hand to each of them. They took it in bewilderment. "Morquinda would have done that anyway...you must not blame yourselves. You have helped us already Harvester, I assure you." She smiled at them and in that one moment she was the old lady Peter remembered from Lambert House.

"You must come with us," Peter said. "We must all get to safety in Kilfanfyn Forest." Isabella shook her head sadly.

"I'm afraid the journey in itself would kill us. No, we must remain here for when the Lord of the Now comes," she said.

"But he will kill you," Sufi said in alarm.

"It is all over for us child. We've been here too long to go home now. Our destiny is here. His rage will be merciless, but we will do what we can to hold him back," Isabella said, slowly beginning to lead them both out of the cave and away from Elyse and Felicia.

There was a strange atmosphere around Peter and Sufi now, an anticipation that their lives would be forever changed from this moment forth. Peter was still trying to come to terms with Morquinda's death, and the realisation that he now had no choice but to immediately put his plans into operation while they still had the element of surprise.

As they shuffled gingerly back down the tunnel, Isabella talked animatedly:

"He fears the Pig-Beast Peter; it is an advantage you must never forget. It is the one living thing on this unfinished world that could genuinely kill him," she hissed conspiratorially. "But you have very little time to prepare yourselves. He has sent out his wild dogs to sniff out your lair, and they will be followed by an army of epic proportions, who will march for Kilfanfyn Forest."

Peter and Sufi looked horror-struck.

"He knows you will be protected now Peter, so he is going to kill everyone around you until you are at his mercy. That way there will be nothing to stop him ending this particular chapter in the Dark Realm's history and starting afresh, on your world Peter."

"But killing me won't help him." Peter was perplexed. "I'm his only link to Earth."

"He has left a Still behind. One which will keep the link open to your world. And I fear he has some prisoners in Stilfanwyn Chasm from Earth as well, though he has not said who they are." Isabella sighed.

Peter had begun to pace angrily. The very thought that anyone from Wick Holm was being held prisoner by that monster left him cold.

"My sister is in great danger," Peter cried. "That Still will pick up her scent now it no longer has mine to follow." He slammed his palm against the tunnel wall in desperation.

Sufi squeezed his arm in reassurance.

"She will be protected Peter, you must have the same faith in her that she has in you," she reminded him. "Isabella?" she continued, turning to hold the old woman's hand as they emerged from the tunnel into the brightness of the sun-streaked mist. "Why are you now suddenly telling us all this?" Sufi looked fondly at her, but her voice betrayed her concern.

Isabella squinted at the brightness, and took a step backwards, out of the light and into the darkness of the cave mouth.

"I have been waiting for the Harvester to come and free us from the oppression of Morquinda. For years I have had to listen to the Lord of the Now spilling his evil plans out to us as though he were offering us sugar. I tell you both now all that I know of his final solution…in the hope that you can save this world from him forever." She paused, wiping a stray tear from her wrinkled cheek.

Sufi wanted to run to her and hug her, but something held her back. Instead she stared with eyes full of pity as the old woman looked sadly at Peter.

"Annabel has not forsaken them Harvester…she is just very tired now. You must ask her for help, she will always answer you. Good luck children, I hope we all meet again someday in a much happier place than this." With that she turned and disappeared into the encompassing dark.

Peter made to go after her, but Sufi grabbed his arm.

"She has made her choice Peter. Now we must make ours." She looked expectantly at him.

The mist was clearing, moving away from the hill, and dissipating over the plains of Carrastorc. Peter stood silently, looking down at his new armour, and the mystical sword which swung from his belt. Finally, he turned his searching blue eyes upon Sufi.

"We have to ride for Kilfanfyn Sufi, there is very little time left." He caressed her cheek with his rough hand, and she smiled.

"You know how to help us, don't you Peter?" she asked, with a glimmer of hope in her eyes.

Peter smiled at her, but said nothing.

15

The Parting.

*T*he Still struggled to stay in close pursuit of the Range Rover. It was not used to such a varied and urbanised terrain.

New smells assaulted its senses at every turn of the road, and alien objects presented themselves in array of alarming shapes and sizes.

It vaulted fences, scrabbled through gardens and attacked random cats and dogs which stumbled across its murderous path.

Inside its head it felt the constant pressure of the Lord of the Now's mind. He was driving the vindictive creature harder and faster than its crippled limbs could stand.

The closer it came to actually catching the Range Rover, the more difficult it became to resist the urge to immediately attack the occupants of the 4x4.

It remembered its attack upon Peter's car, and knew that it would not be difficult to peel away the metal and feast upon the trapped passengers.

But it could not.

They were leading it to the Sacred Mother.

Its vision momentarily blurred as it felt the confusion in the Lord of the Now's mind.

"Annabel Bettany is already dead."

It heard the Lord of the Now's distant voice.

"The scent is of her family. It pleases me to think you will kill them all for me while I in turn destroy Peter Bettany."

The Still snarled, twisting after the accelerating vehicle. It kept moving swiftly along the line of gorse bushes, making certain it wasn't observed.

Although it understood the Lord of the Now's instructions clearly, its own instinct was sending out confusing signals.

It *could* scent the original Sacred Mother.

Up ahead the road was broadening into three lanes and a large functional building was situated at the rise of a small hill.

The building registered nothing to the Still, but it watched with insatiable curiosity as the Range Rover indicated right, and began to approach Wick Holm Hospital at a decreased speed.

🌲

Kilfanfyn Forest looked serene, dipped in the lightest touch of winter's soft fingers, and flecked with the warm orange glow of the late afternoon sun's attentions.

The trees and foliage remained still and quiet, as they had for years and years.

The wildlife of the forest crept tentatively from their various holes, enjoying the peace in the weather, and the solitude of winter frost.

The great oak tree remained proud and prominent, towering above all others as though it were stretching up its branches to reach the fiery heart of the sun.

Everything was as it should be...

Except that, Ethanril was crying.

It was a sound which none of the woodland dwellers had ever heard before. Birds did not flap away in panic, but huddled together on branches to listen to this strange and woeful song.

The trees seemed to bow and creak in response, as though the sound of Ethanril's broken heart was enough to make them fall to the ground in despair.

Below the great oak tree, the Mist Children looked up from their work, trying to understand what such a sound could mean.

High above them all, Ethanril sat huddled on his branch, crying onto the sleeve of his jacket, unable to stop.

His eyes were red and sore, his hair a mess of tangled strands, as he continually ran his hands through it. His lips were constantly quivering as he fought against each tidal wave of despair.

Annabel was hurt. Hurt so badly that he couldn't put her right. He couldn't even go to her side and hold her hand.

He'd finally lost her forever.

The thought made him feel ill, and he clutched his stomach as though in pain.

All afternoon, since Peter and Sufi left the camp, he had fought to repress his emotions. He had watched them both ride away, into a world which held nothing but danger for them, and all he could think of was Annabel.

Normally he would have accompanied them; even if he had had to follow them in secret, just to be sure they were safe. But this time he knew he would have to trust in Peter and let them go alone.

There had been too much to deal with after Peter had left. The endless questions from the Mist Children, too numerous for even Ethanril to be able to answer fully. He had been overjoyed when Taime had actually started defending Peter's decisions with the group. Somehow, seeing the usually rebellious Taime actually fighting Peter's corner, seemed to create something of a turn of opinion.

Before long Ethanril had the group under control, and with Mundo's help he began to read them all Peter's dissertation.

They listened enraptured to the story of Forget-Me-House, and Ethanril noticed that many of the Mist Children seemed to show signs of recognition at various points in the story. They understood that Annabel had saved them from that terrible place, and brought them to sanctuary in the Dark Realm. They also seemed to understand that it was now Peter's responsibility to help them defeat the Lord of the Now. But they could not grasp the fact that this was all the direct result of a story that Peter had written as a child. Or that the Dark Realm had only come into existence through Annabel's dreams.

The concept meant nothing to them. They knew only now, and only the Dark Realm.

It was an innocence that Ethanril envied above everything else.

He had thought long and hard about explaining the complexities of it all to them, about how they were all merely characters in a story which had been brought to life by one very special girl.

But he chose not to.

"Let them sleep at night," he whispered to the trees. "Let them dream…let them live in peace." It was a simple prayer.

Mundo had cornered him after the readings, at the time he had been engrossed in sharpening his broadsword over the edge of a giant boulder near the Tarnwaters.

"Do you know what Morquinda has kept for Peter?" he'd asked bluntly. Ethanril was surprised by his friend's forwardness, but at the same time he understood why Mundo felt he could talk to him like this.

"I promise you Mundo, I have absolutely no idea," Ethanril assured him, running the great blade smoothly over the rock until a spray of sparks glittered into the air. "But when he returns, I have no doubt he will tell us."

Mundo was looking strangely at Ethanril.

"Are you ok?" he asked. The question caught Ethanril slightly off guard, and although he'd laughed it off with a smile and a shrug, it was this small point that had caused the melancholy to descend on him.

After this he had rallied Fess and Pigeon to organise dinner. Amazingly in the midst of all the excitement and tension of the afternoon, he had found the two of them snoozing with their backs resting against a tree and their heads gently pressed together; looking rather like a short, blunt human pyramid.

Ethanril had stolen upon them silently, and with a complete lack of tolerance, clapped his hands loudly in front of their faces.

Pigeon actually shot to his feet and asked a question as though he had fallen asleep in class, while Fess toppled neatly over without Pigeon's body to keep him upright.

"You two never fail to amaze me!" Ethanril had laughed, enjoying the momentary chaos he had created, "you'd sleep through a thunderstorm!"

Pigeon, who had tried to turn his sudden burst of movement into an impromptu exercise routine, and was now innocently humming a tune, stopped and glanced at Ethanril as though registering him for the first time.

"That wasn't sleeping…" he began, seemingly willing Fess to his feet using only the power of his mind. Fess stood up with all the grace of a puppet who had had several of its vital strings clipped. His arms hung loosely by his sides, and one of his legs was half bent as though he were either about to run off, or propose marriage to someone.

"Sleeping? Us? Are you out of your mind?" Fess said, trying to sound outraged.

"Ok…ok!" Ethanril could already see the tissue of lies and excuses he was about to be fed. "If I leave you two in charge of organising some food for tonight, can I trust you to stay alert?"

Fess and Pigeon looked as though they had been mortally offended, and both of them placed their hands to their chests as though to steady their beating hearts.

"When…" they asked, "have we *ever* let you down?"

Ethanril really didn't have time to read out the list.

That conversation had taken place over three hours ago, and it was only now as Ethanril sat in turmoil on his branch, that the faint smells of cooking meat were beginning to drift up to him.

He tipped his head back so his blonde hair rubbed against the tree trunk, and he wiped a strong hand under his sore eyes. He had felt a great deal of physical pain in his lifetime, but nothing compared to the agony his heart was in now.

"I'm so sorry I let you go that night," he apologised to the hazy sky. He squinted into the misty brightness, hoping he would catch a glimpse of her face on the breeze. Something about the tinges of orange in the rays of the sun, reminded him of her hair.

"I wish I'd held onto you…wish I'd kept you from harm."

It was the worst kind of wish. A wish to alter a past that had already happened, and would never come back, and the only answer was one as empty as his heart.

She was gone.

In his despair his mind took him to a variety of places, and made him consider many people. He even spared a thought for Krinn.

He felt almost sorry for him, this confused, lonely boy who had no sense of emotion, because Peter had never written any for him. The only fear he would ever know was fear of his own master. Love and happiness would always remain alien to him.

Krinn had been without doubt Ethanril's deadliest enemy, and though he felt sorry for the emptiness of his life, he didn't mourn his passing.

Ethanril watched the mist rising from the trees, moving away into the valleys like a great silk scarf which had threaded its way across the whole world.

He scented the air, feeling, as always the subtle changes in the currents. The afternoon felt even warmer than the morning, and this meant there would be very little chance of snow. The Dark Realm had indeed changed in the last day, and although he had initially thought that this was because of Peter, it made sense that it was actually Annabel who was helping them.

It was the most encouraging thought Ethanril had had for a long time.

As he gently stretched his legs and began to rise to his feet to watch the rolling mist, he heard the distinctive sound of approaching hooves.

The noise snapped him immediately from his depressive state, and he swung down onto the lower branches, moving with his customary grace.

Peter and Sufi were back, and Ethanril was as keen as everyone else to find out what had happened to them in the cave of the Old Ones.

The clearing was full of movement. The Mist Children were all out either at work or play. Some stoked the blazing fire while others lined and seasoned an array of berries and fruit; they were using the trunk of a fallen beech tree as a makeshift table.

Mundo and Taime had skinned several rabbits, and were in the process of roasting them on a spit, in the flames of the roaring campfire.

The air was full of the comforting smells of cooking.

From the entrance of the Warren, Fess and Pigeon emerged, carrying a tray laden with hand carved wooden cups. These were full of an assortment of freshly squeezed fruit and herbal drinks, which they placed near the campfire to warm.

A complicated snowball fight appeared to be taking place in the far corner of the clearing, and Fess ambled over to join in. The Mist Children had separated into two teams of around twenty, and Fess, for some reason, believed he could handle the odds on his own, without the need to join either team.

By the time Peter and Sufi rode into the clearing, it was difficult to see Fess for the unceasing barrage of snowballs that were being pelted at him.

"Mercy!" he pleaded, realising all too late that he was hopelessly outnumbered. "Pigeon!" he shouted to his friend in alarm.

Pigeon was about to run over to Sufi to make certain she was safe, and Fess's plea for help arrived at a totally inconvenient time. "Can you do anything?" Fess cried as he was broadsided by another vicious attack.

Pigeon had to admit, he had never seen the Mist Children look so happy and at peace as they did whenever they were attacking Fess. He smiled, discreetly collecting a sizeable amount of snow, and compacting it together in his hands.

"Don't worry Fess!" he said with a wicked gleam in his eye. "I'll save you."

Fess looked horrified as Pigeon launched his snowball into the melee. Fess turned in panic, scrabbling through the ice to escape, and Pigeon's snowball caught him a glancing blow on the posterior. He howled with pain, and went down heavy. The Mist Children moved in for the kill, and encouraged by the cries of delight from Mundo and Taime, they buried him in snow.

Lockavarn was whinnying with exhaustion as Sufi gracefully dismounted. She raced over to Jessavarn, and helped Peter down. He was still struggling to adjust to the weight of his new armour, and he practically tumbled off the horse when his weight shifted too quickly to the left side.

Sufi put her hand to her mouth to stifle a giggle, as Peter rose shakily to his knees and settled his wild hair back into shape.

"Thank Annabel you're back." Ethanril raced over from the oak tree to greet them. Sufi hugged him in an affectionate embrace, and he kissed the top of her head in relief she was safe. When he turned to address Peter, he practically did a double take.

The man standing before him, looked only vaguely like the Sacred Mother. Peter seemed somehow to be standing up straighter, his shoulders broader and more defined. With his bristling beard and his hair swept back, he looked every inch a captain-at-arms. Ethanril almost bowed to him, and then he noticed the impressive sword Peter was carrying.

Peter drew it out without a word, and offered it to Ethanril.

"It is the Sword of the Ocean, the weapon of the Harvester," Peter explained as Ethanril weighted the sword in his hand. "Annabel left it for me in Morquinda's charge. She knew I'd come for it one day," Peter continued, as he watched Ethanril examining the cascading water tip of the blade.

"Then the time of heroes is truly upon us, and all the prophesies of the Great Find are coming true...Harvester?" Ethanril said, handing Peter back the sword.

A moment passed between them, of which Sufi was the only witness. It was as though Ethanril were relinquishing all of his leadership to Peter, without question. Peter stared back at him, accepting with a gracious nod. "I have waited for nine years for a captain worth following..." Ethanril continued. "All this time it has been my responsibility to watch over this group, and to keep us together, and alive. I only briefly read some of the writings of the Great Find. This name...the Harvester is not familiar to me, but the coming of a hero was certainly depicted. So I took comfort from that. Now here you are Peter Bettany. My life is yours to command, Harvester." He bowed, and Sufi felt an incredible pride in her brother's gracious behaviour.

Peter looked at Ethanril, finally seeing the man his sister had given her heart to, and for that moment he wished that it was to

Ethanril she had bequeathed the Sword of the Ocean. He knew also, that he now had to assume complete command, or he would be letting down every single one of them.

"We must have a council of war Ethanril, everyone must attend." It was Peter's first command. "How many weapons do we have? Is there enough to arm all the Mist Children...can they even fight?" It was an extraordinary barrage of questions, and for a moment both Sufi and Ethanril looked a little disorientated.

"Annabel provided enough weapons for all of us, we keep them in the Nest, but many of the Mist Children have struggled to master sword skills..." Sufi almost apologised, but Peter seemed fine with this information.

"It doesn't matter, as long as they have a chance to defend themselves, that's all we want. There is so much we must do. Sufi, please summon everyone to the clearing." Peter was actually dismissing her, but Sufi sensed the urgency in his tone and didn't hesitate. As she raced towards Mundo and Taime, Ethanril caught Peter's arm.

"I know something is wrong Peter. I felt it in the trees, and you can taste it on the breeze. The Dark Realm is nervous...why?" His perception startled Peter, but he also knew it was impossible to mislead Ethanril.

"The Lord of the Now is sending an army to Kilfanfyn Forest; somehow he has found exactly where you are hiding. Maybe the wild dogs tracked you here, or maybe he has always known, but never dared to journey here himself..."

"No." Ethanril cut him off. Peter looked surprised. Ethanril was staring at him, his brown eyes contracting as the truth finally hit him. "He followed us yesterday, when we escaped from Myfanwy. I felt a presence all the time we rode, but I was so certain I would have seen something tracking us. He is clever this Lord of the Now, clever and dangerous, but with Krinn gone, he will never be able to cross the Tarnwaters to attack us," he pointed out. Peter nodded in agreement.

"I fear he plans to drive us out, by either intimidation, or starvation. But we have enough food in Kilfanfyn Forest to last for years..." Peter said encouragingly. Ethanril held up his hands.

"But we won't last for years Peter. If needs be he could wait for centuries, until we die out. It is you he wants, and if he can't get you by himself, he will let time do the job for him. He knows you cannot get home from here, not unless Annabel brought you back there." Peter seemed to have already considered this.

"That is exactly what I feared, and Morquinda tells me he has despatched a Still to my world to find her..." Ethanril was on the verge of shouting, and Peter restrained him. "There is nothing we can do." He grabbed Ethanril's shoulders. "I need you here and I need you to have faith that Annabel will be protected," Peter demanded, seeing the rage in Ethanril's eyes. "We have one chance to gain an advantage over the Lord of the Now. We have to separate, and some of us have to leave Kilfanfyn before his army traps us here..."

At this point he was interrupted as he heard Sufi's voice calling everyone to order.

"They're waiting for us," Ethanril said, glancing over Peter's shoulder at the Mist Children all settling themselves by the campfire. Peter looked behind him. The sight of them all made him nervous.

"I'm responsible for all those lives..." he whispered, and Ethanril understood his torment.

"They trust you Peter...I promise you. They understand you now. If we don't fight, we die, so please...tell us what we have to do." Ethanril held out his hand and Peter clasped it again.

With heads bowed they walked into the circle of waiting Children.

Mundo and Taime doled out food and drink, while Peter related his adventures with the Old Ones.

No one spoke as he recounted Morquinda's madness and spoke of her untimely demise.

It was only when he drew out the Sword of the Ocean that there was an audible gasp from everyone, breaking the silence.

"This is the weapon that Annabel had created to defend you all against the Still and the Lord of the Now," Peter explained.

"Does he know of its existence?" Taime asked, crossing to Peter to examine the sword.

"We don't believe so," Sufi answered for him. "That is our main advantage against him. Annabel was waiting for Peter to come back and claim the weapon. He is the only one who can wield it successfully...he is the Harvester of the Now," she said with barely disguised pride.

The group seemed to relax in Peter's presence; something told them they were finally safe.

"But what of this army Isabella spoke of?" Mundo asked, handing Peter a rabbit leg. Peter ate hungrily, sheathing the sword to re-establish everyone's attention upon himself. He cast a rabbit bone into the fire, which hissed and crackled, bringing a hush to the group.

"Our survival now depends upon several things..." Peter began, feeling all eyes falling upon him. "Annabel is still with us, we have witnessed the power she can still command over the weather in the Dark Realm, but she has been weakened by the years she has slept in her coma. We must call to her for help. She will sense us, I'm sure of it...our greatest weapon is faith. If you all focus on Annabel in your minds, and remember how she was when she first came to you...if you pray to her, I'm certain she will find the strength to help us again," Peter assured them.

"But what can she do?" Taime asked, desperate to believe Peter's words.

"She can bring rain," Peter announced, and everyone looked startled. "The snows have not fallen since I first arrived, the weather is changing by the second…it is warmer now, you must have all felt the change?" Peter argued, and several members of the group nodded agreement. "But we need rain. Something which has not fallen in these lands since Annabel created them. You all remember the summers?" Peter queried, and a collective sigh seemed to fall upon the group. "…And you associate winter with the coming of the Lord of the Now. But none of you have ever experienced rain."

"How can it help us?" Fess demanded, and Peter smiled.

"Where I come from, we are seldom without it! It is water, falling from the sky. We know that the Still cannot cross open water, and that any water which is fast flowing will harm them; even kill them if it is in a large enough quantity. So we must pray for rain. Torrential rain, enough to flood the rivers and bloat the lake of Carrastorc…I want it to burst its banks and overflow into the soil…" Peter was becoming excited, and the Mist Children caught some of his excitement. They were looking on with beating hearts as they foresaw the possibility of his plan.

"You mean we could flood Stilfanwyn Chasm?" Ethanril said, his face glowing with pride at Peter's ingenuity.

"That's exactly what I mean. If the rains fall heavy enough, and for long enough, I'm certain the ground will become like a quagmire. The water will leech into the soil, and eventually flood into the Chasm. We can drown them all like rats." Peter took a healthy swallow from his cup as the cheering began. He held up his hand for calm.

"I'm glad you're all enthusiastic about this plan, but I fear that is only one small part of the task ahead of us," Peter admitted.

"If the Chasm floods then the Mist Children, who are trapped in the Hold, would also be killed," Pigeon pointed out in alarm.

"They may already be dead," Mundo argued. A debate broke out amongst the group, and Peter had to shout to restore order.

"I'm not risking leaving anyone to fall victim to the floods, we must go into the Chasm and free any prisoners there..."

"Go into Stilfanwyn Chasm? Do you know what you're asking?" Taime said in alarm. Peter nodded.

"Yes I do, that's why I'm asking only for volunteers, and I will go personally if no one wishes this task to fall to them. Isabella has told me that people from my own world may also be trapped there, and we must get them out alive."

"I'll go with you Peter," Sufi piped up, and Peter smiled at her warmly, but before he could declare it 'agreed' Pigeon interrupted him.

"No Sufi...you're not taking that risk..." he bravely began. Fess looked at his friend in alarm, realising where this sentence was taking him, and finding himself utterly implicated by it. "I'll go. Peter must stay above ground...it's too dangerous to journey into the Chasm. The Lord of the Now will be waiting for you. I'll go...if there's anyone alive in there, I'll bring them out," he vowed.

Sufi was staring at him, as though seeing Pigeon for the first time in her life.

"Are you sure?" Peter asked, amazed by this show of bravery.

"Now...just hold on a second!" Fess was staring at Pigeon as though he feared he had been replaced by an impostor. "Is this for real? Or are you trying to impress someone?" he half-joked, but Pigeon was looking serious. "Well! You can't go alone," Fess said decisively. "You'll be killed! Or more likely you'll get lost and then we'll all be killed...so in order to save us all from a fate worse than Pigeon, I'd better go with him," Fess announced to Peter, looking at Pigeon with a slight smile.

"We'll probably be killed," Pigeon whispered to him, unable to stop smiling at his friend. Fess nodded, looking down at his snowball plastered clothes.

"Pessimist!" he laughed.

Ethanril looked at Peter, his face a mask of worry.

"Two will not be enough to free all the prisoners and fight off any Still left on guard. I know you're relying on the majority marching to Kilfanfyn, but Pigeon's right, the Lord of the Now himself may be waiting in that Chasm," he pointed out.

"That's why there'll be three of us!" a voice close to his ear announced.

Ethanril turned to see Taime standing up and joining Fess and Pigeon.

Peter was overjoyed.

"Very well. The three of you must ride for Stilfanwyn, as soon as this meeting is over. You'll travel part of the way downstream, use the river. Avoid Bayous Ridge and Myfanwy, that is the way the army will approach. You must go over the South Meade Hills and approach Carrastorc that way," Peter advised.

The three boys were already donning their hats, and adjusting their sword belts. "They will be expecting you...have no doubt of that. Stay together, and stay alive," Peter pleaded to them. "If there are any prisoners get them out as quickly as you can, don't linger in that place or you will all be swept away in the flood water. Pray to Annabel, pray for rain," Peter said standing up to embrace each and every one of them.

"What about the Still army Peter? Even if we destroy the Chasm, they will be waiting for us here," Taime asked as he clasped a strong arm around Peter's back.

"I will ride part of the way with you," Peter explained. "I'm going to travel to the Wastelands and find the Pig-Beast." His comment left Taime looking shaken.

"You'll be killed," he said simply.

"I will not...I'm going to make it follow me, back to Kilfanfyn. I'll lead it onto the Still like a fox amongst chickens. They will have nowhere to escape to this time if the Chasm is destroyed. The Pig-Beast will massacre them." Peter tried to sound convinced, but everyone was looking horrified.

"The Pig-Beast isn't a pet Peter; it can't be manipulated like that. I know I led it to the Still last time, but that was an accident. It was trying to kill me. If you go looking for it, then it will hunt you to the ends of the Dark Realm. Once it's disposed of the Still it will turn on the Mist Children. It is an enemy, not an ally," Taime said in frustration.

"I know Taime, I promise you…but it is the only enemy the Still have. It can destroy them just like the rains…" Peter had begun but Taime once again interrupted him.

"How?" he began simply. "How is it that the Pig-Beast can kill them yet we can't?"

Peter felt the eyes of the whole group fall upon him.

"It's because I never wrote the two of them into the same story. I made the Silent-or the Still if you prefer-your enemies, but I never fully established what the Pig-Beast was. So when it encounters anything that is alien to it, it can kill them…anything at all. We must use it to our advantage and then we will destroy it. I know how," Peter assured him. Taime seemed marginally convinced by this but it was Ethanril who spoke next.

"So Sufi, Mundo and I will stay at Kilfanfyn to protect the Mist Children, and wait?" he asked. Peter nodded.

"It will be by far the safer option. You're all needed here to help these young ones stand their ground. They look to you for guidance," Peter explained.

"I can't let you take that risk Peter. You have only ever seen the Pig-Beast once, you don't know its habits, and you carry something too precious to risk you being killed by that monster." Ethanril was talking the way he had when Peter first met him, his authority was absolute. "You will stay here with the Mist Children…you will stay alive. I will go to the Wastelands, and find the Pig-Beast," he announced.

His expression was fixed, and even though a multitude of protests broke out around him, it was obvious the decision had been made.

The meeting broke up into a nervous debate while the chosen four saddled their horses to leave.

∽

Peter watched Ethanril from a distance, knowing he was about to undertake the most dangerous quest of his life. Sufi appeared at his side, holding an apple in her hand.

"I thought he might get hungry..." she began piteously, her hands gesturing hopelessly in his direction.

Peter embraced her, holding her tightly.

"He'll be back Sufi...I promise you," Peter whispered in her ear, closing his eyes in prayer.

Eventually she pulled away from him, looking at a loss as to what to do with the apple in her hand.

"You must have it." she suddenly decided, wiping at her eyes. "He'll be all the hungrier when he's home," she said with a nod and a sad smile.

Peter took the apple and placed it in his pocket, watching her walk slowly over to her brother. From this distance he couldn't hear what she said to him, he just saw them embrace.

He turned and spent some time with Mundo saying good-bye to the boys.

Eventually Ethanril rode into the clearing on Astervarn.

"I will save my goodbyes for another time," he said to his friends. "I look forward to when next we meet, in a more peaceful world." He raised his hand and tipped his hat to them all.

Without another word he rode away into the wilderness.

Mundo gave a shudder to free the tension in his body.

444

"I'll ride with the boys as far as the Tarnwaters Peter, and then I can remain there in hiding," he offered, checking that he still had his spyglass.

Peter nodded agreement.

"You must whistle the second you see anything...promise me Mundo," he pleaded. Mundo nodded, and clamoured onto the back of Taime's horse.

Fess and Pigeon were mounting Ratavarn.

"Sure you wouldn't be more comfortable with us on this one?" they jokingly called to Taime.

"I've no doubt I'll end up on him at some point!" Taime said resignedly. He turned to say his goodbyes to Peter.

"Pigeon."

Sufi was standing a little way off from the leaving party. Pigeon looked at Fess.

"Go say goodbye," Fess said gently.

"Don't you want to come with me?" Pigeon asked. Fess shook his head.

"You say it for me," he graciously offered.

Pigeon climbed down from the saddle, and crossed the clearing towards her. The minute he arrived she began to fuss with his clothes; straightening his hat, and dusting off his shirt as though he were going to school.

He looked imploringly at her, wanting so much to tell her all of his heart's secrets, but he saw the tears in her eyes when she looked up at him, and the words wouldn't leave his lips.

"Come back to me Pigeon." It was a request said in a voice so full of tears that it threatened to evaporate in the air.

Pigeon nodded quickly three times, his own tears rising.

"I promise," he said, embracing her.

Moments later Peter and Sufi were waving off the small group as they rode out of the clearing; none of them looking back to see what they might be leaving behind forever.

"We must busy ourselves Sufi," Peter said decisively. "The Warren entrance will need barricading and the more we can get done now…" He let the sentence tail off, not wanting to finish it.

Sufi just nodded, glad to have something physical to do to take her mind off the emptiness she now felt.

∽

There was an eerie stillness about the Hold.

For almost two hours now no one had spoken and nothing had stirred inside the cavernous prison.

Far below the cages, two Still remained ever vigilant, sitting like waiting panthers listening for the slightest movement. They paid the prisoners no attention, focusing instead upon the Gak Worm's tunnel and the main door which provided the only entrance to the room.

Deep below ground they could sense the other Hybrids working relentlessly on the new tunnel. Soon the Lord of the Now's master plan would be implemented; and the final battle for supremacy of the Dark Realm would be fought and won by the united Still armies.

The cages swung lightly on their rusting chains, making an almost nautical sound in the silence of the vast Hold.

The Mist Children all lay with their faces pressed against the cage floors, gently weeping as though in time with the creaking of the chains.

Lucy Doran just sat, staring down at the unmoving figure of Father Deane.

She was powerless to help him, and although she had tried to call to him, crying over and over again, she had eventually had to stay silent when the Still guards had clamoured up the walls, and screamed at her until she fell mute.

She knew he was dead. Krinn's beating had been merciless.

She was alone now. Peter was a million miles from her, safe in his own world, and the only friend she had left lay bleeding his life away on the floor of a filth infested cage.

She wept at the hopelessness of it all, and prayed death would take her soon.

∽

The stillness of the forest had brought a strange calmness to the Mist Children.

Peter watched from a slight distance as they all sat around Sufi, listening to the wild girl tell them stories from Annabel's writings.

It all sounded so incongruous now, to be hearing these same stories which he had once read while sitting at his sister's dressing table only weeks after he had recovered from the car accident.

Peter remembered those early days in the flat without her.

:He'd felt like a stranger in his own home. An unnerving sense of guilt had remained upon him, a feeling that he was now in someway a consolation prize to his parents. He certainly didn't feel as though he was the lucky one to have survived, it was more a feeling that he was the less-important of the two, and his survival was actually something of an embarrassment to the village.

They were raw emotions, and it was more the shock of losing his once so animated sister, and coming home to such a silent and suddenly claustrophobic place.

He had found it impossible to visit her in the first month. The minute he started to imagine her wired up to her life support machine, his blood went cold in his veins.

He blamed himself for the accident from the second he recovered consciousness.

His sister's room remained like a shrine to her for the first few years after the crash. Nothing was touched, and nothing was changed. His mother would go in every day and hoover and dust, just as if she expected Annabel to walk back through the door that afternoon.

Sometimes Peter would listen at the bedroom door to his Mother talking to her and crying, over and over again.

He did his best to keep the family together in those early years. Staying home more than he ever had, and not immediately mentioning his now recurring dreams about the car crash. He tried to bring a stable normality to the whole situation. Something which even now, he still felt had helped his Mother and Father deal with the unchanging condition of their daughter.

Many times when his parents were out, Peter would steal into Annabel's room and read some of the papers on her desk.

It was his way of learning more about his lost sister, and in many ways keeping in touch with her. Most of the papers he read concerned her dreams, lots of ideas for children's stories and poems. He was impressed at how alike they both were with their writing.

He had barely had time to begin to scratch the surface of Annabel's many papers, when one night they were stolen.

At the time he had thought his Father was finally taking charge of Annabel's room, and tidying away some of her things to make it easier for his Mother. But when Peter was confronted about the missing papers over breakfast the next morning, as though he might in some way have been responsible for their disappearance he finally snapped.

In one angry moment he let all the hurt and pain of the car accident flow over his parents as though they had been totally incognizant to his feelings all that time.

It was the most cathartic moment of his life. Never before had he felt he could be so honest with his parents. He spoke of his feelings of loss, his wishes that he had known Annabel better and finally of his dreams, which he had somehow inherited from his sister.

The outburst ended with the whole family huddled on the kitchen floor with their arms around each other, crying and begging each other for forgiveness.

It was the beginning of the healing, and from that day forth the family started to put their lives back together.

Nothing was ever said of the missing papers again.

:It wasn't surprising, Peter thought, that he had never learnt of the full extent of Annabel's plans for the Dark Realm. Sufi had stolen away the papers in her so-called Great Find, before he had ever had chance to read of the destiny Annabel was preparing him for.

He still felt awkward in the heavy chain mail he was now wearing. He looked down at the monstrous sword hanging in its scabbard from his hip. Was that really the only weapon which would destroy the Lord of the Now? He prayed he would have time to practise more thrusts with it, before the Still arrived.

He moved away from the campfire group, still listening to Sufi's soft lilting voice as she continued with her story.

He thought of their kiss.

It had been so perfect, yet it had felt so wrong.

He had hated having to hurt her, even for a moment, but he could not have lied to her. Not after everything they had been through.

He thought of Lucy Doran, praying she was safe at home, and wondering if she ever thought of him.

He slowly edged towards the belt of beech trees, close to where the Pig-Beast had originally attacked the Mist Children two days ago.

Lockavarn and Jessavarn were lying like Mother and foal, close to the trunk of an ancient forest oak. Jessavarn seemed completely at peace, eyes tightly closed and ears down huddled in front of the prostrate Lockavarn.

Lockavarn looked up as Peter approached, and for a second their eyes met.

"The white horse haunts you Peter Bettany."

He heard Morquinda's cryptic message in his head. Lockavarn shook his mane of white hair, and seemed to nod at Peter in greeting.

Peter still had the apple that Sufi had handed to him in his pocket. He took it out and placed it on a tree root close to the two horses.

Carefully he drew out his sword. He couldn't help but admire the uncertain tip of the weapon again, the water flowing ever outwards as though the sword were a working pump.

He raised the surprisingly light blade above his head and closing his eyes brought it flashing down quickly upon the apple.

It sliced the fruit into two perfect halves, and took a sizable chunk of bark out of the rotting tree stump on route.

Peter opened his eyes, amazed by his own natural accuracy with the blade. He sheathed the weapon and picked up the sliced apple.

Fully aware that Sufi was watching him even while she read; he offered Lockavarn one half of the apple.

The white horse hungrily devoured the proffered fruit, crunching the apple nosily and dropping unwanted chunks from either side of its constantly moving jaws.

Peter giggled at the sensation of the horse's lips on the palm of his hand. Lockavarn's white whiskers were tickling his skin as they brushed across it. He bit into the other half of the apple, feeling happy that he had found a companion of such incredible devotion to share his last meal with.

For a second he wondered if all his friends would ever be reunited.

It was then that he heard Mundo's distress whistle.

Clear and precise, one shrill sound that sent birds screeching into the sky and cut Sufi off abruptly in mid-sentence.

The apple crunched in Peter's mouth like a death rattle.

A sudden hush descended across the whole camp, and Jessavarn woke with a slight whinny of alarm.

"Peter?" Sufi called to him, suddenly in desperate need to hear his voice.

It was the moment Peter had most dreaded. His first and most crucial decision had to be made a lot earlier than he had planned.

He felt the pressure of every child's terrified eyes turning to look at him.

Was he ready to be their saviour, or would all his courage desert him in his moment of need?

He closed his eyes and thought of home. Of Father Deane and all the belief he had in him, of his parents and their unconditional love for him. He thought of Lucy Doran and the need he had inside to see her again. Finally he thought of his sister. Of Annabel's personal struggle these last nine years to stay alive and protect these children as best she could until the Harvester arrived. She had never given up, and he knew she was fighting alongside him now.

Ethanril was racing alone to find the Pig-Beast.

Fess, Pigeon and Taime were going to free the prisoners in Stilfanwyn Chasm.

And Annabel would bring the rain.

He believed in her, and for the first time in his life he believed in himself.

Again the whistle came, harsher and more urgent, but this time Peter was ready for it.

"*They're* coming Sufi," he said, rallying up the two white horses. "Stay here with the Mist Children, I'm going to ride out and meet Mundo." He was already mounting Jessavarn.

Sufi was on her feet, torn between accompanying him, and staying behind to help the now panic-stricken Children.

As Peter spurred Jessavarn onwards, he shot a glance back at Sufi. She knew he was relying on her to calm the Children. She breathed deeply before turning back to them, and with her arms folded behind her back to hide her trembling hands, she began to sing.

It was a soft lilting lullaby, one which she had learnt with Annabel when the Children had been restless many years before.

The Mist Children responded immediately to the singing. Those who knew the words began to join in nervously, while the less confident amongst them clapped in time to Sufi's peaceful voice.

Gradually they began to settle themselves down, and eventually Sufi stopped singing and allowed them to continue unaccompanied. She was looking from one to the next, desperate to hide them all away, but knowing that this was impossible.

She thought of Annabel, and prayed she would not forsake them.

∞

Peter rode so hard he thought his lungs would explode from the acceleration. He kept his chest low to Jessavarn's back as the white horse sped like an arrow through the trees. Branches whipped at Peter's back as they tore through the canopy, and roots were crushed under Jessavarn's mighty hooves.

Mundo heard the thunderous pounding as he lay flat against a giant boulder, close to the shore of the Tarnwaters; but even the knowledge that Peter was riding to his aid did little to lighten his mood. He barely glanced round as the white horse and rider broke free of cover, and Peter jumped down beside him, his boots crunching the shale of the riverbank.

Mundo had one hand clamped to his spyglass, while his free left hand signalled Peter to keep quiet.

By the time Peter joined him on the boulder, he was trembling with fear.

Jessavarn whinnied in alarm behind them, rising onto his back legs and braying loudly. The horse had panic-stricken eyes, as it stared across the Tarnwaters.

Peter tried to control his breathing, and Mundo looked at him with a worried expression. He handed Peter the spyglass.

"Not that you need it!" He was almost laughing. "They've been arriving in droves since I signalled you…I've *never* seen them amass like this before," Mundo confessed.

Peter crawled up the boulder and stared across the vast divide of the river basin.

The Still were assembling along the shore line in ranks of fifty. They crouched in their customary position, all heads staring forward, straight across the Tarnwaters. Their proximity to the lapping river made them nervous, but they stubbornly held ranks, showing no fear in sight of the enemy.

More and more Still were arriving to join them, the march had made them practically uncontrollable with murderous fury. They tore up the snowy ground with their pounding feet, venting their enraged spleen against the trees and shrubs of the copse they ploughed through.

Rank upon rank of Still rampaged out of the copse and made their vindictive way down the riverbank to flank the already assembled army, screaming in rage. The pounding of their clawed feet sent tremors through the ground, and rippled the water of the basin.

"They can't come across," Peter reminded Mundo, moving the spyglass over the army as he sought to find the Lord of the Now. "This is just a show of strength; they're trying to panic us," he reasoned.

Mundo was looking thoughtfully at the ever-increasing cordon of black. Although he knew Peter was telling the truth, he was still concerned as to why they were allowing so many Still to stand guard across the river.

"So this is the army Isabella spoke of?" Mundo clarified. Peter put down the spyglass for a moment, balancing it on the edge of the boulder.

"Undoubtedly," he agreed. "We were lucky to send Ethanril and the boys away when we did. Take some comfort in that." Peter tried to calm him. Mundo was still looking edgy.

"How do we know they didn't run into this army?" Mundo said with barely controlled fear.

"You must have some faith Mundo...please. They are experienced riders; they will have travelled downstream as we planned. They will be far away from here now." Peter was certain of it.

"So why are they here Peter...to try and starve us out?" Mundo tried to work it through logically.

"The Lord of the Now is panicking Mundo. He knows that I'm with you, and that is a huge threat to his plans. He has obviously tracked us to this point, but it matters little, they cannot cross open water. He is just trying to create alarm, make us do something rash. We have to wait it out, as intimidating as it is. He doesn't know of our plans, or of the Sword of the Ocean. It is an advantage." Peter's voice was full of courage and hope. Mundo felt the reassurance of Peter's words and was immediately comforted by them. He watched Peter pick up the spyglass and train it back upon the army. He focused his mind back on Annabel, and prayed for the rains to come.

Behind them he heard more pounding hooves.

Mundo turned to see Sufi and Lockavarn arrive. The wild girl dismounted quickly, covering her mouth to prevent a scream as she saw the legions of Still.

"How long…" she began, her words failing her as she joined them at the shoreline.

"Only minutes…why are you here?" Peter asked looking decidedly agitated by her arrival.

"I've managed to calm the others down, they're singing to each other now…I had to come and see what we were up against." Sufi looked sheepishly at them, but her gaze was quickly drawn back across the river. "Oh Annabel, Peter there are thousands of them," she said in despair.

Peter thrust the spyglass at Mundo and leapt off the boulder to be next to Sufi. He grasped her shoulders in his hands and stared straight at her.

"This is the army Isabella warned us of…" Peter began. "It is a sure sign that the Lord of the Now has reached the end and is panicking. He is trying to scare us Sufi, nothing more. We have to be strong and stand our ground. Ethanril will be back soon with a surprise that the Lord of the Now won't be able to stand against."

Sufi was amazed by Peter's confident air.

"And what of you Peter…are you ready to face him yet?" she asked. The question rolled off Peter like snow.

"It is my duty to put this right," he said simply.

It was then that the first tree fell.

The noise created more commotion than the Still had intended as birds flew into the air and unsuspecting Still scrabbled out of the way of the falling trunk.

The beech tree had been roped high, and dragged over by seventy Still pulling against it. The fell was clean, and the tree had landed with a mighty crash, its top branches striking against the waters of the Tarn.

More Still were arriving with ropes and immediately started to lasso the first belt of beech trees.

"What are they doing?" Mundo cried in alarm, studying the roping procedure at close range with his spyglass. "I've never known them uproot the trees before…" he yelled, and Sufi scrabbled up the boulder for a better view.

Only Peter remained, frozen in place as he heard the next tree fall.

By now the Still were working to a precise regime. The cordon protecting the river's edge remained in place, with just a few breaks in the ranks to allow the trees to fall. The final wave of Still worked industriously upon the trees, heaving them down like bowling pins. Each fell was then pushed out into the waters. Often this process would hit a snag as the muddy bottom of the river ensnared the tree, holding it fast in place like glue.

Above the noise of falling trees a new sound could faintly be heard.

It was the scraping of giant wheels against the rocky terrain of the riverbank.

The carts were arriving.

Sufi and Mundo shared the spyglass, staring in mortified horror as the first cart, pulled by a frenzied team of Still, lurched out of the copse and ground to a halt, right next to the water's edge.

A singular figure abandoned the reins, and clutching a long thin glaive, jumped free of the cart. He landed perfectly on the ground, his black cloak billowing outwards like a dark death shroud.

"It can't be…" Sufi whimpered, snatching the spyglass from Mundo and training it upon the figure.

Almost as if he knew he was being observed, Krinn turned round to face them at that precise moment, bowing obsequiously.

"Krinn is *alive*," Sufi screamed. Mundo felt a stab of panic in his chest as though he had been struck with an arrow. The safety of the water was suddenly ebbing away, as the reality of Krinn's impromptu entrance cast doubt upon all their plans.

"He'll cross the river Peter...he'll come for you himself," Mundo shouted in alarm.

"He would never come alone," Sufi reassured him. "Krinn is too much of a coward for that," she argued.

Peter still had not moved. He was staring across the water at the cart which had borne Krinn to them.

The cart was loaded with tons of rubble and soil.

"He *won't* come alone..." Peter began, joining them on the rock as though he were confirming Sufi's theory. Both Mundo and Sufi felt marginally reassured by this, but suddenly Peter finished his sentence. "He'll bring the entire army with him."

A moment of incredulity passed over Sufi and Mundo. Peter remained apparently oblivious to it, his mind already racing over answers to the situation they were now in.

"The Still can't cross open water," Sufi said with less conviction than before. Peter twisted to face them, his expression one of resolution.

"Very true...but that's why they're felling the trees...and that's why they have a cart...Oh! Wait, forgive me..." He broke off as two more carts lumbered out of the woodland, their wheels creaking in protest. "...That's why they have three carts, sorry. Full of rubble." He turned away from the scene of chaos behind him, feeling the chill as the screaming of the enemy began in earnest.

Sufi and Mundo were just staring at him, their faces asking 'why?'

"They're going to make a dam...a bridge to cross the river," Peter explained. His hands were trembling with fear but his voice was calm.

"We're going to be massacred," Mundo breathed, his own hopes dying with Peter's words.

"That!" Peter shouted back angrily, "is the very last thing we're going to be." He was striding over to Jessavarn like a man possessed. He had to turn his back on them for a minute; his own fear was in danger of showing through. He thought only of Annabel, and found strength in his sister's plight. He clambered onto Jessavarn's back, and turned to look at his two friends.

Across the river, Krinn saw Peter Bettany for the first time. The sight surprised him, but he welcomed the challenge.

"The Sacred Mother is *within* our grasp," he shrieked at the labouring Still. Krinn wondered for a moment how Peter's head would look speared upon his glaive in place of the carved skull. The thought pleased him, and he turned away from the shore and began barking orders at the gathered Still.

Peter could hear Krinn's voice inciting his army to bloody and merciless warfare. The voice chilled him, but he refused to fear it.

"Ethanril will bring the Pig-Beast here in hours..." Peter began, finding comfort in action. "We must hold off this plague of Still until then. This is our only chance of victory, if we fail...all our hopes will be lost," he stressed. "Remember the promise you pledged to me at the campfire...never give up hope. I ask you to act on that promise now. We must fight for everything we believe in, we must fight for everyone we hold dear and sacred to us. And we must fight for Annabel, and she will fight for us. Pray for the rains to fall. They *will* come," Peter cried out, his own courage racing from his body and gripping Sufi and Mundo. They looked back at him with determined eyes.

"Sufi," Peter ordered, "take Lockavarn, and ride back to camp. The Mist Children have to take up arms...they must fight as well," he said sadly. "Get them underground, into the Warren, and have them block up the tunnels as though they were rabbits. It will be safer if you all stay below ground when the first wave of Still eventually crosses. They will try to dig you out but it will delay them, and time is everything to us," Peter said.

Sufi hesitated, she wanted so much to stay and help Mundo and Peter, but she knew she had to go back. Without a word she embraced Mundo quickly, and then looked up at Peter.

"I have no words..." she confessed. Peter smiled at her.

"There will be plenty of time for them later...I promise you Sufi," he said with a nod, as she turned away from him and mounted Lockavarn.

The two of them watched her ride away. Mundo turned to Peter, drawing his rapier with a flourish.

"Are you *ready* to die a hero Peter Bettany?" he asked glancing across the river, as the enemy felled six more trees in unison.

The air filled with cawing birds, screaming Still and the barbaric noise of splintering timber.

Peter drew out the Sword of the Ocean with a single swift action. The transparent blade seemed to reflect the dying rays of the sun, and like a prism, sent blazing streamers of light dancing across the river, momentarily blinding the amassed Still, and causing them to pause in their work for a fleeting second.

"Every story has to end somewhere," Peter said with a resolute smile.

The trilogy concludes in:

HArVESTEr of the NOW: Volume Three: Annabel

Printed in the United Kingdom
by Lightning Source UK Ltd.
133614UK00001B/4-30/A